My Path To Magic

Irina Syromyatnikova

Edited by Amanda Bosworth

Translated by Irina Lobatcheva, Vladislav Lobatchev

Illustrated by Nick Mingaleev

Parallel Worlds' Books

ISBN: 0992055954
ISBN-13: 978-0-9920559-5-0

CONTENTS

PART 5. DEVIL'S DISCIPLE

EPILOGUE

PART 1. THE KING'S ISLAND

CHAPTER 1

Please do not think that I am making excuses; dark magicians are really very respectable people! And well provided for, by the way. Our world is full of odd, inexplicable powers and chilling phenomena that white wizards are helpless against. Commoners want safety and security that is unattainable without the dark magic power. Therefore, a dark magician is a highly paid and scarce specialist; in most counties, for every twenty and even thirty white enchanters, there is only one dark mage. Such was the consequence of an unwise policy of previous years that impaired that particular heritage in the nation. At least their descendants have realized it and repented. Therefore, the situation currently is like this: a genuine, professional dark magician is a very respectable man, but any self-taughts and amateurs are heavily persecuted. This is fair: while a white idiot's mistake results in scorched cookies or hail instead of rain, a screwed up dark spell will trigger a disaster. Zombies, vampires, invisible beasts, ever-burning fires and an epidemic of lethargic sleep are some of the most innocuous consequences of our mistakes. That's why we are all conscripted to serve in the army and almost entirely employed by the government; that's why dark magic is often shamefully called "combat." Our craft is not a good job for idiots!

Now, tell me how a student dark mage is supposed to develop his skills—not to mention some cash on the side—so needed by every college student?!

Well, in my first year I allowed myself to moonlight as a dishwasher and a waiter in a pub, but I gradually learned that wasting so much time to earn scraps was an unacceptable luxury. For the sake of a miserable couple hundred crowns in the present, I risked ruining my "bright" dark future. I had to find a job that for a couple hours a week would earn me the same money; otherwise, I would have looked forward to six years of penance, fasting, and abstinence. A grant from Ronald the Bright's Fund covered tuition and housing, but the cash allowance from my dear family wasn't enough for anything better than bread and milk in the big city where I lived. I could, perhaps, take a credit from the Gugentsolger's Bank secured by my future earnings, as many students did, but that meant I would belong to these crooked penny-pinchers for a whole ten years after graduation from Redstone University of Higher Magic. Hands off me!

Of course, I meant to use my natural talent in the dark arts. I wasn't going to call forth any filth or to flirt with the supernatural, but I could handle some magic. Small otherworldly phenomena were vulnerable to even the most ordinary rituals. I knew when to stop, never took up what I couldn't manage, and even played it safe, relying on spontaneous curses: "donkey ears," "loser's tail," "eviction of violent hobgoblins"—anything that did not carry deadly threat but made life difficult. (In our trade it was called "taking out the garbage".) I charged little and did a thorough job, always taking into account the client's wishes. Alas, it had ended stupidly. One bozo had fantasized that I cheated him out of his pitiful twenty crowns and reported me to the cops. He thought I tried to con him because I called him on the phone, imagine it! As it often happened with the commoners, he was convinced that all magicians were the same, and an image of a decent mage in his mind was that of an ordinary white magician. There were more of them, after all. All the white wizards actively dislike technology since it is unnatural, they think. I am dead serious! They prefer to drag themselves to a client through the whole city or send a courier. But the dark magicians coexist perfectly with any machinery: animated nonlife is right up our alley.

Mad with boredom, the cops had found me right away, but, fortunately, before I did anything. It's not that easy to catch a dark mage with his pants down! I had never worried about a police ambush before, but my common sense has always directed me to carefully consider my surroundings before venturing into something. Thus, they had found no evidence. However, any possible conviction for illegal spellcasting would put an end to my future career, and I had no choice but to deny everything.

Despite my exuberant character, typical for a dark magician, I had never even been to the police before, much less to the Special Department of Magic Affairs. And yet it seemed to me that the government agency should have looked somewhat different. That is, not a filthy basement with furniture bolted to the floor and light bulbs hanging loose on the cords. However, there was no mistake: everyone who worked there sported a badge with the abbreviation NZAMIPS. As far as I knew, this designation wasn't decrypted in any official document, letting your imagination fly. Both the magicians and the townsfolk called this office simply, "NZAMIPS".

At first, as we walked through the corridors, everything looked fine and civilized: inspectors spoke with visitors, couriers scurried back and forth, typewriters snapped, potted ficus trees blossomed. But then we went down to the basement and walked into *that* room: muddy plaster with brown stains, crumbling tiles on a concrete floor, dim light bulb flickering on the ceiling, iron table against the far wall and no chairs. This place had the refined atmosphere of the times when people could be burned alive just on a suspicion of being a magician. I felt as if I had been dunked into a tub of cold water.

Wasting no time, my convoy pushed me to the center of the room and handcuffed me to a chain hanging from the ceiling.

Dear mother! There was a real iron chain with magic bracelets. I had seen such in a movie before. No, this couldn't be real; I was sleeping.

The door had creaked nastily, and a new character showed up.

The new policeman was an ordinary man, not a magician, but with such a build that simply glancing at him made me uneasy. *'That's why all the books depict wizards as weaklings!'* whirled in my mind.

"Well, punk, are you gonna squeal?" this cross of a goblin and a steam train smiled sinisterly at me, rubbing his hairy paws.

Typically, the dark magicians are hostile, but even our militancy has some limit. In abject fear, I forgot everything that I was intending to say.

"Didn't do anything!" I voiced my last argument.

In half of the cases, problems that people bring to magicians are purely of a psychological nature. A soulful conversation and an aromatic candle are usually enough to cure their woes. No wonder that a lot of university courses have nothing to do with magic! Among my clients there were no mages, so the cops couldn't prove the fact of my witchcraft. I just was not sure anymore that they needed any proof.

The investigator slammed his fist on the table, and it became clear to me why the table was made of iron.

"Don't try to lie to me! I see right through you!"

He grabbed me by the shirt and lifted me off the floor.

"Confess!"

It's been a long time since someone dared to touch me without my permission—to a dark magician that was an invitation to fight. Was it any other guy, I would slam his face with my fists regardless of his body size. Even with my hands tied up, I would have chewed off his nose. But not with that cop! Everyone knew the gruesome nature of the dark magicians; no one would believe that I was not at fault. I tried to swallow a curse rushing from my tongue and smother the flames of my Source. To cast a spell on the policeman would be exactly the opposite of what I needed at the moment. Even not being a full-fledged mage, I would have chopped this idiot up like wood.

Meanwhile, it seemed the goblin had determined to commit suicide: he kept shaking me like a ragdoll and then leaned back and swung his hefty fist, aiming at my stomach. Until the very last moment, I had not believed he would hit me. In our modern, humane world, would our police really beat up a minor?! I hadn't been prepared for that—that's why my wheeze sounded especially pathetic.

What had started then was a nightmare: a sacred ordinance called by the dark mages the Empowerment and not similar at all to the Initiation of the white magicians. The difference between them is fundamental: the whites are forced to beg and flirt with their Source to extract its Power and not to frighten it; but our Source itself will scare off, if not drain, anyone. Under normal circumstances, the Empowerment is a long process, the essence of which is carefully concealed from the novices. The procedure requires the presence and assistance of several recognized masters to reduce the possibility of deadly outcomes. I, however, got smacked into this with no safeguards.

For a moment, a dark flame had blinded me, darting to my throat like a hot wave, trying to take away my senses and willpower. It was worse than being in front of a judge: my own Power was ready to crush and subdue me. It was impossible to be prepared for this, as such readiness could not be developed even with time and practice; the Empowerment was a moment of revelation, after which you either remained yourself or ceased to exist. And in that particular case two lives were at stake: a tiny protuberance of the Power escaped from my control would have transmuted the foolish cop into a skeleton. There was no time left for deliberation. Waiting for instructions (from whom?) was senseless; I had to cling to the raging Power with all my claws and teeth and tear, tear, tear... And you know what? That despicable thing was doing the same to me. For a few minutes we were like two grappling cats, my yin to its yang, and then, with an incredible effort of will, in the existence of which I had not believed before, I managed to plug and tame that flow and emerge on its surface, under the blinding light of the bulb.

The attack had passed as quickly as it had begun.

The Source hid somewhere inside me like a dog who had soiled the floor. To teach it to serve me and give me its "paw" in submission required long and hard work, but the process had been initiated. Not daring to believe in my salvation, I cautiously took a deep breath. And then my gaze fell upon the cop, who looked me in the eye with a suspicious gleam of intelligence.

I am a magician, and for the magicians the psychic shocks are worse than physical trauma. The effort that was required to complete the ritual had bottomed out my reserves. All of these terrible things: the walls, the light bulb on the cord, his face—came together in my brain, magnified as if by a lens; I gasped and fell unconscious. The last thing left in my mind was the cursing cop trying to keep me upright.

I do not know for how long I was passed out, but probably for quite a while; by the time I opened my eyes, there were more people milling about. Besides the goblin, I saw a young officer (a dark magician, if my senses are correct), and an elderly white mage with a stethoscope on his chest. On the faces of all three I read a purely medical interest.

"How are you feeling, young man?" That was the old guy. I mumbled in reply something that satisfied him. "The first acquaintance was a success!"

For some strange reason, the attitude toward me had changed dramatically. Even the goblin-like cop hadn't yelled, instead grunting almost kindly.

The next thing that I remembered was a conversation with a pretty woman officer in a sunny and spacious room. Honestly, it would be a stretch to call it a conversation; she gave me a long, heartfelt lecture about the dangers of careless witchcraft, occasionally slipping under my nose disgusting photos from the police files to illustrate her thesis. What she said I knew already in theory and would have preferred to avoid looking at human stumps and giblets, but I did not want to open a lengthy discussion. I nodded and agreed with everything.

Perhaps the shock of clashing with the prose of life added some credibility to my words; ultimately, they believed in my virtue. They put me in a file, warned me that I would be under the watch, threatened to call my dean's office, and finally kicked me out, not caring how I'd get home in such condition.

"Breathe! It will only make you stronger!" goblin laughed. "Join us after graduation—General Miklom will always find a job for a brave kid."

At this point, I was caught up in revelation: I realized that I would never, ever work for the police.

Making my way to the exit of the building, I ran into the stoolie, my backstabbing client. The guy was still giving his testimony, but, seeing me, he became agitated and waved his hand.

"I understand," he began briskly, "you cannot help me today, but, perhaps, on Thursday..."

Apparently, he thought that after all that had happened I would still work for him. Truly, the sweet simplicity is worse than witchcraft.

"I do not understand what you are talking about," I muttered and stumbled away.

Let him deal with the "evil eye" by himself! He will be very fortunate if the "cleaning" service charges him less than two hundred crowns.

Passing through the gleaming glass and copper of the main entrance of the police department, I still could not fully comprehend my luck. My imagination turned window designs into camouflaged jail mesh, and every move behind them betrayed a spying gaze on me. An arch over the courtyard resembled an entrance to a tomb. Having moved away from the police building to a safe distance, I turned into a small park and sat on the nearest bench, trying to put my jumbled feelings in order. The evening had not yet come; from the moment I had entered the client's apartment, four hours had elapsed at most.

But it sure felt like a lifetime had passed.

Thoughts slowly caught up with my stupid head.

Apparently, there wasn't going to be a court trial. Not that I did not understand what I was doing (dark magicians start learning the law while still in high school), but I sincerely believed that I could afford some flexibility in interpretation of the legislation by taking precautionary measures. So typical—how many times do we have to hear that the matches are not toys before we realize that the rule applies to us as well?

"This world does not belong to magicians, either white or dark," I recalled the words of Uncle Gordon (to tell the truth, he was not quite my uncle, but I digress). "Do you think there have not been enough wiseasses trying to prove otherwise?"

Yes, Uncle, there have been quite a lot of them, and it isn't by chance that they were all idiots. Any magic, especially white, doesn't make new things; its essence is an illusion. It won't turn lead into gold or make bread out of sand or wine out of water. Bread, wine, and gold for magicians are made by real people, so you should never anger them—you cannot afford it (and this isn't just some theory, it's a verifiable fact)!

But what to do with our innate nature, our character traits that have long become a byword? For twenty years you learn the rules, but once your mentors are done with you, you immediately forget them and go back to level zero. It's sad to admit, but dark magicians are more receptive to learning lessons through getting their ass kicked, and I was no exception to the rule. I guessed I should be grateful to the cops: they slapped my wrists right on time, halting the development of pathological inclinations in my character.

The only confusing moment left was behavior of the goblin-like officer (of course, he was not an actual victim of a secondary magic mutation, but a striking similarity to a goblin in appearance was there). What did he really want from me, and why did he give up? It was unlikely that my fainting had caused him to stop; if he feared accusations of police brutality, he would not have called witnesses while I lay unconscious. Personal prejudice against dark magicians? Then NZAMIPS wouldn't keep him—if he were not expelled by coworkers, then customers would beat him up for sure. But do I really care for the issues that cops might have?

My tamed Source was devotedly licking my wounds, while I quietly enjoyed the happy ending. Only the dark magicians are able to relax while sitting on a busy intersection. All the white mages familiar to me were obsessed with face-to-face contacts and personal space and could loosen up only in tranquil surroundings. But to me, the impersonal, mechanical movement of the masses had a more profound calming effect. The never-ending city noise I perceived as music.

Carthorses pulling a covered wagon emblazoned with the logo of a famous transportation company sullenly marched along the pavement. The huge beasts, almost three meters at the withers, were bred by magic and controlled by it. An abundance of "horse power" was typical for Redstone. For those who liked speed and weren't burdened with luggage, a merry tram rang along the rails. A rumbling limousine propelled by an "alcoholic's dream" engine had crossed the intersection. I had sniffed after it, hoping to catch a familiar scent of spirits, and enviously watched the car passing by. No comparison with the tram! I had great respect only for the steam engines, but within the city boundaries the trains were not allowed: too many university students were white magicians, for whom a clash with a hissing and steaming iron horse caused severe stress and nervous disorders. Give them any authority, and they would make all of us change back to horses! The municipality was very proud of the fact that all of the power plants had been relocated to the suburbs.

I smiled dreamily, imagining myself in a limousine. A successful dark magician could afford more than that. So far, I hadn't committed any fatal missteps, hadn't been charged with anything, and didn't need to run away. In essence, two ideas were crowding my mind: first, I could be congratulated on becoming a full-fledged magician, and second... how was I supposed to make money now?

* * *

The current chief of the Department of Magic Affairs, Conrad Baer, was a cop of the sixth or even seventh generation. His ancestors began to serve the law shortly after the last king had left Ingernika. They had steadfastly safeguarded their fellow citizens during the awful years of plague and in the times of trouble at the turn of the millennium, occasionally distracted by civil wars and revolutions. The key to the success of the dynasty was the unique physical characteristics of the Baer family: the look of the Department's chief could discourage even the most boisterous dark magicians. Since his college days, Conrad proudly carried the nickname "Locomotive" and was the first member of his dynasty to be promoted to captain. This latter fact was considered a source of pride, but sometimes with a touch of bitterness.

With noticeable relief, the captain took off his anti-magic protective suit. Government specialists made this thing look like a regular police uniform, but it weighed as heavy armor. But wouldn't you put on anything for the sake of saving your own life? Contact with young magicians, possessing unknown powers and temperament, demanded extreme precautionary measures.

Wiping sweat from his neck with a paper towel, Locomotive pulled out a phone and dialed a familiar number. The massive apparatus with brass handle and a pearl insert on the disk liked to play tricks on the captain, but it always connected him to this number on the first attempt.

"Lucky you!" the captain announced to an invisible interlocutor. "I met your godson today."

"How did it go?" someone on the other end wondered vaguely.

"Hard to say. Initially I thought they had messed up his file, attributing him to the mages. He fainted, can you imagine?"

A quiet chuckle came out of the phone.

"Yes, his father was also very reserved. He will become a powerful magician!"

"Strong, that's for sure. I have recorded his aura; drop by when

11

you have time, take a look. We'll pray together."

"Thanks!" the tube commented. "I owe you."

The captain waited until he heard a dial tone but did not put the phone back. Instead, he took a bottle of malt whiskey out of a drawer and measured a cup. Usually, he did not drink during work hours, but today was especially nerve-wracking.

Conrad Baer was not a magician and did not feel magic powers. He understood what had happened in the cell only after viewing a record on a crystal that permanently engraved this event for his superiors. It was then that he decided to have a drink. Due to the proximity of Redstone University, his department had a special covert function: to tease dark magicians in order to get an imprint of their aura. The not-quite-so legitimate procedure was helpful in avoiding problems with their identification later on, but it was recommended before the initiation of a magician and certainly not during it.

The captain, being a knowledgeable police officer with fifteen years of experience, stupidly and foolishly put himself under the attack of the combat magician; any anti-magic protection would not have saved him if the kid had lost consciousness three seconds earlier. It was hard to tell what the thing rushing toward him from the transcendent depths was willing to incarnate into, but the consequences of such events the captain had seen before. The glitter of the walls fused into glass, puffy bluish dead bodies in the police uniform, green pools of slime in the spots where people stood a minute before—that was only a small part of the surprises that dark magic concealed! The boy kept control over his power, and for that he deserved if not full forgiveness of his sins then at least a good discount.

But one couldn't trust the phone with such revelations, so nobody knew about Captain Baer's second birthday, and he had to celebrate it alone.

CHAPTER 2

An echo of the encounter with NZAMIPS reached me on Tuesday, during a lab on alchemy. I had already handed in my notebook with finished lab assignment and idly wondered if I could remotely ignite magnesium shavings in a flask on the professor's desk. Close connection with the Source inside provided me with interesting possibilities... One thing stopped me: I was the only magician in the classroom. That wasn't a joke! Half of the students at the University of Higher Magic were not magicians; our school became well-known for its Faculty of Alchemy instead. It is believed that the alchemic talent is as inborn in people as a talent for magic, only it is harder to find. By the way, I received a scholarly grant from Ronald the Bright's Fund for winning an alchemical tournament. I always liked to watch the pendulum swing, play with lens light refraction, and mess around with chemicals, especially with those that had a propensity for burning and exploding. Unfortunately, due to that, lab classes turned for me into a real torture—I could hardly keep myself from trifling.

Before I had a chance to pull off something nasty, a freshman had opened the door without knocking and cried out: "Provost calls for Tangor!" and ran away.

My mood went sour immediately.

A dark magician in a bad mood is the worst curse possible. Dying of curiosity, my classmates pretended to rifle through their notebooks, but they hesitated to offer any comments. After the bell had rung, Ronald Rest, known as Ron Quarters, burst into the classroom, almost knocking the professor down. Clearly, he wasn't scared of mages, either dark or white.

"What's up, Thomas?" Quarters yelled. "Dragon summons you!"

Thomas Tangor is me. I categorically do not accept any nicknames, because "Tangor" is already short enough.

"Hi," I muttered, unwilling to develop the conversation further.

"What have you done?" Quarters poked about.

"Got into a fight."

"Ooh," he stretched the sound out in disappointment and left.

Yes, a fight involving a dark mage student is corny, boring, and uninteresting. Fits the dark magician image too closely. In contrast to the faint-hearted white enchanters, we love open conflicts, and the sight of blood pleasantly excites us. Not of our blood, naturally. University administrators have always been faced with a tragic dilemma: to order the dark to behave the same way as other students is useless, but to leave such behavior unpunished is untenable. And then some smartass (if I had known who, I would have raised him from the grave!) had found the perfect solution: correctional work. Something like scraping pots in the university canteen or cleaning stables and toilets. To refuse meant a discharge from the university for breach of the discipline code. For three years I was able to avoid this dubious "joy", but yesterday's visit to NZAMIPS seemed to put an end to my fortune...

No, I have nothing against discipline, but I would like to note that some of the so-called "mere humans" turned out to be bigger assholes than any dark magician. Look at Ronald Rest, who got his nickname because each time before getting piss drunk he demands "just a quarter" of booze and, having loaded up, begins harassing all males and flirting with all females. Taught by bitter experience, his classmates learned to leave a pub at his appearance. Well, Quarters perceived correctional work as an outrageous indulgence for the dark magicians.

Anything but the stables...

I came up to the door of the Vice Chancellor's Disciplinary Office for problematic students (a euphemism used at the university to name the dark mages), feeling apprehensively sick in advance. A brass plate on the door announced that Prof. Darkon dwelled behind it.

Contrary to my expectations, the prorector did not look angry or irritated.

"I was told that you spent a couple of hours in our favorite facility yesterday," he winked conspiratorially, while I shuddered at the memory. "Do not take the incident to heart." In response to my puzzled look he explained, "All dark magicians are brought to the police at least once during their studies. This is another law of nature, and you are not the one to break it."

Personally, I did not care about the statistics, but keen interest flashed in the prorector's eyes:

"Did you try your magic on the cop?"

I shook my head frantically. "How could I dare?! An assault on a law enforcement officer with application of magic would be pure suicide."

"Congratulations! Therefore, the first record in your file will be 'very trustworthy'. Believe me, for your career it will mean more than the best references," the professor switched to a confidential tone. "With years of experience behind my back I believe that they aim at driving detainees out of their wits; perhaps, it's the only way to understand a magician's potential. A rather risky way, though."

I parted with the prorector; we shook hands as people united by the injustice we both experienced. I was dying to learn what offense he had committed in his time. After leaving the office, I recalled that I did not mention that Empowerment had already happened to me. Okay, maybe next time. I will just be a little more careful.

Now that my affairs with NZAMIPS had been settled, another problem loomed: making cash. Recount and rigorous calculation of my expenses showed that my savings would last for a month or two. My acquaintance with the goblin was still too fresh in the memory, and I did not dare to earn money illegally.

I had to find a job.

As a man of action, I walked around the neighborhoods adjacent to the campus, looking for a vacancy that would open by summer. The University of Higher Magic was a special school; it did not impose any exams, except at admission and graduation, which was quite logical. The art of magic could not be mastered in a hurry. Education was divided into many, many intermediate control points; however, following an ancient tradition, teachers took a break twice a year: two months in summer and three weeks in winter. During winter breaks, most of my classmates stayed in town, but in summer the university was almost deserted. The time just before the summer vacation was best to grab someone else's place...

Alas! Most vacancies implied a job for white magicians; in rare cases, for ordinary people, but no employers wanted problems with a dark mage student, especially on the eve of Empowerment. Despicable discrimination! If you are a dark magician, do you not need money?

The only real option was to clean the floors in the tram depot at night. No, thank you, when would I sleep then? In the third year, students began specializing. Since I had already been initiated, it made sense to take the full course of witchcraft. To cerebrate over a pentagram after physical work, risking my life? No way, better to hit myself in the head with a stone.

I had two choices: to apply for a credit from Gugentsolger's Bank or ask my family for assistance. The problem had to be solved fast. I decided to start with the family. What the hell? A lineage of hereditary dark magicians could not be poor! I didn't need much—just 50-60 crowns a month; my mother was sending me 20, or occasionally 30 (on Christmas), and sincerely believed that was sufficient. We needed to talk seriously in person, not through the mail. For the first time in two years I decided to use one more privilege of the Roland the Bright's Fund fellowship—a paid roundtrip home.

Actually, summer visits home are more typical for the white mages. I always wondered how they managed to come back on time, if they did not travel in an "iron horse." Ron Quarters was about to leave for the Southern Coast accompanied by two sophomore girls and invited me along, but I stubbornly declined his invitation and spread rumors that I had some serious business to do at home. I desperately did not want to look like a poor beggar in the eyes of my friends.

Purchasing a ticket was easy—the first railcar in the train was not popular among passengers. Very few people traveled to our region in summer, just like in any other season for that matter. For starters, the mountainous plateau at the western extremity of the continent was famous for the worst climate throughout Ingernika. It was neither cold nor hot, the number of sunny days in a year could be counted on one's fingers, and fog was very common. Second, the inhabitants were kind of savages: Krauhard's peasants were full of prejudices and superstitions, they interweaved silver threads into horses' manes and dark cat fur into their blankets, and they nailed ram's horns over the gates. A place of depression, with icy rain and squally winds—the white mages would not be able to stand it. Furthermore, this was the place for the otherworldly creatures. The supernatural manifestations occurred here much more frequently than in any other place. To the local folks, it was a matter of pride and a source of permanent anxiety. Even children knew of the simplest rituals of expulsion; ancient, covered with cryptic signs and stelae were on every street corner, and on clear days one could see from the shore the frightening and alluring King's Island. Hardly a surprise, then, that one in five Krauhardians was a dark magician.

I sat on the bench of a railroad car alone and mindlessly gazed at the passing landscape through puffs of smoke. The thick greenery of the windbreak looked like a tunnel; fields, cows, white cottages, and enormous straw bales flashed through the rare breaks in the trees. With hidden impatience I waited for the evergreen trees to be replaced with low-lying shrubs and weeds, and fields with rocky wastelands and deep ravines, but the first greeting from the motherland came as rain. Of course.

I slept through most of the trip, and the time of our arrival—despite its early hour—was cheerful and fresh. Luggage-wise, I had almost nothing: a small backpack and a wicker basket. I also could not resist the temptation and had bought a couple of gifts for my mom and younger siblings, firmly sending my finances into the red. The conductor, heroically restraining his urge to yawn, courteously unfolded a ladder onto the platform. He helped me off and sincerely wished me a good trip, while thick, milky fog reigned all around.

As soon as I dove into the moist, faintly roiling haze, I realized how badly homesick I was. All that I liked in urban settings—the fumes of vehicles and their never-ending movement—was only a poor surrogate for this mysterious, enveloping pseudo-existence. The steam engine, invisible in the fog, whistled pitifully, the departing train faintly clanged, and I strode along the platform, past the "Wildlife Outpost," trying to remember the location of the descending path.

The fog started barely breaking away from the ground; in an hour there would be no trace of it. Thanks to its lift, I first noticed feet of people meeting me and only later discerned their faces. I was greeted by a pair of ladies' shoes on low heels (simple and worn-out), men's boots of the type "not afraid of mud," and four horse hooves. It was the hooves that I recognized—you do not often see a horse with all four legs of different colors.

"Hi, Mom!"

A woman in a black knitted jacket rose out of the fog. I would have recognized her anytime and anywhere. She stood up on her tiptoes and kissed me on the cheek.

"Hi, Tommy! How are you? How was your trip?"

"Excellent!"

"Hello, Thomas. The children have been waiting for you for three days; all the neighbors know that their brother is coming back. Don't be alarmed."

Before turning to the speaker, I took a deep breath, bringing myself into the state which I commonly used when communicating with my clients: detached benevolence, respect without familiarity. I was sure I was better at it now than two years ago. He stood next to my mother, smiling, one of only three white magicians in Krauhard. My stepfather.

"Let's go," my mother hurried me to a horse carriage.

I caught myself thinking that, while imagining this meeting, my memory had been skipping over, in some tricky way, a man I had known for more than ten years; that is to say, not even a sole thought of him had arisen in my mind. Perhaps the brain cannot remember what it does not understand. My stepfather climbed onto the coach box, and my mother sat down next to me, while I, smiling, was still striving for a sense of recognition.

Dark and white magicians cannot unite in a single family. These are two different species of people, different universes. As common interests, we had food only; indeed, we even slept in different ways. Regarding to my upbringing, my stepfather could not argue with me at all, and punishing me was completely unrealistic. Since our first acquaintance (me—eight, him—thirty-two) he was just Joe to me, but I was Thomas to him (at first, even Mr. Thomas). I always considered myself senior to him. The reason did not lie in any magical metaphysics, because my dark talent was still asleep, and his white one was never too strong. Personalities, attitudes, perception of the world—everything was different between us as night and day.

He liked to sit by the fire and read a book, while I showed up at home only long enough to eat. He tended and nurtured flowerbeds with exotic daisies; I repaired a lawn mower in the barn. He brought a good-natured rough-legged horse to our house that took pleasure in carrying our family to the market and to neighbors on weekends. I had bought a scooter on my first salary, awfully rattling and reeking of alcohol, and, whenever I had time, rolled it out to the driveway in front of the house and cleaned, adjusted, and fine-tuned. That way, we grated on each other's nerves for long six years after his marriage to my mother. Only now, after studying at Redstone University for two years, did I understand the nightmare he had been living in. The day I received a scholarship from Roland the Bright's Fund must have been the happiest day of his life.

"Well, how are things at home?" I tried to be polite.

"Fine. Thomas," my mother hesitated, but I patiently waited, "we need to have a serious talk."

When she called me by my full name, I knew it was something

serious.

"Yes?"

"Lyuchik has revealed a talent," she took a deep breath. "A white one."

"Congratulations!"

What else could I say? A young white magician is like a naked nerve, totally susceptible to any outside influence. A wrong word, a sharp look, and the kid would fall into deep emotional distress. Later he would grow older, stronger, but right now... And moreover, his brother, a dark one, came to see him.

"You see..." my mother began in embarrassment.

Now, after two years at Redstone, I was genuinely able to see.

"I'll be careful!" I promised sincerely.

I was sure of myself, but what about the others? There was no place less appropriate for a young white mage than Krauhard.

"How will he cope in our village?"

The best for them would be to move away from here; it was long overdue. Mother shrugged:

"We are trying to accommodate him, but with our income one cannot expect much."

"Has my father left nothing? I cannot believe that a dark magician did not know how to make a living!"

"You probably do not remember... We did not struggle like now when he was alive. There were some savings, but when your father... died so suddenly, I could not find what he had invested his money in."

A silly situation, isn't it?

"We had a state pension previously, but when you turned eighteen, they took us off the payroll."

And a family of four was left to live on only a schoolteacher's salary.

"You should have mentioned that to me; I would have sent you money!"

She smiled: "What kind of money does a student have?"

Indeed, what money was I talking about? Oh, the money...

"I would have thought of something!" I replied stubbornly.

"Do not spout nonsense; you need to focus on studying. You are very talented! Your father would be very proud of you."

The cunning plan to increase my monthly allowance failed splendidly. Well, now my conscience would not let me take a cent from her. It was a blow... But if I did pick up something from the white magicians, it was their ability to treat all setbacks philosophically. A very important quality! Well, I will enjoy my vacation in Krauhard then.

The horse hoofs clicked loudly on a cobbled road, and the old carriage's springs creaked in accompaniment. The fog thinned, revealing moss-covered granite boulders, curved trees, and trailing shrubs. It was summer and bindweed was in bloom. The carriage had passed a cleft, and a valley, fairly wide for Krauhard, opened up in front of us. Its gently sloping southern side was covered with greenery, cattle grazed in the pastures, and the windows of houses with roofs of brown shale glimmered happily. Another half an hour, and I would be at home!

The reception was cordial and loud. Lyuchik, all grown up, shouted and jumped as if there were four of him, although his

22

younger sister barely remembered me at all and felt shy. But virtually nothing had changed. It was the same country house with boisterous chickens in the yard and a neat small front garden, where my stepfather tried to grow roses in a climate perhaps only suitable for sagebrush.

I noticed small, colorfully painted boxes in the garden.

"What is it?" I asked, shuddering inwardly, already suspecting the answer.

"You know, while you were gone, I thought..."

"Bees," I stated in a suddenly sunken voice.

If there are any creatures in the world that I cannot stand at all, it would be those nasty, buzzing, biting insects. Yes, it will be a fun summer.

My mother prepared a table on the open patio. And when I say open, I mean indeed, open for everything and everyone. In addition to the expected guests, the smell of freshly made bread and baked apples attracted the unwelcome visitors. The joy of my return home was spoiled, not to mention my appetite.

The bees treated me with suspicion. Small aviators flew around me with a thoughtful humming, trying to get in my face.

"Do not fear them!" Lyuchik tried to persuade me.

A young white magician was comforting me, an initiated dark! If I relax for a moment and they bite me... I didn't want to think about it! I knew nothing about taming my Source, and its second awakening might be much worse than the first one with the cops. The lecture of the female police officer came alive in my memory with an amazing clarity—especially the photos with bodily fragments. I have to control myself; I cannot harm people I love, whether they are white or dark. But that was easier said than done.

I had to spend only half a day there to understand that the night when something would buzz over my head would be the last one for all dwellers of the house. It was not a joke. I urgently had to consult with another dark magician; luckily for me, they weren't exactly hard to find in Krauhard.

"Ma, I'll drop by Uncle Gordon's to say hi. He hasn't moved out, has he?"

"Where would he go to, that old bore!" mother snorted. "Go, go. He already stopped by here today and asked about you, but the bees scared him off."

Poor Uncle Gordon.

My desire to visit the old man did not surprise anybody—he was closer to me than my stepfather; he was a second father to me. It is an axiom that raising a dark mage requires another dark; even ordinary people do not cope well with the task, not to mention white mages. This was the case when you had to be firm and flog a child severely for seemingly innocent pranks to discourage the youngster from trying something nastier next time. Don't preach to me about the fragile psyche of children, I know what I am talking about! While growing up, you begin recognizing your wrongdoings at some point, but you are yet too young to have the strength to cope with the dark nature. Having been beaten, you give yourself a solid pledge—never again!—and sometimes you even keep your word.

As far as I can remember, Uncle Gordon has always been a friend of our family. I owe him my love for alchemy and a relatively flawless character. He was also the only inhabitant of the valley who built a house on the northern slope, among stunted trees and lichen. It was not because of his nature: he had a lot of machinery in his yard and barn—Uncle was the village mechanic. When I showed up, he was tinkering with his broken-down truck; the clunker puffed even more smoke than two years ago, if that were at all possible. Uncle noticed me and waved to go straight to the kitchen, where he appeared a few minutes later, wiping his hands with a cloth. He smiled with a tint of malice:

"How do you like your home?"

"Uncle, do not even start!" I brushed him off and then put the question squarely. "We must do something, or else I'll kill them all!"

Uncle Gordon jerked his brow.

"Are you that edgy?"

"I can barely control the Source."

"But your initiation is supposed to happen in the fall!"

"Has happened already."

He put his chair in front of my own and ordered: "Speak!"

Well, I told him everything. I did not think that it would be quite so unbearably shameful to narrate to him my shady dealings. But Uncle was not angry, he was deathly serious: "Don't tell anyone else about it! Got it?"

"Why?"

"Because an uncontrolled 'wild' Empowerment means an almost guaranteed ban on practicing magic. At best, they will expel you from the university, at worst, put the shackles on you, and you will have to register with NZAMIPS office every week."

"But why?!"

Uncle Gordon sighed.

"Have you read about Bloody Baldus? About Crom the Ripper?

An uncontrolled Empowerment brings Power with unpredictable properties; the most common spells in your case could act as the armory curse. Mental instability and risk of madness go hand in hand with it. Who would allow such a risk?"

"But... what should I do?"

"Keep silence!"

"Is that legal?" I was amazed. Uncle usually didn't give advice with a criminal tinge.

"Look at it this way: the authorities keep silence about what has happened to you. These bloodsuckers have recorded an imprint of your aura. The moment of the Empowerment should be clearly visible on your chip, but had they admitted that you were injured because of them, someone in NZAMIPS would have been in big trouble. Their chicanery annoys many, believe me! They are waiting for you to wag your tongue or lose control on the official test, and then you will never be able to prove their guilt."

"I needed to speak out right away..."

"No, you have done everything right! You were alone, you had no witnesses—especially mage-witnesses—and you will never get access to your aura crystal. They aren't stupid! So why should you be the one taking the fall? I'll show you how to fake the Empowerment on the official test. Of course, from now on, you will have to be very careful, think a hundred times before doing something, and visit an empath upon noticing any deviations, but your life does not have to end here."

"Why are you telling me this?"

"You are Toder's son. I owe much to your father and hate to think that they will destroy your future to cover their own

26

mistakes. Keep your pecker up! In the past, all dark magicians went through spontaneous Empowerment, and it worked out fine; only a few of them had problems."

I immediately thought of Baldus the Bloody. Uncle went to the kitchen, rustled with something in the closet, and returned with a small opaque vial in his hands: "Here it is, drink this. It'll suppress all your magic abilities. A folk remedy. Though the stomach will feel a little twisted for a while."

I sniffed the bottle suspiciously—the liquid inside had a scent of garlic.

"Stay at home for a couple days so that NZAMIPS won't become suspicious. Then I will get you into an expedition."

"Where to?"

"Where necessary! Some morons from Ho-Carg came to our village, some kind of archaeologists from the capital. They are going to dig on the King's Island and are looking for seasonal workers. Of course, no locals will work for them (no fools here), so they will grab someone like you immediately. I suppose I will also have to go with you..."

Having heard that, I gulped down the content of the bottle with no objections. The strange liquid flowed into my stomach as if it was lead, but it did not cause any immediate catastrophic changes. In fact, it produced no changes at all. No matter how much I tried, I could not detect in myself a sensation of decreasing Power, or any kind of internal weakness. Uncle noticed my anxiety, smiled, and told me to go home.

Yes, it was time to go home: night was falling, and the village was not illuminated. What could you do? The countryside isn't quite like your typical city. I ran home following a long familiar path (directly across the rocks, the creek, and by the gardens), and my thoughts swirled around the strange turn of my fate.

From whatever side I looked at it, Lady Luck smiled at me. Please get me right, I don't give a shit if I can't practice dark magic (I am going to be an alchemist anyway), but the general public is suspicious of people that are under NZAMIPS' supervision. For them, the mere existence of surveillance implies psychopathic behavior. I would have died from the effort of trying to explain that I wasn't the one to blame! But the problem had been solved even before it manifested itself.

And then, as if in compensation for my anxiety, an exotic excursion materialized on the horizon. Holy crap, the King's Island! Well, who of the dark magicians wouldn't love a chance to feast their eyes on that place? How timely was my arrival in Krauhard!

CHAPTER 3

My summer vacation, so troublesome at the start, returned to normal: Uncle's potion spoiled my appetite but seriously improved character. I never thought that fluctuations in the Source could so strongly influence my mood.

The potion happened to be very timely: now I could handle my younger sister and brother without irritation. No, I'm not against children, but two years ago, when we were on equal terms, the little ones had not pestered me that much; their attention was mainly focused on our parents then. Now little Emmy was teaching me to recognize different flowers. She was taking me to some buttercups, poking at them, and saying something like, "This is a chicken gizzard plant!"

I was much more worried about zoology than botany: my stepfather cast a spell on my room's window that repelled the bees, but the little beasts caught up with me outside the house. For two days none had stung me, but I was afraid that my luck would not last long.

Lyuchik ran around, happy and shining, and talked about everything. Literally, about everything. It was an unhindered flow of consciousness, the sense of which I could not catch, even when I tried. Unusual behavior for an eight-year-old boy. If those were the symptoms of an awakening white Source, then what did the awakening of a dark one look like? I tried to remember what I used to do to get on my relatives' nerves at his age.

"You know, when we just discovered your dark talent, you tried to control everyone," my stepfather Joe said at lunch, following his offspring with a look full of adoration. "Virtually everyone, even cats. That was so endearing..."

It was a blessing that my memory hadn't retained these events.

For two days I was miraculously showcasing self-control and restraint; even the pickiest empath could not say that I fell short of the image of a perfect genius Big Brother. On the third day, Uncle Gordon, as promised, told my parents about the expedition. We enjoyed tea on the deck that was under a spell of repulsion against bees. The brazen creatures flew to the edge of the spell's shield and hung out there, buzzing ponderously. I was pouring honey over my pancakes. I did not like bees, but I loved sweets, and the idea that the treat was taken away from the hated insects and spiced with their corpses improved the flavor for me.

My mother responded to Uncle's offer without enthusiasm.

"Thomas came here to relax..."

I tore myself away from the pancakes: "Ma! It's the King's Island!"

"Besides, the kid could make some money," Uncle said into his cup. Money? I had not thought about this aspect of the expedition.

"How much do they pay?" Joe became interested.

"Seventeen crowns per week," Uncle said. "Plus three meals a day."

Fifty crowns for three weeks! My look must have said everything: I already saw that money in my pocket. I already felt the weight in my hands. My mother sighed.

"Stop it, Millie!" Uncle smiled. "It will only take a month. You'll still have time to enjoy each other."

"Are you going to the island with the ghosts?" Lyuchik widened his eyes.

"Do not be afraid, kid!" I scoffed. "If they appear, your brother will seal them all."

"Nothing has been going on there for a hundred years now," my stepfather took my side.

"Because no one has been living there for a hundred years," mother pointedly replied.

They argued a little longer, but the last word, as always, was left with me. Was I a dark mage or not? Mother sighed and started packing my things for the trip. Joe was getting in our way, greatly irritating both me and my mom. One thing was good: on the day of my departure it rained in the valley, and the bees did not see me off.

The whole way to the coast Uncle and I drove in silence, but not because there was nothing to talk about—the old wreck jumped on potholes like a jerboa, howling on the rises and rattling deafeningly downhill. Any communication under such circumstances could cost us our tongues. A few travelers that we saw on our way quickly jumped to the side and incanted averting spells, cows started kicking, and horses were rearing up. Ha, imagine what would have happened had they known where we were going to!

As far as I knew, the island had always been closed for visitors. Under the old government, there was a prison, the most horrible place in all of Ingernika. The current authorities closed it out of compassion for the warders, but since then a belief had sprung up that the souls of the dark magicians came to live there after death. About a hundred years ago a chain of enchanted beacons emerged around the island, scaring off fishing boats with their sad ringing. Opinions regarding the reason for the strict prohibition against visitors differed: some thought that there were gates to the underworld on the island, while others claimed that the authorities guarded the tomb of the island's namesake king. Others, referring to the legends, hinted that the king would be fully able to protect himself. The island had never been a tourist destination, any interest in it was discouraged, and I hadn't seen its picture even once.

Still more surprising was the appearance of dandies from the capital in Krauhard. What could attract their interest in a place where no one ever lived?

Archaeologists were going to sail to the island from a tiny fishing village with the strange name of Canine Beach; I do not know about others, but in my mind that name was associated with corpses and garbage. Uncle and I were the first to arrive at the village. I sweated hard in my thick knitted jacket hoping that it would be as cold on the sea as promised.

The employers showed up when it was already past noon. A hefty truck, nearly new if judged by its exhaust, rolled up to the pier, and a paramilitary off-road minivan (only the army used diesel engines in small vehicles) followed it. Movers and security guys jumped out of the truck, while our future bosses slowly poured out of the minivan.

"These guys have money," Uncle remarked thoughtfully.

I did not try to sustain the conversation; the hangover from the anti-magic elixir was surprisingly miserable.

"I won't give you more," Uncle said at the time of departure. "Taking this elixir for a long time causes hallucinations and bouts of schizophrenia."

I nearly choked.

"Why didn't you warn me?"

"Did you really have a choice?" Uncle argued. "Let's not draw attention to us. The elixir's effect will end in two days, and we will start training. Let me warn you: I am no good as a teacher, so do not expect too much. You are not a fortuneteller like Coy Gorgun; your task is to learn how to confidently call upon and dismiss your Source, and even an idiot can cope with it after practicing. Got it?"

I nodded; my head did not ache yet then. The prospect of making money, walking around the forbidden island, and learning a little more magic looked quite attractive. Who knew that I would be feeling so sick?

Besides us, three more workers were going to the island, and, judging by their clothing, they were not local. Nobody wore shirts with short sleeves in Krauhard, not even in summer— health is more important than comfort. The guys did not attempt to make introductions, but I realized that all of them were students, either from the capital or from its suburbs. They took swigs out of a large leather flask and laughed; they looked like they knew little about the King's Island. I had already pictured in my mind a company of cabinet scientists committing a raid on historical places on their university's budget, when the paramilitary truck approached the pier. A mountain of bales, boxes, and barrels grew rapidly on the berth; a couple of burly men in uniform overalls received the cargo at the pier and chased the curious away; one of the two had a nightstick hanging on his belt, and another one had a knife tucked in his boot. The ship that lazily dangled off the coast started steaming.

I tried to fight off nausea and think sensibly: the car, the boat, and the guards implied that the superiors of the expedition were not just after the money, they knew what kind of place the island was. I started wondering:

"What are we going to look for?"

Uncle just laughed in response: "I did not ask. Do not worry, nephew, we'll be cautious."

The students roared, welcoming the director of the expedition, a short, lean, and remarkably ugly woman. Hers was one of those cases when even a white magician would not be able to help: having proper facial features and smooth, ivory skin, she sported heavy eyelids of a habitual drunkard and a sardonic smile that would have scared a crocodile. The director was followed by a man a head taller than she, deliberately overdressed and bearing the obvious signs of a dark magician.

No surprise there; bringing a specialist in the supernatural to the island was a very wise decision, but we all knew how costly the services of a dark magician with military bearing were.

"Gentlemen," the lady-crocodile began her greeting speech, referring mainly to the two of us, "I am your queen and god for the next four weeks. Please address me 'Mrs. Clements' and nothing short of it. Just so we are clear, I will not tolerate any drunken debauchery during our expedition," she pierced me with a glare, though the flask was in the hands of the students, "and I am warning you: all that you will see or find on the island is the exclusive property of the expedition. Got it? Those who do not agree better stay on the mainland."

"Everything is clear, Mrs. Clements!" Uncle sang in a tone that was typically used for courting an obstinate mare.

The lady-crocodile jerked her head in a rather horse-like manner, but the man who stood behind her coughed politely, and a scandal did not unfold.

"Next to me is Mr. Smith," she said through her teeth, "he is our safety expert. Given the specificity of our place of work, I am asking you to report to him any oddities or unusual events immediately."

All of us nodded, but I became a little disappointed. What, I wouldn't be able to tell anyone about the island?! The trip was turning out to be somewhat schizophrenic from the outset.

A lifeboat with a crackling ethanol engine cast off from the ship. Local fishermen that gathered on the shore watched the boat with interest: would it stall or wouldn't? If the alcohol was local, then it surely would; I tested it on my moped many times. Either the climate here was very humid, or vendors were particularly shameless, but I failed to achieve any stable engine operation. It would be dubious fun to get stuck in the middle of nowhere.

But on a bright sunny day the boat looked good, and it flew— not sailed—across the waves.

"Roll call!" Mrs. Clements captured my attention again. "Pierre Acleran..."

Students readily raised their hands, Mr. Smith and the two guards were accounted for too, and someone called Mermer was marked as being on a ship. Uncle and I were the last on the list.

"Gordon Ferro..."

"Present!"

"... and Thomas Tangor."

"Here," I raised my hand for clarity. Mr. Smith gave me an interested look.

"All aboard!"

Mrs. Clements was hasty, of course, when she commanded everyone to board: only four people and a couple of boxes at a time could fit onto the boat. Mrs. Clements and the students went first, but I did not envy them: the three of them would have to receive and arrange all of the expedition's belongings.

On the shore, Uncle was able to maneuver so that he involved everyone in the loading, including the guards and the driver of the truck. Naturally, we finished the job faster. The last boat (already free of its boxes) took to the ship those who lingered over on the shore. Mr. Smith sat down across from me and stared at me during the ride.

"Why have you joined the expedition, Mr. Tangor?" he asked finally.

"Money, sir!" I smiled broadly. A universal reason.

"What about you, Mr. Ferro?"

"Someone has to watch my nephew."

"Hmm."

"Why are you going there, Mr. Smith?" I could not restrain my curiosity.

He jerked his eyebrow in surprise. I wondered what his expectation was when he started a conversation with a dark mage.

"My job is to ensure the safety of this stupid expedition!" he admitted with surprising sincerity.

"I feel sorry for you," Uncle intoned.

But Mr. Smith stubbornly shook his head: "Everything is under control. There won't be any problems."

As they say, Let us pray, Brothers and Sisters.

But perhaps that was a perfect example of a rational approach based on knowledge rather than on local superstitions. I have been pestered with safety rules since I was five; I knew about the supernatural manifestations so much that I could lecture at Redstone University. Yet in my memory, nothing occurred in our valley like what was depicted in old men's stories. Well, a couple of imbeciles had been injured, of course... Cattle raged at night as well... But against Krauhard's sinister reputation it was hardly noteworthy. Perhaps, rumors exaggerated the King's Island's danger too. It happened now and then!

It took us almost twenty-four hours to reach the place. Of course, we could have sailed faster, but nobody wanted to land on the island in the dark. I slept soundly under the quiet whistle of a steam turbine, the nausea was gone, and my mood could not be better. Time to look around—assess where exactly I ended up.

The ship slowly and cautiously made its way through the fog that was much thinner over the water and smelled subtly of the sea. There were no birds; the only sources of sound were the boat and the surf slowly roaring somewhere nearby. We had passed the beacon line at night, and now there were jagged cliffs and boulders, stretching to the right of the ship, protruding from the sea as if guarding some ancient fortresses. I idly watched seaweed floundering about in the foam between the rock teeth. The members of the team who were not struck down by seasickness woke up and got out on the deck. It was at that exact moment that the island chose to surprise us.

The shore cliffs snuggled close to the ground, revealing a large cleft: water and wind corroded stone, and the rock broke like a bad tooth. A metal castle appeared in the inner cavity. It was perfectly exposed before our eyes. My jaw dropped. Almost untouched by rust, massive metallic plates enclosed the structure from the outside; where the rocks had overcome the metal, the eye caught layers of inner levels in a jumble of steel construction. Years had stripped away the extra stuff, and whatever resisted belonged to the centuries, millennia, eternity. The castle seemed to be tired of solitude, and it leaned out of the rocks to look at us with its dark maw. Below the castle, a ledge sprinkled with crushed stone was sticking out above the shore line, and powerful steel trusses could be seen under the ledge. From the ship, it seemed like the cliffs were but a false front, lined with stone and hollow inside.

"A gorgeous place!" the words escaped my mouth unbidden. Indeed, if the expedition let at least one picture leak to the world at large, no enchanted beacons would hold people back.

The armored plates over a foot thick suggested such reliability and power that you just wanted to sink your teeth into them. Was there anything left inside?

"Get out of here! The place is ugly as hell," one of the students gasped.

I raised my eyebrow unwittingly. I thought he was pale because of seasickness. Was he scared by the island?

"Ah," it dawned on me, "you are the white, aren't you? I got it."

"What did you get?" his companion protested.

"Nerves," I shrugged.

Uncle struggled out from the hold and, having discerned the shore, began to rub his hands involuntarily: "Wow, how deliciously captivating! What's inside?" he asked Mrs. Clements.

"It should not concern you!" she said coldly. "The ruins are under the state's protection, and you will not approach them."

What a witch... Uncle saddened noticeably.

We quickly left behind the mysterious construction, but I was still puzzled, trying to figure out in what era our ancestors could build something like that. As an alchemist, I knew how heavy one such plate could be, and it was incomprehensible how the plates were assembled in such a big stack. And how they worked from the inside, not the outside. History wasn't my strongest subject, but I always thought that in previous centuries people lived somewhat simpler.

The situation intrigued me; surprises on the King's Island were in store for all.

"As you know, I do not like to hire locals!" Mrs. Clements thoroughly stirred a spoonful of white powder in a quarter of glass of water and swallowed the resulting mess in one gulp. The taste of the medical medley made her shudder. Her conversation partner lazily mumbled something from his bunk.

"Especially those, who are also wild drunks," she hid a box of medicine in a leather case. "You get little help but problems through the roof from them."

"Do not rush to conclusions, they were not drunk," Mr. Smith got up on his elbow. "As to their uproar... Both of them are dark—a huge fortune! Hiring those two in Ho-Carg would have eaten our entire budget, but here they will work for us almost for free. Let me deal with them, okay?"

"No problem!" Mrs. Clements easily agreed. "I do not think that we will need their skills. The last commission had worked on the island three years ago, and their review was favorable. The caretaker still lives in the castle, and NZAMIPS would not have allowed this if they had any doubts."

"The last three years... These three years have been too strange," Mr. Smith sighed, "but I hope you're right. That will be better for all of us."

CHAPTER 4

The island rejected us. It became clear from the very first minute of our stay there.

The fog cleared when we reached our destination. The sun did not show up; instead, the sky was filled with a translucent pearl-gray haze—a common phenomenon for Krauhard. When the monotony of the landscape became tiresome, the cliffs parted, revealing an entrance to a deep bay, the ancient name of which had been reliably forgotten long ago, and for the last three hundred years it was known simply as the Prison Bay. On the far side of the island one could see buildings of the type more common for Ingernika: rough masonry made from local stone, guarded windows, rusty stains on the walls. The buildings were subtly immersed in landscape, pretending to be a mirage; only their roofs of red tiles dotted the background of gray rocks. There were no external walls - the place had never been used as a fortress. And who would ever think of guarding the King's Island? From the outset, the complex was built as a prison, Vale of the Doomed—a name that had become a household word. If memory served me correctly, it was the first specialized institution of that kind; before, criminals were either flogged publicly or had their heads lopped off, nothing in between. Indubitably, given their particular character, there were far more dark mages held there over the years than anyone else, and that brought about all sorts of silly superstitions. A black slab of some unknown material, obviously predating the construction of the prison, served as its foundation.

Crossing the natural breakwater, the ship gave a signal. Then another one. And another. Then the noise of the engine changed: the team started backing up; it seemed that the captain did not dare to approach the pier head-on. After a short meeting, they lowered the dinghy on the water and Mr. Smith went ashore with one of the guards. They returned two hours later and, after another meeting, the ship finally moved forward. Lady-crocodile, as if nothing had happened, began directing the unloading.

I drew two conclusions from what was going on: first, something went wrong, and second, mere mortals were not supposed to know what exactly went wrong.

"Keep your eyes open," Uncle whispered to me.

The unloading made me set my concerns aside for a moment. Students, cursing, hauled a cart with the expeditionary belongings to a building (at least we had a cart. Without it, to carry that mountain of stuff over would have taken until the end of summer). Uncle Gordon and I, armed with poles, rolled barrels with fuel for the generator up the hill (not really a difficult task, but it looked technically daunting from outside). That white guy was busy with the dynamo-machine in the outbuilding. I couldn't believe my eyes: didn't they find a dark mage to send?! After the third barrel, I really wanted to ask what he was doing there for so long. After the fourth one I acted.

The outbuilding strongly smelled of oil; the white had managed to fuel the tank. Burnt fuses lay on the floor: an emergency breaker was triggered, but, at first glance, neither the generator nor its winding looked damaged. The student was yanking the start-up handle again and again to no visible results. The poor fellow was in a trance; the machine was not working. I needed to rescue the guy and myself. Literally. That was one of the most annoying traits in the white mages—if something really upsets them, they could cry for weeks. More than once had I witnessed a funeral of a broken cup, not to mention of dead mice and birds. The most unforgettable spectacle for me, though, was a man gently carrying a caught cockroach into the street. Imagine: the cockroach must have been captured first and then carried outside without being hurt. In short, I was not thrilled with the prospect of spending four weeks in the company of the emotionally shell-shocked white. Much less so, on King's Island. Ha!

"Hey, make way for an alchemist!"

He sulked and started looking like Lyuchik.

"Don't lose heart!" I patted him on the shoulder. "I will fix it right away."

The problem was as simple as a stump and wasn't related to alchemy at all, but rather to the "science of shitty contacts"—that sorry excuse for a mechanic had not pushed the fuses far enough into the slots, causing the generator not to start up. When the machine started, the student genuinely lit up.

"If something else happens," I smiled amicably, "call me. I'll try my best to help!"

He nodded and smiled.

"Mr. Tangor! What are you doing there?" Mr. Smith barked from somewhere.

"I'm taking out the garbage!" I yelled out the first thing that came into my mind, winked, and was gone.

As it turned out, Mr. Smith yelled for a good reason—the weather had changed dramatically. Although the day was at its height, a strip of thick fog crept out from the sea to the shore. It looked utterly suspicious. Our superiors began fretting; we were ordered to grab and drag everything that could be damaged by dampness into the house and leave the rest outside in its place. The boat started backing up to anchor somewhere in the middle of the bay, out of harm's way. By the time the trembling white curtain of fog reached the shore, the doors of the prison's only residential building had been closed tightly, and the members of the expedition had made their home as comfortable as they could.

We were given a corner room overlooking the prison yard, though we couldn't see anything because of the fog. In the light of the day, such as it was, the room looked cozy, just a little dusty. Uncle checked for ward-off spells on the windows, clicked his tongue, and did not change anything. The thick fog splashed outside, like milk, and poured into the water; the sun illuminated it from within, and the air seemed to glow faintly. An infernal spectacle that we, Krauhardians, did not like to admire.

"Uncle, don't you feel that something is wrong here?"

"The supernatural," he nodded with the look of a connoisseur. "It looms so close to the borders of reality that it presses on our nerves. Actually, our whole venture is starting to smell."

"Well, they ought to have known where they were going to."

"Are you sure?" Uncle chuckled. "The situation can change very quickly. They expected to be met. Have you noticed? Who was supposed to meet us, and where is he now?"

I shuddered involuntarily. So far, I hadn't met anything deadly dangerous that could take away a man's life. The only guests from the other world in our valley were ignes fatui—flashes of light that wandered in fog—quite a harmless phenomenon, as long as you didn't touch them.

Somebody knocked on the door politely.

"Come in," Uncle offered.

The white mage from the generator room timidly peeked

through the door and said: "Mrs. Clements has asked for everyone to gather downstairs."

"We are coming!" I tried to remember where I put my shoes.

"What's the urgency, I wonder?" Uncle grunted and pulled out of his bag a pair of felt slippers. Alas, I lacked the foresight to bring the same.

"Maybe she wants to bid us farewell?" I giggled hysterically.

Perhaps, the prison's administration used to live in this building at one time: rooms were spacious, narrow hallways with multiple doors were absent, and a spacious hall was right behind the front door. There, among a heap of unsorted equipment, Mrs. Clements decided to gather us. In the absence of chairs, we had to sit on the luggage. The atmosphere at the meeting was quite peculiar: there appeared to be no immediate danger, but something strange was certainly going on. The problem, in my opinion, was that the capital residents thought that otherworldly threats were severely exaggerated (you can afford an attitude of that sort only if you live on top of salt marshes—the supernatural doesn't like salt). Nobody seemed to realize that there was nothing alive, not even rats, on the King's Island. Intuition stubbornly kept telling me that Krauhard wouldn't forgive such an attitude.

Two students conversed in hushed tones, the white from before (I remembered his name now—Alex) looked depressed. Uncle was the only one who showed up at the meeting in slippers. Mr. Smith looked like he just crawled out of some hole and smelled musty and dank. Only Mrs. Clements was cheerful and unfazed. I thought the audience was in for a lecture on the rules of safe conduct, but instead she delivered a speech about the necessity of hard work: "The expedition has to work on a tight schedule; attaining our goals will require a thoughtful and responsible approach to the job from everyone. Simple execution of assigned tasks will not be enough. Upon successful completion of the project there may be bonuses."

"What are we looking for?" I could not resist asking.

She glanced at me in irritation: "If you permit me, Mr. Tangor, I will get to it in a minute."

The students readily giggled. I shrugged; two years in Redstone had taught me to ignore simple jabs.

"This island safeguards the sanctity of the mysteries of the most ancient civilization in the world," Mrs. Clements informed us loftily and launched into a lengthy description of someone's work, citing authors and the results of their excavations. Students were hastily scribing it down.

My attention to the lecture quickly wavered. History was never in the sphere of my interests; I failed to see the point in gathering thousands of useless things. The idea that from these fragments one could draw pictures of the lives of past generations seemed funny to me (will you agree? If not, try to assemble even an ordinary alarm clock from scattered debris), and the aesthetic value of shards and fragments was even more arguable. Archeology, in my eyes, was a costly foolishness based on insatiable human curiosity.

"...and to assess the level of the technomagic development of that era," Mrs. Clements finished her next premise.

That brought me out of my stupor: "Alchemy?"

Mrs. Clements gave me a scornful look.

"Tech-no-ma-gic," she repeated almost syllable by syllable, "differs from alchemy in its ability to manipulate very delicate structures of matter, and it allows the execution of these fine operations thousands and hundreds of thousands of times, without any deviation from the original."

I pulled from the pile of things a box of fuses that survived contact with Alex.

"Like this?" I asked. Let the one who thought that it deviated from the original cast a stone at me.

She scrunched her face: "No! On a much more subtle level, commensurable with the effect of magic!"

"The lost alchemical techniques," Uncle Gordon concluded competently.

I shrugged and decided not to push the argument; there are people who have an irrational aversion to alchemy. Usually, they belong to the whites, but you can also meet them among ordinary people. And their ostentatious dislike for the "artificial" nonetheless sits perfectly well with love for products of white magic, like all those trans-horses, trans-rabbits, and trans-cows. Mrs. Clements belonged exactly to that category. My Redstone experience suggested that an altercation with such personalities was pointless and unproductive.

After a lengthy lecture about the grandeur and uniqueness of the technomagic, we finally learned what we were here to look for: the audience was shown drawings, diagrams, and reconstructions of ancient objects. They looked like small, angular beetles with varying numbers of legs and no distinction between their front and rear ends. The latter fact amused me a lot, but I managed to keep myself from laughing until we were back in our room.

"Don't cackle," Uncle remarked, watching my convulsions. "If they find at least a dozen of these, it will more than compensate for the cost of the expedition. These things used to be called 'sand gnats', and their artificial origin was discovered not too long ago. Ever since then, they have been in sharp demand by everybody: the military, academia, private developers. No one knows what they are, but they are wanted by all. I heard that one of their intact nests was sold for one and a half million crowns."

"One and a half million..." my mirth left me in a flash.

"Don't even think about it!" Uncle warned me. "Why do you think this island hasn't been ransacked yet, despite all the bans? Remember the castle. Inside it is dark all around; there has been no light for hundreds, if not thousands, of years. Understand my point?"

I caught his meaning, and it made me sick. I recalled a theory to that effect: the longer an otherworldly phenomenon existed, the stronger and more evolved and unpredictable it became. It explained why there was such a strong magic ambiance here! For thousands of years even a primitive ignis fatuus could turn into a fiery phantom, not to mention the more complex entities. What a fabulous island this was...

"We are waist deep in..." I began.

"Ah, you got it at last!" Uncle rejoiced. "Don't fear! Just mind your surroundings; there is little hope for help from our companions. Those two blockheads are just mirror images of the king's godfather, and the woman is probably the same."

In Krauhard's mythology, the "godfathers of the King" were the doomed ones, people carrying the mark of impending death. In this case, the nickname was a good match, too good, even. Unthinkable! Why did NZAMIPS let us come here, a pack of civilians accompanied by only one official dark magician? From childhood I had been taught that, when confronted with otherworldly forces, your main weapon is stealth, but a big expedition invading the island could only remain unnoticed through pure chance. I came to the conclusion that somebody was set to kill us.

I am still young; I don't want to meet the King just yet!

"Uncle, perhaps we should get out..."

"Practice your power, kiddo!" he proclaimed sternly. "You might need it very soon."

I was "overjoyed", as they say.

We agreed to get up early, before breakfast, to start the training that I needed so badly and that had gotten me in this deep shit.

"Not too early?" I clarified.

"No, otherwise it will be too late."

Now I recalled how annoyed I was as a child at the way Uncle Gordon "comforted" me: he used to say, "Torn pants aren't a big deal," adding, "you'll get flogged once or twice for the sake of propriety, so what?" I wondered if he realized that his nephew had grown a bit.

Breakfast was set at eight, and we went down to the shore at seven in the morning; we grabbed our towels and pretended to be going for a swim. Why not? The bay's water was warm in summer, and its cleanliness around the island was almost assured. Yesterday's fog had left no traces, the day promised to be sunny and warm, and shoals of fry flashed in the waves, immune to the dark curses.

"Climb!" Uncle requested, pointing to a lonely rock protruding from the water.

"Maybe I'd better practice on the beach?"

"Well, only if you wish to summon all the neighboring undead..."

I sighed, undressed, and jumped into the water. By the way, the water was really warm. Climbing on a slippery boulder wasn't an easy task; teetering on the top, I called out, "Now what?" Immediately after, I felt a pebble hit my back. "Hey! What are you doing?"

"Invoke your Power!" Uncle ordered.

"How?"

"As you did the first time."

The next pebble struck me on the buttocks.

"Invoke your Power."

"Give me at least a minute!"

I tried to recall the circumstances that surrounded my Empowerment. Should I get angry or scared? Another pebble!

"Stop it! Are you crazy?"

"Do what I said."

"I'm doing it!"

"You are not. Emotions facilitate the call, but they are not part of it. You need neither anger, nor wrath, but Power! Let me see it!"

"Wait a minute!" I frantically tried to figure out what to do. Go down there and try to kick his ass? He was older and still stronger than me.

"Better. Go on!"

What exactly had I done? Again a pebble!

"Don't relax."

I strained myself so heavily that almost fainted and then began projecting something outward, so hard that my brains felt like they were leaking out.

"Go on, more confidence!"

Preserving some degree of pressure, I ventured to open my eyes: a black mirage floated in front of me—the same black flame that blinded me during the Empowerment. And then I lost my breath, saw circles swirling in front my eyes, and fell off the rock. Uncle pulled me out of the water.

"Enough for the first time," he concluded, "rest now. And remember, if you try to suppress the dark Source, you'll cease feeling a difference between the presence and absence of Power, and thus you'll lose control over it. An attempt to forget your essence always ends in madness for a dark magician. Empowerment is a one-way road only. You don't have a choice; you ought to call your Power again and again until it is no longer associated with any particular emotion, and until it reveals itself fully. You must learn to treat it like your arm or leg. This can only be accomplished through continuous training and repetition. Got it?"

"Yes, Master!" I tried to catch my breath, lying on the rocky shore. Colored circles floated before my eyes.

"You spend too much energy on the call, but that's for lack of habit; you'll get used to it."

I very much hoped so! My nausea had subsided, being replaced with weakness and trembling of the muscles. And it was only seven o'clock in the morning; we still had to work all day!

"Get up!" Uncle kicked me in the ribs. "Break stereotypes. You're not tired physically; it's a mental illusion."

Screw that, an illusion!

We left the shore to get breakfast. I was wet and angry; Uncle was also wet, but filled with a sense of accomplishment.

Damned tutor! If I had a choice, would I have allowed him to treat me so?

At breakfast our life became more interesting: Alex sat down next to us. The dark power still paced in me, and I barely restrained myself from insulting him.

"What's the matter?"

Alex hesitated for a while, eventually uttering, "May I move in with you?"

His question surprised me so much that I even forgot to get angry: "What the hell?"

"I... okay, forget it!" He attempted to leave.

Without any explanation? No way! I immediately changed my tune, letting in a note of confidence and irony: the whites are almost all empaths, which means they subconsciously perceive the moods of people close to them. They also tend to mirror other people's emotions and the younger the magician, the worse he controls it.

"Don't be rash now. We do not mind." I glanced at Uncle who merely shrugged, "It's just a little unexpected."

Alex, not sensing that he was caught in a trap of the master manipulator, relaxed a little, but didn't open up immediately. He looked a bit crumpled, and for empaths, their health depends heavily on the overall emotional ambiance...

"Are your friends scaring you?" I guessed.

He nodded quietly.

What did I say before? Ordinary people could be worse than any of the dark magicians. They could have picked a better place to screw with their friend's nerves! Odds were, if I left him alone, he would eventually go nuts, lose his temper, and pay for their jokes with his blood. Indignation dilated my nostrils and awakened my urge to beat someone up.

"Uncle?"

He shrugged again: "Let him move in! Just one thing: give him the 'safety instructions' to avoid surprises."

For the remainder of the leisure time after breakfast, we moved Alex's belongings over under the pensive gaze of Mr. Smith. I instructed my new friend: "Don't fear! You can feel that something strange is going on around. But I know some simple rules, and if you follow them, you will minimize your risk. Believe me! I grew up in Krauhard."

"Do you think there are the otherworldly here?" the white mage asked with an unhealthy interest, packing into his bag the sundries that he had unloaded before.

"I guarantee! It's the King's Island, after all. Remember, you cannot go to a place that lacks light, even if you carry a lantern. The places where sunlight does not reach are especially dangerous—caves, cellars, and such. Don't let your curiosity trap you, especially if you are alone. If you notice any strange sounds, rustles, movement—skidoo and run to Mr. Smith. And do not hesitate; he is a dark mage, he will understand. If it gets worse, remember the sea is your salvation; no otherworldly creature can sneak up on you over the salty water. Another rule: if you see any humans, ask them to name themselves, and if you do not get a response, run. The mute do not live in Krauhard. Here they are killed in infancy as unholy spawns. And surely, do not open cursed doors, do not break protective signs; if you mess anything up, just call Mr. Smith immediately. He is paid to provide our protection, so let him do his job. Got it?"

"Yeah." He put his bag in the corner of our room and looked

around with interest.

"The main thing is to follow the rules all the time, regardless of circumstances. Imagine that they are the laws of nature, and you cannot break them physically, no matter who asked you to."

"And run away to Mr. Smith at once," he smiled.

"Well done, chap!"

On that day we worked long hours. The job, from my point of view, was moronic: we hand-sorted rocks at the dump. When clearing the site and erecting the prison's wall, ancient builders had produced a mountain of debris, which they piled up right there, on the beach, without thinking twice. Before making a raid to the core of the island, Mrs. Clements wanted to know whether there was anything interesting that had been dug up earlier and discarded as useless. To assess the treasures in the dump, we chose a few sites to go through stone by stone to the solid rock beneath, carefully recording our findings. Alex was paired with me. Two other students dug together, and Uncle and the guards continued to unload the ship. Guess which of us worked longer?

Alex was again in good spirits and full of enthusiasm. Luckily, yesterday's worries had no serious impact on his health. He lectured me about the subtleties of archaeological research, without asking whether I needed that or not: "Rocks in these parts of the dump can be distinguished by color and size; clearly, they have been brought from different places. If we find something, we might be able to track its source and understand where to focus our attention. We are short on time!"

I nodded and diligently, one by one, shifted the rocks to the cart. So far, in front of me, there were rocks, rocks, and more rocks.

"Here you are!" Alex showed me a fragment with jagged scars on the edge. "The material was clearly treated with a chisel. I think our section contains masonry waste; it's unlikely there is anything else of interest."

Who would have doubted that! I was sure that Mrs. Clements would not entrust me with such an important task, since I was so skeptical about the technomagic. The hill of displaced rocks grew; Alex found time to tell me what university he was a student of, about his interests, why he joined the expedition, and how cool it was to be an archeologist. My habit of ignoring idle chatter, practiced to perfection on my younger siblings, was the only thing that saved me now. He gibbered and muttered like rustle of wind and rain, occasionally dropping meaningful phrases. According to him, Mrs. Clements was a rising star of archaeology that got the wealthy and the military interested in her studies, though I had already figured that out myself. The subject of her research interest was the most ancient of the known civilizations, presumably found in Capetower (Capetower was the steel fortress we had seen) but little studied. Among the apparent reasons for that was the antiquity of the culture in question, as well as its clear connection to the supernatural manifestations; the majority of the excavations were visited by archeologists once or twice at most, and every time with serious risk to their lives. It was incomprehensible that a white magician would choose this line of business.

At the depth of two feet the soil suddenly changed its properties. The rough stone fragments were replaced with tightly packed sand with splashes of colorful scales and large debris; among the inorganic dust I noticed a white spot—it was a fish skeleton. Oh my, a fish that had been eaten three hundred years ago! I sure had found a treasure. Alex hopped enthusiastically around the pit: "This is it! The stuff that was taken out of the ancient ruins before the construction! Now we'll know how it all looked before!"

What an optimist! Mrs. Clements approached us, praised Alex

(hey, what about me?), and began explaining to him how to keep proper records. The boundaries of the excavation had been changed; now envious students had to dig close to us. In all this activity, time was flying.

The King's Island waited in ambush. Nothing strange happened, the fog did not return, and the days were sunny and warm. Uncle and I went to "swim" every day and, I had to admit, my skills were improving noticeably. The food was good (Mr. Mermer turned out to be an excellent cook), our work wasn't difficult, and entertainment was present as well: Uncle Gordon began arguing with Mr. Smith. I expected that to happen as soon as I saw them together, but I hadn't imagined them to quarrel with such enthusiasm.

It all started on the third day when I, once again having fallen down from the rock, was recovering on the shore. I was basically sunbathing.

"What a brazen face he has..." Uncle muttered suddenly.

I half-rose on one elbow and looked around the rocky beach. Pierre Acleran was approaching us through the boulders.

"Mr. Smith is looking for you," the student told us gleefully.

"It's still a quarter of an hour till breakfast," Uncle cut him off.

"You tell him that!"

We did not rush: the sea salt had to be washed off (we brought a bucket of freshwater with us). We poured the water on our bodies, dried off, and put on our clothes. That is to say, we arrived barely in time for breakfast.

Mr. Smith met us on the path leading from the beach to the prison quarters. His eyes were shooting lightning bolts: "You will not leave the camp from now on!"

"Unlikely," Uncle smiled calmly. "Or you believe that the prison has not been shut down yet?"

"These places are..." Mr. Smith began talking.

"My home," Uncle finished for him. "I've lived here twice as long as you have existed. I do not need to be taught cautiousness. Instead, you'd better give a lecture to your students—they swarm over the ruins with a simple lantern."

The oil lantern was a child's toy; to feel safe in this neighborhood you had to carry a special lamp, enchanted with blue light. Mr. Smith gritted his teeth and left us to brainwash the capital fools. It was fun to have three dark magicians in one place!

That day I barely followed the development of the conflict; my thoughts were busy with some other stuff. Frankly speaking, the problem I faced was unusual: the night before Alex had advised us that the following day the ship would sail back to the mainland. He asked if I wanted to send a word to my family.

"Why?" I had never written letters to anyone; even the date of my return home I reported by telegram.

"What do you mean?" Alex became surprised in turn. "They are probably worried."

Mom was surely worried. The day before I merely shrugged at Alex's words, but since then a thought about sending her a letter visited me with obsessive regularity. Of course, my mother knew me inside and out, and if she loved me so far, nothing would change that.

I was troubled by this question for half a day, watching with annoyance as Mr. Smith hounded Uncle on trifling issues. The old contrarian loudly criticized all of the security measures taken. The two fools began attracting attention, but no one wanted to give ground. Doing so would mean accepting the other side's superiority. They stood on their haunches, eyes shooting sparks; it was a good thing that they did not reach the stage of throwing curses at each other. In fairy tales, dark magicians always lived in towers alone and were never in anyone's service. I wondered how the military coped with schooling its contingent. Judging by Mr. Smith, they didn't.

Alex tried to draw my attention to the conflict, but I brushed him off and advised to turn his back on the problem; they would sort it out by themselves. I had a more serious question: what to do with the letter. To write or not to write? In the end, it was worth a try, at least. During the lunch break I borrowed some ink and paper from Alex, set myself up on the steps of the residential quarters, and began doing the most unnatural thing in my life—corresponding.

Right off the bat, it turned out that I did not have any idea how a letter should look. Well, I sure knew how to address an envelope. But what about the contents inside? I vaguely recalled the contents of an official invitation that came to me from Redstone University.

'Hello all,' I wrote at the top and paused again.

In principle, the guiding reason behind my decision to write was my mother's concerns. What should I write to calm her worries?

'It is good here.'

'Where is here?' I crossed out the last words and wrote differently: 'We have arrived on the island without any problem. I'm sending a letter at the first opportunity. The situation is good, the food is excellent. I swim in the sea every morning; haven't caught a cold yet.'

I was pleased with the result of my efforts. It was brief,

informative, correctly spelled. Legible. I could have wrapped it up right there, but I began enjoying it. What else could be written about?

'You're probably wondering why I left home to come here.'

What if she got offended? I spent just three days at home before leaving for the island. It was worth it to add a bit of candor: 'Joe's new hobby caught me by surprise.'

It was a gross understatement!

'Please get me right, I do not want to limit his self-expression. I just need time to prepare for it mentally.'

And physically, if the dark Source could be considered a physical phenomenon.

'I am sure that by the end of the expedition I will be able to control myself sufficiently.'

...And to control my power too. At least, Uncle Gordon was confident about it.

'I guess I should have warned you in advance about my coming back.'

Unfortunately, some things you understand only in hindsight. It was good that I hadn't asked them for money via telegram! My mother would have sold everything and left my little bro and sis without their sweets. How would their older brother look in that case?

Deciding that my duty was fulfilled, I signed the letter and went to look for Mrs. Clements; Mr. Smith was not in the right mood to play the role of a mailman. The rest was simple: in the mailbox there was a whole pack of letters with Alex's neat handwriting. The white mage had probably written to all of his acquaintances whose addresses he was able to recall. I added my modest contribution to his titanic work and lightheartedly went to poke around in the dump.

Meanwhile, the war between the mages was flaring up. In the evening Uncle had attempted to recruit me into his army but was sent to hell. In the morning Mr. Smith went to the beach with us and, instead of training, we were forced to actually swim. During the day Uncle had caught students in an attempt to get into the basement of the watertower, and for a while criticized Mr. Smith for not watching them properly. In the evening—at midnight—the security expert showed up to verify the integrity of the protective spells on our window. With his own lamp.

The nerves of the audience broke down first.

"Why are they doing this?" Alex asked plaintively. The white mage still shared our room; he was in no hurry to leave us.

I sighed heavily: "They are the dark."

"You are a dark as well, yet you do not behave like them!"

"I am not just dark, I'm... smart." When I talked about myself, I didn't sell myself short in front of the audience.

What sense did it make to turn this into a circus, confirming the scandalous reputation of the dark magicians? I'm not talking about how much worse it made things, but those two removed any room for maneuvering, clashing head-to-head like a pair of mules. Now they were left with no other way to solve the conflict but banal fisticuffs; the question was just how soon they would overcome the aversion to violence diligently drummed into every magician's head. I made a bet on Mr. Smith: he was a military guy, they were taught differently, and he could give Uncle a decent head start both in physical shape and in magic power. So far, they both still remembered that fighting was not good, and that kept them angry and others anxious.

The return of the ship calmed the brawlers down for some time but did not solve the dilemma—someone's blood had to be spilled. I waited with interest; I had never seen a fight between adults, let alone between initiated magicians. Would they risk using magic? And what would the island's response to it be? I'd better prep the lifeboat, just in case...

And then came the day that promised to be "the one". Noticing the signs, I quietly took Alex aside and asked him not to talk with Uncle, not even to say hello. Actually, there was no need to alert people. Uncle disappeared in the morning, and at lunch both magicians looked so spiteful that even the meanest of the students, Pierre, did not dare to screw around. During the day, Uncle Gordon was digging furiously, muttering something inaudibly (he was probably counting the offenses he had incurred), and Mr. Smith was milling around the shore looking dispassionately at the sea (probably doing the same thing as Uncle Gordon, but silently). For the final collision they had to be brought closer. Alex wanted me to help them, right?

Seizing the moment when Mrs. Clements called Mr. Smith over to inspect some findings, I dropped my basket next to them as if by chance and asked, as though making small talk: "If we find any bones, will we be able to figure out what had killed their owners?"

"No," Mr. Smith muttered over his shoulder.

Uncle's snort was deafening: "They can't do anything now, but in my time this could be done very easily."

"How?" I took a lively interest in it, since I didn't know the answer.

"Raising the dead and asking who had killed him and why! There is no such thing as an unmarked grave in Krauhard."

"Shut your maw!" Mr. Smith snapped at once. "Are you going

to teach necromancy to a child, you old fart?!" And addressing me, he shouted, "Don't you dare even to think about it, it's illegal!"

The old magician broke into a cheeky grin: "Excuse me, I forgot! The capital fools had invented rules for themselves in their infinite wisdom, and now they are all like a bunch of castrates—understand everything, can do nothing."

Mr. Smith tried to pull himself together: "One more word, and you will continue your speech in front of your watch officer at NZAMIPS."

The threat did not even faze Uncle: "Naturally, you know them so closely—same office, tea breaks together! It's true what I was told: the dark cannot serve in NZAMIPS. Their brain leaks out of their ass in the course of their duties."

Mrs. Clements, who listened to the squabble perplexedly, did not understand Uncle's attitude toward his superior. She was outraged, "Watch your tone!"

I sighed in frustration—she could have been the last straw. Why was she trying to get into the middle of this?

"Let them bark at each other, Mrs. Clements! This is a kind of dark magic sport. As they say, being fools is in the darks' nature."

The lady crocodile seemed to understand what I was talking about. She snorted disdainfully and walked away, sashaying her hips. Mr. Smith coughed in embarrassment, glanced at me gloomily, and hurried after her.

As soon as he had passed out of sight, Uncle also started coughing, "You know you shouldn't treat magicians like that!"

"What have I done?" I was genuinely surprised.

"That... You know."

Damn it! Both were mature, initiated magicians: what could I tell them about dark magic that they would not know already?

After the incident, the conflict sharply died down, as if a bucket of water was dumped on brawling cats. I did not know whether it was the role my words had played, or Mrs. Clements had managed to cool down her subordinates' souls, but common sense unexpectedly prevailed over magic. They began treating each other in a formal manner ("Mr. Ferro", "Mr. Smith"), speaking in a jaw-twisting literary style. I sighed furtively; other members of the expedition stayed quiet. Yes, that's what happens when the number of dark magicians per square meter goes overboard. Will I grow up the same? How sad that would be.

CHAPTER 5

After a week of digging in the dump, we found a variety of items, but they were all related to the period of the prison's construction and didn't have any historical value. Talk started that there were no sand gnats on the island or they were apparently not associated with Capetower. Mrs. Clements categorically disagreed with that view.

"We need to expand the boundaries of the excavation," her eyes burned with fanaticism. "The commission's report talks about ruins five kilometers to the south. There we will surely find something!"

More ruins and uninhabited at that. Magnificent! Intuition told me that we might find something there that we did not expect.

Mr. Smith took Pierre as an assistant for the initial examination of the new place, and the fool was terribly proud of it. Strangely enough, they both returned safe and sound. Mr. Smith was carrying a chest, the contents of which he did not show to anyone but Mrs. Clements. There was something important in it, no doubt, because all discussions had come to an end, and our redeployment was scheduled for the next day.

Uncle Gordon and I, and Pierre and one of the guards, Gerick, volunteered. I noticed that the base camp remained without any dark mages, but I thought that Mr. Smith knew better where we were needed most.

"What, they didn't take your bootlicker?" Uncle remarked venomously.

It took me some time to realize who he had in mind.

"I never thought that you would have such a thirst for power, nephew! I would never be tempted to lord over that pale worm."

Was he talking about Alex? I hadn't noticed any ass-kissing in the white—it was just his admiring nature. Of course, I was flattered that the guy only a year older than me recognized my authority. The point was not in lording over him, but rather in my Big Brother complex, an attitude that awoke in me after visiting home. I hadn't previously known how much I would like the feeling of being in charge of the family. But why was Uncle sticking his nose into my business? "Jealous?" I asked innocently.

Ha! He was jealous and even blushed! Yes, Uncle, you used to be the first guy in the village, but it won't stay that way forever: young people are nipping at your heels. Call me wicked, but to be an object of envy is an awesome feeling! Uncle, realizing his mistake, did not touch this subject any longer, but harm had been done already: for the first time I clearly realized that we were the dark too, which meant that a time would come to sort things out between us. Not yet; right now my Source of Power, threats of the King's Island, and the ever-present money shortage problem were on the agenda. No time for rearranging our hierarchy! I needed to figure out how to divert Uncle from thinking about it. Maybe I should confront him with Smith again?

As it turned out, I worried for nothing—the King's Island found a way to distract us. The new excavation site was located in the most inaccessible part of the shore. How the notorious commission had managed to discover it remained a mystery. Nevertheless, it had been found, identified on maps, and even given a name: Cape Solitude. We landed there almost as a real military unit, on a dinghy from the main ship, literally squeezing through the coastal cliffs. I was a little worried that we would have to commit such a feat every day. Behind the rocks there wasn't even a bay, but just a shallow lagoon, where remnants of an ancient road began. Nobody could guess when, why, and by whom it was built; it would have been impossible for a cargo ship to access that place. Our goal was located well above sea level, on top of a mountain with a cut-off summit where geometrically proportional heaps of sand and gravel signified the remains of three or four large buildings. By size they resembled Capetower, the steel fortress; apparently, that was the reason why Mrs. Clements liked them. For about twenty minutes we clambered up to the top like beasts of burden and quietly swore. After I dumped my first cargo load on the ground, I allowed myself to breathe and wander through the ruins.

Close up, the ruins looked rather chaotic. The landscape was typical for the King's Island: rocks, rocks, and more rocks. Not a speck of green, not even moss. The walls of the ancient houses had settled and collapsed unevenly; in some places there was only debris lying in big heaps, while in others you could guess the contours of the first floor. There were no steel plates, but we came across broken glass, thin and opaque, and once I spotted something resembling a weathered bone. Everything else… did not look like people ever lived here. The place lacked many small details, traces of human hands; it had almost returned to the silence of the primeval wilderness, became dissolved in time.

I was overcome by a feeling of something unnatural, but I could not quite pin down its cause. After a walk around the ruins, the strange feeling hadn't left me but rather increased in intensity, as if I had seen something odd but could not place when or where. Drawn by the hard-to-explain concern, I entered the remnants of the ancient edifice and looked around: a mountain of rubble towered to the right, presumably the former top floors of the structure; to the left small stones ran down the stairs to the entrance of the basement. Darkness glowered at me through the basement's doorway slit. The silence was soft and promising. At night it was probably quite ugly here; if anything happened, there would be nowhere to run. I cautiously peered down and began actively disliking the place.

The stones cracked behind my back—Pierre stepped into the ruins after me. "What, are you scared?" he snorted and pretended to push me into the basement. My elbow in his stomach was quite real: some things you just don't play around with. "What the..? It was a joke!"

"You're an idiot!" I was furious. "There's something... someone over there! I feel it!"

Uncle came close at the sound of our quarrel, looked down into the basement, and turned very gloomy: "Call Smith over here! There is something otherworldly in there, but I can't make out what; I am only the sixth level."

At Redstone, you couldn't get higher than a lab techie with the sixth level. Why in hell did Uncle pick a fight with a combat magician then?

Our overseer was unhappy that we distracted him from the unloading, but when he looked into the hole, he didn't just turn pale—he became downright green. "Get out of here immediately!"

Pushing puzzled Pierre aside, I ran head over heels to the shore; when a dark magician orders you to take off, you obey quickly. And cowardice has nothing to do with this.

"Into the boat, into the boat!" Mr. Smith must have torn his lungs up screaming. "Abandon equipment, leave now!"

I got there first, charging up the slope in a record-breaking six minutes; Uncle was not far behind me, and Mr. Smith bravely walked last, almost backwards, though the day was bright, and the supernatural wasn't supposed to haunt us just yet. What had we discovered there?

"If we're lucky, that was Rustle," Uncle growled, answering the unasked question. "If not..."

It was difficult to imagine something worse than Rustle, except for a gang of ghouls: the latter could chase you even in the day time. Had Pierre entered the basement, Rustle would have marked him and, perhaps, let him go the first time. But after a few days the victim would have experienced an unbearable urge to come back and, preferably, not alone. Children were particularly susceptible: there were times when the first victim of the monster's hug came back accompanied by ten to fifteen people—friends, acquaintances, parents. In contrast to the predatory echo, Rustle was a mobile creature, which meant that it could try to catch us in the darkness.

"Are we going back to the base camp?" Gerick inquired.

"No!" Mr. Smith interrupted him. "We'll go directly to the Trunk Bay."

Surely, they suspected Rustle. Moreover, quite active Rustle, because they didn't notice the otherworldly on their first trip, but it was present now. Suspicion of possible contact with the creature was enough to hold us in the Trunk Bay for a month—there was a local NZAMIPS' center and a special hospital for victims of otherworldly creatures. For those victims who were still alive, of course.

"Will the quarantine days be paid for, sir?" Uncle took a businesslike tack. "My nephew and I are surely clean."

"Are you going to argue with NZAMIPS' officers, Mr. Ferro?" Mr. Smith narrowed his eyes.

Uncle Gordon shrugged. Shit, that was it for my salary! We will be paid, at best, for one week. Well, at least I had seen the King's Island; not many could boast that. The ship passed by the prison wharf, hanging its flags and giving a signal, but nobody appeared on the shore. Mr. Smith ordered the ship to slow down and climbed to the signal mast to examine the camp with binoculars.

"It looks like we have to go there, sir!" Uncle approached Mr. Smith while the latter came down. "They should hear us by now."

Smith stared intently at the pier.

"A couple of hours, that's all we have, sir," Uncle nagged.

"I know! You'll go with me."

Their eyes met. The issues of hierarchy were left behind, disagreement forgotten—they had a common enemy now, and that reconciled dark magicians better than any preaching.

"Let's take my nephew—his eyes are better than mine!" Uncle offered generously.

I wasn't particularly happy about his suggestion, but did not object; they could use an extra pair of hands, and people insensitive to dark magic should not go there. Mr. Smith was giving the final instructions: "Whoever tries to follow us should be tied up and watched after—very likely, he is infected. Do not approach the bank, even if I myself call to you. On our way back to the ship, call us; if we don't answer, do not let us come close, just go to the open sea. Do not wait till sunset. Go to the Trunk Bay and ask for help."

The captain nodded hard, while Uncle Gordon filled large flasks with sea water. It is salt, not silver, that is most effective against otherworldly entities of low caliber, while the stronger ones are basically immune to common rituals with salt.

We approached the shore at the slowest speed. Uncle steered and Mr. Smith looked for all sorts of threats on land. As a result, it was me who noticed a strange something at the moorage. Something floundered about in the water. A corpse? Uncle brought the boat almost to the shore, where the surf hissed on the boulders, and a strange white object rolled and pitched in the waves. Mr. Smith sorted it out at once and cursed; it was Alex, alive but nearly frozen to death. We dragged the poor guy into the boat (he could not move) and tried to bring him back to life. One look was enough to realize that he was not just swimming. Alex got into the water fully dressed, even in his shoes, though one sleeve of his shirt was practically absent. He had a long white scratch on his cheek. That couldn't be from a fight; these weren't the type of people to brawl. Alex wasn't in a condition to explain the reasons for his grievous state; he was desperately shaking and had managed to bite his lips until bleeding. He kept pointing in the direction of the prison and moving his hands up and down.

"The tower?" Uncle guessed.

The white mage nodded, though it looked more like a convulsion.

"Follow me!" Mr. Smith jumped onto the dock.

I gave my jacket to Alex, shouting, "Stay here! Do not go ashore; if we show up, call us. If we do not come back until sunset, go to the ship, but first call them, too. They are all on alert now."

The expedition camp was suspiciously quiet: no one walked, no one talked. The generator stalled again, which implied something serious. Keeping the jars of saltwater ready and trying to stay away from windows and doorways, we advanced into the prison, where sounds of scuffling could be heard distinctly.

The water tower was the only structure that the prison's architects decided to leave as it was, probably because they were not going to live there. Actually, that thing should have been called "a water tower pond": the tower wasn't stuck in the middle of the yard but was adjoined to the rock; above the construction there was a huge reservoir, half of which rested on man-made supports, and another half on the rock. The reservoir was filled with streams flowing down from the mountains after rain—the only source of water on the island. If the developers had limited themselves to a plain dam, their descendants would have had no problems, but the former owners wanted to squeeze in a distribution system with pipes and valves. That was why the ancient foundation was raised and fortified, and the tower itself was tightly packed with stairs and bridging. No space left for windows, and oil lanterns were the only source of light inside. The place turned into a cozy, dark room, as though specifically designed for otherworldly creatures. At the time of the expedition's arrival, the tower had stayed unlocked for over a hundred years, and any protective or ward-off spells had long worn down.

Near the entrance to the water tower we found a crowd of people: the guard that remained in the camp, the cook, and the student, whose name I could not remember. Mrs. Clements did not let them go inside, clinging to the door with a dead man's grip. The ensorcelled people were not smart enough to grab her by the arms or to bend down and get past; they stupidly pushed and impeded one another. Still, there were three of them, and she was alone.

"Hold on, Rina," Mr. Smith gasped.

"It's Rustle, and it's everywhere!" she croaked in response.

Uncle popped open a flask and splashed into the darkness. We heard a sound resembling rustle of many dry, falling leaves; a lantern above the door flashed brighter, and the attack of the enchanted people subsided.

"Grab them!" Mr. Smith ordered and jumped first, pulling out from the heap a burly security guard and wringing his hands behind his back. I focused on the cook—he was shorter.

Mrs. Clements, dirty and tired, followed us. "I thought it was the end," she groaned. "They were dragging me with them!"

"When had it found time to seize so many?" Uncle puffed (the student he dealt with began to resist). "We've been here for only a week."

"Knuckleheads!" Mr. Smith hissed through his teeth. "I told you, you should have hired only local workers for the expedition, or the dark mages, but not these donkeys!"

Yes, in Krauhard only a small child could fall prey to Rustle's charm.

"Arguing now is pointless," Mrs. Clements sighed. "The caretaker disappeared before our arrival. In this place, Rustle's activity grows stronger than elsewhere; this should have been taken into account."

"Here is your caretaker!" Uncle announced in a cheerful voice.

On the shore, between us and the dock, stood a man, dead by all indications. The lower half of his face was missing completely; the wound had had time to dry out and turn black, and there was no fresh blood left in him. Softened tissues melted off the bone, kept in place by the skin only. As such, the body could only be preserved on the King's Island—the place was almost sterile. For some reason, I did not want to know what this corpse was capable of.

Mr. Smith squeezed the guard's neck and lowered the unconscious man to the ground, "Rina, watch him!"

The dark magician stepped forward, blocking the dead man's way; threads invisible to the naked eye danced around his hands, a whole lace of black silk. There it was, real magic! When the weaving had been done, Mr. Smith threw it forward, as if it were a catching net. The body of the deceased caretaker was instantly fettered with black strands and began to sink. Nothing could keep it upright, the bones broke through the skin, and the smelly, bubbling mess plopped to the ground.

"Move, move, move," Mr. Smith muttered, turning to the guard again. There was no need to persuade us. I enjoyed the spectacle of the dark magician performing enchantment. The group of people, enchanted by Rustle, had slightly sobered up, so it did not take much time to tie their hands and place them on the boat. The sun had touched the water by the time the ship picked us up, and the King's Island sank into a deep shadow. It was clear to all that the expedition had come to the end.

Perhaps, those who had bet on the deceased King were right—he really knew how to stand up for himself.

We were leaving the accursed island, having lost no one, but having gained nothing (except for the valuable life experience, of course). Expeditioners, affected by Rustle, were tightly bound and locked in the hold, while the ship's crew was making warning signs against us. Uncle looked like he had single-handedly saved all of us and triumphed over the King himself. Mrs. Clements cried on the shoulder of Mr. Smith for the rest of the trip to the Trunk Bay (six hours at full speed). He stroked her hair and whispered in her ear something soft and comforting. I did not dare to ask about their relationship; there were questions that a dark magician would not hesitate to give a box on the ears for.

CHAPTER 6

Early the next morning, our ship entered the Trunk Bay; signal flags hung off the mast, and a dull, monotonous warning bell, ringing loudly from the ship, carried the plague alarm. The guard towers winked with lights through the morning fog, and at the entrance to the channel we were met by the iron gates that quickly reminded me of Capetower, though the gates were opened this time. Our captain was nervous, Mr. Smith impatiently tapped on the rail, and it took a good half hour for the quarantine staff to wake up, notice us, and point to a berth for mooring the ship.

Contrary to our expectations, the expedition's appearance did not make a sensation in the Trunk Bay. The head of the quarantine service and concurrently the chief of the local NZAMIPS' office took news of the death of the prison's caretaker with gloomy fatalism, "We were telling him: 'Get out of there while your head is still on your shoulders,' and his response always was: 'Everything is under control, everything is under control!' "

The chief of NZAMIPS, Mr. Harlik, was a longtime friend of Uncle Gordon and a man of good sense, so in the quarantine zone we were immediately enlisted into the conditionally healthy and employed as civilian nursing assistants. Surprisingly, the staff had almost no dark magicians. Chief Harlik, chronically suffering from misunderstandings around there, poured his heart out to us, inviting for tea every evening.

"Will you be expelling Rustle?"

"Where would I find it now? This abomination preys on people and then goes into hiding at once. No, I will collect the caretaker's remains and conserve the building; now, finally, the capitol authorities won't argue with that."

"How had people lived there before?" I wondered.

"Before... three years ago our hospital was nearly closed—no patients; nowadays we are building a new one. Not enough beds. Before, we were barely surviving. Now, we live."

It was difficult to argue with Chief Harlik—he knew too much about everything. For me, twenty-eight days at the Trunk Bay was a real vacation: full board, comfortable rooms, and a rich cultural program. Chief Harlik was an expert in Krauhard's folklore and a very sociable man—a rarity among the dark. He willingly offered his insights on everyday happenings, did not ask any questions about my training with the Source under the guidance of Uncle Gordon, and taught me basic expelling rituals (just in case). How simple could life be when your superiors were of your own kind!

I wrote a letter to Mom, delighting her with the news that the work on the King's Island was over, and complaining that we would have to wait a bit for the transport to go home (she did not need to know about the quarantine). Meanwhile, my theoretical knowledge of the otherworldly was enriched with practical content: doctors began inviting us for reception of new patients and suppression of the most violent—only the dark magicians were able to react properly and quickly enough to the attacks of the consciousnesses, plagued by the otherworldly. I dealt with children: many, many children with smiles, jerky movements, and unpredictable mood swings. In each of my little patients I seemed to see Lyuchik, and soon I clearly understood that my white family must move out of Krauhard.

"The kids come from the Brand's Valley," Chief Harlik explained. " A town with a lot of foreigners sprang up there in the last ten years. Now the rules of dealing with the supernatural are taught in schools as the main subject; I would have started teaching them even earlier, but parents are against it—a child's psyche is unstable and all that stuff. So now children are being taken to us, while their parents aren't; they die on spot because they don't know the rules half as well as their kids."

Well, at least regarding knowledge of the rules, I wasn't worried for Lyuchik. For our voluntary assistance as nurse aides, we had accrued salary of one crown per day. Together with twenty crowns, earned in less than two weeks during the expedition, our total amounted to nearly fifty. Please note that it was earned through honest hard work! Still, that money couldn't come close to solving my financial woes, and I started crying to Uncle about my bitter fate. How could it happen that my father, a dark magician, did not leave any inheritance to his son?

Uncle shrugged: "If you want to, I'll ask Harlik to find out what happened. In his last years your father had no contact with me, but you're right, it does look strange. Me—I am a mediocre alchemist, but he was a real magician, tough and mighty. What happened to him?"

It was so great to have good friends, even though for the dark it was the exception rather than the rule. We returned home with less than ten days left until the end of my summer vacation. Joe hid the hives somewhere (though the bees were flying in the garden), but they didn't bother me anymore. I had become a real dark magician, tough and brave.

The time left before my return to Redstone was spent tastefully: I drove a moped around, scared cows, told stories of the King's Island to the younger ones (that were nothing like reality), helped Uncle Gordon catch up with the work that had accumulated in his garage over the past month, and collected rumors about events that took place in Krauhard. Chief Harlik was right: everything pointed to the return of the ancient, legendary times. I finally decided to talk about it with my stepfather.

"Joe, I heard rumors that Krauhard is getting restless of late. You ought to move somewhere closer to Redstone or to the capital."

My stepfather sighed sadly: "We should. But we have no money to move, Thomas, even if I immediately find a job after the move."

"Then at least Lyuchik has to be sent away. To some boarding school or maybe to your relatives, if you have any."

"I'm thinking about it."

I put my honestly earned fifty crowns on the table. "Take this! When I'm back at Redstone, I'll send you more. Think harder."

He hesitated, but didn't rush to take the money. Another helpless white on my hands!

"What now?"

"You are so concerned for the family, you do so much for the kids... and I have never apologized to you!"

"For what?" I did not understand.

"I invaded your house, took the place of your father... perhaps, you're angry with me."

I sighed. How typical for the white to apply his standards to everybody. And I thought he was an empath.

"Have you not been lectured about the psychological differences in the school of magic?"

"Yes I have, of course. I always tried to... well... to treat you

76

with understanding..."

But he never understood me fully, anyway.

"If my father had spent enough time at home to be remembered. If you had come to our house when I was eight, not eleven. If you had tried to preach to me. If you had forbidden me to buy that damn moped. If you had bought those fucking bees before I left... Anyway, if you had done things differently, I would have hated you to the depths of my soul. But you hadn't... I think blood parents also don't always understand their children, but somehow they do well."

He smiled. "You have become more mature. Wiser."

Just one thing left now: I had to find a job. Oh, money, money...

The day I was leaving for Redstone turned out to be noisy and senseless. On the eve of my departure, I went to the station and performed a little trick: I sold my express non-stop railroad ticket to one lucky guy. I was going to return to Redstone by suburban railroads, changing them at every town. It was not quite legitimate, but that way I would save an extra eighteen crowns. The bad thing was that the way back by the suburban railroad would take twice as much time.

My mother kept trying to shove a jingling worn-out wallet in my backpack, and I kept taking it out.

"Tommy, please, take it for your trip!"

"I don't need money!" I was dead set on that. "You need it more. I can always make money in the city."

If I only knew how!

At the last moment it turned out that the train I needed did not stop at the Wildlife Outpost, and Uncle Gordon had to give me a ride on his jalopy through two mountain passes. There were pros to it—no time for a teary parting, and cons—I did not manage to talk to Mom about my father again.

I started my irritatingly slow travel via local rail lines that departed rarely and stopped at every shabby station. Good thing that Mom had shoved some grub into my bag, and Joe had poured a calabash of mead of his own make (it was so much more fun to travel with that drink). It took me 26 hours to reach Ekkverh Junction. From there, trains to Redstone departed twice a day, and I had to waste another three hours between routes. Taking a nap at the station was fraught with troubles, and I did not want to squander money on a baggage locker, so I sat in the waiting room, hugging my backpack and dying of boredom.

At first, I entertained myself by visualizing a speech that I would be making in front of Quarters, who would certainly want to know what I was doing the whole summer. Should I tell him about the island and the quarantine? Then on my last penny left after the ticket purchase, I bought a local paper from a newsboy (you could put it under your ass, and the seat wouldn't be so freezing cold) and read it from cover to cover. The contents of eight yellow pages captured the essence of provincial life: a harvest festival, local news, anecdotes, obituaries, ads, and crosswords (the latter turned out to be amazingly stupid).

I quickly looked through the ads: farmers selling cattle, furniture, tractors and equipment, unusually few suggestions to buy puppies and kittens, and an entire section at the end devoted to magical services. Three dozen wizards offered local townsfolk remedies for male potency, cockroach extermination, improving the tempers of horses, and the treatment of root rot in roses. Naturally, there were no dark magicians among them: which of us would voluntarily agree to live in the boonies? The dark mages are irresistibly attracted to big, crowded cities, full of amenities and devoid of insects. There was no work for NZAMIPS here as well, and I sympathized with the poor fellows who operated the local "cleaning" service—they must have been sent there for some mortal sin. However, if the situation in Ekkverh was changing the same as in Krauhard...

And then, as though an invisible hand squeezed my mind, the sense of a touch on the back of my head became so vivid that I turned around.

Surely, in this preserve of white magic, there wasn't a single NZAMIPS' office (perhaps, local farmers didn't even know what that was). For the whole county, there was one on-site inspector, and he lived somewhere in Redstone. Hardly any of the locals knew the subtleties of the licensing of dark magicians and the limitations that NZAMIPS imposed on our practice— they used to pay cash after the work had been done without asking for a receipt or invoice. You couldn't meet representatives of the government there even by accident, and a bit of competition wouldn't hurt the local "cleaning" service.

I carefully pulled off a newspaper coupon for a free ad, took a pen from a news vendor and filled in: "A dark magician, specialist in the undead and otherworldly phenomena. Pricelist available. Warranty. Free consultation." As a contact number I provided the phone of a girl I knew who worked in the answering services. She was the half-blind girl with well-developed vocal strength who was a secretary for three or four small companies that were too poor to keep a separate office. She was valued for her good telephone manners: the girl never asked stupid questions like: "Who are you looking for?" Another advantage—she lived near the university, not far from me to check for the news regularly.

Finally, I fell back into my old ways. As they say, you can't wash the stripes off a zebra.

Part 2. PRIVATE PRACTICE

CHAPTER 7

Redstone University occupied two complexes or, as people said, "territories". The new territory was located on the outskirts of town, across the river, and consisted of a noisy dormitory and laboratories for the Faculty of Alchemy, as large as factories. They say there were greenhouses and stables somewhere behind the dormitory, but I never dealt with that side of the university's life.

The old territory and the heart of the university was the Redstone School of Magic, the first educational institution to teach dark and white magicians together—the pioneering attempt to reconcile the opposites. The founders of the university discovered a magic formula for the successful preparation of magic art specialists: joint education with ordinary people in some disciplines, like alchemy and pharmaceuticals. Nowadays such arrangement is considered standard, but in the past the innovation was regarded as revolutionary. Since then, the classic "apprenticeship" has fizzled out—graduates of specialized alchemical and magic institutions lagged seriously behind ordinary university graduates in their skills. It was assumed that the joint training allowed ordinary people to actually get acquainted with the logic of magic (an important life experience was presented at the right time in their lives) and helped magicians better integrate into the society. Also, the dark, being in the absolute minority, were unable to bully the white, which was a huge bonus for the latter. The Redstone school quickly grew into a university, regularly supplying society with talented alchemists, the mightiest white magicians, and the strongest combat sorcerers. Soon I will join them. This year, twelve dark students expressed an intention to undergo the Empowerment. If you trust statistics, among them there would be at least one master, a couple of generals, and one genuine archimage.

I sat on the square in front of the faculty building, waiting for my turn to take the Empowerment (that day there were three others scheduled for the ritual) and getting annoyed at mere trifles. My dear Uncle (kick the bucket already, you old goat!) refused to explain the essence of the ritual, despite the whole summer of my practicing with the Source. "If you know it in advance, you will fail it for sure! Just remember: you should refrain from using your power for as long as possible. Got it? For as long as possible!" That was all that I was able to shake out of him. Now my peers were preparing for the most important moment of their lives by fasting and taking special herbs (Uncle forbade me from touching them), while I stupidly sweated in anticipation of troubles.

The shadow of the sundial had crawled to noon when I noticed a guy that was supposed to take the ritual before me. I did not know his name; the dark rarely get to know each other. The newly-made magician threw a gloomy look at me and, without saying anything, disappeared in the direction of the main building.

I was next.

All students learned quickly the place occupied by the Faculty of Dark Magic; this was the area where you'd better not walk in the evening. Beginners often mistook it for a utility structure— against the background of the main building with tall lancet windows and colored tints on precious finish, the three-story box looked weird, resembling the prison on the King's Island. The university's authorities regularly considered transferring the faculty to the new territory (the city municipality was all in favor of that idea), but it did not budge; to build such an institution from scratch required a shocking amount of money. The current monstrous building sported a unique magical structure that was capable of retaining and absorbing the fatal consequences of student errors and, in fact, carried that function out regularly. According to the stats, two percent of dark magicians died in the process of learning. But today the townsfolk could rest safely; for the whole week the building was at the juniors' disposal.

A dark carpet runner was spread in front of the entrance, pennants with the wise sayings of famous combat magicians hung on the walls (could you believe it—combat mages were able to speak eloquently!), and crows, consorts of plagues and wars lined up on the roof, attracted by emanations of magic. In the lobby I was met by the dean and an instructor with two assistants. Representatives of the city authorities—the same goblin-like cop and an unknown dark mage—were silently present as well. Nothing unexpected so far.

"You have finally decided to go through the Empowerment," Mr. Darkon said, looking a little sad.

I was still pondering that question prior to the incident at the NZAMIPS' office, but afterwards it became a must-do thing.

"I'm not going to quit alchemy."

"Everybody says so."

The instructor politely cleared his throat: "If you are aware of the risks associated with the Empowerment, please sign here!"

That was the disclaimer—the university pledged to do its utmost to ensure the safety of the ritual, but it refused any responsibility for injuries received in the process. On top of that, there was my own written application, a letter from my immediate family (I hadn't reached twenty-one yet), a health certificate... At one time, just the list of the necessary paperwork was enough to discourage me from becoming a magician. I hated bureaucracy! But I didn't have a choice and signed the disclaimer without looking.

I was tapped on the shoulder, wished success, and escorted to a large door that was upholstered in black leather. I tried to figure out what would happen next, but the instructor immediately began lecturing me about historical parallels and my responsibility to society, reminding me of the incessant babble of the white kids. I was not in a mood to argue on a day like this and patiently waited until his speech dried out.

Just through the doors the corridor broke off at a spiral staircase that led down to the second underground level. That was quite logical—rituals of this kind had to be conducted in a lab with the highest safety level, and regulations prescribed that such places must be hidden in basements. I had never been there before. My imagination painted a secret temple with torches and pentagrams, but in reality the place turned out to be quite prosaic: the clanking iron staircase ended in a tiny dressing room with a single bench and a coat rack for jackets. There, I was asked to change into the ritual costume (it looked like a black pajamas), and from thereon I continued barefoot, pretending to be a seasoned mage, because a dark magician arriving at the ritual in socks with holes didn't strike me as comical.

With great effort, the instructor swung open a door made of cast iron (like a vault), but there was no temple behind it—just a small room without sharp corners. Bluish-white lights glared on the walls of polished silver. If there were any magic wards present there, they did not stick out. One of the assistants went ahead of me, the other breathed down my neck from behind, and the instructor showed the way, occasionally tugging me by the sleeve and annoying me greatly.

I hated to be grabbed or pulled! The door locked behind us with a dull clanking sound that caused my heart to skip a beat anxiously. Why did the door need to be locked?

"This important-for-every-dark-magician day..." the instructor monotonously droned. He managed to maneuver so masterfully that I noticed our destination at the last moment: it was a short iron table with four leather bracelets.

"Perhaps..."

As though by accident, he took my hand and started pushing me down onto the polished surface. All my instincts howled at once. I rushed to the door but was adroitly intercepted by the second assistant and laid on the damned altar. That it was an altar was as clear as day.

"I have changed my mind! I do not want to go through the ritual!"

"Too late," the instructor replied after catching his breath, "You'll leave this room as a dark magician or won't leave at all."

"A-ah!" Damn! The walls were thick there; furthermore, it was the basement. I tried to pull myself together (figuratively speaking, because my hands were fastened behind my head). Today two other students had taken the ritual before me and both were alive and intact; I even saw one of them. Though the color of his face was...

"What will happen next?"

The assistants tinkered with something in the corner, while the instructor examined me with the look of a professional surgeon.

"You will acquire Power."

I tried to discern what they were doing, but failed. It drove me crazy.

"There won't be anything cruel, right? Nothing special?"

The instructor's eyes met mine, and he declared solemnly: "There will be!"

"You have no right!" I tried to speak decisively, but my voice trembled and broke.

He leaned closer to me and winked conspiratorially: "We do."

My dear mother! I fell into the hands of maniacs. The police persuaded them, and they would kill me right here and now and blame the ritual. What could I do? SOS! The assistants mounted a few black candles along the altar and lit them, murmuring indistinctly. I started feeling an uncomfortable tingling in my hands and feet.

"The spell is called 'Odo Aurum', " the instructor told me amiably. "It will help you to call your Source as soon as possible. We'll wait until the spell starts operating."

I instantly recalled where I had heard that name. The spell was used by inquisitors to increase the sensitivity of their victims to pain, making obtaining any confession trivial. I broke out in cold sweat at the discovery.

Please understand me correctly: I did not hesitate to jump into a fight, and I never worried about skinning my knees. But being tied to the table, helpless...

Wait. Helpless? I was practicing all summer!

"Hey, freak, let off me now, or I'll slam you with a curse!"

"Try it!" the instructor smirked.

I hesitated for a moment, feeling a disgusting tingling that climbed along my spine, remembering pictures of the injured from the police collection, and fighting with a feeling of mercy and humanism, awakened at the wrong time. Should I try to contain my temper further? No, damn it! With familiar effort, I mentally squeezed my Source and drove the Power outward, trying to crush any malicious magic or, at least, break the damn bracelets. A white shroud flashed before my eyes for a second, and when it had faded, all the unpleasant sensations disappeared at once.

"Not bad. Very good, actually!" the instructor's voice lost its threatening tone. "Fourth level on your first attempt. Now dismiss the Source!"

I gently released the Source—my feet had already been freed.

"What, is that all?"

"Yes," the instructor announced cheerfully, "but I have to remind you that you must not disclose to anyone the essence of the ritual. If our actions lose their surprise factor, we would have to go much further, up to the actual harm. Do you understand me?"

At that time I was ready to understand anything in order to cut and run. One of the assistants offered me water and energizers, and another advised me not to hurry, but I brushed off their help and broke through to the door. Already at the exit, I ventured to ask: "Why we are not allowed doing it ourselves?"

"If you hadn't noticed, a modulating spell is set on the room. It directed the energy of your call and helped create a secure channel for your Power. The first time the control is very important; after the Empowerment had happened, it would be almost impossible to change the characteristics of the Source. Don't worry! The ritual took place almost without deviations."

"Deviations?" I instantly tensed up.

"Judging by what I've seen, you will show one particular talent."

"Which one?"

"If you attend your classes regularly, I will tell you at the end of the year."

What a bastard! It must be a common feature for those who teach dark magic—the ability to drive a student into frenzy. Oh, yeah, I will be attending his lectures! And he will regret that.

That was it—no more secret rituals. Screw that! Having climbed the steep stairs, I literally tumbled out into the hall. I was greeted with ceremonious applause. Quarters smirked brazenly behind the backs of the university authorities. Who let him in on the event for the dark? Dean shook my hand; the instructor slipped me some sort of paper to sign and a numbered token that would be exchanged for a magician's seal upon graduation. I no longer had to fear wearing the shackles of deliverance.

The goblin in the uniform gloomily watched the process of my legalization. I smiled. A smiling dark mage is quite a sight! He couldn't do me any harm now! Officially, I had just been initiated; to prove the opposite he would have to bring the memory crystal and explain why he had not done that before. This subtle psychological point was taken into account by Uncle Gordon and me. Had the brave cop's sense of duty prevailed over his selfish interests, we would have found ourselves up a creek without a paddle. But the dark mages are quite selfish and measure others' corn by their own bushel. In short, we bet on his cowardice and didn't lose. The goblin waved at me, calling me over. Others sharply stepped aside.

"How are you," I welcomed him.

"Fine... Captain Baer."

With some delay, I realized that the captain was him. "What can I do for you?" I inquired politely.

"I... would like to offer you an apology."

"For what?" I replied lively.

"You know!" the captain-goblin cut me off.

I shrugged: "I forgive everyone!"

Goblin looked me up and down, and then pulled out a plain business card with NZAMIPS logo. "If you have a problem," he nodded meaningfully, "do not hesitate to contact me."

"Thank you, Officer!" I grinned.

He paused for a moment, thinking (I was prepared to use the instructor as a shield), then nodded and returned to his place. I looked around, trying to determine what effect I produced on others. They all stared at me somewhat strangely. Assured that there wouldn't be any speeches given, Quarters took me by the arm and dragged away. I didn't have the strength to protest. Everyone wanted to lay a hand on me that day...

The assistants with businesslike looks tramped past us—went to search for another victim. At this point I clearly saw why the secret of the famous ritual had remained veiled to date. The thought that every past and current dark magician had been tricked into this, and that every future magician would be, filled my heart with inexpressible satisfaction. You forget your own troubles, enjoying others' misfortunes. Psychotherapy, damn it!

Quarters wasn't perceptive enough to understand these subtleties. "Wow!" he exclaimed. "Do you know who he is?"

"Captain Baer."

"Chief of Redstone's NZAMIPS! You were rude to the inquisitor!"

I shrugged and said what I thought about Captain Baer, generously employing Krauhard's folklore and many other slang expressions. Quarters gaped after me, trying to remember the phrase that took his fancy. "Well, as you wish!" he concluded. "Let's have beer." Seeing me tensing up, he generously added, "My treat!"

* * *

A dark magician in the police uniform was righteously indignant: "As I said, it was idiocy to go there! A mage from Tangor's family is not so easy to catch! He went to the Trunk Bay for a reason. It's Krauhard! They cover for each other, all stand united; there is no tripping him up."

Conrad Baer listened to him half-heartedly, briskly looking around. They marched to the gates of the university, and the majority of oncoming students abruptly changed course at the sight of the police officers. All were guilty!

"Come on, stop it," the captain dismissed his subordinate. "The guy worked hard on self-control, found himself a mentor. I think he won't be trouble."

"A nonstandard channel of power will manifest itself during his training. Two years of intensive practice, and he will be off his rocker!"

"Hardly," the captain did not support his coworker. "Larkes examined his crystal, and the configuration was quite stable."

The magician chuckled, "Sir, I think Coordinator Larkes has his own stake in it."

"We'll see!"

A student standing in a group of people that gathered at the university gates suddenly took to flight, having discovered the presence of the police. Captain Baer barely suppressed the desire to pursue the fleeing man. NZAMIPS must strengthen intelligence work at the university! So many cases could be closed at once.

CHAPTER 8

Believe me, not every magician can become an instructor in combat magic! One must have a special talent to make a gang of young dark beasts nauseate and sweat their guts out. Precisely a gang, because the university's program did not provide private lessons, and precisely to the point of sickness, because practice with the Source required incredible effort at the beginning. I, thank god, passed that stage. In my case, dearest Uncle Gordon stimulated my brain with pebbles, but a university instructor could not afford to beat up his students; otherwise, he wouldn't leave the auditorium alive. However, Mr. Rakshat coped with the task well: he cursed like a drill sergeant, thrashed his cane on students' desks (making a sudden incredible noise over your ear-- it's an unforgettable feeling), threatened to put you in the shackles, and hoarsely whispered what fate would befall you at the slightest mistake. I admit, I used to have a finger tremor after three hours of such training.

That was why we had so few dark magicians! No one in his right mind would agree to such a travesty—if he had a choice, of course. From this reasoning followed a sad conclusion that all those present, except for me, were insane.

Mr. Rakshat wasn't particularly spiteful with me, but he did not improve my mood; perhaps, I was the only dark in the university's history who fell into the autumn depression. My finances were dwindling like golden leaves falling off trees; it didn't matter how frugal I was; money could not multiply in the absence of income. Add to that the cost of supplies, essential for a novice magician, payment to the "chatterbox"—my answering service, a fine for the violation of municipal bylaws (for drinking with Quarters), and you will understand that I was on the rocks long before the foliage had flown off.

My mulishness did not allow me to ask for help from the family. I had already borrowed from Ron and a few other friends with the promise to pay it back at the end of the month. Students were short of money after summer vacations and lent with reluctance. The day that I went to bed hungry for the first time in my life inevitably came. That fact impressed me deeply. No room left to maneuver; reluctantly, I set a date for an appointment at Gugentsolger's Bank and tried to figure how much money they would snooker from me. Apparently, I would give them back twice as much as I would borrow.

The first call came at the peak of my desperation.

The "chatterbox" handed me a piece of paper with the address and name of the client.

"I said that your next free day would be Saturday, and they didn't mind. I don't know what you're gonna do, but good luck to you."

I laid out a course on the map and was making a detailed plan of the campaign all of Friday; a trip through the fields and communication with the client needed to be thoroughly prepared for. That day I ate only two pies stolen from a freshman's bag (shame on me); hence, I approached the preparation with the uttermost care.

My bitter experience suggested that it was not enough to be a dark magician—you ought to look like one. So when I approached the farm gate, I was dressed in a shiny black raincoat (on a perfectly clear day), official business attire from a rental shop, and wore black dance shoes (brand new; it was a gift from my mother on admission to the university). That was exactly how a classic dark mage should look. One my hand played with a bunch of keys from storage lockers with a shiny nickel-plated pendant shaped like a car, another held a spacious gripsack, borrowed from the university's amateur theater. Let people think that I came here by car rather than guess that I walked ten miles from the station!

A little girl sat on the grass before the gate and played with a rag doll.

"Good afternoon," I hissed coldly, "how can I find Mr. Larsen?"

She squeaked and ran away. A minute later a middle-aged gentleman in traditional farmer clothes (plaid shirt, homespun overalls) came out from the house (I suspected an uninitiated white mage in him). He looked at me childishly, with a mixture of fear and admiration. "Wow! A genuine dark magician!"

I smiled sternly and condescendingly, imitating the most hostile teacher from my school, and then demonstrated a silver business card with my initials and indistinct logo (I had a whole five of them with me).

"Have you called our firm?"

"Yes!" he breathed out, stunned.

"'Neklot & Sons': we will solve all your problems!" I proudly announced. "I understand that you believe your house is cursed. Can I take a look around?"

"Yes, yes, of course! Will you allow me to take it?" he held out his hand toward my gripsack.

With pleasure, I handed my heavy baggage to him and added strictly: "Be careful with it! Inside are my tools."

Just one look at the interior of the house was enough to

understand—this task was beyond my skill level. The supernatural was certainly present there: all corners were covered with thin black gossamer, visible on the walls in some spots and translucent on the glass. That was phoma, one of the simplest manifestations of the otherworldly, a brainless mold. It was dangerous if it struck roots—in that case it was easier to burn the house than to clean it. Almost no time remained until the moment when all isolated pockets of phoma would merge in a deadly black cocoon.

"Has anyone died already?" I tried to stay as indifferent as possible.

"No, no," he shook his head.

Well, it would not stand true for long. In any other circumstances, I would have smiled sweetly and buzzed off, but the money wasted on renting the suit was big enough to make me cry. And then, the phoma was primitive; I knew curses to expel it (though I never used them—Chief Harlik taught me the basics, but he was not stupid enough to teach the youngster anything serious).

"Have you seen our price list?" I asked him in order to buy some time and gather my thoughts. "Have a look at it! Your case is number five."

He took out of my hands a piece of paper filled with letters of elegant gothic font.

"Three hundred crowns?"

I shrugged, rejoicing inside: if he refused, I would retreat without losing face.

"If you are not happy with our prices, I would recommend calling the local 'cleaning' service."

The farmer shook his head: "He had already been here and done nothing. Let it be three hundred! Will you do the job?"

If the local mage had been here and found nothing, he had to be burned—not as a sorcerer, but as a charlatan. So, he will not notice my mistakes and won't be able to track me down.

Three hundred crowns...

I feigned the most disgusting smile I was capable of.

"Who do you think I am? Our company guarantees the expulsion of any dangerous phenomenon and warrants no otherworldly recurrence. Of course, if you manage to curse your house twice, we won't be responsible for that."

He quickly nodded: "I got it! When can you start?"

"I would like to finish everything today—I don't really want to come this far twice. And fuel is not cheap these days..."

"Good! Is there anything you need?"

I nodded: "Remove all people, pets, and plants from the house. I will start working after the dusk, so you have time. It would be better if you stay overnight at your friends' place."

All inhabitants of the house (there were many) sprang into motion. The farmer harnessed two heavy carthorses into a hefty three-axis cart. Then they loaded it with everything they needed for a sleepover. Cats and kittens, puppies and dogs, rubber plants, violets, two boxes with a collection of cacti and a cage of parrots, an aquarium, and what not! A pile of pillows, embroidered by hand; a porcelain set, carefully packed in a basket; bundles of albums with pictures of family and bags of clothes—as if all of them were just waiting to be taken away. Perhaps the people subconsciously sensed the approaching crisis and were glad to get out of there at least for a short time.

Ignoring the hustle and bustle, I watched for the phoma: it was a clear day, and the otherworldly was quiet, but such violent activity would wake it up early.

The sun had not touched the horizon yet when the farmer's family was ready to leave. The owner came up to me, questioning, "Are you sure...?"

Tell him that I was not?

"Do not worry. Come back after the dawn, check the results, and pay me for the job. You may want to bring along some experts, although I wouldn't recommend that you rely on the local 'cleaning' service."

"Yeah, sure!" he breathed out and ran to the cart with his family. He was obviously happy with the opportunity to foist his problem off on someone else.

I waited patiently until the creaking of the wheels, the shrill cries of children, and the dog barking subsided. I needed silence to calm down, call the Power, and stop thinking that the work would be simple; overly self-confident dark magicians died young, slowly and painfully. A fight with any, even the most innocuous, otherworldly is a battle for life and death, and let that death not be mine.

I took off and carefully folded my suit, wrapped it in my raincoat, and put it outside the gates, where the precious clothes would be safe. I left dressed in black sports pants, a faded T-shirt, and some rubber boots that I borrowed from the farmer— nothing valuable. If by morning I should turn into a spot of black slime, my financial situation would not be affected. The only cause for concern was mosquitoes. (I hate insects! The first thing I will do when I get back to the university will be to learn a spell that will repel mosquitoes or exterminate them on approach.)

Now it was necessary to set the boundaries of the battle zone. I took out of my gripsack an enchanted compass and a bunch of knitting needles, with pieces of shiny foil screwed to their blunt ends. Ideally, I should have used mirror fragments, but I had not figured out how to drill holes in the glass and did not dare to purchase ready-to-use enhancements—for reasons of conspiracy. Following the compass needle, I walked around the house, marking my way with needles and cursing the damned insects (the ritual didn't allow hand-waving or accelerating one's pace), then moved into the house and drew lines with crayons around all windows that were within my reach. The battlefield was set.

Settling in the room that I felt was the center of the phoma's expansion, I pulled out of my bag a portable altar (a simplified model, designed for students) with an embossed coordinate grid that greatly facilitated the drawing of pentagrams. Charting a ward-off symbol took no more than a minute. Then I chose three candles from the set: red, black, and white (the latter not to be confused with colorless!), and slightly melted and attached them to the surface of the altar. (Tipped over candles caused injuries in dark magicians more frequently than even the otherworldly itself). Then I settled down to wait for night to fall.

The sun had not set completely when the phoma showed signs of awakening to its mysterious non-life. It was big, hungry, and irritated by the lack of conventional food sources. When the clock boomingly struck 11 p.m., I decided to light the first candle.

The flame was tiny but of the white shade that could not be produced by the combustion of any ordinary matter. Only white magicians made that kind of candles and used it to keep off the melancholy that so often beset their delicate souls. I found a better use for those things. Touching the white tongue of the flame with my finger, I ordered: "Flame of the fire, listen to me! What I name, I want to see. Phoma, phoma, phoma!"

The problem of simple spells is not their low efficiency, but the side effects. If the phoma had not been nearby, the temporarily animated candle would have cruelly taken revenge for my audacity: I would have lost my magic power for a few days and hallucinated phomas everywhere. But the supernatural's presence was assured in that room, so the candle's spark grew twice in size and flowed upward as a luminous white smoke, outlining the contour of the invisible monster. I kept waiting. After about half an hour, the pattern of infection became clear.

The farmer was lucky—he had left home in time. The otherworldly was almost ripe. Its isolated pockets of mold grew up into thin cilia-tentacles, ready to connect and form a solid body trap. It was foolish of them to let the phoma evolve into its current condition! Those peasants grew fat, became relaxed, and forgot to worry about invisible threats. I should have left everything as it was and let those boobies be eaten.

But three hundred crowns...

The next step would be to entice the undead and seal it off; in this procedure, time was of the essence. I should activate the seal after the entire phoma was within its boundaries, and I could not let the creature just eat the bait and get out. Focusing and alerting the Source, I touched the red candle and ordered: "Flesh, burn!"

In accordance with the theory, the candle emitted an inimitable, unique flavor that attracted the otherworldly to the live beings. The smell of food irresistibly beckoned the brainless thing. The phoma did not possess a real body of weight and volume, and the creature that filled the whole house with its snake shoots instantly shrank to the size of a roll of wool and tightly entangled the bait. At that very moment, when the last smoky process slunk defeated into the boundaries of the pentagram, I grabbed the Source by the scruff and tossed it directly into the black candle.

"Dangemaharus!"

The true meaning of this word had been lost to the dark ages, but it is known that for a simple force attack one could not think of anything better. The black candle exploded into a ball of fuming flame that instantly filled the contour of the pentagram. Among jets of fire, the phoma rushed as chaos of black lines. I squeezed the Source with all my strength, arousing to life the most destructive hypostasis of dark magic—the Infernal Flame. The latter was too strong for the inferior otherworldly, but I hadn't yet perfected other methods of expelling. The phoma squeaked and vanished in a green flash, no grueling hours-long struggle; I spent more time taming the fire and preventing it from splashing on the floor. I did not know if I killed the being that was not alive to begin with, but the phoma wasn't there anymore. So, technically, it was dead now.

I spent another hour making sure that no other supernatural beings were left in the house. Along the way, I discovered the source of the phoma—an old, beat-up dresser. I did not know where they found the dresser and why the otherworldly occupied it for such a long time without manifesting itself but I, personally, was not going to buy anything from flea markets anymore. You never know what you will bring home!

While I was cleaning the room, tearing off candle-ends from the altar and wiping magical signs off of windows, dawn was breaking. It did not make sense to go to bed. I fired up the wood stove in the kitchen and made coffee from the farmer's stock; then I finished the food left over in a pan and disposed of a pastry that had been thoughtlessly abandoned on the table by the owners. Life was getting better; what still remained, however, was to get paid.

The owners arrived at nine in the morning, when the sun was already high. I met them at the door of the house (with the suit, raincoat, and model shoes on and the gripsack in hand), smiled to the farmer, and coldly nodded to his companion, a withered priest of unknown confession (to be honest, I am not religious).

"We have solved your problem. Please inspect the house!"

They came in and, judging by how quickly the farmer's face brightened up, he sensed that now all was well. The old priest roamed about the rooms for some time, but he was forced to admit that the dwelling was completely safe. Wildly shying, Mr. Larsen handed me a weighty bag of coins.

"You cannot imagine how thankful we are to you! I thought this nightmare would never end."

Well, in a couple of days their nightmare would have ended anyway, but I wasn't going to upset the client who paid money. I feigned a dry, cold, very dark magic smile and nodded: "Our staff does not make mistakes! We have recently entered the market in your area and would be grateful if you recommend us to your friends." I gave shining business cards to both of them. "I ask you for a small favor: please do not give our contact info to the magician who examined your home before me. Dark mages are very sensitive to outsiders in their territory. I fear that he would try to hide his blatant incompetence through an ugly scandal."

The farmer and the priest nodded so vigorously that I guessed that the local "cleaner" had already managed to manifest his appalling side.

"A word of advice. If you buy second-hand items, soak them in salt water or, depending on the nature of the object, pour rock salt and leave it on for a day. This will help you avoid trouble in the future. Seeing me off is not necessary!"

I moved off, proudly keeping my back straight and not turning around. I walked along the trail that wound through the hills and fields. Next time, I will get a cane and learn how to handle it elegantly. A cane with a knob in the form of a skull.

The trip to the station would have to last a whole day, and I intended to take classes at the university the next morning. The noticeably weightier gripsack didn't get on my nerves any more, and the thought of three hundred crowns warmed my heart.

My visit to Gugentsolger's could be postponed for a while.

* * *

A black lacquered carriage drawn by a pair of well-fed trotters stopped in front of a large farmhouse. Four children of different ages played inside the gates in the company of a sprightly red dog and a melancholic pony. Two people sat on the box of the carriage, and one more man—a passenger— sprawled on a leather seat and looked bored. The coachman stayed with the horses, and his satellite jumped down from the box and quickly went into the house. This man's appearance could not generate any sympathy: he was lean and thin-boned by nature, with a puffy face, swollen eyelids, bluish-gray nose and cheeks from a mesh of burst blood vessels. His black coat was quite worn out and shiny on the elbows, and his pants looked chewed and stretched at the knees. The passenger from the leather seat gave him a contemptuous glance, stood up, causing the seat to squeak sadly, and slowly followed the first man. That passenger was tall, dressed in the impeccable suit of a public bureaucrat, and his bearing reminded one of a guard officer; upon his appearance, the red dog hid behind the children's feet and began growling with displeasure.

The owner of the house wasn't happy with the arrival of the guests.

"Look, that asshole is back again!" the farmer said through his teeth, watching the approaching people through the slit in the curtains.

"We did not call him!" his wife stepped in.

"That's right. Take the children out of sight; I'll meet them."

Meanwhile, the owner of the coat reached the porch but did not step on it.

"Mr. Larsen!" he called in a quavering falsetto. "Mr. Larsen, may I talk to you for a moment?"

The farmer went out to the porch, staring gloomily at the visitors. His wife slipped behind him, gathered the children in the yard, and took them into the house.

"What is it, Mr. Kugel? We seemed to agree that my house was none of your business."

"You misunderstood me, Mr. Larsen! I said that I could not help, but today I have brought a colleague of mine who is able to... "

"We do not need your help!"

"You misunderstood..."

"Do I need to repeat it?"

"I apologize," the tall gentleman stepped in, pushing hapless Kugel aside, "But if your house does have a supernatural contamination, as it was reported, it is a threat not only to your family, but also to your neighbors. Such beings do not go away; they cannot be ignored. Saving five hundred crowns, you drive them to the stage when they become dangerous to your loved ones, and the house has to be burned down..."

"Don't you dare come near my house!"

A white magician in a fury was a rare and atypical phenomenon, and the consequences of that could be—oh-ho-ho! The tall gentleman raised his hands in a conciliatory gesture.

"I beg your pardon! I used an incorrect expression, excuse me! I just want to make sure that the threat does not exist. It is my duty; I must react to the report. I only need to have a look; I won't give you any trouble!"

The farmer pulled himself together with visible effort.

"You may enter. But I repeat: we do not have any problem, and we do not need your services."

The tall gentleman went into the house and almost immediately came out. Mr. Kugel still hemmed and hawed at the door: "I don't understand. I was sure..."

Subtly swinging, the tall gentleman slapped him in the face with such force that the unfortunate guy flew to the ground head over heels.

"What a knucklehead! Why the hell do you work here? What do they pay you money for? You could not expel a phoma; you needed help, yeah? Had it been the phoma, it wouldn't have left even the bones of these people, while we were driving here! This was your last day at the office. Gather your stuff; I fire you. Your luck that they found someone smarter than you; otherwise, you would be sentenced to life in the mines. What a muddle head!"

The boss kicked the mage—who was crying in the dust—with the toe of his shoe and strode toward the gates. The coachman did not wait for the latecomer, and Mr. Kugel had to go home on foot.

CHAPTER 9

My memory saved that winter in torn half remembered fragments, with some episodes looking like they occurred to someone other than me.

Everyone knew that the first six months after the Empowerment was the most difficult period for a dark magician. Searching for equilibrium with the Source, a mage changed internally and externally (I don't mean growing hooves and horns); this was true for both the dark and the white. Previously, I was amused by the looks of the third-year students, roaming the university with stupid smiles, hopping and skipping, or "saving" autumn leaves from puddles. A magician in the period of temporary insanity was a favorite topic in student jokes. Now I understood that the targets of jokes were only the white mages; no joker (fortunately for him or her) saw the dark ones in that state. Persistent rumors about zombies, circulated by the Faculty of Combat Magic, suddenly made sense.

Future masters and generals headed home from the faculty late at night, in complete darkness, without stooping to offer vulgar wishes of "good night". That was the way the genuine darks had to behave in their own circle! But my old habits were so strong that I could barely keep myself from giving a parting gesture. One wizard wrote that the dark developed a nasty character as a means of self-preservation—that was the only way to withstand the day-to-day pressure of the hostile Source. I definitely didn't have enough bitchiness. Perhaps only blind faith in my invincibility protected me from a complete collapse of personality.

Not good to be a dark, grown up among the white.

Leaving the gloomy walls of the faculty, I used to drop into the nearest pub, where I ate, not tasting the food, and drank without getting drunk, and then the pub owner called me a cab. Yes, I could afford a ride, not a walk, to the hostel now! I did not know how other dark students managed to find their way in such condition. The thought that the next day would be entirely devoted to alchemy helped me to sleep without nightmares.

In fact, I could have every other weekday off—the Roland Fund's awardees were eligible for benefits for the first six months after the Empowerment. But they wouldn't have done me any good. Had I not alternated magic practice with alchemy courses, I would have lost my mind. After the painful efforts of practicing with the Source, alchemy was like a balm—cool, clear, sincere. Predictability and accurate calculations, beauty of formulas and knowledge of the true essence of things, tamed power of the elements loaded my hands with work and didn't strain the brain. My admiration for alchemy reached the stage that I shed tears watching the delightful precision of the work of the turret lathe. Quarters sympathetically patted me on the shoulder. Perhaps, other students did not get tired so much, because they were smart enough not to become engaged in illegal practice.

Meanwhile, my underground business gained momentum. I wasn't greedy, I did not have to advertise at all, but people were calling and calling. My previous clients put a bug in their neighbors' ears; that system worked especially effectively among rural residents. It just boggled my mind how many terrible secrets were hidden amidst peaceful bucolic landscapes! Phomas, birth curses, water spuns, anchutkas, brownies, quiet plague, and even predatory echoes. It seemed that somebody multiplied the supernatural there. Once or twice a week the answering service received a call from a customer, tearfully pleading to save his or her Uncle Peabody or Aunt Triffani. I mean to save in a literal sense, since not even once I came across a case of primitive psychosis that I used to see so much in Redstone. A couple of times I was called when the clients had a death in the family. It was not about the money any more—I did not have time to spend it. Even if I were a dark magician in the power of three, hard-hearted and tough, I could not fence-sit on a woman, sobbing into the phone, whose son had picked up bone rot at the cemetery. It would be physically impossible, at least for me.

Not good to be a dark, having grown up in a white family.

My "chatter-box", Ms. Fiberti, responded to my problems with surprising understanding. I obtained a corner in her apartment to keep an escritoire with filing cabinets and workbooks, a rack for my gripsack, and a hanger for my business suit (the suit and the gripsack were my own now). Every evening the hostess made amazingly delicious strawberry tea and allowed me to speak out, and I was immensely grateful to her for that.

I approached the rate of "two calls per weekend", and geography of my trips became more and more complicated. Leisure time disappeared—I hardly slept enough those days. Long walks and lengthy waiting times for the train turned into a sophisticated form of torture. After falling asleep on the platform and almost freezing to death while waiting for a train, I realized that I needed my own transportation.

I couldn't choose which one. A horse was no good—I had no place to hold it, and horses would die from such loads. Alas, I wasn't able to afford a large black limousine with leather seats; the only other option that came to mind was a bicycle. After counting my savings and finding the crazy amount of fifteen hundred crowns, I decided to become more creative in my search - to show off, putting it simply.

The only car dealer I knew was located across the river, just opposite the dormitory, and from a distance it looked like a long shed with a skylight. I didn't intend to buy anything there—just to get an idea of what was on the market. That place seemed like the right one to start with. I wanted to stretch the nerves of the salespeople, touch and test-drive the machinery, and then buy secondhand through classifieds and hope that I was lucky enough not to get a lemon.

I took a day off from my studies, slipping away from a lecture on magic theory; I didn't anticipate any problems with that discipline. The sun was shining, light frost hardened the dirt, and a feeling of unexpected freedom intoxicated me as in spring. I wasn't dressed officially (that business suit and tie were making me sick), and I looked like a funny anomaly strolling among well-dressed crowd. Middle-aged gentlemen, women with children, and old ladies with dogs leisurely sauntered along the promenade. Skinny, cheeky students didn't belong there.

Was there a festival of some kind that day? Or was it just a popular place?

A lightly renovated barn displayed the proud name of "Plaza". Most of the visitors, like me, came there just to browse. All of the car models could be viewed right in the hall, without going outside. The sunlight beat through the windows, and the room was surprisingly warm.

Two dozen brand-new cars were lined up against the long wall. Frustration gripped me when I looked at this exhibition of harlequins. Surely, I knew that cars were toys for wealthy townsfolk (rural residents preferred horse-powered carts and carriages, and for seasonal work they used awfully smoking tractors, powered by rapeseed oil), but I had no idea how far it had gone. All cars had been puffed and curved with an abundance of chrome and gold, in cheerful colors, and some came without a top. Just looking at them caused subconscious aversion. In addition, they all had a very low clearance; such toys were of no use in the places where my clients dwelled. A dark magician who had to be pulled out of potholes with a rope would become a disgrace for the whole profession! I felt an unbearable urge to buy a tractor and drive it back and forth all over the "Plaza".

"Do you have anything military for sale?" without much hope I asked a pimply young guy with the badge of sales consultant. "For rural areas?"

He pursed his lips stiffly.

"We do not sell agricultural machinery!"

Look at that, a self-conceited flea!

"I know where I can buy trucks," I smiled dryly. "I wonder if there is anything worth viewing at your place."

"Hello! How are you?" his boss immediately smelled a brewing conflict. The young guy caught his glance and quietly disappeared. "Are you interested in anything special? Not everything that we sell is on display in the hall."

I sighed. The dark mage profession had its advantages and drawbacks.

"I need an off-road vehicle that I could drive everywhere, small and black."

"Would you like to browse our catalogs?"

I reluctantly agreed; his suggestion to look at the pictures meant that there were no suitable vehicles on display. The boss took me into his office behind the garage. The place turned out to be quite remarkable; all the walls were plastered with posters bearing images of machinery: engines and steam engines, cars of all makes, racing bolides, squared-off army trucks and tractors— anything that moved without the use of muscle power. A glass cabinet was filled with tiny copies of the most prominent models. I paused at a moped, resembling my own like two peas in a pod, and even blinked with pleasure—the owner had good taste.

"To find what you want," the salesman said busily, putting thick binders of magazines on the table, "you need to articulate what you want. What you expect your vehicle will do, its operating conditions, fuel, your financial means, all of it. We will get you any model for the right price."

"I frequently travel to the countryside. There are no roads there, none at all. I need to move quickly. Comfort doesn't matter. I figured I could buy some used military equipment."

"It's feasible," the salesman nodded, "but the military flogs their vehicles to the ground. You'll get financially broken fixing their cars, but a brand new unit will cost you a fortune—their machines aren't in demand among civilians. It ought to be a custom order."

Shit... what I wanted was quite unique. Nobody, nobody thought of the needs of talented dark magicians, who had to work at the top of their bent! But the merchant already had his eyes fixed on the ceiling, digging hard into his memory; he seemed to be honored to satisfy the exotic request of his customer.

"Come on!" he started up suddenly. "You must see it."

We left the garage, watched by his staff.

"I think an ethanol engine won't work for you; it's difficult to find dry alcohol briquettes in the countryside, and diluted spirit will stall the engine every other kilometer..."

I remembered my own experience with the moped and wholeheartedly agreed with him.

"So, we're looking for something that works on oil," he

summarized. "Diesels are more complex in operation, but you have some experience, I believe..."

The salesman artfully taxied around the complex in a yellow two-seater car, simultaneously introducing me to the particulars of the automotive industry: "A couple years ago, Domgari Motors promoted cars with diesel engines, but their vehicles did not do well: except for the military, nobody showed any interest in them. Noisy and expensive to maintain, they were difficult to ignite in the cold weather and had really large dimensions. In short, the design was stalled. But the company managed to produce some prototypes..."

A hunting excitement awoke in me. Could it really be true that there was something in this world that could serve me and only me?

We drove into the suburbs, an area of warehouses and workshops.

"That's it! Our surplus stock."

Five vehicles were tightly stuffed in a dusty barn: small trucks, limousines with abnormally elongated hoods, and even a mini-bus.

"What's the catch? Why did nobody buy them?"

"I'll start them up, and you'll understand," he went to search for fuel oil.

I stayed to inspect the collection. All the cars were a bit too big compared to their usual counterparts, and at least three of them had a rather high clearance to fit the definition of an off-road vehicle. Oil was cheaper and more widespread than alcohol; consequently, there would be fewer problems filling up the gas tank. I noticed in one corner a smaller vehicle covered with a dusty tarp. The thing smelled strongly of dark magic.

"Oh, that!" the salesman approached me unnoticed. "A perfect beast. See for yourself."

I pulled off the tarp. There was a motorcycle under it, so hefty that I dropped my jaw.

"A pitiful dead-end design," the guy shook his head in sincere sorrow. "It's not just the size. The engine is operated by dark magic; a single failure, and it would be cheaper to throw it away than to fix it. You know how expensive dark mages' services are!"

I knew, because I provided those services myself.

"May I test-drive it?"

The salesman smiled: "Go ahead!"

The unit had been conserved skillfully; one could just wipe the dust off and fill the tank to drive it. Dark magic that gave the engine a kind of pseudo-life ate half of the oil in the tank at once and contentedly rumbled. My God, it was a mechanical zombie!

"Don't go to town," the guy asked.

I nodded and pulled the starter. The engine didn't clatter, it roared. The motorcycle vibrated impatiently, almost jumping under my hand. I grinned, then turned on the gas and rolled out of the hangar.

The effect was stunning! Quietly talking salespeople turned their heads toward me in shock, sleepy technicians dropped their tools, and drivers of heavy trucks frantically clanged to the steering wheels, preparing to tame their raging beasts.

I toured around the hangar, creating terrified screams and unhealthy excitement.

This monster was capable of killing a white mage by its mere appearance—all the more so by the sound of it. Therefore, I could not ride it around the town; the last thing I needed would be fines for violation of road safety regulations. I would have to rent a garage somewhere on the outskirts of town to keep that monster... because I had made my choice.

The salesman welcomed my return with a mixture of irritation and excitement on his face.

"Hey, man! How much does it cost?" I shouted, bellowing over the roar of the engine.

"Four thousand!" he shouted in reply. "But you could buy it with a two-year installment plan!"

"I'll take it!"

That was how I became the owner of the most monstrous vehicle in the whole Ingernika.

The motorcycle became the breath of air, the fresh stream that allowed me to get out of the stupor caused by the Empowerment; the vehicle merged my old and current lives— the awakened Power and the acquired freedom. I think I was the last student in our group to recover. Seeing me brisk and angry, Mr. Rakshat sighed with relief and began drilling us with renewed energy—there should be no dropouts in our group anymore.

My monstrous machine (prudently dyed black by the manufacturer) settled in a shed at a junkyard (the yardman owed me). The convenience was many-sided: first, no one could see it; second, no one could hear it; and finally, it was cheap. The junkyard dwellers would not dare steal from a dark magician, even under the death penalty; they were very superstitious people. So it all worked out splendidly, except for the yard's stench. The roar of the rumbling engine didn't let me fully enjoy my night rides—anybody could track my routes just by the sound. It did not help to keep the secrecy of my trips (remember, remember NZAMIPS!). Since buying another vehicle was out of the question, I had to modify the vehicle. I was an alchemist, after all! Though, my gut feeling was telling me that alchemy alone wouldn't be enough.

The motorcycle was an advanced model that used a spell to operate the engine: it was a brilliant solution that relieved the owner of problems with the ignition and idling. The design fell short of perfect just a little bit. The solution came to me on the way to Redstone from a client's: it was getting dark, but the headlight refused to light up—the spell that controlled the engine decided to ignore the dynamo-machine. The spell just disliked the dynamo! The engine heated up like a stove, but it could not incandesce one little steel hair in the bulb—the spell was rejecting intermediates, the wires and coils. The problem was fundamental: the dark spell was not an alchemical structure, created by a sorcerer once and for all; the spell existed as an equilibrium of flows, in constant movement, pseudo-alive. The engine was like an organism with its own rhythm, but it perceived the dynamo as an alien structure with a wholly different logic of being; the stronger body cast off the foreign one. They had to be designed as two separate modules, independent of each other, but coming in contact through a simple material buffer. Thinking about the design of the lighting block, I inevitably came to the issue of energy source. And then it hit me: the alternating current!

I made the alchemical parts of the new design in the workshop myself. As for the magic components, I hesitated for a while, but didn't dare draw a pentagram in the garage. I asked Mr. Rakshat for a spot in the lab. The instructor was clearly impressed by the extent of my responsibility; he gave me the place and even advised periodically.

"I do not know why you need this amulet," he hinted pointedly.

"Oh," I brightened up, "it would be a revolution in the mufflers!" Let him suffer from curiosity.

I called Quarters to come and appreciate my exceptional skill and unique talent. By that time the device had already been installed and field tested twice—riding the motorcycle felt much more comfortable now.

Quarters respectfully looked around my machine.

"Cool bike! Does it run fast?"

I brushed him aside: "You've got that wrong. Look at this. Better - listen!"

I turned the starter, and the ground trembled.

"Wow!" Quarters shook his head, unaccustomed to my vehicle.

I grinned and turned an invisible lever on the panel. The roar was cut off immediately, transforming instead into a deep growl, and the headlight mounted on the handlebars beamed rays of blinding light.

"Wow!" Quarters' eyes were glued to my motorcycle. "How are you doing that?"

"Dark magic."

Quarters raised an eyebrow.

"Well, how do I explain it to you... the movement of pistons creates a light wave instead of sound."

"Apply for a patent!"

"What?" I did not understand.

"This. Needs. To be. Patented," he repeated slowly. "The first person to see it will instantly steal it."

"Come on..." I did not want to get involved in such an enterprise. I do not like bureaucracy.

Quarters instantly caught my mood: "Do you want me to attend to it? We'll split the profits 50/50."

"Agreed!"

Half is better than nothing, right? Quarters was more knowledgeable about such things, his dad was wealthy, and instinct for money was hard-coded into my friend's genes, he believed. Well, we'll see about that.

My life was filled with colors again: money (lots of it), a fury of battles with monsters from the other world, the taste of victory, and the realization that I was a "genius" (according to Quarters). What else does a dark magician need to be happy? A silly question: of course, the news that NZAMIPS was shut down! And Captain Baer hung up.

CHAPTER 10

The window in Conrad Baer's office looked to the west: the setting sun was peeping through. An old tree protected the room from direct sunlight in the summer, but now its leafless branches only introduced chaos, casting a net of weird shadows on the wall. However, the owner of the office wasn't going to draw the blinds—he preferred to add some anxiety to the atmosphere. Having climbed to the rank of captain, the policeman nicknamed Locomotive willy-nilly learned some professional tricks.

The senior regional coordinator arrived from Ho-Carg at Redstone; another one, not Larkes, whom Locomotive more or less got used to. Larkes had been moved into another position, and nobody knew whether it was a promotion or the former boss was sent to a distant place like the King's Island as a "cleaner". The new coordinator, as rumored, possessed dark power at the master's level; he was young and pathologically active. Having arrived in town on the five p.m. express, he requested an urgent meeting in one hour. The captain did not invite to the meeting any of his own mages, but he dressed in the highest level safety suit (just in case) and replaced his secretary with an agile guy from the guard (there was no reason to risk the life of a mother of three kids). The senior analyst, the head of the investigation group, and the on-duty patrol officer were called to the meeting as well.

It remained to be seen what the new boss had in mind.

The senior coordinator (young, perhaps too immature) appeared at the meeting together with a youthful woman, carefully maintaining distance between them. She had an inconspicuous appearance, with clothing that was strongly reminiscent of an archive servant, but an amazingly penetrating green-eyed gaze unmasked her. Locomotive displayed a blank face; his entire look lent to that. It was not his first meeting with a white empath; he guessed that this girl was a walking X-ray.

The coordinator's move went down the drain: Conrad Baer was not the son of a glazier. But the question remained: what caused a dark magician to work in cahoots with a white? Strange winds must be blowing at the top...

"Senior Coordinator Mr. Satal. Ms. Kevinahari," the captain introduced the newcomers. "Mr. Vosker, Inspector Shtoss, Lieutenant Hamirson. May we help you with anything?"

The coordinator looked around the room with evident displeasure. Having plenty of experience dealing with dark mages (they accounted for a quarter of his staff), the captain had arranged the furniture in his office in such a way that the visitor from the capital would not be able to take the place of the office's owner. Baer did not care how weird the arrangement looked. If he did not stop the instinctive proclivities of the coordinator from the very beginning, he would have to quarrel with the dark all the way, figuring out which one of the two was the boss.

The guest hesitated for a few seconds but did not wade through the bottleneck of chairs. His companion smiled faintly and sat in a chair pre-arranged for her.

"The reason for our visit is the alarming news from the suburbs of Redstone."

"...And management decided to satisfy our request for more staff?" Baer continued for him.

Mr. Satal angrily shrugged: "It's about outrageous lawlessness in Redstone County!"

The coordinator said the magic word "county", and the captain relaxed a little: formally, his mandate ended at the town's boundaries, and the county office had not reported any problems lately.

"Could you provide more detail?"

It was a tricky question, because Locomotive recalled outright dozens of incidents in the county office that could be characterized as malfeasance, but he did not want to ruin the career of the chief of the county's "cleaners"; the old man deserved his honorable retirement.

"A case of illegal practice. Five episodes minimum!"

The captain instantly caught what was going on. No, he did not have his own agents outside the town, but a large part of the Baer family lived in remote rural areas. Regular visits by his cousins and aunts were enough to keep up with all the gossip. It did not make sense to deny the facts, and the captain allowed himself to correct the coordinator cautiously: "Probably, closer to two dozen cases."

Mr. Satal crept: "Do you know what's going on?"

"Only rumors, sir. The suburbs are outside my jurisdiction."

For some time, the coordinator contemplated what was said, and Locomotive waited patiently to continue. He was surprised at the speed with which the news reached the capitol; generally, their superiors used to respond to the most urgent requests in a year, maybe a year and a half. The impression was that the couriers met in the middle or that a spy worked somewhere in the neighborhood, and his information went to the authorities directly.

"What exactly do you know?" Ms. Kevinahari finally gave tongue.

The captain shrugged: "Rumor is that any otherworldly problem could be solved without calling the "cleaners". Inexpensive, fast, with a warranty." Not to mention that the unknown dark magician was polite and gave a discount to families with children.

"Nobody questions him about his certification and license," the captain sighed.

"Do you consider it normal?"

Locomotive shrugged again: "Someone has to do the job!"

Locomotive did not want to inform on the county's "cleaning" service or, rather, did not want to risk his life; the guests would leave, and he would stay. He knew firsthand the heart of the problem: townsfolk, faced with the boorishness of the county's "cleaners", often sent their complaints to the captain, and he and old Yudter, the chief of the "cleaners", had to actually use their authority a few times to make the mages move their butts. At least a little bit. Alas, military status allowed the Division of the Supernatural Phenomena Liquidation (the official name of the "cleaning" service) to ignore opinions of the chief of the civil division of Redstone's NZAMIPS. The "cleaners" paid him no mind, regularly and with pleasure.

"In some sense, you're right," Mr. Satal suddenly confessed. "All who approached the mage-infractor had direct or covert written rejections from the county's "cleaners". My team of internal investigators is working there now, and I guarantee that heads will roll. What an almshouse here, at taxpayers' expense!"

That was the answer: the capitol authorities intended to instill the fear of superiors into the "cleaners" and stumbled upon the dubious magician right away. Locomotive remembered the ugly face of Colonel Grokk and cheered—the chief of the "cleaners" was cruising for a bruising!

Mr. Satal switched to a business-like tone again: "I hope I do not need to explain what our duty is?"

"To give this guy a medal?" the captain suggested.

"To give, but not a medal!" the coordinator exploded. "This man has gone crazy with greed: he conducts expulsion rituals at five-six day intervals. He is leaving no time for basic recovery. We must stop him before he destroys himself and others!"

Locomotive nodded sadly. Dark mages are essentially all the same: loosen the reins a bit, and they over-speed. It would be strange if a crook poking under the nose of the county's "cleaners" were any different.

"Do we have any complaints?"

Mr. Satal's face literally blackened; the captain even got frightened. A nutty boss was the last thing they needed here...

"We will act preemptively," Ms. Kevinahari quickly interposed. "No use waiting for the situation to end in disaster."

Locomotive nodded readily—let it be preemptive. He was not in the mood to test the reliability of his safety suit.

"We received neither complaints," the coordinator pulled himself together, "nor certified testimonies. One might as well start a conspiracy case!"

Baer imagined peasants that suffered a great deal from the cleaners' meanness "greeting" NZAMIPS agents, and he silently sympathized with the coordinator: his people, carrying out their duty, felt spit at up and down. It remained to be seen how they intended to look for the mage, with no statement or witness testimony...

"We don't have an imprint of his aura," Ms. Kevinahari added to the conversation. "He uses a portable altar and the most basic spells and always thoroughly destroys all traces of divination. Even if we get a search warrant, unlikely we will find any specific proof."

"The prudent son of a bitch," Mr. Satal sighed.

"By the way, he is a good psychologist, too," the empath seemed to be amused by the difficulties before her colleagues. "For a dark, it is a very rare skill! Nobody saw him without a black coat, leather shoes, a handbag and, more recently, a cane. These flashy attributes of the profession attract all the attention: the witnesses who agreed to speak with us cannot describe his facial features or even his hair color."

"Perhaps he doesn't operate alone?" Locomotive suggested cautiously.

"Can you picture a cohesive team of dark magicians?" the coordinator hummed. "No, his style is too unique, precisely because of his elusiveness. The guy works not only with magic, but with people as well: he says what they want to hear, does what they expect from him. He is so convincing in this role that even the white don't feel false; on the contrary, they would rather not trust the police. You have no idea how difficult it is for a dark to achieve this!"

Captain Baer had some ideas.

"That is," he concluded, "you can only catch him red-handed."

"That's it. The county's office is now trying to find his contacts."

Locomotive figured that Mr. Satal would wait for a long time for the results from his old friend Yudter: the chief of the county's "cleaners", being a seasoned pro, didn't fear resignation and criticized the politics of the capitol's authorities, using foul language. He would need to talk to the old man in person;

acting together, they would be able to prevent the bloody denouement of the story. The captain didn't doubt for a moment that the end would be bloody. After the mage's arrest he would petition the court to mitigate the punishment and, perhaps, even offer the enterprising guy a full-time position at NZAMIPS. But he had to be found first.

"Have you already got some details?" the captain asked.

Ms. Kevinahari took the floor again: "We were able to establish that our smart guy uses public transit for traveling; the analysis showed that the starting point of his routes was, most likely, Redstone. In addition, we noticed certain periodicity in his actions; for example, he never goes to clients on Wednesday. We may, of course, suggest some sort of superstition, but most likely he is engaged in some legitimate work at this time."

Redstone! That's why they came to him. Locomotive tried to figure out which one of his charges could have gotten involved in this venture and shook his head: "Redstone is a big town; there are a lot of dark magicians here. Furthermore, there's the university. This guy just needs to change clothes to mix with townsfolk."

Mr. Satal reluctantly nodded: "We have a chance to track him down at the station—a man in a black coat, with a cane and handbag should be eye-catching."

"How many people do you intend to involve in surveillance?" Captain Baer said half-heartedly, weighing his resources.

"Two!" Ms. Kevinahari calmed him down. "It would look strange if I wait at the station alone, without a companion."

In a quarter of an hour they had created a plan for the operation. Locomotive admitted that an ambush with the empath's participation was the surest means of solving the problem. The coordinator himself wasn't going to take part in the ambush, but he couldn't wait—his eyes thirsted for action. Captain Baer hoped that Mr. Satal would direct his energy at the county's "cleaning" service. The guard on duty, who replaced the captain's secretary, called the garage for a car. The fierce coordinator and his empath were shown out to the hotel.

When thick cabinet doors closed behind the visitors, Mr. Vosker loudly gasped; the senior analyst of Redstone's NZAMIPS was a nervous man that grew pale simply upon hearing the words "dark magician". Meeting with the new boss made the poor man lose heart.

Inspector Shtoss cleared his throat: "Hmm, a very energetic man."

Captain Baer just smiled: "He is exactly what is needed to whip Colonel Grokk into shape. Listen," he turned to Hamirson, and the lieutenant melancholically raised his eyebrow, "Do not do any favors for the county's "cleaners", and order your people the same. Everything should go through me! All inquiries should bear signatures, all papers—endorsements. The same applies to the rest of you." His subordinates nodded with understanding.

"Grokk will twitch now like a man hanged on a rope; I hope he won't drag us with him!"

* * *

In the evening the NZAMIPS' office was empty and quiet. Mr. Satal marched proudly to the exit door, glancing disapprovingly at tubs of ficus plants and flowerpots; his empath kept an impenetrable silence. The coordinator broke their quiescence first: "What a sleazebag," he said through his teeth. "How did he manage to become an officer with such a mug?"

Ms. Kevinahari smiled slyly, but her voice was serious and reserved: "Conrad Baer has been with NZAMIPS longer than I've been alive, achieved a perfect career record, liquidated an incident in Nintark, and was awarded a medal twice. A skilled and responsible manager."

"How does his current behavior fit with the massacre in Nintark?" the coordinator snorted.

"He showed no enthusiasm today," the empath admitted, "but I cannot say that he does not understand the problem. Rather, the captain chooses the lesser evil. Obviously, the situation with the supernatural is so serious that he is willing to pay for twenty successful expulsions with lives of the mage and those nearby."

"What a bastard."

"He is cynical," the empath agreed, "tends to manipulate others, but he is dedicated to his job. He will go after our guy."

"He wouldn't dare not to."

"I would like to point out to you that any reference to the 'cleaners' causes inadequate reaction in all respondents."

"You bet!" Mr. Satal almost spat in a fit of temper. "I'll be damned if any of those scams remain in the service!"

"The capitol is partially guilty," Ms. Kevinahari recalled. "We should have foreseen that ten years of peace would badly impact the team that was made up entirely of dark magicians."

"They had enough fun for the last three years, the frequency of manifestations has been quite high."

The empath did not argue. Mr. Satal paused on the porch steps, intently eyeing the street, as if expecting to see the man wearing a black coat and a cane.

"I haven't been here since the day of my graduation," he said quietly. "Nothing has changed. The province, what else can I say?!"

"Would you like to change anything?" Ms. Kevinahari moved her head.

The senior coordinator paused before replying. A tram rolled along the neighboring street, banging and clanging; soft music was heard from the pub on the corner. Second-shift NZAMIPS' staff was leaving the office with relief, excitedly discussing something—it was Friday.

"No, I wouldn't," the magician said very seriously.

They did not discuss this question further.

CHAPTER 11

"An incredible monster—huge, black, and one-eyed—raced down the road, frantically snarling. Blinded by the light of the evil pupil, a child stood stock-still, barely seeing a brave knight that sat on the back of the monster and firmly held the creature by the horns. Having noticed the boy, the beast reared; then, tamed by a firm hand, the beast obediently froze after roaring one last time.

'I am a dark magician. Who called me?' a stentorian voice resounded.

'There are... dead... many...'

'Show me!' a fearless magician commanded sternly, grabbing his crosier with right hand and a magic valise with left.

The boy seemed to hear the magician mutter under his breath something like, 'Every time in deep shit' but, obviously, it was a sound hallucination."

I could not read further. Ms. Fiberti was crying from laughter.

"Who wrote this... such..." I had many epithets for the content of the article in The Western Herald, but they were all quite obscene.

"What do you want, Thomas? Not every day a dark magician can stop an army of ghosts!"

"What crosier, damn it? I had a cane, a walking stick! I thought it would be handy to cope with furious dogs."

"A cane and a crosier are similar things. Oblong..."

"How about the valise? Where did they take the valise from?"

"The magic valise," Ms. Fiberti giggled again.

"Other magicians will be reading that! The dark ones! I look like a complete idiot in there!"

"Don't worry; they haven't mentioned your name. Imagine what people will say about 'cleaners' after that!"

I pictured how tough combat mages from the "cleaning" service would be reading that nonsense... and neighed like a horse for ten minutes, unable to stop.

Although the situation did not seem quite so funny last week.

That day started badly: the route I planned out on the map did not match what was in the area. One of the selected roads simply didn't exist; the other one ended in a ruined bridge. There were no people coming from the opposite direction; in short, all of the attributes of a "bad place" were present. Mindful of how bold travelers end their life, I did not try to go straight through the low ground, overgrown with rotten wood and, making a huge roundabout, approached the target of my trip from the diametrically opposite side. With a powerful engine and new tires, I reached the place long before the onset of darkness. And why my motorcycle always has a headlight on, you already know.

I drove along a broken dirt road in the late afternoon, seeing the property on the hill exactly as described by the caller, and I was happy that I didn't have to spend the night in the field. Suddenly, a kid jumped on the road out of nowhere. A motorcycle is not a limousine; I could pass a pedestrian even on a very narrow road, but it was a risky move on the boy's part, anyway. I stopped and counted to ten. What would have happened if I had touched the kid with the shields? They stuck out for half a meter from the base and could hit hard. After some thought, I decided that the boy was sent to meet me and asked him: "Have you called a dark mage?"

The boy was pale, shaking; his shirt and pants were ripped with blood spots in front and on the back. Furthermore, one was struck with the impression that his clothes were torn with teeth. This misfortune looked at me and murmured: "Dead, dead, they're all dead!"

I thought some kids had been hit by a spell while playing. Familiar story - pitiful, but nothing could be done. I grabbed my gripsack and cane (the latter because there were always dogs on bigger farms) and pulled the string, converting my jacket into the coat—a typical military clothes' modification.

"Well, show the way," I told the kid calmly.

As far as I remember, I even took the time to apply the cleansing spell to my clothes. The owner of the estate was an ambitious man from a big city; you could not come in dirty shoes to a guy like that!

Why should I be nervous? I did not know at that time that zombies had been slaughtering the inhabitants of the estate for three generations in a row, and the day before a "cleaner" came in and awakened all the nonlife around. I walked to the house and suddenly noticed three ghouls, approaching me from the opposite direction. They were typical fully matured undead, dripping with green juice, a head taller than any man, with claws and fangs of the size that no living being could possess in principle. Moreover, they were moving despite the day time, very quickly, and I had neither a drafted pentagram ready, nor a flame-thrower in hand.

Students learned combat curses only in their senior year, at the very end of their studies, as juniors, we practiced how to call and hold basic spells, but the deadly threat fantastically sped up my learning process. Since the case with Rustle in the Prison Bay I knew how the combat curse should look (from the view of an objective observer). Terrified, I squeezed out of myself some quivering form, crumpled it into a sort of Shadow Sickle, and crying: "Hishu hara!" tossed it into the ghouls.

Naturally, my curse did not incinerate them, but I managed to delay the zombies; in some places, where my weaving touched the monsters, their bodies were severed into long, stirring rag-like tentacles. Not that it hurt them; rather, they were puzzled. While they were deciding whether to fix themselves or stay cut up as they were, I grabbed the kid under my arm (all this time he was hiding behind my back) and ran away.

Students of Redstone University maintain good physiques!

I hid behind a shed and recalled that ghouls only pursued objects visible to them (they were unable to keep images in their memory long enough). I paused to take a breath and realized that I missed something: there were four ghouls, not three—the fourth being a dog, raised from the dead.

A quite fresh corpse. It stood and watched.

When the creature was alive, it was a big, prick-eared dog of the kind farmers of the valley liked to keep. The invasion of the supernatural had already changed the dog: its bones and muscles stretched, its skin burst in some places, and teeth protruded from its mouth. Naturally, the otherworldly that had animated the dog did not want to cripple it; the supernatural just did not know—could not know—how to create a truly living thing. The deviations were not strong yet—little time had passed since the death of the dog. At the whim of the supernatural, a wave of pseudo-life touched not only the body, but also the brain of the animal (it doesn't happen often). The animal even slightly wagged its tail. While alive, the creature must have been very kind. Now, it probably started feeling urge to tear and gulp living flesh to satisfy its hunger. The dog used to take food from people's hands, and it wasn't so crazy yet as to hunt them down.

The fourth ghoul waited for me to feed it.

I had two options. I could smash its skull with my cane and move on, forever remembering the glance of the deceived dog that remained so faithful to people, even while dead. Or I could complete the process, correct the errors committed by the supernatural, and turn it into a genuine zombie that would not eat flesh and blood, but would require revivifying spells regularly. Had anyone found me doing something like that, I would have been burned alive.

Not good to be a dark magician that grew up among the white.

I called the dog by quietly whistling, let it sniff my palm, and put my hand on its back. Completion of the transformation was surprisingly easy: the life meridians had not cooled down in the body yet. I passed the spell over them. The dog liked the actions that I made; it wagged its tail and tried to lick my face.

So, the three ghouls left on the agenda, but I couldn't perform the same trick with them—they were transformed long ago and irreversibly. I turned to the kid, who watched my actions with intense interest. The boy was so exhausted by fear that he wouldn't run from me, even if he wanted to.

"Pull yourself together, man! I need to know what happened, or they will eat us here."

Experience with my stepfather and younger white brother helped me to get out all the details I needed without beating the unfortunate kid. Things couldn't be worse: his parents bought the estate six months ago, after something bad had happened to the former owners. Almost immediately they applied to the local "cleaning" service, but the bastard cleaners put them on a waitlist, not even bothering to find out the reason for the complaint. Two weeks ago, a representative of "Totars Energy" was supposed to pay them a visit to give a quote for hook-up to the power supply network, but the guy didn't show up; later the company declared his disappearance. The police didn't demonstrate any enthusiasm in searching for him; the new owners of the estate learned from the officers that people disappeared from that place regularly throughout the past one hundred years. The kid's father's patience had exhausted, he called me, and we agreed to meet.

But yesterday the long-awaited "cleaner" with a team of assistants and police officers finally visited the farm. I did not know what this parody on the dark troopers was trying to accomplish; they decided that the poor tradesman was killed either by one of his own, or by a tramp, or by the farmer. These psychos didn't bother to evacuate the family; instead, they rushed to the woods that I had bypassed. Two local policemen flatly refused to participate in the suicidal event. Thanks to those two, there were still people alive at the estate: when ghuls and ghouls, new and old, came to the front from the forest, the brave rural boys met them with heavy fire. Alas, bullets (any bullets) could not stop three ghouls, each a century old. Only dark magic was effective against such creatures, and the senior "cleaner" returned from the forest as one of the zombies.

It would be best to pick up the boy and run away, but, according to the kid, his family was still hiding in the house, along with the two courageous policemen and an assistant to the "cleaner", who had not gone to the woods. As soon as the sun dropped behind the horizon, the zombies would become stronger and more resolute; they were not stupid, just their mind, affected by the supernatural, manifested itself erratically and unpredictably. People's lives depended on whether I could resolve the situation before the nightfall.

The zombie-dog whined and rubbed my knee.

"Now, kid, I need your help. Do you know your neighborhood well?"

He nodded.

"Is there flat ground, roughly the size of a croquet field, nearby?"

He thought and shook his head.

"Any spot, more or less level? I need to draw a pentagram."

He nodded and walked me around the house. The zombie-dog disappeared in the bushes, but I didn't worry about it. The level ground was a barnyard, overgrown with weeds. Without complex preparation I could only use a patch of a hundred square feet in size. There was no way that I could seal all three ghouls at the same time.

"Listen, does your father keep spirits here?"

Oil was not well suited for cremation, but the spirit would do the job just fine. The boy pointed toward the house.

"Excellent. Now climb the tree and look sharp! If anything moves, knock, whistle, or shout to me."

I hoisted him onto the lower branch. At least, one of us would stay safe now.

Drawing a pentagram proved easy, but the next step—lighting a black candle—I postponed: before commencing, I had to find some weapon. In the driveway, I stumbled upon a phaeton without horses and an army truck with a canvas top; the team of the "cleaner" must have arrived in them at the manor. A fresh ghul was sitting motionlessly in the cab of the truck. I carefully climbed into the truck's body. They ought to bring some weapons with them! I managed to find a flare-gun (an exotic and funny device) and a pack of flares. There was also a spare canister of oil; all the rest the policemen had carried away. I took the flare-gun and slowly spilled oil all over the truck, then soaked a piece of cloth in the fuel, turning it into a great wick. To attack the three mature ghouls with one flare-gun would be stupid, so I had to go around the perimeter of the house in hopes of finding something else. Fortunately for me, the owner kept a barrel of spirits that leaked slightly, and I managed to find it by smell in the barn. It was getting dark outside with almost no time left until sunset. I made three trips, filling large buckets with alcohol and placing them along the path to the barnyard. Then I loaded the pistol, said a prayer, and hit the truck with a flare.

The fresh ghul, not quite used to the role of a zombie, panicked and forgot how to open the cabin door. It cried almost like a man and burned for a long time.

The three mature ghouls emerged rapidly. Had I not strained all my senses, I wouldn't have gotten away from them. Only on the second attempt did I manage to pour over the most active zombie with spirit. Rushing into the barnyard, I set fire to it with the pistol. The zombie caught fire unexpectedly well and burned brightly, with fountains of sparks (which was very handy, because in the darkness I could miss my own pentagram). There was no time left for any mistakes: the other two zombies attacked me practically together. I lit a black candle and stood behind the pentagram so that the drawing separated me from the undead. The second one was moving directly over the pentacle.

"Dangemaharus!"

And I shut the trap. A dense column of fire filled the pentagram. When the flame had subsided, the zombie disappeared without a trace. And the black candle went with it.

It burned down at once, and the pentagram became useless. The last ghoul was safe and sound: it was too far away, and the flame did not touch it. I turned around and ran to the tree, knowing that I wouldn't get there in time.

The situation was saved by the zombie-dog, clinging to the loins of the undead with a belly growl. How could I not believe in good deeds?! I climbed to the tree and together with the kid watched as the dog tore the ghoul; the two deserved each other. I thought hard what to do next: the sun was about to set, and I did not want to find out what that third ghoul was capable of at night.

"Will you save my mother?" the boy asked cautiously.

"Of course!" I habitually lied. "Let Max wear the ghoul down a bit."

The zombie-dog excitedly attacked the ghoul.

"Max?" the boy repeated doubtfully. "Actually, its name is Archie."

"I hate to tell you, kid, but your Archie has died. It's Max now. And if anyone notices Max, the 'cleaners' will kill me."

"Why?" he did not understand.

"Why did they let all these people die?" I asked reasonably. "Because they are not capable of controlling the supernatural creatures! They can decimate them one way or another, but to control—no chance."

"What about you?"

Should I tell him that I was doing this for the first time in my life?

"Sure, I can. I am the most powerful necromancer in Ingernika!

Secret knowledge is transferred in our family from father to son for a thousand years. Naturally, we use it solely to protect people from the supernatural."

I thought for a while. It was vital to take Max away from that place: the zombie-dog served as proof of my crime; no one should see it. Also, I needed to convince the boy to keep silence.

"Listen, let's make a deal. Give Max to me! I'm going to take good care of the dog. It has a real talent for hunting ghouls; it would be shameful to bury Max in the ground!"

The boy hesitated.

"In order to 'live', it must be constantly fed with dark magic, and you are short of it in this place. Without a necromantic ritual it would stay 'alive' only until the next full moon."

The position of the celestial bodies had no significance whatsoever, but the phrase sounded meaningful.

"Okay," the kid decided, "I'll tell Max to go with you."

"Thanks, man! You'll see, your dog will become a hero."

That was dependent on the condition that we stay alive until the dawn. Meanwhile, the prospects of that were dim.

The zombies fought at the far end of the barnyard in the dilapidated stables. The dog successfully limited the mobility of the ghoul, and that gave me some room for maneuver. I had one more bucket of spirit and the flare pistol that was buried somewhere in the weeds. I waited until the ghoul turned its back to the tree and smiled at the boy: "Well, I am going! Wish me luck."

Now the flare-gun was within my reach, but the bullets got lost somewhere; just one remained that I managed to drive into the trunk. The bucket leaked, a little more than half left inside. I hoped that would be enough. Having approached the fighting zombies, I managed to pour the spirit over the ghoul. The monster attacked me, but the dog hung on it as a wriggling and snarling anchor. I retreated to the tree and ordered: "Max, to me!" and fired a flare point-blank at the ghoul.

It burned to death, but not instantaneously. For a couple more minutes the zombie was running after me in the yard in the agony of death. When it was all over, I gratefully patted the dog's ears.

"Good for you, doggie! We made it."

"Do not come down!" I told the boy. "I need to check if there are some other zombies here. Until I get back, do not dare go down to the ground."

The boy nodded. It is in silly fairy tales that people do everything the wrong way round, but in reality, when they find themselves face-to-face with death, they become placid and obedient.

We reconnoitered together, the beast and the dark mage. The zombie-dog trotted briskly ahead, carefully sniffing. I was sure that it would notice a ghoul before me. The truck had already burned down, twilight passed into the night, but it was quiet and calm—the kind of silence that suggested the danger had passed. I made a torch out of the materials at hand because I had no idea where to look for the lamp. The owners were quite wealthy; they even had their own electric generator (fueled by oil, not by alcohol). It wasn't running—they forgot or hadn't wanted to turn it on. I checked the contacts and pushed the switch—it worked. The yard became lit with light bulbs, but the house was dark. It was not a good sign.

I told the dog: "Bring me my gripsack!" and cautiously came

closer to the house to peer through the windows. I found the cane under my feet—I had almost forgotten about it.

A minute later I heard panting—the zombie-dog brought me my bag. I began to like the beast.

"Hide!" I ordered. "People should not see you. Meet me at the motorcycle."

It disappeared into the darkness.

First, I lit a candle, but it attracted no zombies; only the dog rustled and breathed noisily in the bushes. Then I walked around the house calling: "Is anybody alive?"

About fifteen minutes later a pale spot flashed in the second floor's window.

"Who's there?" a voice shuddered.

"Have you called a dark mage?"

"Beware of the zombies!"

"They are in the past. Do you remember how many of them were there?"

A movement in the window, and another voice answered me.

"Twelve men had gone into the forest. Then I saw seven zombies come back, but we were able to decimate one or two of them."

"How many were the old ones?"

"Three."

"Then the worst that is left is a couple of zombies straight from the tin, lurking in the corners. We can look for them in the morning. Is there light in the house?"

"Have you indeed killed three ghouls?"

Judging by his knowledge of terminology, it was one of the "cleaners". The ghul relates to the ghoul as a lap-dog to a wolfhound. The ghuls that are many years old are called ghouls; years of being undead give them strength. I restrained myself from displaying a contemptuous smirk; the "cleaner" would not see it anyway.

"Yes! And without much effort. Plus one of the young zombies in the truck. But I had a problem with reagents—I did not expect to meet an army of zombies. Who was the idiot that raised them?"

He stayed silent in response; the "cleaner" did not want to acknowledge his folly but could not refute my words.

"Okay, never mind. Stay where you are now. I'll take the boy to the nearest farm and come back in the morning. We will talk about my fee."

"Is Mihas alive?" it was a troubled woman's voice.

"Yes. Are you his mother?"

"Mihas! I must see him!"

I heard a noise that sounded like strife. Oh-ho... I'd better run from here and let them sow their wild oats by the morning.

"In short, we'll take the road to the east."

"Mihas!"

I had to take the kid to the house and let her cry it out. The boy was surprisingly quiet and very seriously tried to persuade his mother to wait until the morning. When we left, she was still sobbing.

"Is she from the white?" I asked, turning my motorcycle around.

"No. My grandfather is a white."

"I see. A family trait!"

"What is the family trait?" the boy felt hurt.

"Weak nerves."

Receiving my command, the motorcycle's magic breathed fire into the cylinders and spun the shaft; the engine roared, and a dazzling cone from the headlight punctured the darkness.

"Hold on tight!" I ordered pulling the strings of the coat, and we moved east, followed by the quick shadow of the zombie-dog.

I didn't return to the farm; my suspicions were correct and freedom was more important than money. It seemed unwise to allow the "cleaners" to see my face: they could quickly take me to NZAMIPS. I explained to the boy that all the zombies were gone from the farm, and the police would investigate the case. I reminded him not to tell anyone about the dog.

"...Unless asked directly with no other option; outright lying is not good."

He nodded in accord.

The owners of the neighboring farm, alarmed by news of the ghouls' attack and reassured that everything would be fine from now on, agreed to take care of the kid and let the police know about the incident. Halfway to the highway, I saw from a distance a column of military trucks with the NZAMIPS logo, stirring dust from the opposite direction. I cheerfully turned into the bushes—did not want to renew acquaintance with my "beloved captain."

A day later, back at home, browsing through the headlines of the morning papers, I realized what had happened. It turned out that one of the policemen did break alive through that same cursed forest and managed to call for backup. A regiment of NZAMIPS' troopers drove there all night because the three active ghouls were horribly dangerous (originally there were four, but one of the killed "cleaners" managed to sell his life dear). The military convoy was pursued by a pack of journalists, willing to risk their lives for an opportunity to observe the fight. I saw a few of them thumbing a lift on the roadside, but intuition prompted me not to stop. Well, they were in the right place, and no ghouls—not even a poor ghul—were there. All were decimated.

It was then that the folktale of the "dark knight on a horned monster" was born.

Mass media went on and on, relishing the story of a private magician that successfully replaced a battalion of "cleaners". More sensible people questioned how the ghouls could hide for so many years in the heart of a densely populated land, repeatedly attacking unsuspecting villagers. Casualties of "cleaners" and policemen (the ghouls had eaten the big boss) added savor to the story. The chief of the regional NZAMIPS' office gave an interview, in which he regretted what had happened and remorsed, regretted and remorsed, and swore on his life that everything would be fine in the county from now on.

It was then that I became a wanted criminal. Initially, NZAMIPS' officials hinted at a reward for the "knight" for saving people, and then they publicly offered me to come and get it (did they think I was an idiot?). Finally, a reward was promised for information about me (well, go interrogate the ghouls!). Ms. Fiberti, my "answering service", was visited by some guests, but she was a willful woman and chased them all out. Emotions gradually quieted, but it was clear even to journalists that the dark magician, practicing for almost a year in the county, was from Redstone.

The day after the incident, I left the university after the second lecture reporting myself sick, and went to my "answering service". There I was handed a new issue of The Western Herald.

"Ms. Fiberti, we need to talk seriously."

She knowingly nodded: "Do you want to shut down the business?"

"After what happened, NZAMIPS will comb the entire county. I do not want trouble."

She sighed, "I'm sorry that it's over; I liked working with you. May I," she adjusted her glasses in embarrassment, "write a book about you?"

"A book?"

"A novel. Naturally, I'll change your name."

"Do you think it would be interesting to anybody?"

"I believe so."

"Fine!" I generously agreed. "Just let me browse through it when you finish. I don't want to look like a complete idiot."

Ms. Fiberti made me tea; I packed up the filing cabinet and neatly folded my business suit.

"Will you have problems because of me?"

She grinned: "If anything, I will say that I rented out a room with the phone and did not know who lived there."

So we parted.

I wrapped my black gripsack in a white towel and went to the junkyard, where my horned monster slept peacefully under the protection of the zombie-dog. If someone stumbled into those two, the gripsack would be my smallest concern. How could I manage to get into such a mess? I thought I didn't do really bad things... at least I did not plan... most importantly, everyone was happy, and then suddenly—hop—I was a danger to society (according to NZAMIPS). It was time to stop illegal activity. I vowed to myself to find Captain Baer's business card in the pockets of my old pants, frame it, and hang over my desk as a constant reminder to stay away from adventures.

Part 3. INTERNSHIP IN ALCHEMY

CHAPTER 12

"I'm a good-hearted dark mage, I'm a very modest dark mage, I am very, very..."

Should I stay quiet after what happened at the farm, or behave like everyone else? Don't get me wrong—I am, of course, very intelligent—but acting is not my element. I could convincingly simulate simple and natural reactions, but a sophisticated reconstruction of behavior was not my milieu. That was more up the white magicians' alley. How could I behave myself if I didn't know what would be best in my situation?

The question was relevant, because Redstone buzzed like a disturbed beehive. I did not think that a couple episodes of my half-illegal business would make so much noise. Interestingly enough, the townsfolk's reaction to that matter was diametrically opposed to the official view. Apparently, people did not support the authorities. I could imagine how irritated NZAMIPS' officials were! I was praised, I was recommended as a role model, I was admired and, you know, the dark are suckers for flattery. For obvious reasons, the mage remained anonymous, but I knew whom they were talking about. The only thing that kept me from running through the streets shouting, "That knight is me! Me!" was the zombie-dog. Such a trick no one would forgive.

University classes turned into a real test for my nerves: Quarters looked at me with a sly eye (what on earth made me show him my motorcycle?), and whenever at least three dark got together, they immediately began discussing "that same incident".

Nothing agitates the dark as much as another's glory! All of my fellow students were confident that they would have done "the same", but better. One twit even tried to move from word to deed, and Mr. Rakshat beat him so seriously that the guy had to go to the hospital. Any other measures wouldn't discourage the dark; therefore, the teacher's over-reaction was considered adequate. It was clear even to the white.

Due to such cases the university offered a lecture - a review of supernatural phenomena, mandatory for all dark mages. The ones who did not attend would not be allowed to take final exams. The lecturer, sent by NZAMIPS, was a lady of colorless appearance, shy and embarrassed, who told us about the history of the scientific study of otherworldly powers, uttering phrases like "lethal" and "witnesses did not survive" with a slight stammer. The officer vitalized only when she started a demonstration of heinous exhibits, spreading the disgusting stink of formalin throughout the entire room.

And I saw some of these exhibits without any formalin...

After the lecture it became clear to everyone—even to me—that the accomplishment of the feats, overblown by the media, could only be done by a well-trained otherworldly liquidator, a retired "cleaner", or an aged master looking for a meaningful death. I didn't understand why I was still alive. Logic dictated that either I embodied the Spirit of Holy Salem or the lady-lecturer slightly distorted the truth.

Since childhood I have been catching hints well, but my case did not require special subtleties: I ought to put a big, bold cross on my underground business. That was, perhaps, for the better: how much longer could I risk my life? Yes, I still owed money for the motorcycle (five hundred crowns) and needed to help my family. I could not leave them without money—Lyuchik was going to a new school. In a pinch, I could sell some stuff; the business suit was worth no less than a hundred crowns.

It was time to get more serious about my life—in the next month I would be twenty-one. No more allowances for non-age. At this stage, good students looked to make contacts with future employers and earn work experience instead of riding a motorcycle around the county with a magic gripsack at the ready. It was time to decide which was closer to my soul: magic or alchemy. Mr. Darkon was right: the majority of initiated dark mages chose the career of a combat mage (it was always easier to earn a living with one's hands, not one's brains), but I tested it and discovered that the job of a "cleaner" was rather monotonous. To my chagrin, I did not have any employer in sight for a career in alchemy.

What about Quarters?

"Hey Ron, how is our patent doing?" I asked my friend.

"Excellent! If Dad doesn't show a bit of generosity, I'll sell your invention to Domgari Motors. Old hags still think that a student is a sort of free slave. Don't piss! You will be rich."

"What do you think: can I mention the patent in my resume?"

"You aren't going to be an alchemist, are you?"

"I have always been planning to become an alchemist."

"Weren't you going to learn magic?"

"So what?"

Quarters shrugged and immediately perked up: "How about making some money?"

"Don't even ask!"

"I've got some friends," Quarters hesitated. "In short, they started a business..."

"Do they need a draftsman?"

"They need brains! Oh, and a draftsman too. They've signed a big contract: the optimization of gas generators."

"Shit tanks, you mean?"

Ron chuckled: "Tom, you have no idea what dough swirls in this business! Do you know how much shit this town produces a day?"

I snorted. Wow, what a start to my life! Though, why not?

"What are the terms?"

"You'll like them."

Of course, compared to the income of a dark magician, it was no money at all, but I certainly couldn't become too choosy. From a student's perspective, everything looked damn attractive, and from the point of view of a wanted criminal, the job was excellent camouflage. Ron shared a common belief that alchemy was not the place for an initiated dark mage.

* * *

Edan Satal's career as the senior coordinator of the Northwestern Region began with resounding failure and public humiliation. The excuse that it took some time to gain full control of the situation was poor consolation. Had Satal caught the ill-starred mage in the heat of the moment, tortures and a murder would have been added to the other sins of the coordinator. But the hero of Satal's humiliation was wisely hiding somewhere.

Care for the mental health of decision makers was the direct responsibility of empaths in the public service. Ms. Kevinahari was confident that, whatever passions boiled in the soul of the dark magician, two or three weeks of hard work would melt them in dry pragmatism. If nothing else happened. So far, the only side effect of the scandal was the transfer of the regional

NZAMIPS' office from Gerdana to Redstone.

Ms. Kevinahari presented an investigatory report on the Fitsroten Estate to the coordinator personally: "In some sense, we have been lucky this time—he drew a pentagram on the ground. But some... dog... dug all around and even peed all over. Having examined... this, our best expert... I don't even know such words! In short, he came to a conclusion: the power channel of our mage is nonstandard. That's it."

"Perhaps, I'd better speak to the expert myself?"

"No, no! You would kill each other. Seriously."

Mr. Satal kept silence, and even the empath could not say whether the coordinator thought of the emerging issue or cherished his annoyance.

"Would you like me to communicate the results to Captain Baer?" Ms. Kevinahari disturbed the quiescence.

"No!" the coordinator startled.

The empath refrained from commenting, but Mr. Satal sensed some disagreement (or his teamwork skills improved) and found it necessary to explain: "Weren't you surprised that he switched transportation methods at exactly the time that we set up the ambush at the railroad station?"

"Yes, I was," Ms. Kevinahari admitted. "Prior to that, he used trains so often that conductors thought up a nickname for him. But Captain Baer is not a traitor, that's for sure!"

"I didn't mean him. Lots of people work in his office. I want to close all channels that information could leak from."

The empath reluctantly nodded, admitting that he was right, and immediately livened up: "Do you think that our mage has a support group?"

"Rather, a nonsupport group," Mr. Satal grimaced. "Talks of the Artisans started again in some circles, meaning there will be sacrifices. But I am not Larkes! I'll be sentimental with no one. If they stick out, they will pay dearly for that!"

Ms. Kevinahari conciliatorily shook her head: "The rebirth of the sect requires a certain incubation period, if there is still anybody left. Or do you think the incident at the estate was their work?"

"You mean Grokk?" the coordinator raised eyebrow. "Nonsense! The old knucklehead ran in the ghouls' jaws to cover up his wrongdoing. When he was in charge, seven (that we know about) were lost in that place. He had to prove to everybody that the danger was exaggerated."

His brief analysis perfectly complemented the image of a fattened and brazen dark magician, who was introduced to Ms. Kevinahari as the chief of Redstone County's Division for the Liquidation of Supernatural Phenomena.

"Perhaps I should try to establish connections with the local white," the empath decided. "Also, I need information about Redstone's artisans, if they were here."

"Tell my secretary to prepare a request; I'll sign it..." the coordinator suddenly faltered. "There is one more thing, Ms. Kevinahari..."

"Rona...Rona, for short," the empath smiled.

"Oh?... Thanks! Then... I am just Dan."

Rona Kevinahari smiled at him and left the senior regional coordinator's office that was temporarily stationed in the Redstone division of NZAMIPS.

That day they took an important step forward: the move to informal communication meant that Satal no longer perceived her as a suspicious spy. Trust has been established! Perhaps the higher-ups weren't mistaken on the new coordinator, for a change. The dark could control himself, he was easily appeased, he was ready to adapt to teamwork, and his excessive aggressiveness in the current situation was more of a bonus than a disadvantage. She needed to reflect this in her report!

In the hallway, Ms. Kevinahari exchanged bows with Captain Baer, noting that the chief of Redstone's NZAMIPS looked particularly melancholic (no doubt he was hiding something), and hurried to the door—she was going to visit the university and give two review lectures today.

Locomotive followed the empath with an indifferent glance. When he was told that the regional coordinator would occupy his office, the captain could not believe his ears at first. Was the complex of buildings, taken away from Grokk's "cleaners", too small for the coordinator? It had so much room—you could let a rail line run through. Alas! The captain had to reshuffle and condense his staff in a smaller space, because the senior coordinator wanted to take over Baer's office, and the captain was forced to move to the former accounting room. In a sense, the idea proved not to be so bad: women-bookkeepers started aggressively courting the single man, and some of them were such beauties that o-ho-ho! But losing his office pained Baer anyway!

On the other hand, the authorization of documents happened at a phenomenal rate now, as in the approval of increased funding for intelligence work at the university. Locomotive was not sure if the coordinator took his arguments seriously, but the logic was compelling, and Satal did not risk arguing about it. It was easier for him just to give the money.

The unlicensed dark mage was not found yet. The captain agreed that such a successful otherworldly liquidator was unlikely to be a novice. Unlikely, but not totally improbable.

First, according to the assurance of his own experts, the unknown magician used a single spell, the Fire Seal, in all cases. It would be hard to find a simpler curse, but what a great effect he had achieved. Second, all of Redstone's magicians minimally suiting the description of the Knight had already been checked. Oh, and third, what mage in his right mind, apart from a student, would agree to stake his life for money?

"A novice," the captain confidentially whispered to the coordinator.

"A student?" the coordinator winced with displeasure, trying to dodge off the bulky body of Locomotive. "With such skills? Three ghouls simultaneously, practically with his bare hands, improvising as easily as scratching his foot's heel! It's a shame to admit, but I don't know any combat mage so powerful."

"A gifted student!" Locomotive hung over the dark mage as a big warm cloud.

And Mr. Satal surrendered: "Okay. Talk to the faculty members whether they have a young genius in mind."

"A genius with money."

"Right. If we don't catch him red-handed, then at least we will watch him. We'll need to recruit this kid."

To recruit! First, they needed to find him. The intuition of the experienced police operative hinted that they would have a good run to accomplish the task. Captain Baer wandered around the office with a businesslike appearance and without a specific purpose, but not because of thoughts about the Dark Knight. He was not a magician (and did not possess any Source), but years of service and life woes taught him to perceive approaching troubles, even when the others found only occasion for fun. Now Locomotive was haunted by a feeling that the situation had acquired an irregular shape.

Thinking logically, events in the county were supposed to undermine the reputation of NZAMIPS and dark mages in one fell swoop. All preconditions for disaster were present: a dismissed team of "cleaners" headed by the fat idiot, long-time ignorance by the central office (perhaps too long) of the activities of the Redstone division, the novice coordinator, not knowing yet how to put two and two together, and the mass media—always waiting for a scandal. The situation bore distinct traces of serious planning, and here an adventurous unlicensed mage emerged on the scene, walked over some sore spots, fixed them in passing, and transformed a minus into a plus. And the worst was that the former coordinator Larkes definitely played some role in this. Captain Baer felt the upcoming troubles in his gut, though he could not rule out the possibility that it was all about him changing the room.

CHAPTER 13

I never had a chance to work in a team, except for the expedition to the King's Island. The future belongs to large research institutions and corporations; the time when alchemists worked alone in garages has forever gone (my motorcycle is a different story). Therefore, I had to learn how to get along with co-workers or become so brilliant that I would be forgiven for anything.

Overwhelmed by those thoughts, I bought a penny-worth pamphlet titled The Business Etiquette from a hawker's tray, read it, and realized that it was written by a well-wisher whose intent was to help prostitutes reach the level of a secretary. A more useless idea was to ask Quarters' advice. No, he would have answered, but god forbid I follow his recommendation!

It would have been easier if the employer had interviewed me; we would have looked at each other and understood who was worth what. But Ron conveyed that Mr. Polak preferred to test me in action. Did he think, 'Every dark is the same?' Or was it our patent that impressed him? On the other hand, they offered so little money during the probation period that it wouldn't matter who was at the drawing board; even with a monkey they would not lose much.

The situation was kind of confusing to me. I could have guessed then what was the matter, but, as a naive student, I wasn't versed in business.

And then the day came: the first day of my grown-up life.

I went to work in a business suit (in my opinion, I had to be dressed up), though I didn't put a tie on; I was fed up with neckties. The bureau occupied the third floor of a cheap office building. A dusty sign on the door declared "BioKin". That name did not shout association with alchemy. Behind the doors there was a huge hall. Two drawing boards, pushed into the far corner, and desks with rolls of drawing paper on top of neighboring thick folders hinted at the creative process that was taking place there. A boy in uniform and two girls (I immediately recalled The Business Etiquette) were having coffee at the only unloaded desk. One of the two was red-haired and giggling cutely; the other, a searing brunette, flashed her astounding blue eyes from under long bangs. Not without regret I interrupted their fun: "Where can I find Mr. Polak?"

The redhead pointed her finger at the distal end of the hall, where the deposits of folders and drawings were particularly high. I confess, I did not notice a man behind them. He did not see or hear me, but not because he was busy with work: Mr. Polak was sweetly napping with his head on a pillow of folders and his legs stretched into the aisle.

"Hello!" I called gently.

He started, looking around with bleary eyes. I waited patiently until his face took on a meaningful expression.

"You booked an appointment with me at three p.m."

"Is that so? Oh... of course! Mr. Tangor?"

I suspected this guy wouldn't be able to pronounce the word "mister" twice in a row. Not because he woke up two seconds ago. Bewildered, I looked at the man who was steering the whole company: he wore a plaid farmer shirt and overalls, like a handyman from a farmyard. (If not for the quality of the fabric, I would have thought that he had just come out of there). On top of it all, a brilliant earring gleamed in his ear.

And then the revelation hit me that my first boss was a classic, double-dyed representative of the nerds. Shit!

"You can call me Thomas for short."

He smiled radiantly and introduced himself: "Geoff. Would you like coffee?"

"Thanks..."

"Girls, girls! Coffee!"

I tried to avoid stimulants in the afternoon, but it was impossible to get Geoff off of the idea. The courier quietly disappeared; the secretaries stopped giggling and started intently rattling the dishes.

"By the way, you don't have to dress up. Our company has adopted a casual style," he pulled a strap off of his overalls.

Okay, he might think of me as a hick, but I would not allow myself to wear such junk on the streets, except maybe to use as work clothes on the job. But they could make me look like I had an attitude, not to mention that there were no lockers or places for a clothes change.

I forced a smile, feverishly looking for a way to turn his offer down.

"I understand, Geoff," I looked down, pulling on the lapel of my jacket. "But this is a gift from my Mommy!"

Knockout! He could not dispute that argument and tried to hide his embarrassment under a business-like tone: "Do you already know what our company develops?" That was Mr. Polak's first question.

"Equipment for sewage factories?" I ventured to suggest.

"Not only that, not only that!" he jumped up in indignation.

"The application of modified micro-organisms will open up a new era in the progress of civilization!"

And Mr. Polak poured down on me streams of strategic information about market conditions and future developments in this field.

I desperately tried to extract the nitty-gritty about the firm and my future responsibilities from the torrent of words. Why was he telling me all that stuff? I came here to earn, not to donate money!

"Do you understand now?" he smiled encouragingly, sipping his coffee.

"I do," I nodded stupidly. "But at this moment you are working on a gas generator."

"Yes," he did not deny the obvious.

I struggled with a desire to run away without explanation— absolutely everything annoyed me about the place. And I wanted to have a heart-to-heart with Quarters...

We began fine-tuning my work schedule: it was not supposed to interfere with my studies. Polak was surprised to learn that my classes ended at midnight twice a week.

"What program are you taking at the university?"

"Alchemy and the art of dark magic."

"Uh..."

I waited patiently—which one of my skills would he question? I swear I was ready to cast the Odo Aurum spell on the spot!

"Have you been engaged in research and development previously?" Mr. Polak asked cautiously.

In my opinion, the boss began catching on to whom he was speaking.

"Yes," I nodded, "I have a patent in the engineering field."

"Right, they told me..."

'Why did you ask then?'

He clapped his hands: "Well, let's try to get down to business."

"Let's try" was an apropos phrase in this context.

Polak gave me a sketch made by hand, and ordered to transfer it to a Whatman paper. Then he left, probably going back to nap in some other place. First of all, I dragged one of the drawing boards to the window, mercilessly hitting a desk cluttered with pots of violets. The secretaries, pointedly clanking their heels, moved the pots to another windowsill.

For two hours I transferred the sketch in fine lines and then went to a familiar pub to have a showdown with Quarters. That malicious serpent! To draw his friend into this...

"Ron, who did you send me to, you bastard?!"

A guilty expression appeared on Quarters' face: "Tom, I've got a cousin working there, and she is crazy about Polak. Be a sport and give them a hand!"

"Redhead or brunette?"

"She usually wears curls. Listen, they've been breaking their backs for two years with zero result. My uncle will fire them soon."

"What do I have to do with that? I would have to spend a year just to delve into the topic! What could I do that they haven't done already?"

Quarters rolled his eyes: "Had they done anything, the situation would have been different! Have you met Johan?"

I tensed up: "What, is he worse than...?"

"Yes, he is—I don't have the words! My uncle had hired stars of academic science for the firm. Think for yourself: who can get carried away by breeding shitty mold, except for a white mage? They do breed mold there! But they haven't been able to make a working device. Polak chatters, Johan writes articles, and an alchemist of theirs, Carl, raises a fuss: 'Give me ideas!' Tom, do you remember how you excelled at the seminars? Do the same with them—make them run!"

"How can I excel in white magic? I am an alchemist! Those two fields have almost no connection."

"Well, bring this thought up to them. Tom, I'll pay you from my own pocket!"

"Two hundred."

"Agreed."

"Per month."

"Agreed!"

I realized that I made a bad bargain. As a bonus, I managed to shake out of Quarters his understanding of the problem. Ron knew nothing and didn't care to learn about the improved microorganisms. The company was formed two years ago in the wake of new developments, promising, according to experts, fantastic profits. The work was funded by Ron's uncle who owned a sewage disposal factory and was an extremely pragmatic and meticulous guy. Well-versed in profit generation, he knew little about employing academic nerds. How he managed to maintain patience for two years was incomprehensible, but Quarters was aware that BioKin had ignominiously failed tests more than once. If I knew then what the failed tests meant...

Well, becoming a killjoy for the staff was not complicated, and no one would cope with the task better than a dark magician. It remained unclear whether the firm's goal was feasible at all; people from the academy like to work on the undoable! I feared the work would be such that I wouldn't want to put it in my resume, but two hundred crowns from Quarters were guaranteed to me anyway.

Better to take the money up front...

* * *

Captain Baer was busy creating a network of agents, a task that would take years, not months, and certainly not days. Locomotive believed that he was the only one in the office engaged in real work.

The whole of Redstone's NZAMIPS searched for the mysterious sorcerer by the sweat of their brows. For heaven's sake, who did he do harm to? The chief of the division saw the heart of the problem and pondered: if a mean trick on the "cleaners" and the capitol's raid on the regional NZAMIPS were cover-up operations, what would be the next move of the enemies? What would have to occur after the media stirred up the townsfolk with chilling stories of the supernatural frenzy in the neighborhood? Half of NZAMIPS higher-ups would immediately lose their jobs, but that would happen on the surface. Following the onset of panic, a muddy wave of forgotten customs and strange superstitions—superstitions that the state had been eradicating since the time of the Inquisition— would flow from the cracks. And somebody hoped to ride that wave.

Mysticism! The word that decent people do not say. An echo

of primitive times, when people were ruled by Fear with a capital "F", great and comprehensive Fear, Fear consisting of many small fears: fear of the elements, crop failures, animals and neighbors, and most importantly, fear of creatures from the other world. A multitude of false gods awaited unwary minds on the back streets of memory, captivating them by the beauty of rituals and enticing by promises of love; but, whatever their adherents alleged, they brought only more fear into the world. It didn't matter what people asked of ancient magic; they could get what they wanted just by chance, if they were fortunate, but the beggars always paid for the asking. It seemed that by now people had become more reasonable and forgotten their silly belief in fairy tales. But logical magic was inaccessible to all and was not omnipotent, and, therefore, again and again under different pretexts people returned to a naive belief in miracles.

That is, the belief is naive in the beginning. Captain Baer caught one such wave that coincided with the abolition of the Inquisition: under sweet moans about love and goodness, latter-day priests reveled in the power, demanded offerings, and then dragon tears, unbridled orgies and human sacrifices took their turn. The troops hesitated to enter the city, whose residents declared the foundation of Heaven on Earth; a couple months later, the same troops were engaged in the removal of forty thousand corpses, fighting off the few surviving monsters (who, typically, ate only human flesh). The ruins of Nintark remained inhabitable...

Knock on wood! Why scare yourself ahead of time?

Locomotive gained enough experience and decisiveness in dealing with "non-formals" (a vague term used in reports for any non-normal humans), and the bylaw mandating "gatherings of no more than three people" hadn't been canceled yet. The authorities had not forgotten how badly such gatherings could end. It was enough to reinstate the licensing of public events, and NZAMIPS chambers would be full of the homegrown gurus. Someone worked hard feeding those psychos with appropriate information, motivating them, taking them under his control, but so far all his efforts came to naught. The inopportunely-appearing dark magician tamed the supernatural in the region, turning the bloody drama into a comic scene—an occasion for jokes. With perverted pleasure, Captain Baer crushed the results of someone's long-term work with a steamroller of police forces.

A big prize wasn't long in coming.

In the blue light of the balls mounted on portable tripods NZAMIPS experts dismantled the ruins of a brick outhouse. Soldiers in protective suits and masks cautiously stacked clear glass vials with glowing contents into sealed containers. Locomotive's hair stood on end just from looking at them.

The dragon tears! The first batch in seven years. But experts claimed that the recipe for the cursed potion had been lost. Was the source an archeological excavation? Foreign intervention? Even the scent of this potion resulted in a state of euphoria for a commoner and summoned a desire to trust and obey, not thinking about the consequences and repenting for one's deeds. Booze for killers! In the white mages the potion caused irreversible addiction; the dark reacted to its action much more simply—they just puked.

All the residents of that house would have to be investigated regarding their involvement in the sales of that stuff. The distributor of the poison escaped the interrogation: upon seeing the police, the psycho maniac blew himself up in the boiler room that had been converted into a warehouse. The poor fellow did not know the specifics of the building code. The main apartment building only lost its glass windows; in the outhouse, the roof got blown off and one of the outside walls destroyed. There were no casualties among the NZAMIPS team; two were wounded by fragments of the roof, but the suicidal maniac died on site.

The poison served him right! Surely, he was hooked on his own potion, and they wouldn't get anything coherent out of him in the interrogation anyway.

"You are to be congratulated."

Before turning around, Locomotive drove a smug grin off his face.

"Yes, sir! The operation went off almost flawlessly."

Mr. Satal nodded gravely, looking over the luminous scattering: "This will make the capitol authorities fuss around. But they will start asking difficult questions."

Locomotive shrugged indifferently: "I have requested forty-four times an increase in funding over the last ten years; I can show you a copy of each of them."

The coordinator angrily shook his head: "I don't give a shit about your papers! What will we do when inspectors arrive here? They can stick their noses anywhere, and I don't even know what you and Larkes have done."

For some reason, Locomotive didn't think of that. It isn't enough to be honest, you must look honest. Any normal organization inevitably accumulates a couple of episodes that appear ambiguously untrustworthy. As soon as the auditors dug out something like this, he could kiss his captaincy goodbye!

"I ... will do the cleanup."

Mr. Satal nodded with satisfaction: "I'm glad we understand each other!"

Captain Baer worked with superiors of a dark nature for years, but it was the first time that he was so frankly offered to commit fraud. He was almost ordered to...

"And one more thing," the coordinator stopped halfway to his limousine, "I didn't have time to go into the details of our main investigation."

Locomotive snorted mentally. Indeed, he didn't have time!

"There is an opinion that our mage developed an unconventional power channel. We are not talking about a wild Empowerment, but, perhaps, university instructors remember an unusual student. Let's say, over the past seven years. I think it will be easier if you talk to them," Mr. Satal concluded.

Naturally! All university instructors of dark magic were traditionally salaried NZAMIPS part-timers. An unconventional channel... And then Captain Baer thanked all the gods that the empath wasn't anywhere near the coordinator. He knew one magician whose power channel was guaranteed to be nonstandard, and he knew him very closely...

"Clean up the tail, Mr. Satal? We will do that, sir!" Tail? What does that mean?

CHAPTER 14

For my next work day at BioKin I arrived ten minutes early just to watch the others coming. Bummer! All employees were already at their workstations (as far as I knew, because I wasn't officially introduced), but they weren't doing any work. They all were in a mourning mood, suffering in silence.

I wondered if someone died there.

Upon closer examination, I was the only one who dressed more or less decently, in the sense that I had neither trousers that were stretched at the knees with fringe around the lapels, nor pseudo-artistic patches on my shirt, nor a hairstyle as if I had run across a stray camel. Naturally, that put me in opposition to the team, and they immediately attempted to humiliate me: the red-haired secretary (Quarters' relative) brought me utterly cold coffee. When I tossed a warming spell into the cup almost without looking, nobody else showed a desire to joke.

No one tried to make me a closer acquaintance, either. Well, I easily figured out who Johan was—the guy Quarters mentioned, because there was only one white mage among them. A guy in leather pants could pass for the alchemist Carl (with the last name of either Fartsing or Ferting) and a younger lad with bright red hair - for his assistant; a chubby little man, sitting closer to the coffeemaker, resembled an accountant. Boss Polak and his secretaries needed no introduction.

I could easily picture a white mage in depression here, but it remained a mystery what or who could have driven seven people into a stupor. If all my future employers are like these, I'd rather go back to the garage business to fix motorcycles. I'm sure that will be a very profitable business! But since I took money (and twice for the same job), decorum demanded that I help them. The Tangor are proud, and reputation can be lost only once.

Pretending to be an emotionally dull dark jerk, I went to the boss to find out if my previous day's work was done correctly. They paid me for something, right? Mr. Polak looked at me painfully, but I was deaf to his suffering. I myself had to invent the next assignment: "Maybe I'd better learn design of a particular node and focus on it? Or work on the gas generator system as a whole?"

"I'm not sure if you will understand the scheme..."

I smiled politely: "Coupling alchemy with magic is my strong point!" It was true, at least for dark magic.

Once more he looked around the tables in confusion, and I finally grasped it: "Perhaps, your drawings are not systematized? I could do it. Orderliness helps a lot in work!"

He perked up a bit, nodded, and asked me to organize the documents in chronological order. Unfortunately, most of them had no dates, and, armed with archaeological methods, I had to arrange the papers in layers. Periodically, I tried to obtain advice from Polak, then from Carl, and soon they got fed up with me. Polak deserted first, followed by the rest; by lunch time, I was left alone in the office (except for the secretaries). Finally, that got me. "Girls, what happened? Or have you been like this the whole time?"

Ron's relative rolled her eyes, enjoying an opportunity to show her awareness: "They are in depression since yesterday!"

"Do not keep me in suspense! What happened yesterday?"

"A test at the sewage factory," the brunette stepped in and sniffed. "Another one!"

It explained a bit of the situation.

"And how did it end?"

"As always!" That meant they failed it. I could have guessed that.

By the end of the day I managed to go through almost a third of the documents and get acquainted with the subject of the work. Polak was wrong when he said that I wouldn't understand the scheme. Drawings are typically made according to the same set of standards; otherwise, manufacturers wouldn't be able to use them. And it doesn't matter what you put in the fermentation vat—beer or sewage; from the alchemical point of view, it is all the same, as soon as it is organic. As well as I understood it, they tried to design a complex nonlinear control mechanism as a set of perforated drums, to which the device was supposed to turn under a specific combination of input parameters (like through a set of locks). The idea was beautiful, but it did not work for some reason. I wasn't sure that I could figure out why the design was failing. Two variants of different complexity were presented in the piles of papers, and, judging by the contents of the documents, both schemes of perforation were developed by the local white mage, Johan. I don't mean that his schemes were wrong, but he was guided by the logic of the magical process, and the limitations of such an approach were seen very well in the design of my motorcycle. That gave me some hope that the problem could be solved...

Coming to work the next day, I caught Johan stiff drunk.

My coworkers pretended that it was nothing out of the ordinary. I tried not to pay attention to Johan, blend with the team, but it was beyond me. I decided they didn't understand what was happening. Okay, as to the dark mages, there are few of us in Redstone, and the dark from the university do not talk much to the townsfolk. So the latter do not know what is normal for a dark. But the white ones are a different story. There ought to be as many of them as dirt here! Was I the only one who knew how Johan's drinking would end?!

A white magician who goes on a drinking bout will usually not come out of it alive. Well, maybe he will, if you resort to involuntary hospitalization. Their psyche is considered to be fragile and not adapted to the ills of life. Once unable to cope with the nervous shock and falling into a chemical relaxant, a white will drown his mental anguish in wine again and again, and he will have less and less willpower to get out of it. But the physical condition of a white is directly related to the mental one...

Perhaps, the firm just wanted one of its developers to die? No, that was a bad joke on my part... But I needed to save the man, no kidding!

Driving off the secretaries, I made killingly strong coffee and went to bring the guy, with a runny nose, to his senses; I took his hand and put the cup in. Regretfully, I had no egg yolks and pepper handy, but I threw so much lemon in the coffee that my eyes started watering. "Have a sip, please! You have to drink it out."

White mages respond to physical contact differently—a touch sets them on an intimate footing and makes willing to trust. Given that alcohol intoxication increases suggestibility, I hoped that he would do as I said. "In one sip, opa!"

He gulped and painfully winced. A very good effect! I continued to hold his hand and looked him in the eye (it usually helps to be more persuasive): "Hey, buddy, you must go home! Rest well today, gather yourself up for tomorrow. Everything will be fine, I promise! We need your help. You will be okay! Do you want me to take you home?"

He shook his head drunkenly, stood up, and firmly went to the door; drunken whites first lose their brains before the rest of the body gets poisoned. I hoped that he would be able to pull himself together.

After Johan's departure, the average mood in the office improved by two degrees. Probably, no one dared to start discussion of failure in the presence of that poor guy. After waiting for five minutes to make sure that Johan was gone, Polak loudly clapped his hands: "What do you think, guys, about a five-minute coffee break?"

Employees perked up, and their chairs began creaking. I nipped in the bud their attempts to sit on the drawings, so we all gathered around the secretaries' table, ousting the unhappy girls. The table was quickly serviced with coffee, biscuits, and salted nuts, and even with a bottle of homemade liquor—which I generously poured into the coffee without delay.

"I cannot hide, my friends," Polak began, "that the test results have been a big blow for us. But it's not the end of the world. Who has ideas about the causes of the latest failure?"

Depressed silence reigned at the table. "Come on, my friends, go ahead!"

"Magic cannot be coupled with alchemy," Carl said gravely.

"Why is that?" A sip of liquor made me long for communion.

The alchemist glanced viciously at me: "Because those fields are unconnected!"

I pointedly raised my finger: "They interact through the material world! The main problem is to find the common ground, the points of contact."

"Points? In the vat of shit?"

"What is wrong with the vat of shit from the alchemical point of view?"

"It does not work!"

I patted myself on the chest: "I have a patent for a device, in which a magical unit is built into an alchemical one, and it f*cking works! Although in the beginning, the conjunction was monstrous." Should I actually show them my motorcycle?

But Carl did not want to listen to my success: "What do you think we ought to do?"

"Usually the problem can be solved by splitting the system into parts," I shrugged.

At least, that worked for me once.

"Which parts?" Carl muttered angrily.

I shrugged again: "I'll say when I have studied the process!"

"Carl," Polak stood up for me, "let the boy learn the process in more detail!"

For the "boy" I would have beaten him in the face, but Mr. Polak was my boss. I had to smile.

The alchemist proudly turned his back on me. I couldn't care less! Quarters' relative poured liquor into my cup as a reward (the girls definitely did not like the alchemist). The conversation turned to non-serious topics: attending the spring festival and the company's barbeque in the countryside. I watched, listened, and attempted to figure why Ron tried so hard to put me in this company. Kindergarten! I felt like I was among children!

"Why don't you have a job as a magician?" the brunette cautiously got closer, thinking that two cups of liquor would have made me soft.

I feigned a warm, fatherly, and smug smile: "One does not interfere with the other, darling!"

She cutely pouted her lips and tried to take a seat on my lap.

The next day Mr. Polak sent me on a "business trip" to the client's factory. Well, you could guess where to. I admit, only then did I realize what exactly caused such severe depression in the firm's employees.

It is hard to give an adequate description of a sewage disposal factory. Not that I did not know before how sewage is treated, but little smelly tubes in the lab did not provide me with insight into the scale of the system that was capable of processing the wastes of the whole city. Dark magicians do not like such things, but I was personally impressed by the magnitude of it: rows of giant pumps, pipes of my height in diameter entangled in staircases, vats with spikes of thermometers, and a constantly dancing flame of emergency exhaust above the pipes (can you guess what gas was burning?).

I was not welcome there. I have to admit, I did not immediately realize why.

"What, BioKin again?" the manager grimaced.

"Yes," I shyly confessed.

"In relation to what occurred three days ago?"

"Right."

He did not want to deal with me and passed into the hands of the shift master.

"What are you doing here?" the worker squinted suspiciously.

It seemed to be unwise to introduce myself as a new employee in that situation.

"I'm an independent auditor!" I arched my chest. "Investors want to know feasibility of the project."

"This is long overdue... Office rats!" the master expressively presented his point of view.

"Let's do it like this: you'll help me understand what's going on, and those smarty pants will no longer disturb you."

'Because they are about to be swept out with a dust broom,' I added to myself. We shook each other's hands, and the staff became much kinder to me.

It quickly became clear that our office wanted to design a prototype of the control block for a fermentation vat, the main production unit of the factory. Every vat was fed with filtered and stirred sewage, and illuminating gas and a tarry substance—used as a raw material for all sorts of chemical products—were received as output. Oh, plus lots and lots of water. The essence of the problem was that the super proliferative bacteria, modified through white magic methods, were extremely sensitive to the composition of... hmm... culture medium. Much, much more sensitive than the unpretentious wild strains! As soon as the microscopic workers, invisible to the naked eye, got overheated or overcooled, they lost their activity, and the vat had to be stopped. And cleaned. My visit to the factory coincided precisely with the cleaning event, and I could tell you: a ghoul one hundred years old compared to that would be like a walking scented candle. The half-treated sewage had to be stored somewhere else for the cleaning of the fermentation vats, and that added flavor to the situation.

I could kill people guilty of triggering even one such event, but if BioKin was the cause of that at least twice... then the workers' sincere hatred was understandable. I did not want any more visits to the sewage facility, but intuition told me that the solution of the design problem could only be found at the factory. There was something in the enhanced bacteria that turned their inoculation into quiet sabotage. If I wanted to work off Quarters' money, I had to find that intangible factor.

Nothing distracts one better from evil thoughts than hard, creative work! The object of work in this case is irrelevant. In a few days, I totally forgot the events of the past few months, as though the whole saga about the Dark Knight had nothing to do with me.

Not surprisingly, when I noticed the chief of Redstone's NZAMIPS waiting at the university gates, I did not linger my eyes on him for a second. All the more so because Captain Baer was in civilian clothes. Maybe he was waiting for a girl there?

No, the captain (Quarters told me that his nickname was "Locomotive"—he was like a steam engine: slow-witted, narrow-minded, and impossible to stop) had other plans. When I caught up with him, he hissed: "Hey! Slow down."

I slowed down and exhaled a disgruntled huff: "Any questions for me, sir?"

"We need to talk." He took me to a dark cafe and offered a seat at the far table. I did not mind—I preferred that other people did not see me with him. Otherwise, it would be the talk of the town. "I want to re-record your crystal."

My eyes may have popped out: "Why is that?"

"Because I can replace it without any problem, but they'll have my head if I lose it."

"I don't get it!" I was being honest.

The policeman frowned crossly.

"Look here! I have gotten a new supervisor recently. I worked with my previous boss for fifteen years; naturally, I helped him a few times, did some favors—I couldn't stay that long on his team without that. But God forbid I should trust any of the dark mages; I know your brothers' nature very well. My boss had personally covered up the case of your "breakdown", saying that the channel was stable and there was no reason to panic. I did not mind; there was no point in arguing with the boss. Had I gathered an expert commission to investigate, both you and we would have endured a lot, but the conclusion would have been the same. It's a different story now: he is no longer my boss, and I can't pin his words to the file. I've been thinking and realized that I was a fool—I shouldn't have believed a dark magician. It's not about you personally, it's just that you guys have differently rotated brains; you cannot take other people's interests into account."

"Why, we can!" I replied touchily.

"Not in this case," the captain dismissed my comment. "In short, the entire division is looking for one smart ass, browsing crystal records, fussing around everywhere. The new boss will see your crystal sooner or later, and it will be better if he doesn't find the "breakdown" in it. Do I have your interest?"

I clearly understood that the chief of Redstone's NZAMIPS was offering me to collude. And it was more important to him than to me! "I do not agree if it's for free."

"What do you want?" Locomotive growled in an unfriendly manner.

"I want to know everything!" I joked.

"Then you'll die early," he promised.

I shrugged: "Maybe. You won't pay me anyway; after money, information is the second most valuable thing. Let's agree as follows: you will fully answer one of the questions that interests me, we'll record a new crystal, and you'll give me back the old one."

"Ha!"

"Come on! You don't really believe that I'll blackmail you, knowing what is at stake for me, do you?"

"Then why do you want it back?"

"Are you kidding? That was my real Empowerment!"

He paused for a moment, staring at me with blank eyes. I never thought that a man with such a dull appearance could have a bright mind. Now I knew.

"Agreed," the captain decided. "The crystal hasn't been numbered; after it has left the storage, nobody will be able to discover where it was recorded. You can't present it as an imprint of another mage's aura; your name was engraved on it before the recording."

"I have never even thought about giving to a stranger!" I reassured him.

"You will come to my office tomorrow—here's your notice."

The timing was perfectly appropriate: he was obviously aware of my class schedule.

"I will," I hid the notice in my pocket and suddenly asked him, "How do you feel about zombies?"

He gave me a hard look. "In theory, I mean!"

"Don't be a smartass!" he threatened. "I'll watch you closely, you theorizer, son of a bitch!"

Why did he mention my mother? Ugh. I just had to find a place for my dog.

CHAPTER 15

Only in a week I managed to leave the sewage factory and come back to the office. I expected to ask Johan a couple of questions, but the white mage's desk was empty.

"He took a vacation," Polak tried not to look at me, "to recover from sickness. During his time off, we'd better put things in order..."

The white magician started commanding my respect—he decided to ask for help! Let's face it: these guys do not always have enough spirit to understand their own problems. A good reason to roll up my sleeves.

"Can I take the test records?"

Polak pointed to a cabinet full of folders. I wondered whether it had the same chaos in the records as in the drawings.

Thick, bound folders kept records of all BioKin's deeds. The project had a brisk start two years ago: a team of three magicians and four alchemists gathered together to make a unit that would utilize the advantages of the enhanced bacteria. As its basis, they took a standard fermentation vat and four of the most promising strains. The process worked beautifully in the tubes, but when they tried to scale-up, failures came one after the other. To be more specific, the record uptime of the new gas generator was one month. The alchemists deserted first, quickly figuring that they wouldn't get a free ride, and then followed the magicians, one of whom was Johan's student. For the last six months, BioKin worked with less staff, fine-tuning (seemingly) the final nuances of the design. With no result...

The project looked quite hopeless; it was the right time to quit. But I had already squandered Quarters' advance and didn't expect any more money to come. If the unit could not work, I had to explain why, at least.

For three weeks I pondered the problem, viewing it from different angles, focusing mainly on the actions of people who managed the fermentation vats, not on the charts provided by the bacterial engineers. Summer break at the university facilitated my task: I spent all my days and nights at the factory. Soon I realized that the gas generators in general were surprisingly stupid; that is, the time elapsing between the turn of the control switch and the response of the culture was quite long, up to fifteen minutes. According to the experiments' records (and I had no desire to repeat them again), the inoculation of advanced cultures into the fermentation vat was like trying to run a tractor engine on nitroglycerin. No way would it work! The fact that BioKin managed to keep the unit stable for the whole month was a masterpiece of alchemical thought! In order to substantiate my feelings, I read all of Johan's articles and lecture notes on the theory of operation control and came to the disappointing conclusion: the application of the new BioKin design for the control block was impossible without an essential modification of the vat's design.

The latter idea I presented at the next coffee break, now taking place regularly (Johan, who had put on weight and regained some of the pink color in his face, was back to work).

"How should a 'perfect vat' look, in your opinion?" Polak smiled encouragingly.

"A long, small diameter tube."

Carl snorted.

"It will cool down too quickly!"

"It can be warmed from outside," I snapped.

"What if we use a self-heating culture?!" Johan unexpectedly helped me out.

"How about cleaning them?" Carl did not stop.

"We can combine multiple tubes into a battery and clean them one at a time." Strings of digits and design schemes were already spinning in Polak's eyes, who shouted, "Smaller volumes are easier to handle!"

"And use diverse strains simultaneously," Johan stuck to his guns.

The team took heart, and the work began in earnest. Carl drove me off my favorite drawing desk—that was the first result. Wouldn't it be fairer to drag his own board to the window? I protested but soon realized that on a wave of enthusiasm he would do all the hard work for me. I quietly retreated and returned to leisurely sorting the drawings.

Polak knocked in money for the model (simple, one pipe) from the client, and it was a feat worthy of inclusion in the annals. Making the buyer fork out for yet another pilot device after two years of total failure... Polak had a phenomenal talent for persuasion, though, perhaps, Ron contributed to his success, too. We hoped that the new gas generator would be tested by the end of summer.

I wondered if I should quit before running the tests or wait for the results. I was sure the unit would work as designed, but feared another meeting with the shift master from the factory.

Just after the drawings of the new design had been sent to the factory and we had learned that there wouldn't be any problem with assembly, Ron invited me to the wine cellar "Three Students" to celebrate something. I did not mind and greatly hoped that he would buy us something stronger than coffee—all that creative rigmarole wore me down even more than combat with ghouls.

"Dance!" Quarters demanded.

"Want a kick in the teeth?"

He asked touchily: "Why have you gotten so angry?"

I would have explained why, but I did not want to start all over again. Ron could not keep his news secret for long: "Our patent is bought..."

"Hmm..."

"For twenty-five thousand crowns!"

"What?!"

"And a crown from each machine that installs the device. Can you imagine how many diesel cars they make per year?!"

"But our device won't be on each one; dark magic is expensive."

Quarters squinted his eyes: "Man, did you show your amulet to anyone?"

"Well... to Rakshat, for example."

"Did he tell you that your design was a 'transmaster?' "

"No."

"I am telling you that! It does not use the Source, meaning it can be installed by any magician. Dark magic is only needed to create the inverse template, and then any white dolt can rubber-stamp the amulets. Done!"

I was flabbergasted. I felt like a cat that someone dipped in a cold bathtub.

"Didn't we sell it too cheap?"

"Are you kidding? We sold only the principle; design and production are not our problems."

I already knew what the realization of a basic idea would cost, and I understood that we got rich almost for nothing.

"When will I get the money?"

Quarters solemnly handed me a check: a large, multi-colored paper with gold lettering and metallic sheen. The money. A lot of money. Almost without any strain on my part. I love that so much!

"How will you spend it?" Ron was curious.

I brushed him aside. For now, I just wanted to look at the check, carry it with me, and show it to everyone.

"Interest will go to your student account."

"Ron, you are a genius!"

"Come on," Quarters was embarrassed. "If you think up something like this again, let me know!"

And then I noticed a funny thing.

"Listen, the check was issued two weeks ago."

"So what? It's not a fish; it won't rot."

"Then why didn't you give it to me right away?"

"So that you wouldn't lose the incentive to work."

When the meaning of his words reached me, I almost lost my speech.

"You son of a bitch..."

To kill him! To wipe the bastard off the face of the earth and leave him without offspring!

"Quiet, be quiet! Why get worked up? Everything turned out excellent!"

"Shit!"

For a few minutes I unsuccessfully chased Quarters around the pub, but he refused to meet me in a fair fight. He locked himself in a bathroom stall. Breaking my way into the bathroom was kind of awkward, and I returned to the table, meanly determined to eat all of the food without him.

That rascal... god save me from working under his command!

In about ten minutes Quarters got bolder and came out of his hiding place: "You got mad at me for nothing, Tom!" he proclaimed emotionally (I had already finished all the pork ears on the plate by that time). "I only wanted the best for everybody."

"Go to hell! All because of a cool chick?"

"Are you kidding?" Ron took offense. "I bet with my uncle I could make the device work. Thirty percent of the shares in his factory if I win."

What could I say? He definitely had a talent! Sort of dark magic, just more profitable.

PART 4. RUSTLES AND WHISPERS

CHAPTER 16

Reading biographies of famous combat mages didn't fascinate me, but I heard that all of them were motivated by external stimuli. Typically, we, dark magicians, find a compromise between our natural instincts and reasonable opportunities to satisfy them (if we can't, we die) and reach a certain balance in our existence. Ordinary people get used to everything—even to ugly, pugnacious, vindictive, and heartless dark magicians, and life gets back to normal. But some dark have no such luck. Certain unavoidable circumstances don't let them settle a warm nest, prompting painful and unnatural efforts such as a struggle for power, defense of the fatherland, or perfection of the art of dark magic. What's the point? Instead of a simple desire to be at the top of their local hierarchy, they take responsibility for the future of the nation, the sovereignty of economics, or (god save me from such fate!) health and safety. Some quirk of the psyche fancifully changes the nature of the unfortunate guys; poetically speaking, they hear the Voice of Destiny. That's the story people tell about the celebrities.

I need to confess: I didn't hear any such voices. In my case, it all began quite casually, with a funeral.

I was notified of a telegram from home. It was strange, because I did not expect any correspondence: at the beginning of summer Joe wrote to me twice, asking to come home, but I excused myself, referring to the new job. Did he decide to try again?

The telegram was drafted without any attempt to save money on punctuation marks (most likely, my mother sent it); it briefly stated that Uncle Gordon had passed away, and the funeral would be in two days. Not that the message was incredible (we are all mortal). I just couldn't understand why he died now. Last summer the old man looked quite cheerful—magicians generally live long. The dark mages cannot grieve keenly in principle; we all will meet out there sooner or later. But I had some plans for Uncle, and they would have to be changed now. And one more thing: will Chief Harlik agree to tell me what he promised to find out for the old man?

In this philosophical mood I came to work, barely responded to the greetings of my coworkers, and sat down to meditate over the bills. All of my drawings were finished a week ago, the calculations - checked and rechecked. Carl personally controlled the assembly of the modules; I was bored and wanted to follow Polak's example: hide somewhere and take a nap.

Perhaps I looked gloomily detached.

"Something isn't working?" Johan began to worry.

"No," I waved my hand dismissively, "my uncle passed away."

I shouldn't have said it to him. The white began clucking around me, and within a minute the whole office knew of my loss. They grieved over the death of a stranger more than me, who had known him all my life.

Mr. Polak decided that I must urgently take some time off and go to the funeral. I didn't care about the obsequies, but didn't mind a few days away. It was summer after all!

"Will you be okay without me?" I put on an act that I did not want to go.

"Family is your first priority!" the boss cut me short. "The model works--what's left is the assembly—and we'll sort it out."

Excellent! And if they fail, I will be away—nobody could blame me.

To get to the funeral in time, I had to leave right away. It turned out that only one ticket was left for the Krauhard Express. It was in first class, for the outrageous sum of one hundred and twenty crowns, but dinner was included. I sighed with relief, and the cashier raised his eyebrow in surprise. He didn't know that, given availability in economy class, greed would have forced me to buy the cheapest ticket. Then my zombie-dog would have to stay in Redstone, and the revivifying curses I imposed on it could fall off before my return. To come back to realize that the city was quarantined because of my dog would be... unpleasant.

For Max to get on the train was a piece of cake: under the guise of a bale of fur (it was incredible how tightly you could pack an animal when it did not resist). In order to get the dog off the railcar at the desired station, it was enough to just throw the bale out of the window. The next morning I sat on the express train, riding in the direction of Krauhard. I was going to arrive at the funeral just in time.

Krauhard met me with its usual fog and empty platform, but some things did change, yes. No one could say that a dark magician takes the death of a relative lightly! I adjusted the lapel of a deliberately fashionable, beige-plaid jacket without a single black thread, but with a bright red tie. Tribute to tradition! Black, as well as white, is not considered a mourning color in Krauhard. In the past, people didn't think much about funeral colors, but they settled on purple-red in the end. It was elegant, practical and, on top of that, red was the symbol of "pure death", death not defiled by a supernatural touch. (Anyone who saw ghouls would understand my point.) But Krauhardians don't practice a parade of mourning colors. A tribute to passed away is paid by arranging a lavish funeral and taking custody of dependents of the deceased (especially young children); his or her pets (horse, dog, or cat) receive special treatment as well. Krauhardian funerals served as a favorite subject for jokes: newcomers often confused them with weddings. From a stranger's viewpoint, they were almost the same, except that people sang different songs and had no cake on the table. To me, there is nothing wrong with the similarity of the events— both require some optimism from the family. I, for instance, never understood the popularity of mourning and grieving at the white funeral. Would a normal deceased want his or her relatives to weep and tear their hair? Only a pervert would like that, and what would be the point of crying about him at all then? Uncle Gordon didn't have close relatives, especially underage; at least, we knew none of them. The village alchemist did not keep pets or cattle, so that simplified the entire list of things to do. Just the booze. In fact, I had hoped for that.

Touched by the moment, the gloved conductor passed onto the platform my large leather suitcase with small iron wheels. I gave him a crown.

"Oh, Thomas!" mother clasped her hands. "You look beautiful!"

"How are you," I shyly welcomed them, hiding a smug smile.

Joe scratched his head, trying to decide where to put my luxurious case.

"Throw it in the back," I solved his problem. "I'll clean it by spell later."

The main thing was to preserve my polished look for the occasion, while invited funeral guests were still coherent enough to notice anything—that would be until afternoon. The success of Uncle Gordon's apprentice would honor his deceased mentor!

In his last journey Gordon Ferro was escorted by all of Krauhard. I managed to arrive at the time of the bearing out, walked to the cemetery in the morning chill, waited until the priest had performed all the rituals for the final rest, and threw a pinch of salt on the coffin. I looked like a walking advertisement of the benefits of education, and even threw off a speech to thank my first teacher Gordon. Those present nodded understandingly and embarked on a return trip to the tables, set in the machine yard in the open air. First songs and the rousing rhythm of a tambourine sounded; the most beautiful Krauhardian girl—the daughter of the village's headman—raised a pennant symbolizing the funeral of a dark magician. The street festivity was also part of the tradition: whatever deity was in charge of the now deceased, it ought to take into account how many relatives the dead had done favors for.

Uncle Gordon's funeral feast passed with enthusiasm: toasts and wishes of luck to the old man in hell or heaven were heard everywhere. Some recalled with especially acrimonious toasts that he left important stuff of theirs unrepaired (I took note of them; it would be a good dead on my part to fulfill the promises of the passed away). In general, people were optimistic regarding the destination of uncle's soul and the prospects of their village (after all, someone was going to replace the deceased alchemist). They offered me to take his vacant place, but I pleaded that I was still studying. The tradition was observed at its best.

My neighbor across the table fascinatingly depicted the mischief and tricks that Uncle Gordon got into when he was young. I experienced difficulty meshing those adventures with the image of the bilious and pedantic alchemist.

"By the way, why was the coffin closed?" I wondered.

A neighbor hissed: "He passed away suddenly, on the street. Animals ate his body a little."

It was strange. Around Uncle's home there were always ward-off spells that turned small animals away—the alchemist did not like his furry neighbors.

"Where did he die?"

"He was found behind his garage."

It was sounding stranger and stranger. What would he have been doing there?

The gathering was over before the darkness fell; the villagers used to spend their nights at home in Krauhard. That is another local exotic feature: all drink, but virtually without getting drunk. Or next day there would be a new funeral. Generally, thoughts about eternal rest are very sobering. Wives were slowly taking home their swaying husbands; my neighbor across the table was given a ride in a wheelbarrow. I managed to stay up until the end without falling under the bench and soiling myself with salad from head to toe; aside from me, the only two sober were Joe and the village elder, a very proper man for Krauhard. Of course, others started asking us for help. Catching that moment, I pretended that I was going to pee and quietly hid behind the outbuildings. I didn't want to be covered with puke! Another half an hour to make sure that I escaped the dubious honor, I decided to spend on something useful. I took a walk to the place of Uncle's sudden death to check the condition of his ward-off spells.

My head was pleasantly spinning. The houses on the other side of the valley were bathed in sunlight, but the northern slope was cold and quite dark. There were no bushes around; otherwise, I would have gotten lost in them. To find out where exactly Uncle died was impossible—all the rocks looked the same, and, indeed, I did not feel any spells. Why was that so? Perhaps, the disappearance of the spells was the reason the old man had climbed there; usually, he did not show any passion for mounting.

I decided to walk up the hill a bit further and look for seals, the round granite washers that usually serve as anchors for household magic. Guess why they are granite, but not lead, glass, or gold? I didn't know until Mr. Rakshat explained: that way they won't be stolen. Though the best materials to absorb a curse are silver and copper. The rough rock washers showed up almost immediately; each of them carried a ward-off rune meaning, in theory, that no any filthy animal, real or supernatural, could come close to the dwelling of the alchemist and desecrate his corpse. I had found the only explanation—the contour wasn't closed. The seals were set quite frequently, so that the theft of one or two washers would not affect the performance of the runes. I felt an urge to check the entire perimeter, but common sense suggested choosing another day for the investigation.

For example, a day when there would be more time before sunset, because overly self-confident dark magicians do not last long in Krauhard. And I needed to be sober, too...

I sighed, pondering how fast city life had weaned me from cautiousness, and started slowly making way back. A warm bed was already dancing before my eyes; if I sang Joe a story about poor me, tired from the trip to Krauhard, he would surely agree to give me a ride home in his carriage. A wheelbarrow would suit me fine as well... Having almost reached Uncle's home, I came across two strange guys, poking around some junk machinery under the awning. But the excess of food eaten and drink imbibed did not permit me to understand what they were doing and why their faces looked unfamiliar. A lot of people had gathered for the funeral—maybe these guys were the guests of some villagers? Muttering, "Excuse me, dudes," I passed them, but as soon as the strangers got behind me, something stung my side. What the hell...? My legs gave way, weak-willed corpse collapsed—not on the ground, but into the clutching hands of that duo. I was quickly pulled behind the garage.

"Well?" one of them asked tensely.

"Nothing," the other said, thoroughly searching my pockets.

"Damn! What was he looking for here?"

"F*ck knows. What should we do? Two corpses in the same place would be suspicious; we don't want cops' attention."

The first one thought for a moment. "Drop him into a gully," he made a decision. "They'll think he was drunk."

All my sensibilities howled in protest: the mountain's slope was cleaved through by the gully right behind Uncle's property, which was kind of a canyon in miniature, all in narrow cracks and wet boulders. If I fell into it, my bones would be broken, and people would find me by smell a few days later. Alas, despite the roaring power of my Source, my muscles were limp and motionless, and I wasn't able to concentrate on spellcasting. Another mess I got myself into!

Max came to my aid: it raised voice. The growling of the zombie-dog was as music to me. I do not know what those two had managed to descry, but in a moment only a quickly subsiding sound of footsteps reminded of their existence. I lay there, slowly grasping the horror of my situation. I couldn't send Max for help; anyone in Krauhard would immediately recognize the zombie in it. What the drunken bums were capable of doing with the dog, I was afraid to think of. My only option was to wait for the poison's action to end. I hoped I would be all right. Dark magicians are surprisingly overconfident! I mentally ordered Max to watch for the two strangers and prepared to wait.

Minutes dragged on slowly. It was getting dark, or maybe

darkness was just growing in my eyes. I was running out of breath; all the power of my Source was not enough to drive away the nasty, pulling cold that was getting closer and closer to my heart. And then I realized that Uncle Gordon died exactly like that—alone on the cold rocks, knowing that his murder would be declared death from senile weakness. The two strangers were the cause of his death. To kill them! But while I lay here, they would be far away, and Max seemed not to hear me.

The cold escalated into a dull ache, and fear of suffocation started pestering me. How soon would they notice that I was missing? Joe, perhaps, decided that I had gone home on foot. It would take a while until they figured out that I wasn't there... Logic dictated that they would begin worrying only in the morning; a dark magician was more likely to survive at night than drunken rescuers.

I tried not to panic and think optimistically. To recall my job, focus on my plans for the future (I had so many of them!), focus on my eccentric family that couldn't manage without the help of the pragmatic dark mage. The rustle of blood in my ears lulled so sweetly... but I needed to stay awake. Stop! Since when did blood rustle?!

I made an incredible effort to turn my eyes, dried out from not blinking, and noticed that something flickered on the edge of the cleft, vaguely resembling a pile of foliage whipped by the wind.

It couldn't be worse.

Meeting a creature from the other world was the last thing that I needed now, precisely at this moment. Indeed, Rustle did not forget the heart it had heard. It came after me, but I was so young yet! On the other hand, to recall my life before dying wouldn't take much time; I didn't live long. First of all, I shouldn't show the creature my fear. If my illegal practice had taught me anything, it was the conventional wisdom that the undead learned about its adversary's power by how fearless the adversary was. Maybe it came after me to avenge its deceased comrades? What nonsense got into my head... I was not going to surrender without a fight, but my power, suppressed by the poison, would be enough for just a friendly slap. The monster would guzzle me, no question, and maybe choke as well. I would torture it with heartburn!

I needed to think about something cheerful. What was nice in my life? My motorcycle, short-term anonymous glory, my cute zombie-dog, Lyuchik who wanted to tell me something—all day long he had been bobbing around me. The two scoundrels searched for something, but what? Family honor required me to find and seize the treasure. By now every heartbeat in my chest caused sharp pain, my dried up eyes burned, and a string of pictures from the past day (so bright!) floated in my mind, mixing with episodes of the busy last year, events of the previous summer, recollections of the first meeting with Rustle.

I got scared only after realizing that I was staring at myself from outside, from the ruins, bottom-up.

CHAPTER 17

The auditors from the capitol did arrive, as Mr. Satal predicted, but Locomotive was not afraid of them. His office was like a storefront—transparent and shiny; it screamed, "Look, but don't touch." The rigorous auditors would see papers in ideal order, friendly clerks, guards in polished uniforms, and an almost complete absence of rank at the office: everyone was on an assigned task. NZAMIPS was snowed under with work!

Never before had so many operatives obtained vacations in early summer...

Locomotive did not deceive himself: had the auditors set a goal to get to him, they could have easily found or invented a case. Perhaps, that occasion wouldn't be serious enough for a full internal investigation; in the worst case, it would lead to a reprimand or a record of "incomplete conformity". Unpleasant, too, but he was used to that. No one could hang blame on him for the appearance of the banned potion on the market.

Judging by the displeasure with which the auditors examined the results of the police investigation, they were well aware of the situation. Yes, the case of dragon tears had already gone to court. Ms. Kevinahari had given the captain a tip, and the lab was quickly caught red-handed; however, the mastermind of that crime had fled and, by Locomotive's estimation, was already quietly killed somewhere. Such failures could not be pardoned. In the hands of NZAMIPS investigators there were two haywire white mages and a few small fries who distributed the poison under the guise of a stimulant. Without regret, Captain Baer addressed capitol authorities on the question of how the criminals had gotten the recipe for the most dangerous venom—it was outside his jurisdiction. The villain, declared wanted, had moved to Redstone from the East Coast just a year ago, so let the central office find out what he was doing here.

For the auditing period, Mr. Satal, the senior coordinator of the region, defiantly left the city; upon returning, he was astonishingly well-informed about everything that had happened.

"We got off easy," Mr. Satal briefly summarized the result. "Captain, I was told that they had a direct order to fire the higher-ups in Redstone's division but could not find anybody wishing to take your post. So do not consider it a success. The Dark Knight still hangs over our heads, and no empath can predict what he is capable of."

"It is unlikely that he will do anything crazy," the captain said thoughtfully. "He has a new source of income now. Why would he run the risk?"

The dark mage glanced at the captain indignantly, and Locomotive regretted that he hadn't put a protective suit on.

"Confess, you sleazebag, who is it?"

"Uh... a student, I think. I warn you, I have no evidence!"

"To hell with the evidence! Are you sure it's him?"

The captain shrugged: "He has a non-standard channel of power. He was involved in illegal practices. For three years he lived in a dormitory, paying fifty dollars per semester; now he rents an apartment. He wears suits that cost my monthly salary, each! He is originally from Krauhard. Earlier this year he bought a black motorcycle in the 'Plaza'. "

Locomotive did not mention the incident with the crystal, nor the fact that he had begun making inquiries only after he had seen a gentleman that the poor scruffy boy, ready to chase brownies for twenty crowns, had turned to.

"Hmm," Mr. Satal blissfully squinted his eyes. "Introduce him to me!"

"Why?" Locomotive became tense.

"I want to look him in the eyes," the senior coordinator fidgeted in his chair. "Don't you understand? He's a genius! A gold nugget. Forty-four episodes, with no insurance and not a single misfire. Ordinary mages are not capable of such things. Just Tangor the Second, you know!

"Tangor?" the captain stiffened.

"Yes! Tangor was a coordinator about twenty years ago; at the courses he drove our brains up the wall... He served here, too."

That was why the student's name seemed so familiar to him! Locomotive strained his memory: "Toder Tangor?"

"Exactly. How do you know?"

"We worked together. I was already a lieutenant then."

Captain Baer belatedly realized that he was almost twice as old as his boss, and questions of seniority for the dark were a sore topic. But the danger had passed.

Mr. Satal pointedly raised his finger: "He was also a genius!"

"Sorry that he ended badly."

"All because of his own people," the coordinator's face suddenly hardened. "But that will not happen to me!"

The captain politely stayed silent. Everyone has his own hang-ups! However, didn't Baer himself rave about conspiracy of the elite? They were from the same office, and long service in NZAMIPS used to affect brains of its employees.

"By the way, the student's name is Tangor. Do you think he is a relative?"

"All people with the surname Tangor are relatives, but it's unlikely that our student is close to Toder. That coordinator lived in Finkaun."

Locomotive breathed... and gasped: he did not have enough courage to tell the coordinator of the rewritten crystal.

"What?" Mr. Satal squinted suspiciously.

And people say that the dark mages cannot feel people!

"Aren't you surprised with all this?" Locomotive blurted the first thing that came into his mind. "I mean the repulsive behavior of the "cleaners", the ghouls, and dragon tears—all that in one place after ten years of quietness? Keep in mind, I had repeatedly reported about the doings of Grokk, but nobody reacted. As if nothing out of the ordinary was going on. F*ck with him, deceased! Nowadays our prison is overcrowded with dissidents. And what is interesting is that half of them are immigrants. They lived normally somewhere, and then about a year ago decided to move to Redstone. What was the reason? Some kind of festival? Maybe I missed the poster?"

The senior coordinator frowned thoughtfully and folded his palms as if making a house of cards.

"There is an opinion swirling around," he began cautiously, "that some of the events bear traces of premeditation."

Who would doubt that!

"Aliens?"

"No, our own people."

"What do they hope to accomplish?" the captain got interested.

Mr. Satal shrugged: "Power. Wealth. Satisfaction of their brutish instincts. What else can they get by fishing in troubled waters? I don't know whether you follow politics," Locomotive chuckled knowingly, "but suggestions to 'improve' the social order of Ingernika come regularly."

"Can't we just bring these wiseacres to reason?"

"Unfortunately, the people who generate the ideas and the ones who implement them are not the same; so far we can't prove a connection between them. And an attempt to ban debate would have violated the principles of democracy. Our options are education and prevention of violence and destruction."

"Don't you think that letting them stay on the loose is kind of... dumb?"

"Risk is inevitable, but our society must prove its historical sustainability continuously, whether it wants to or not."

The dark spoke about the problem as if he were reading a piece of paper, quietly and impartially, perhaps exactly as he perceived it. Locomotive was an ordinary man, and he couldn't detach himself the same way. He thought about casual witnesses, innocent victims, children whose lives would be crippled by their fanatical parents. How many of the forty thousand inhabitants of fallen Nintark really wanted to participate in the large-scale magic experiment?

The coordinator noticed a shadow on the face of his subordinate and nodded: "There will be victims. But that's the distinguishing feature of our adversaries' regimes—attempts to avoid casualties at all costs. You already know the results that come of their actions. We are required to limit the death toll to the members of the risk groups."

Who would be in those groups? A few days ago Locomotive was visited by a relative, who promised to show her children the zoo during summer break. The cop's little niece (his second or third cousin from the side of his mother's sister's husband) told him with excitement that the Dark Knight came to their town in winter, ousted a ghost from the town hall, and gave the children a ride on his motorcycle two times around the church. The captain checked reports regarding the incident and realized that he could never have met that relative of his again. And the one to blame would be Grokk and, through him, indirectly, the people who carefully planned and organized chaos in Redstone county to achieve their filthy goals. Therefore, whatever the dark mage had said about historical necessity, Locomotive hoped to find the villains and render them harmless, even if his actions would be excessive.

God knows, it will strongly improve the social order.

CHAPTER 18

Lyuchik saved me.

Our novice white mage and his buddies snuck their way into the funeral feast to watch the boozers. Please don't think that Krauhardians often get dead drunk. He watched me going behind the garage, but did not see me come back. Despite the risk of being punished for lewdness, Lyuchik went to the elders and demanded to find me. When a group with charmed lamps (we take them everywhere in Krauhard) turned round the garage, Rustle disappeared without a trace. Thus, one brother saved another.

Then Joe gave me CPR and heart massage for forty minutes without a break until the headman's truck reached the county hospital. (Anyone who has tried giving CPR even once would understand Joe's heroism; I would have lasted for a maximum of fifteen minutes). I regained consciousness after two days in intensive care, and for the first five minutes I was convinced that I woke up in heaven: everything was white, luminous, and slightly hazy. I seemed to see angels even... Still not sure whether it was my imagination or something else.

Nobody was able to understand the depth of my problems there. I bent over backwards to convince the healers that I was healthy, but the attending doctor proved the opposite with perverse pleasure. And he called himself a white! By the end of the week I got sick to death of his saying "my friend". In part, he was right: for a couple of days my eyesight occasionally weakened and sharp pain pierced muscles on any attempt to get up; but eventually all these symptoms were gone.

"Do not argue with me, my friend," the doctor lisped good-naturedly, tapping me on the knee with his knocker. I was lucky that he didn't use needles! He laughed, "The injection you received would have killed an ordinary man on the spot, but dark mages are exceptionally strong bastards."

If the doctor said so, I had to believe him. As a result, he forbade me to cast spells at least for another two months; he even wrote a letter to the university to that end.

"Why are you in a hurry?" Chief Harlik asked when he came to interrogate me. "We called your boss, he reacted with understanding, and you are free until the beginning of the semester. I wish I had a boss like yours!"

Should I explain to the man that if I do not renew the revivifying spell, Max would bite half of Krauhard's residents? I did not want to teach cannibalism to my dog.

"So, what happened then?"

He listened attentively to my story and confirmed with a nod the suspicion that Uncle was poisoned, but did not share the progress of the investigation: "We will find those two. It's a pity that you did not descry them better. Do you know what they were looking for?"

"I have no idea. I thought Uncle had said something to you."

He pursed his lips.

"We'll return to that later. Two days before his death, Gordon had received a parcel, something small and light. Do you know from whom?" Perhaps he understood my answer by the expression on my face. "Okay, have a rest. Talk to you later."

And then I decided to ask a very important question: "How do people die from an attack of Rustle? I've wanted to ask for a long time."

He shrugged: "Hard to say—there used to be no witnesses. Typically, only bones and a puddle of brown foam remain on the spot."

At that moment I recalled the caretaker on King's Island. On the other hand, I doubted that he tore off his own jaw.

"How do you treat the victims?"

"We don't! Just wait until they will recover on their own. The victims show a positive reaction to the presence of the supernatural in their bodies for life. Rustle, you know, does not forget the ones that it has marked. I hope that was a rhetorical question?"

I raised my eyebrow: "A professional one. We had a lecture about it at the university."

"Yeah, I heard that story!" he perked up. "Some dude from the dark had fun there, didn't he?"

I winced: "NZAMIPS shook up all the dark mages in the vicinity after that."

"It's only for the benefit of our kind!"

He went off, and I was left to ponder about the vanity of vanities. Had I told them about Rustle, they would have simply locked me up for forty days; by that time my zombie-dog would have gone berserk. On the other hand, no one else saw the monster; if I showed a positive reaction later, I could always say that was the result of my visit to the King's Island. Go prove it! I just needed to be more careful and leave quicker: bones and brown foam were not my style.

The next day I was discharged from the hospital and found out that I couldn't leave for Redstone right away.

My relatives all came together on the spacious headman's truck to take me home. Lyuchik was as happy as if I had returned from the dead (which was almost true), and my mother cried on my chest. I am, of course, a dark mage and surely heartless, but I couldn't leave them just by saying "ciao!"—my sudden departure would not fit the situation logically. I had to stay with my family for at least a week. And not go anywhere at night.

"What a terrible thing happened!" I did not know how many times my mother repeated those words. On the way home she calmed down, but clung to my hand as if I were about to be taken away. "Somebody tried to break into Gordon's house: they broke the windows and left."

I knew what had scared them off. They must have had fantastic cheekiness to appear twice in the place, guarded by the zombie-dog.

What were they looking for? Certainly they had not found it, or wouldn't come for a second time. Small, lightweight, measuring just over the size of a notebook—that was how Chief Harlik seemed to describe the thing. My fantasy didn't go further than a hundred thousand crowns in bonds or a confession from the Prime Minister's wife, though hardly anyone would be killed over the latter. The poison still reared its ugly head in my weakness and difficulty in concentrating attention. I got tired on the short trip home, as though I were walking on foot through all of Krauhard from end-to-end. Joe even had to help me undress. I hadn't experienced such weakness since I was seven years old! Yes, I was obviously sick, and home care would not hurt; perhaps it would be a good idea to rest for a week or two—home cooking, full relaxation, and no visits to the shit factory. As a typical dark, I couldn't care less about the doctor's ban on spellcasting; as to Rustle, I was inclined to think that it had missed its chance to reach out for me.

A man can hope for the best, can't he?!

The last week of vacation was horrible—my own weakness angered me, and the thought of a valuable treasure being found by others led me into frenzy, as if I were going to give away something of my own. All my spare time was split between the hunt for a cache in Uncle's house (under the pretext of sorting out his stuff) and the interrogation of witnesses. Not every police officer was capable of obtaining a simple answer to a specific question from a resident of Krauhard (whether dark or not), but I was relentless, like a runny nose. The fact that I was the only alchemist in the valley now was helping me in the investigation; with all their problems, the villagers were forced to go to me. The postman remembered that the parcel Uncle received two days before his death had Ho-Carg's address. An old tippler who confided in me at the funeral feast said that Uncle had lived in the capital for some time and returned to the village about twenty years ago, without explaining his circumstances.

Mom was upset, saying, "You work too hard," and Joe gently assented to her. I smiled sweetly and asked my stepfather to join me in doing everything that I could think of. It was my little revenge for the insects that were still flying around the garden. The little beasts could not bite me anymore because I prudently stocked up on an amulet that turned away bees, mosquitoes, bugs, and all other creatures that could attack the human body; even Quarters lost desire to pat me on the shoulder. That was the true power of magic!

Max had the best time of all; the zombie-dog felt blissfully happy in the tall grass, having fun studying rodent burrows and chasing butterflies.

The murderers did not show up anymore.

Uncle Gordon's house was gradually emptied. First of all, I dragged his large oak table to our attic. I loved its beautiful design. In Uncle's toolbox I found a chic set of lock picks; in the bedroom—cute cupronickel beads, the mandatory attribute of a dark magician: each bead could hold a couple of spells, easily capable of replacing a combat curse. Uncle must have been unable to manipulate the flow of Power. My booty was his workbooks, the last record in which was made twenty years ago. I hoped to find inside a recipe of the potion that inhibited magic power and pour it into Mr. Rakshat's tea. To delve into Uncle's stuff was not tedious, just a little sad. That kind of work reveals the true nature of death: you can change nothing after you have passed away; all that was dear to you is left at the mercy of the alive. I sorted out my findings into three piles: stuff that would go to the trash, commemorative things that I would keep in memory of Uncle, and the rest that could have a useful application. In the end, the house would become devoid of any individual touch; it was about to be occupied by a new alchemist in a week. I did not want to wait for the newcomer just out of precaution, because I did not know if my pernicious nature would accept an outsider. My huge suitcase was ready for the trip and the chic suit waited on the rack for its hour, but my conscience was burdened by a small, though urgent, task: fixing up the ward-off spells around Uncle's home. Their absence was becoming noticeable—mice appeared in the garage. That would be the last thing I could do in honor of Uncle to observe his traditions.

On the day of my departure, I woke up very early from a sleep in which I was fixing some strange alchemical devices capable of flying without wings. I was awakened by the smell of fresh pancakes and by Lyuchik, of course. My grown-up brother was running around the garden with a problem, the gist of which could be grasped only by a white. Maybe he worried that the burrow had gotten too narrow for the mice? I should bring him a cat as a present next time...

I was not given a chance to stay in bed.

"Breakfast!" mother's voice came from downstairs.

Squeals and clatter signaled that I would not be the first at the table. Not good! Having pulled on my pants hastily, I left my bedroom.

Despite the early hour, the entire family was at the table.

Joe was sipping milk from a beer mug with a satisfied air. Little Emmy used pancakes as an excuse—she licked jam off of them and asked to put more on. Hopefully Mom would be able to wash her off afterwards. Lyuchik, excited, did not see what he was eating—a surprisingly active child. Bees left the sugar bowl with a displeased buzz upon my appearance.

"Are we going to the station together?" I wanted to clarify, just in case.

"Yeah," Joe nodded genially.

I needed to change plans. I wouldn't dare load Max on the train for all my family to view. Joe was unlikely to poke his nose into my business, but little Emmy would want to flatter my "fur" pet for sure. I sensed my zombie-dog would have to run home on foot. It should be okay as Max was a clever beast (I sometimes wondered why he was so highly intelligent), and the dog could cope alone with the trip.

Lyuchik barely managed to finish his meal and started telling me a story about his new school, friends, and some white mage (or was it just beard of his teacher that was white?). That became almost a ritual at the table. I nodded with a straight face and enjoyed quickly decreasing hillock of pancakes. My little brother wasn't embarrassed by the fact that he had told me all his stories about twenty times already. We had just approached the most disappointing part—his classmates did not believe that his brother was a dark magician, when a truck wearing the NZAMIPS logo raced with a terrible roar past the passage into the valley. All of us, without saying a word, fixed our eyes on the truck.

What was that? New clowns or Chief Harlik to visit us? And my zombie was running around out there...

"Good for you!" I habitually complimented Lyuchik (little white mages should be praised frequently). "I'll drop in at Uncle Gordon's; I forgot to fasten a padlock on his door."

All nodded understandingly.

My first worry was Max, who had saved my life twice already. The dog met me at the edge of the village: it rustled in the grass, patrolling and snapping its jaw in an attempt to catch butterflies. I hobbled slowly down the path, enjoying the overall harmony of life. The truck that I had spotted in the morning shone with its emblems halfway to the passage to the valley. That was for better: I did not want a company of combat mages.

So, mice were on the agenda. Because of them I had to climb into the gully: the ward-off spells at the bottom of the slope were in order. I deliberately delayed the ascent, trying to catch if some kind of unhealthy interest in Rustle's temporary lair would arise in me. It didn't. That day was remarkably clear for Krauhard; at such an early hour the sun slightly touched the roof of the garage, slipping into a crack between rocks. After fastening the padlock on the barn, I whistled to Max and reluctantly plodded to the place where I had endangered my life so stupidly. A typical dark won't let such things happen to him, even when he is drunk!

Now it was easy to find the place where they killed Uncle: yellow flags appeared on the rocks. The police tried to mark the pose in which the body had been found. I grasped why the two strangers were worried—the spot where they attacked me was a mere twenty steps away from the location of the murder.

Everything seemed to suggest that the old man fell, climbing up the slope, coming back from the gully to the garage.

I glanced down, tensely aware that I might start feeling an involuntary urge to continue the walk. The gully was deep and dark; any place that the sun never reaches is definitely a dangerous one, by Krauhard's standards. If the cause of the damaged ward-off curses was sitting there, I wouldn't risk my life again—let the curses stay unrepaired!

But mice are the eternal enemy of alchemists. They gnaw the wiring, make their nests in the most important parts of machines, and leave their droppings in the fuel oil, thus spoiling it forever. I do not count their stamping and squeaking at night. I will never forget how I found a dead mouse in the milk—I have been unable to drink any white liquids since then.

All pests need to be exterminated!

I walked back and forth around the gully. The line of seals was well visible even from the top. One washer clearly stood out among the old stones for its newer look and different texture— clearly, someone was tempting me to climb down there. Who? Why did I decide that it was Uncle? One couldn't accidentally get into a place like that—sane children do not play there, and the insane do not survive in Krauhard. Should I call Chief Harlik?

If I called him, I would lose the treasure. No! I did everything possible to secure myself: I went back to Uncle's house, explained the situation on a piece of paper, and shoved it into Max's mouth with the instructions to deliver it to people if I didn't return before noon. Perhaps my desire to check the washer was all Rustle's call, and if it proved to be true... I habitually clenched the Source, and it nervously vibrated in response. If so, then the creature would regret touching me!

Cautiously descending the scree, I picked up the washer to examine it. The ward-off curse, rustling, closed around me.

I did not understand. Truly, I did not understand. It seemed that Uncle climbed down there not to fix the spell, but to break it. That would be stupid! Why would anyone want to damage the rodent traps? I inspected the seal—on its underside somebody had scratched an arrow that pointed to a mountainside, where the gully converged into a narrow slit with a trickling stream of water. If it was a tip, who had made it? And for whom? I did not believe that some stranger, unfamiliar with the spell, could unlock it so cleverly to engrave the hint; that meant the strange message could be left only by the former owner of the house.

I pondered it for a while. Couldn't Uncle have been affected by Rustle when manipulated with the washer? The fact that he was a dark magician did not provide automatic protection from the supernatural. And why would some place in the rocks be a better cache than a compartment in the attic or in the basement? Perhaps, the reason was that the tip could be discovered only by another mage, and the two strangers were not magicians. I would have to climb there, no matter how reluctant I was. And if the mysterious seal was just a silly joke, I would spit on that comedian's grave!

Repeating the previous order to Max, I cautiously stepped onto the slippery rocks. I managed to reach the bottom without hurting myself, figuring that I had totally lost my mind. It would be so stupid to get into that shithole, guess Uncle's obtuse clues, and die on the way back! The treasure that he hid must be really valuable, or I must have completely misread Uncle. And his cache was the most disgusting place you could imagine—only a burial vault would be worse. No wonder that Rustle hid there.

At the bottom of the gully, two steps away from the slit, two boards lay on the rocks, and a rope hung from the top. I didn't grab for it—it wasn't clear what was fixing it in place. Getting wet and dirty, I finally reached the slit and stood stock-still in surprise.

What the hell!

Immediately after the narrow orifice, the slit expanded to the size of a small cave. Sunlight just barely passed through to the center, and eternal darkness swirled in the corners and behind rocks. A huge chest towered in the center of a bright spot on a water-washed rock. Judging by its size, the chest must have been assembled on the spot. The place reeked of dark magic in its most ancient and gloomy sense.

I cautiously entered the cave. The cache had been made a very, very long time ago, and not by Uncle. Certainly, there was some supernatural being nearby, because my hair stood on end the entire time I was there. The most superficial examination of the chest revealed three layers of magical protection: from the water, from the fire, and from all living things. On the top of the chest I found an amulet-key with an ornate monogram of the capital letter "T".

Wow, that was the Tangors' secret lair!

My mother and I lived apart from my father's relatives; therefore, I did not know the Tangor's legends. Who and when made the cache and how Uncle discovered it was unclear. My curiosity overcame common sense; I took the key and climbed into the chest.

Two-thirds of it was filled with strange stuff: unusually shaped knives, inlaid polished skulls, and flutes made from bones. Had I brought some of these things to the university, I would have been instantly apprehended for necromancy. In a separate niche I found books, entirely written on parchment, bound in suspiciously fine leather, with meaningful runes on the cover.

Surely, those were the treasures of a dark magician, a necromancer, an ancient one. What the dark were doing in the past, I don't have the right words to describe. But by today's standards, the collection was of no use, except as antiques. A mail package, tied up with string, lay over the dubious treasures; I took it and left the lair, slowly and cautiously backing to the exit. I never thought that such a probably wrong word to use here place could be in our valley! And it was only mine now.

The zombie-dog watched with interest as its master clambered over the rocks, using one hand only. At some point my nerves could not take it anymore (I was still far up the slope from Uncle's house); I aimed my find and threw it toward the barn wall. It wasn't glass, after all! Having climbed down, I disemboweled the parcel, untying the string and unwrapping it. There was a return address! The postman was right; the parcel came from the capital. Inside, there were several sheets folded in half—a letter—and a small book, ancient in appearance; I immediately grabbed it, opened it, and...

And couldn't understand anything.

Incredibly thin, translucent pages were protected by so much magic that they had become almost metallic—elastic and solid. Blue squiggles of handwriting ran over a yellowish background; no magic runes, circuits, or signs were there. Some letters looked familiar, but the meaning of the words remained a mystery. That must have been one of those ancient relics that Mrs. Clements had been looking for, the same one hundred thousand crowns—not in bonds, but in one piece. I did not think that Uncle was involved in business with rarities! An explanation had to be in the letter, but I didn't have time to read it—while I was searching the cache, the NZAMIPS truck moved from the pass to the village. My family waited for me at home, and some of my kinsmen could drop by Uncle's house at any time. I needed to go back.

But I had to protect the book: Uncle was murdered for it, somebody tried to kill me, and who knows what else they would do. I did not want to carry it in my luggage; there was another way... I put the letter and the address, torn from the wrapper, between the magically protected sheets of the book, and re-packaged it. Then I shoved the parcel into Max's mouth with instructions to deliver it to my garage at Redstone. That method of transportation seemed to be the most secure to me: no one would notice the zombie among bushes and rocks and, even if someone did, he or she wouldn't catch the dog. And the zombie didn't have my name on it. I could always say it wasn't mine.

Finally, I was ready to leave Krauhard. With calm soul and conscience, but with agitated nerves. All the way to the village my palms and shoulder blades were itching so much that I wanted to bob up and down like Lyuchik. The enthusiasm of the white is contagious. And I couldn't tell anyone...

Returning home, I found Chief Harlik drinking tea on the veranda with the leftovers of cold pancakes (there were no bees). It was outrageous—in my absence my mother let another man in and fed him my meal! I was about to revile the NZAMIPS boss, but Mom deftly put scrambled eggs in front of me. My dark nature was pleased—my meal was bigger. Harlik gave a sour look toward my plate, but did not say anything; yes, he was older, but it was my home.

"I see you've recovered."

I allowed myself to swallow a piece of egg and then replied: "I have!"

"We have found those murderers," Harlik paused meaningfully. "It's a pity that we couldn't interrogate them."

I felt like the scrambled egg got stuck in my throat. Hmm. I wondered what Max was doing yesterday. I had not watched the zombie at all.

"Wolves?"

"No, Rustle."

So, that rascal hadn't gone far away. Supposedly, it was waiting for me!

"Obviously, they weren't local," Harlik explained when I did not respond. "They came in the evening, hoping to get to the village at night. That's when the otherworldly caught and killed them."

Yes, only barbaric townsfolk could do business in Krauhard at night. Well, even if they saw my dog, they wouldn't be able to tell anyone about it now!"

"Bad luck," I mumbled, returning to the food.

"You don't look very upset," Harlik noticed.

"I am not upset at all," I agreed, chewing non-stop. Mother sighed softly, and I had to explain my point to her, "I know what Uncle had gone through before he died. Rustle is far too humane for them!"

I reminded myself not to blab out to the chief that I was now personally familiar with Rustle. Joe cautiously approached the veranda: two dark magicians at a time were too much for his nerves.

"I am leaving," Harlik stood up. "Call me, if anything."

Mom gently nodded.

"What was he talking about?" I asked suspiciously when the back of the chief was out of sight.

"He is worried that the interest in Gordon would pass onto us," she answered serenely.

That was unconvincing. Though why would Mother lie?

And I threw Harlik out of my head; I had far too many impressions today.

* * *

Locomotive wasn't able to take the student to the coordinator: the enterprising kid had left town right before the authorities expressed interest in him. The captain flirted with the idea of contacting Krauhard's department of NZAMIPS, but decided against it: fables of mutual cover-up and conspiracy among the local dark could be true. None of the dark magicians was ever caught in Krauhard for the entirety of NZAMIPS' history. The captain had to wait until the guy returned to Redstone on his own.

Mr. Satal reacted to Locomotive's misfortune quite emotionally: "What the hell! Next time I should be the first to know, got it?"

"Yes, sir," Locomotive did not argue.

Morning briefs of NZAMIPS higher-ups became regular, and Captain Baer had to attend them alone—his subordinates were losing their operability after meetings with the senior coordinator.

It was difficult to say whether there was any benefit from the meetings. The coordinator wished to know everything that was happening in Redstone—Redstone alone and nowhere else. Sometimes Conrad Baer asked himself: was the situation in his town unique? Had anything similar happened before?

"A new informant let us approach the elder who acts in the southwestern part of the town. His name is Godovan Boberri; he has been detained for illegal practice of magic. Boberri is clearly a priest and had a few disciples, three of whom have been arrested."

The coordinator nodded in satisfaction.

"The source of the rumors about a 'rebirth' has not been found yet. Our analyst emphasizes the high quality of the underlying theory; he is of the opinion that they will soon move from words to deeds. His recommendation is to pay attention to the corpses of young men, including the ones who died of putative suicide or accidents; they could attempt to hide the real cause of death."

Mr. Satal frowned: "This topic had already been discussed in the ministry. We have been advised to stay calm and wait, meaning that we should use information resources only after finding three-four corpses. Try not to miss them!"

Captain Baer refrained himself from swearing, though he was confident that he didn't need recommendations on how to do his job. The captain himself had complained that his superiors were not interested in his work, and he started regretting that now.

"All editions of the pamphlet 'The New Way' have been confiscated; the reason formulated was the 'promotion of dangerous magic practices'. The publisher has been detained; the chief editor is under investigation. We are checking why they decided to print the editions without the visa of the NZAMIPS censor."

The coordinator sighed: "Share responsibility. If your censors are choking, pass on part of the work to our department. Ms. Kevinahari has a group of six experts, and it would warm them up."

"Thank you, sir!" Locomotive made note to contact the empath; his censor was truly overloaded. His whole division was overwhelmed with work—their weekly load was higher than their monthly load a year ago.

"Now for the oddities."

The coordinator put his elbows on the desk and folded his palms as if making a house of cards—the gesture meant he was extremely interested and attentive.

"There is a connection between Boberri and Fire Mage who was arrested two weeks ago: both used trusted aides of similar appearance—it seemed to be one and the same person. The aide uses different names and dress styles, and the two groups belong to different religious confessions, but a few white witnesses quite emotionally described a man with a piercing gaze who smelled strangely. What was interesting in case of Fire Mage is that the aide insisted on more serious sacrifices than a few candles."

"Excellent!" the dark magician echoed. "It looks like we are nearing the center point."

Locomotive grimly nodded: "All of these 'elders' are just protective fog around a group that is up for some really serious stuff. Minions are lost sooner than their leaders expected them to be, and now they have to risk the lives of higher-standing agents."

A haze of meditation covered the dark magician's eyes: "We need to find them, Conrad! Before they are ready. We must strengthen the work at the university. Tell your guys there. Freshmen from the province will be their first target."

"We think about the same," Baer stated grimly.

Mr. Satal's voice broke out in a hissing whisper: "The artisans! Or a similar sect that just calls itself differently. They preach that the nature of man can be changed—that man can be turned into a different being. As soon as you eat and drink something special or say 'yes' in the right place, voila, your soul and body are purged. First, they invent some kind of threat, then they require sacrifices to fix it; and the greater the sacrifice, the more followers believe in the existence of threats. But in the end no one can remember for the sake of what it all began."

"And reckless magical practices," Locomotive couldn't keep his concerns to himself.

"Naturally!" the coordinator agreed. "If they don't respect the boundaries of their own nature, why would they limit themselves in the application of the elements? The insane cannot master the concept of responsibility. But we'll get them, Conrad; I will prove that we can do that!"

"Are you going to declare the theological threat?" the captain clarified.

Mr. Satal could hardly get back to reality: "No. Then they will start all over with the same people, but in another place. And they will take into account the errors made in Redstone. Do we need that?"

Locomotive did not answer.

"Have you read Redstone's artisans' file?" the coordinator was curious.

Captain Baer nodded: "I took part in the preparation of those materials."

"Then you know that the inquisitors couldn't get the artisans' higher-ups, five-six people that lay low after Nintark. Our job is to lure them out of their shelter."

Locomotive applauded the idea, but he didn't like that it was planned for Redstone. "Will you let them frolic in freedom?"

"No!" Mr. Satal resentfully shook his head. "We will be beating them, but... awkwardly. We'll win, demonstrating our helplessness, as if by accident. We'll look ridiculous, as though all that separated them from success was the incompetence of their junior officers."

"Do you think that normal people will buy such nonsense?"

"Do you think that the artisans are normal people?"

Locomotive shrugged: "Well, if we are going to beat them anyway, I am in!"

"I didn't doubt for a second!" Mr. Satal chuckled. "By the way, you can call me Dan for short, but not before subordinates."

Locomotive was always moved by the ceremoniousness of the dark, often demonstrated at the most inopportune times. "And I am just Conrad," he suggested placidly.

CHAPTER 19

How much does a dark mage need in order to be happy? In fact, quite a lot, but there is some minimum which makes life bearable. That summer I regarded as successful.

I decorously parted with my family on the platform, three times pledged to Lyuchik to come to his school in winter, and encouragingly patted Joe on the back ("keep an eye on everything while I am away"). Then we barely pulled my suitcase into the railroad car.

The circumstances of the eventful morning were still settling in my head (to collect thoughts in the presence of Lyuchik was just impossible), so I had to act intuitively. I checked in the heavy suitcase with deliberate carelessness and took into the compartment only a basket—it was large, see-through, and allowed visual inspection from all sides. Everyone could see that I didn't carry any ancient artifacts with me. The train's buffers clanked, and we slowly sailed off through the starting drizzle—Krauhard's summer was over. My family waved at me from the platform.

There is some benefit to having relatives, especially when they are compassionate.

I sat on the bench, plunging into meditation—not for the sake of spellcasting (it was forbidden for me), but simply to get my thoughts in order. Not often did I have such a need.

The passing summer was very special: it scared, surprised, angered, and delighted me. I would have never thought that a dark mage could experience such a diverse range of emotions! I almost died and was saved, suffered from helplessness and triumphed, was outraged and intrigued. But in the end I became bigger, wider, and longer. Something of that kind. For a magician it is very important to see and perceive the world in all its diversity, and for a dark magician it is also very difficult. We always impose our own view on reality and dislike accepting objections, so reality intrudes into our lives in one way only: by force and without asking.

In a burst of feelings, I promised myself that I would start a new life. I would pay greater attention to what happened around me, so that no more enemies could approach me from behind. I would start thinking not only about myself... One year left until graduation from the university, but I didn't know any better entertainment than joining Quarters for his pub parties. It was shameful! Please understand, I had no desire to make this promise a major life turning point; it was momentary insanity, a second of weakness, born from thoughts about my white family. Thinking about spiritual perfection, I moved the basket closer to sort out the delicious grub that Mom had put in - there was too much food to finish it at once, anyway.

That night I didn't dream about alchemical designs. I saw Redstone, not as always, but in some strange, very alien way. Everything was colored in dust and dirt; buildings had trembling outlines, as if drawn by a frightened hand, and they were almost indistinguishable from each other. Acrid smoke, hanging low over the pavement like a ghost, hot stuffiness, and lack of shades: that must be the way a completely feral white mage would perceive a city. It hurts to think of the white at night!

I liked the feeling I experienced during a night dream; it had a sort of gentle exotic touch. Funny what kind of brains one must have to imagine buildings with inclined side walls. Houses could not stand that way, after all. And strange orange stench... Fireplaces in residential areas were stocked with pressed briquettes, and they gave off a bluish, slightly tart smoke with scent of straw and manure. The closest things I had ever seen in real life were the yellowish acidic evaporations of smithy and leather workshops in the southeastern outskirts of Redstone. Only a white was capable of confusing the blue smoke with the red one. In a burst of rare complacency, I tried to make the image more realistic by running cars and trams along the streets of my dream. I spent the rest of the night doing just that.

And then the night dream continued in reality.

I stood silently on the platform, hugging my suitcase with the basket, and realizing that I did not recognize the station where I had been plenty of times. It was a completely strange place now. I didn't forget the details; I just did not see them. Normal daily life seethed around me, but the crowd seemed to look strange now: people were replaced with some kind of blurred contours that flashed iridescently with unnamed colors (either shades of emotions or reflections of intents). No, the contours did not merge, did not lose individuality, but I couldn't say what those people wore even under pain of death.

Did I eat something poisonous?

All moved and stirred, exchanged momentum, lit up, and faded. My eyes caught two almost monochromatic figures among the iridescent sea of complex natures: one of them came off my train and another awaited the first one at the end of the platform. For some reason I thought it would be unwise to look at them.

What was going on, eh? I seemed to know which tricks those were. Too soon had I rejoiced that Rustle hadn't touched me! I thought I dreamed those interesting dreams, but it was Rustle, picking up the key to me. Now I understood behavior of patients at the Trunk Bay hospital—things like that could really make you lose your mind. I shouldn't panic—the train station itself did not change a bit, and where the exit was one could guess by the direction of the crowd's traffic. I ought to stick together with all the people...

Then I noticed a vividly pulsating silhouette heading straight toward me. I did not have a lot of friends of such stature, to be precise—I knew just one.

"What's up, lad!" the silhouette said with Captain Baer's voice.

"Hello, sir," the effort required to pronounce the words allowed me to focus and pull myself together.

It took a few seconds for the familiar shapes of buildings and platforms to stand out of the veil of strange beings. I felt better.

"I heard you had a problem," the chief of Redstone's NZAMIPS noted genially.

He came to the train station wearing his posh uniform.

"There were some," I did not argue.

"Let me give you a lift!" he proposed generously.

Very well! I guessed I was about to get sent straight into a madhouse. With a dark mage who did not understand where he was, they would deal shortly.

He took my suitcase by the handle and went forward, pointing the way, and the crowd parted before him like waves before a ship. I stomped after, carefully freeing my consciousness of the stranger's influence. I sensed that what was happening had something to do with my promise to think of others. Not without reason had I dreamt of white mages all night! If they saw the world halfway like that, then how they could survive at all? However, all that could just be an illusion, charmed by Rustle because of its mean nature.

I ought to keep myself in hand! Forty days had not passed yet; it seemed that the most interesting would be ahead.

When we left the station, only a slight tremor of my right eyelid reminded me of the strange visions.

Captain Baer ignored a line of cabs and headed to the parking lot. I expected to see a striped police car, but he brought his own auto.

I felt like I was kicked in the stomach, just thinking that he owned a car.

"Get in!" the chief of NZAMIPS clicked the lock and took my basket, not paying attention to the fact that I was morally destroyed.

Oh, that was a real car! Of course, not a black limo, but still quite impressive: big, bright, conservative blue, without a single scratch on the mirrored polished body. Captain Baer effortlessly lifted my suitcase and put it into a roomy trunk, onto some neat terry rug. Not wasting any time, I got inside. Leather seats! The back ones were like a sofa bed, with enough space to comfortably sleep; in the middle there was a little extra strap, probably for children. Subtle echoes of cleaning spells suggested that they were used here on a regular basis. Not a cheap thing, by the way. I was impressed; no, I was shocked. Someone else owned my dream. NZAMIPS wasn't, of course, a poor institution, but I always felt that government officials were supposed to look and behave like humble gray mice. What a surprise...

I squirmed in my seat, trying to soak into my skin the flavor of the luxurious leather. Yes, my motorcycle was also quite stylish, but of incomparable comfort. And no one around was surprised that the chief of Redstone NZAMIPS loaded my luggage; probably, the townsfolk took his clothes for a certain type of driver's uniform. For a moment, I imagined that was true: my own car, my private chauffeur—I felt good! The captain finished with the basket and took the driver's seat.

"Do you know where to?"

"Yes, I do."

Well, okay. It would be strange if the boss of NZAMIPS was not able to obtain my new address. The captain was driving out of the station square's crowd to the boulevard, and I relished my new experience.

In such a car I could drive and drink champagne without risking knocking my teeth out and even without splashing a drop. There was definitely some magic in the car; I didn't know of any suspension that could provide such soft movement over the pavement slabs, tram routes, and central alleys covered with cobblestones in imitation of the antique style. Nothing in common with Uncle's clunkers. I would buy myself the same model! I would do anything to buy it.

I felt like my dream came true, but somewhere halfway down I realized that we were driving to the town's junkyard.

Oops.

Yes, Thomas, you feared the wrong things...

Silly thoughts frantically rushed through my clever head. Maybe I should threaten him with disclosing the story about the crystal? No, it would not work. I thought about hitting him on the head and jumping out. Yeah, an attack on a NZAMIPS officer would look great on the list of my sins! Or maybe the situation was not so scary? He didn't bring soldiers along; he came without fisticuffs; what if we would be able to come to an agreement? Maybe he just needed money.

Hopefully Max had not reached home yet...

When the car stopped at the rickety wooden gates, I decided not to step up with initiative and instead followed him in silence. If the captain wanted to make a show, I should help him with that.

The junkyard itself (the junkyard, not a dump!) was quite a remarkable place. On a space the size of a small field, there were long piles of incredible stuff that was sorted by a gang of idiotic personalities, though they were quite friendly. What exactly their business was like I didn't know, but the junkyard owner shipped carts of various items daily and immediately filled the freed space with a new batch of stuff. Part of the territory was occupied by illegal housing—junkmen's sheds, workshops of amateur alchemists, as well as garages of car enthusiasts, less wealthy than I was. Knowledgeable people found the place very convenient: in the junkyard one could get parts to almost any obsolete device, starting with a wall clock and ending with a locomotive (for the first time I came here for that very reason). The owner of the junkyard charged a few copper coins for the right to own a squalid tin can and watched that no one lived there seriously; despite the cheap dilapidated gates and fence, the junkyard was well guarded.

That day, the maze of rickety ruins was particularly quiet—the local old-timers sensed troubles well. The captain stood beside the familiar garage and looked at me expectantly.

"Have you been inside?" I asked.

"I looked through the crack."

I sighed and opened the door. It was never locked. In the garage there was my huge black motorcycle; my merry dead dog sat right next to it. Well, of course! Why would it be somewhere else?

Max, wagging its tail, ran toward me and began to swirl around my legs (that's right, the captain and I came together as friends, and the zombie did not have any reason to worry about the stranger). I patted Max on the back, routinely refreshing the revivifying spell. No point in hiding it! The chief of Redstone's NZAMIPS calmly watched the spectacle. The man had iron nerves!

"Why did you make this zombie?"

I shrugged: "Not on purpose, it just happened so!" Max shoved its ears into my hand to stroke and looked at the stranger in a quite friendly manner. "The dog saved my life. And it was also a victim of the ghouls."

By the way, the dog resisted death much longer than the afflicted people.

"Okay, what's done is done," somebody grimly announced behind me.

That was a mage. A dark. An adult. Something clicked in me, and to the very roots of my being I realized the truth: I'd better not start a fight with him—I would lose. Max pressed tightly to my knee, folding its ears as if making a house of cards.

"Calm the beast, hold it by the collar. I do not like dogs."

I firmly grabbed Max by the skin, though I was sure that without my word it would not move from the spot. Scenes in which I had dealt with other dark magicians face-to-face flashed through my mind. There were not many of them: Uncle, Mr. Smith, and Mr. Rakshat, that was about all. None of them was really tough, but this guy was truly strong—no need to go to an empath. It wasn't easy to assess his age, but I felt that the mage was no older than forty, and my imagination persistently pictured him in general's epaulets. An abundance of power gives a dark mage's face a specific expression... Who did Captain Baer bring along?

The magician stared at Max. "Are you interested in

necromancy?" he asked calmly, without shuddering, as if someone's interest in necromancy was nothing out of the ordinary!

"No way! I just felt sorry for the dog."

It sounded silly. They would think that I was a nutcase and send me for treatment.

The magician raised his eyebrow: "Have you asked its opinion?"

Max and I exchanged bewildered looks: "The dog did not seem to be opposed."

"What did you use?"

It was the hardest question. If I was not prepared in the necromantic ritual, then how did I manage to accomplish it? I had no other option but to shrug: "It happened somehow."

Captain Baer expressively snorted.

The magician turned his attention from the zombie to me. In principle, it is difficult to find something that will scare a dark mage, but there were so many minor sins in my heart (starting with the same Rustle) that I couldn't meet his gaze imperturbably. He enjoyed my embarrassment. What a bastard! I had to endure his sassy staring in silence, because all my skills were nothing against a real combat mage. Max would hold against him for about ten seconds; meanwhile, Captain Baer would attack me from behind and strangle to death—such a hulk could not be stopped by a curse. It was unbearable to stand like that knowing that you couldn't even hit him in the face!

It must have been something like a test. Assured that I was not going to start a suicidal attack, the magician lost his interest in me and melancholically nodded to his accomplice.

"Well," Captain Baer began, "by the end of the week you'll report about your adventures in detail to me personally. Got it? If I see even one deviation from my own data, you'll be arrested."

"And then what?" I clarified cautiously.

"At this moment we... how do I put it... don't want more sensations. We will watch for you, you son of a bitch!"

Why did they give no rest to my family? I made a valiant effort to conceal a sigh of relief. All turned out well! I did not feel myself guilty, but I was a little worried about Max.

"One more thing," the magician added quietly and softly.

All my hair stood on end.

"If you come into the spotlight once again or some rumors will start, then blame yourself!"

A faint dark shadow gently touched my skin.

I quickly nodded and the mage, contented with the effect he produced, slowly went somewhere, dodging around piles of rusty scrap. Amazing that two dark magicians parted without a duel! The unnatural simplicity of the incident made me a little dizzy.

"Come on, I'll give you a ride to your apartment," Locomotive chuckled.

"Thank you, I'll manage myself."

"What, you'll manage your suitcase as well?"

Yes, the suitcase was a problem. Very well then, he had brought me in, let him take me out of here. I slapped Max, sending the dog back inside the garage, pinned the door with a wooden leg, and returned to the car.

* * *

The meeting the captain promised to Mr. Satal didn't go as planned. During the operation, Locomotive did not doubt his superior's orders, but when they got back to the office he couldn't preserve his composure: "We have to..."

"No."

"Well, at least..."

"No."

"Sir, necromancy is the most heinous of all the crimes that a dark magician is capable of doing. And to ignore it would be just... just..."

"Want me to give you a written order?"

Satal was the captain's first superior, who suggested taking some responsibility off of Baer's shoulders.

"No, Dan," Locomotive was deeply moved, "I do not mean that! The guy went too far, seriously, and not for the first time. He cannot live like everyone else; we either ought to recruit him or apprehend—there are no other options."

"Don't fret!" the dark magician ordered calmly. "Everything is under control. As the senior coordinator of the region I can authorize the use of necromancy, in particular, for operational purposes, of course, if he signs a contract, albeit retroactively. He has nowhere to go but to us—a dark mage cannot change his nature. The kid exposed himself twice, and he will do it again—that's when we'll recruit him. He won't feel pushed into the corner and will be thankful to us. And considering that even his zombie frolics like a sweet puppy, I am not afraid for the innocent people. Have you seen a frolicking zombie before?"

Captain Baer snorted: "It's impossible! The degeneration into a zombie cannot be stopped in the middle. It does not matter how fresh the corpse is."

"Let's say it is feasible, but very difficult to accomplish; that's why it is almost impossible. I will take him as my disciple! Why not? He has talent, the basics are excellently provided by the university; what remain are the details that I will help him to master. He will call me 'Sensei'..."

Locomotive gazed at the dreaming magician and rolled his eyes. The dark! He needed to tell Ms. Kevinahari about their conversation and let her do her therapy.

CHAPTER 20

For the rest of my vacation I scribbled reports for NZAMIPS.
For the first time in my life. I punctually expounded events,
checking and rechecking my field notes. I dared not lie, but
strongly suspected that the truth would seem like first-class
taradiddle to most. And then what? Surely, I did not want to
finish my days in the jail for especially dangerous magicians;
according to rumors, it was an abominable institution. On the
other hand, there was seemingly no reason to break into a run...

An ordinary man would have gained a myocardial infarction
from such an experience (not to mention a white mage!), but I
was just tormented by hopeless irritation. I felt angry that
NZAMIPS so quickly got to the bottom of my case. I should
have gone into denial mode! Confess nothing: that wasn't me,
the motorcycle was mine but the dog—no, no, though it could
all take a turn for much worse than now. Now only my self-
esteem suffered. I would survive. However, the strange pliancy
of the unfamiliar mage suggested some kind of a trap.

Anyway, the captain received the folder with my report in time
and did not even read me the moral code. The latter frightened
me—the policeman knew the nature of the dark magician. The
absence of a strong reaction confuses us, dark magicians, and
produces a feeling of permissiveness—virtually guaranteeing a
relapse. Did they want to provoke me to commit a crime? I
decided to act out of spite and not succumb. I would be quiet,
polite, and modest, at least until graduation—about a year was
left to wait. I had a lot of money, nobody asked questions about
my Empowerment, and nothing else kept me from fully
focusing on alchemy. I wanted just that! As a bonus, I received

four typewritten sheets with guidelines for "zombie upkeep". The guide advised one to give a zombie a special mineral broth periodically. It was time to visit my favorite firm and ask Johan for the necessary chemicals.

Had I known how it would end, I would have surrendered the zombie to NZAMIPS for experiments, and let them feed it with what they wanted.

At BioKin's office, I met a sobbing Bella (the blue-eyed brunette). What was going on now? The design seemed to be working. Carl and Johan danced with a tambourine around it, day and night, so that my presence wasn't necessary. And I didn't believe that she would be crying because of issues with the fermentation vat.

I decided to stay away from the secretary's problems (I have little experience in dealing with weeping women), but no such luck. Her sobs reached me everywhere in the huge office and stabbed my brain like red-hot nails. I sensed that Rustle was having a blast, exacerbating my ill feelings, and for half an hour I meditated, trying to isolate myself from the alien's influence. I wasn't going to allow some otherworldly stinker to teach me how to live! Nothing positive came out of it: the place in my body that had been taken by Rustle was not available to my conscious mind yet (I became a real magician only a year ago, after all). The cry even intensified in my mind, overshadowing all other sounds.

I pondered if I should perhaps take some time off. Less than two weeks remained until the end of the conditional quarantine; if I locked myself up in the apartment and drank, I would hold out. But then some ominous purple glow came under my eyelids, and I understood that playing the fool because of some stupid chick did not make any sense. I sighed and went to show my consolation for others, the hell with them.

The girl carefully concealed the tear-reddened eyes with her palm.

"So, what happened?" I muttered, trying to sound friendly.

She did not answer, turning to the window.

"Maybe I can help."

"No..."

"How do you know? Do the dark magicians often offer you help?"

It sounded convincing.

Soon she started talking. As it turned out, she was worried about her fiancé, a guy named Uther. I saw him a couple of times in the office; he worked part-time as a courier—a typical uninitiated dark mage, restless and boisterous, but with a sense of humor, a rare feature in people of our kind. Bella's mother was against the guy; she requested that he get medical treatment with some doctor she knew—and who wasn't even an empath— to "correct his character". The fiancé was truly noisy and quarrelsome, but the girl liked him, and his excessive obstinacy wasn't vicious. Uther agreed (I could not believe it); together they went to the clinic, and Bella watched him sleeping after the procedure, being so calm. Two days passed by. Yesterday he had to return home but could not be found anywhere, and the girl was no longer allowed in the clinic, and they didn't answer her questions. What else could she do to help him?

"What did they mean by the 'treatment'?" Something in her story alerted me.

The charming secretary did not know anything about magic. She tried to recall diligently the explanations given to her, using terms like "dissection of the contour" and "setting the axis". I carefully listened, gradually realizing a nasty thing: she could say goodbye to Uther. When the poor girl, biting her lower lip from effort, drew on a piece of paper the sign used in the "procedural room", my doubts were confirmed.

"They used the shackles of deliverance on the uninitiated magician," I concluded. "Your boyfriend is already gone."

Her eyes opened wide in indignation.

"There's nothing you can do about it, dear, that's life. You may think of him as passed away, and if he is still breathing, it is not an indication that he will live. Any mage will say the same thing to you."

"No, they would not harm..."

"This is another issue: how they dared to perform that on him. What kind of a doctor was that, who didn't know the basics? Have you seen his license?"

She visibly shivered and timidly shook her head: "No, I haven't. It was Mrs. Melons' Medical School..."

"I do not care about the school—the license of the healer is what is important. Magic is as much a part of the human being as is the liver or the heart. An initiated magician is taught how to separate the Source from himself; magic is like his third hand, so it can be cut off. That would be unpleasant, but not deadly. For an uninitiated mage, an attempt to remove the Source is equivalent to a strike by a hammerhead in the chest: the mind and personality get broken into debris and the body is still breathing, but the mind isn't functioning. The body without the soul does not live long."

Bella seemed to grasp the meaning of what had occurred.

"Yeah, dear, they killed him. I do not know purposefully or not. It was like hitting him with a knife, only there was no blood. If his relatives have not yet reported the case to NZAMIPS, being in your shoes, I would have done it immediately so that those charlatans won't kill someone else."

She became very pale and began to fuss, grabbing her purse, then her phone, then her purse again.

"Go, I'll let Polak know," my generosity knew no bounds. "NZAMIPS head office is on Park Road; tell their chief that I referred you."

She sniffled, jumped up, and ran away.

Blessed silence!

I got back to my desk, habitually rubbed my cup to warm the coffee, and braced to familiarize myself with the shape the sewage tank had acquired in my absence. My enjoyment was spoiled by waves of approval from Rustle. Can you imagine— the revenant wight had demonstrated high ethics norms! Had I known how, I would have killed it. By the way, I should delve into the literature; perhaps there is a way to get rid of the monster.

It was mind-boggling how the brainless creature managed to find the only weak spot in the dark magician. If Rustle had dared to pester me with visions of burning cities and the walking dead, I would have laughed. But since childhood I have been told that helping people is a must! Normally, I more or less ignored the unnatural impulses, pretending not to see anything heartrending, but Rustle pitilessly poked me into a conflict between my white upbringing and my dark nature.

Too bad to be a dark raised in a white family.

I didn't see Bella the next day—she picked up her stuff from the office and disappeared forever. Quarters said that the girl burst into asceticism and devoted her spare time to studying; she was going to be a doctor. A useful thing to do!

But my involuntary humanism resulted in some consequences.

Surprisingly, NZAMIPS reacted vigorously to the incoherently mumbling girl: when the assault squad broke into the dubious clinic, the ill-fated Uther had already been dead and prepared for cremation, and there were two other dark children waiting in line for "treatment". NZAMIPS apprehended everyone from the director to the floor cleaner, but most of the staff were peaceful herbalists, unaware that the owner of the establishment was playing with forbidden divination. The tabloids came out with headlines like "Revival of the Inquisition" and "Police Lawlessness"; however, that did not stop the prosecution. Authorities announced that the clinic would be closed and demolished, as the building had been desecrated by the sacrifice.

"Can you imagine—I had been there," the unusually serious Quarters twisted an almost full glass in his hands, "and saw that woman."

"Wanted to get a treatment?" I was sarcastic.

"Bite your tongue!" Ron got angry. "You're in a better position than me—your folks are far away, but mine see me every day. Mother was a girlfriend of Melons'; they're now organizing a club of supporters."

"Supporters of whom? Bella or Uther?"

"You won't understand," he brushed me off. "Melons was... well... a typical white!"

"White is not synonymous with good," I said instructively.

"I know," Quarters frowned, "I did not think that everything had gone that far."

"Rent an apartment!" I advised sincerely. "There is nothing better than life without neighbors."

Especially when you have the financial resources for that.

Uther was buried on the first day of the new school year, and not even one f*cking newspaper put a line in about him! It was outrageous!

We railed in unison with Rustle; the result was frightening. I did not know what Rustle was going to do, but I went to the university and personally asked every dark magician whose name I was able to recall (it turned out that I remembered quite a lot of them) whether he was aware that a white mage had killed a dark. And guess what? Everyone showed the liveliest interest to the case. That was when I first heard the strange word "Artisan". The oldest teachers spoke the word through clenched teeth with such hatred that I was ready to believe in the reality of a war between the dark and white. By the end of the day, someone had painted on the walls of the central building the distinctive sign of a blood feud with the words, "Nintark is not forgotten!" I wondered where that was.

White mages whispered in the corners about their enchanted friends, kidnapped and enslaved; freshmen, eyes round with terror and delight, questioned each other about some priests, but I had no clue about the artisans whatsoever. It must have been something that I was supposed to learn through my family, but I never knew my father-dark, and Uncle did not condescend to enlighten me (though I shouldn't speak ill of the dead).

I tried to shake my classmates; it didn't pan out. Nobody wanted to elaborate on the topic. And then I recalled who owed me a favor.

Ironically, Captain Baer was not opposed to a chat.

"Remember, you promised me an answer to one question?"

"Yeah, you jackanapes!"

"I am what I am. So, is your boss aware of the crystal?"

"Not yet. What do you want to know?"

"About the artisans."

"That is a banned topic."

"Then lift the ban!"

For some time we looked into each other's eyes, and I got suspicious whether Captain Baer was a veiled uninitiated Dark.

"Why do you want to know?" he sighed, conceding.

"They could be a threat to me."

"I won't show you any documents, of course, but I can tell you if you pledge your word of honor. Okay?"

"Fine!"

"Do you know the history of the First Period?"

I thoughtfully frowned.

"Okay, let's get more to the point, what is Roland the Bright famous for?"

"Isn't he a saint?" I ventured to suggest.

"Not only that," the captain sighed. "Well, let's try a different approach. Imagine that someone in Ingernika still believes that the source of the supernatural has been the dark magicians."

"Ha-ha!"

"Have I answered your question?" he raised his eyebrows.

"No, of course not."

"Then shut up and listen. Do you think NZAMIPS deals with

the dark only? Hell, no! Our main contingent is white magicians. Don't laugh. Try to picture for yourself what a white mage is. I don't believe you can succeed, but try, at least! They put other people on a par with themselves—and not only people. They perceive both positive and negative emotions, without discrimination. Do you understand?"

I recalled my experience with my own family and involuntarily winced. The captain slightly brightened.

"It's good if a white mage grew up in a village; they see how nature works and learn about real life. In a sense, they know that rabbits eat grass and people eat rabbits, and they do not put an equals sign between their family and the cows, for example. A city-grown mage cannot put a rabbit in a cage (the animal would feel bad). Their reactions are aggravated to hysteria, and they can do nothing with that—such is their nature. Of course, NZAMIPS does its job, and empaths help, but the issue cannot be fully resolved. Ordinary people laugh at the problems of the white; it's the theme of jokes. And that is a mistake!"

The captain raised his finger: "A white takes on the entire pain of the world, and the desire to get rid of the pain is a very strong stimulus. For such an incentive they would give away their life. Most of them adapt somehow, especially the initiated ones— they can mute their Source. But some can't or don't want to, or were stressed too much in childhood. The latter becomes a problem: a request to ban eating meat, a fight for the rights of pets, a fight to take sewer rats under protection. Or worse: they bother people and want to teach them how to live 'rightly'. Those latter are our clients."

From his frequent repetition of the word "white", Rustle's tricks began to revive in my mind, and I decided that it was time to finish the verbiage: "What do the artisans have to do with that?"

"A lot! The artisans and the like are sects relying on mentally unstable people, mostly from the white mages. They exploit the legend of White Halak (read about it—this topic is not banned) and promise to build a world where everyone would be happy. An ordinary man cannot understand the danger they carry. The dark are almost impossible to manipulate; they're too independent. But the white are trusting, suggestible, and industrious. Before you know it, you are already opposed to the crowd of fanatics who firmly believe that they are fighting for the happiness of all humankind. As a rule, they begin trying to 'treat' or simply exterminate all the dark within their reach."

"Sweet."

"And pointless. One could build a world without grief only by annihilating all who could feel compassion. These homegrown saviors are simply unable to grasp the simplest truth: life is suffering; life includes birth, disease, and ultimately death, and that is realistic."

So, all my visions had some basis, but it remained unclear whether that was good or bad. However, I didn't have deep sympathy for an abstract white—abstraction lacked personality. To Rustle with them!

"Are these idiots able to accomplish anything serious?"

The captain shrugged: "People don't really care. In my youth, it was fashionable to believe in good intentions, and the artisans had become almost an official organization. The upshot was that they had covered a whole city by a spell, thinking to save its inhabitants from evil thoughts."

"Is this possible?" I was shocked.

"It is possible, but for a very short time. The real White Halak had existed for around seventy years; Nintark hadn't lasted over eight months. They had lost forty thousand 'trial' people and another eight hundred men from NZAMIPS, standing in the cordon."

"I do not understand. Was that an effect of the white spell that killed them...?"

"No, it wasn't. It was an unidentified supernatural phenomenon. White mages are absolutely helpless before the otherworldly—even more helpless than ordinary people. The revenant creatures tend to crash a party, and they do not require dark mages to spawn them. Therefore, we will fight these 'activists', no matter where they'll show up and what they'll call themselves. We'll cry and sympathize, but beat them. Got it?"

I hesitantly nodded.

"Now answer me," Captain Baer frowned, "was that you who blabbed about Uther?"

I straightened up shoulders and militantly jerked chin: "Yes, that was me!"

"Thanks."

I was taken aback: "For what?"

He shrugged: "We could have missed the boat with that case, because Mrs. Melons was a doctor. And the capitol authorities advised us not to panic... So, thank you. You did well."

"You are welcome!" I could offer plenty of such services to them.

At night I had a dream about White Halak; the fact that I had never seen the town, even in pictures, did not hinder me. People, no different from the ghouls except for their red blood, walked along its streets. They were as the blind—"see no evil, speak no evil"—because they could not even imagine that someone may (and had the right to) grieve, experience pain... die.

They weren't compassionate; no, they wanted suffering to disappear, and these are two different things. All people should have been healthy and happy, or shouldn't have been at all—the happy zombies did not tolerate the elderly and sick among themselves. In my dream I saw the mighty zombies that protected the borders of the fairy kingdom of White Halak by simply killing any creature that attempted to cross them. The same zombies worked at the factories and fields, because the residents of Halak weren't able to put forth the effort needed for regular work; that is, work when it was necessary, but not when they wanted. Why work? The thirst for deeds could be satisfied in other ways. They walked, ate, and painted strange scrolls on canvas and felt touched by them; they multiplied useless things and sounds; they slept together and did not know what to do with the resulting children—often getting rid of them before their birth. I couldn't picture how the upbringing of children was done in their world, unless they assigned that job to the zombies too: to raise a full-fledged person is hard work, impossible without the use of some coercion.

Later, the history books talked about the flourishing of arts and sciences but, in fact, the inhabitants of White Halak were not capable of doing anything that required the throes of creation, any somewhat serious effort, or complicated training. And they did not need it—they lived a pale imitation of life.

That strange perversion of human nature did not horrify me (by the way, the real undead did not frighten me either), but I felt disgusted. No, better let the white be what I had gotten used to: harmless nitwits. They are not so useless if you take the time to think about them. I would treat them cautiously (I succeeded with Lyuchik), protect and indulge them, and they wouldn't create any extraordinary troubles for me.

That would be idyllic, wouldn't it?

CHAPTER 21

Finally, the forty days of my quarantine were over. No, not like that. They had ended!!!

The last two days were especially difficult—the damned otherworldly settled in my head and enjoyed it as much as it could. I physically couldn't stay at home days and nights: clocks had started ticking too loudly. But on the streets a glance at any living object caused in my mind a rapid string of images of his or her past, present and, at times, future. Why the hell did I need to know what the neighbor's dog ate in the morning, why a kitten was hungry, or how a hangover pained Mr. Rakshat? And, as a final touch, I could not read a book about the eviction of Rustle—my vision was failing me.

I had never believed before that a dark mage could seriously think about suicide.

I barely managed to last until the end of the forty days, but after the magic date had passed, the problems with the monster abruptly went down. My mind became acclimated, maybe? Bleak hallucinations and moments of sharpened hearing made me shudder a few more times, but then I realized that the problems were gone. The only left over issue was that a thought of the white was giving me willies and reminder that the Rustle-inspired memories would stay with me forever.

Why did I need alien problems? I had plenty of my own.

I felt blissfully happy, gradually tying the broken threads of my former plans and events, pondered where to find a buyer for Uncle's rarities, and fondly looked forward to the terrible revenge that I would strike upon the wretched creature. The encyclopedia said that Rustle was practically the only otherworldly phenomenon that a dark mage could summon at will (there were precedents). I wondered how many Rustles existed, and how would I choose the right one? I will challenge them one by one and torture, tantalize, crucify...

The people around me didn't know the nature of my problems and guessed that I did not have enough sleep. I couldn't care less; let them think what they wanted. I did not see or hear their thoughts anymore, and that made me feel immensely happy.

But the world had lost its familiar simplicity. The euphoria and temporary insanity that I was awarded by Rustle could not hide the unpleasant fact that people started gazing at me strangely. Did I carry some signs on my face? I asked Quarters straight out and received an unexpected response: "You've, sort of, crossed the road to the artisans."

"When?!"

"Did you not get that?"

I fell deep in thought, sifting through the events of recent difficult days. Well, people with a fairly sick imagination could perceive my talks about Uther as a hostile attack. On the other hand, no malicious sect could surpass Rustle in its meanness; it wasn't realistic. Anything that was less evil I didn't care about, I declared to Quarters.

"Whatever you say, Tom," he shook his head. "I can't understand you, the dark."

Brave bully Quarters... scared?

As it turned out, he was not alone in that. Outside the university, the white moved only in groups of three or four now; they had gone through some kind of "safety" training and became atypically anxious thereafter. Freshmen were counted twice a day, in the morning and in the evening. Students self-organized into patrol groups with men on duty, and these guards imposed the dormitory curfew. I wondered how they intended to make the dark mages observe all these rules. Especially the novice magicians, who were finishing regular classes well after midnight and by the end of the day were in such condition that no artisans were necessary.

Organizing the dark proved to be easy. They were offered a cab and a free dinner daily. With beer. Freebies! All the dark students appeared right on time, by 12 am, without fail. Even I felt the temptation to freeload in the dormitory and barely suppressed it. Are we, the dark, so predictable?

These extraordinary measures fostered a serious mood. For a while I honestly tried to scare myself, picturing that I was being hunted by freaks, but could not continue in that vein for long—it was boring. What could they do to me? Kill me? The most horrible thing I could imagine was a burnt out light bulb at the porch and Rustle waiting for me at the door, but that could not happen in the city (knock on wood)—too many ward-off spells were pinned around, and NZAMIPS was on standby. The maximum that I managed to achieve was to develop a habit of looking on both sides of the street and staying sober in unfamiliar places.

I was not allowed to attend dark magic classes—the doctor from Krauhard informed the university about my injury (what a pathetic snitch; one excuse - he was white). I spent spare time in the library, as a good student.

I had two topics of interest. The number one was Rustle. Certainly I wasn't the first dark magician it infected; people must have tried to get rid of the creature before, and some reports on the progress made should exist somewhere. I couldn't believe that one of my kind had successfully expelled Rustle and hadn't bragged about it. However, material on the most dangerous otherworldly phenomenon was surprisingly scarce. The reasons for that could be twofold: either Rustle was of no interest to anyone but me (nonsense!), or the results achieved were "not for mere mortals". I needed to ask the captain about Rustle, but instead I inquired about some white idiots.

Second, Uncle's book burned in my hands. I asked Johan's advice without going into detail and learned that the address on the parcel wasn't even a building—it was a botanical garden. The name also seemed suspicious, for Pierrot Sohane was a character in a fairly well-known fable. Combined, the two facts pointed to a white magician who lived in solitude and kept neutrality. Clearly, he wasn't a merchant, because a seller would not name a buyer "my precious friend" and wouldn't complain, "I hadn't hoped to find you alive". Moreover, he would not persuade in his letter that he "solemnly kept without any selfish interest an 'unnamed something' just for the sake of continuity". A rhythm of these phrases stuffed up my ears, and I wasn't eager to meet the "insignificant master of mirrors". Thus, I needed to figure out what I had in hand not to be strangled at the first attempt to sell the rarity. And what if the book was stolen?

To identify my treasure was no easier than to pin Rustle down. I couldn't match the text with any known writing style and could not exclude the idea that the content was simply encrypted. The only recognizable elements were numbers at the beginning of each chapter, though there was a chance the numbers were dates, and they would be current in a couple thousand years. My research revealed a similar font in one place, in a copy of the legendary The Word about the King. These were the most ancient extant chronicles, and my treasure looked like a luxurious notebook in comparison. To focus my search, it wasn't enough to just browse through its illustrations—I needed to attain a thorough grasp of the subject and honestly tried, but it was impossible to achieve.

Of all the historical nonsense discovered, I was pleased with one interesting fact: it turned out that Roland the Bright was a holy dark magician. Funny, Ronald the "Bright" was dark! Well, at least not "white". How this man could stand such a moniker was mind-boggling.

* * *

The senior coordinator of the region sat in his office, happy and well-fed, like a big black tomcat. Shadows of thinning foliage fluttered on the walls, creating a feel of the jungle. Locomotive knew that he would never occupy that room again—associations would be too strong.

"One is apprehended," Satal rumbled.

Captain Baer gently shook his head: "Why have you decided that Melons was one of the artisans? She is accused of illegal practices and a murder, but that is just one episode. We didn't find any evidence that somebody was behind her. What if she is just another red herring?"

"She confessed to the murder too lightly," the coordinator hemmed. "There was a chance that she managed to impose the shackles of deliverance on the first attempt, but why did the peaceful herbalist place the pump-sign on the table top?"

"The means of inorganic estrangement of the channel," Locomotive corrected habitually.

"Forget about the terms!" Satal brushed him aside. "There is only one application for the Source that was detached from its managing will—the armory curse. Especially powerful. A peaceful herbalist? Ha!"

"You propose a special interrogation?"

"Wanna bet?" Satal snorted. "She will die in our hands under the interrogation, and all the newspapers will shout about the 'police brutality'," the coordinator obviously mimicked someone and was pleased with that. "Let everything go its normal way."

"Unauthorized use of the shackles," Locomotive stated, "and theft of the Source."

"Death penalty," the coordinator confirmed, "and I will not permit any advocate to find extenuating circumstances in this case. She was a certified magician and could not be unaware of what she was doing; the fact that the kid died before they managed to find an application for his Source was pure luck. Our luck."

The dark magician enjoyed the hunt for invisible artisans amidst the stone jungle. The beast followed the trail of another beast— they were human beings only partially... Locomotive blinked, driving off an ugly image. The dark could not behave differently, but Baer was a regular human being—he had to take care of people instead of Satal.

"Our guy came into the spotlight in this case."

The coordinator got a little distracted from his triumph: "Leave him. You won't do anything."

Locomotive frowned: "I do not understand what you mean, sir."

"You do," Satal dismissed. "He is dark; you can't say to him, 'Go here but don't go there.' If you start taking care of him, he will resist and become less manageable. Hopefully, the sect will be disoriented without Melons, and we will apprehend them before they get ready for some serious steps. Let's go back to work, back to work!"

Captain Baer shook his head again.

He participated in the arrest of Mrs. Melons and watched the doctor at that very moment when all her plans were dashed. Her face, the face of a white magician who deliberately decided to kill, stuck in Locomotive's memory, and one word swirled in his head: "witch"! The captain was accustomed to the intricate logic of the dark, to the delirious talks of the street preachers— but a normal-looking person, behaving as if she lived in another dimension, was something new for him. The relativity of good and evil was brought to absurdity when the good was measured not even by profit, but by some unattainable and unknown ideal that, for some reason, justified any crime. He was there at the moment when Melons made a decision that determined her future behavior and confessions, and he could swear that this story wouldn't end well.

The armory curse. God save us...

CHAPTER 22

I was bored. I couldn't get drunk, unless I did it at home - it was safe in there, but the pleasure wasn't the same.

The biggest problem of any dark mage is what to do with his spare time, particularly if a reliable source of livelihood has been found already.

My work at BioKin had come to a halt: Polak negotiated the acceptance of the prototype of the gas generator with the client, and we all awaited the result. Johan, in his work time, scribbled an article about the new approach to the application of advanced micro-organisms and pestered me with questions about the alchemical part. Carl scoffed at the fermentation vat, throwing into it all sorts of rubbish to test. We both knew that a device with such parameters would thresh any sewage with the equanimity of a pinion, and all these "tests" for the machine were like spitting in the locomotive firebox. The red-haired cousin of Quarters went on maternity leave, the father was an alchemist's assistant (also red-haired), and their child would probably have fire-red hair that one could only touch with mittens. The future father was present at work only as a piece of furniture; his thoughts hovered somewhere far away.

I brewed coffee for myself and counted days until the moment that I would join my magic classes again. I never thought I would miss them! Of course, I could quit and forget the entire shit business, but I was expecting triumph ahead, and it would be a disappointment not to share it.

My third wish was to find new sorts of fun; Rustle heard it but did not fulfill.

I decided to act rapidly; I bought a ticket to the theater for a play with the neutral name "The Road to Exile". And I liked it. After the first three scenes I began quietly giggling, at the end of the first act I already roared with laughter, and in the middle of the second act the attendant requested that I be quieter.

"I do not know what you have found so funny about the drama, young man," an elderly gentleman, sitting right next to me, noted after the performance.

Still twitching convulsively, I explained to him in what condition a dark mage must have been to start talking with his crosier. Again, a crosier! A purely phallic symbol. The idea of its magic properties must have been introduced to the masses by combat mages, but I knew that the only real use of that thing was beating enemies on the head (which, probably, was widespread entertainment in the past). An ideal object to store spells has a round, at most cylindrical, shape; one object can't hold more than one spell at the same time. So, a really mighty magician is a man, adorned with silver beads from head to toe, but on the stage he would be mistaken for a homo.

I could give a thumbs-up to the theater as my new entertainment, but the next play was called "The Rose of the Wind" and created an unwelcome association with the white. Well, to hell with them!

To visit the horse race, maybe? But I had no spare money to waste.

I decided to join a student club; it was kind of late - a year left till my graduation. They didn't let me into the "Green World" club—pushed me out the door. Quarters suggested a yacht club, but I declined—I disliked moisture. I went to a meeting of fans of antique mechanics, and for two days I dreamed of gears. I even promised to find authentic weights for clocks. Surely, I could find something at the junkyard next time. The historic club offered a series of lectures on the origin of magic; I went there to ask about Roland (why he was nicknamed "the Bright"), got into a dispute about northern shamans—to prove my point I quoted an excerpt from the book "The Word About the King"—and made all feel jealous.

Captain Baer came to me and spoiled the mood: "I know that you do not care, but bear in mind: the Melons trial is over, but she has friends. Before, they wanted to appear good-natured, but now they will seek revenge. Watch out!"

And what am I supposed to think about the police after that?

I bought a ticket to the theater one more time, again for a tragedy—"King George XIV", and guessed it would be as laughable as the previous one.

But Polak saved me from the bizarre escapades with unpredictable consequences: once, closer to the end of the day, the boss came into the office shining like a brass chandelier and said that BioKin had successfully handed over the gas generator to the client. The concept had been approved, the firm was commissioned to design two versions of industrial-scale devices and soon, as the finale of the two-year ordeal, the team would have a grand banquet. Well, finally!

Nothing warms the heart of a dark mage more than plenty of free food and drinks of the sort that he cannot afford, and a chance to strut before a gathering of cultured people, knowing that they won't be rude or get into a fight. The only fee for participation in the event was the obligation to silently listen to the solemn forty-minute speech by the owner of the sewage factory and the invited mayor of Redstone. The floor was given to no one else; Quarters said that this way his uncle could emphasize that he had wiped the noses of all the skeptics. He had the right to!

Then all knocked back, and the party went on. I methodically tasted the contents of all bottles and decanters on the table, discovering how much I had missed of life. What could I taste in my Krauhard? Beer. Mead. Once-tried moonshine at the fair. Uncle told me a story: someone in our valley made homebrew once, but the drink had attracted chariks (a supernatural thing, plentiful as mosquitoes in Krauhard), and he no longer risked it. There was no demand for hard liquor in Krauhard! Even in Redstone, I acquired no taste for strong booze - did not like to lose consciousness. But there were white, red, fruity, wormwood drinks... Though, I must admit that after the third glass the difference between the drinks disappeared.

"Hey Tom, don't drink anymore," Quarters took the glass out of my hands.

I was stunned with surprise: "Why?"

"Because! I briefly saw one guy here. He used to hang out with Melons; I do not understand what he is doing at the party. He was not invited! You can get into trouble..."

Damn it, what bad timing! Why am I so unfortunate with banquets?

Quarters was already grogged; caring about me in his condition was surprisingly touching.

"No more!" I sincerely promised and switched exclusively to appetizers; they were also very good at the sewage tycoon's soiree.

The party proved to be no worse than at home: snobbishness quickly evaporated, the guests danced to music and without it, loudly talked and laughed. Johan, who drank only apple juice the entire evening, entertained a group of white mages in deeply philosophical conversation; Polak danced around another sponsor. Some plump little man pestered me with the question of whether I got paid enough.

It was close to midnight when a waiter came over with the message that the requested carriage had arrived. It must have been Quarters who ordered it for me. Actually, I intended to spend the night at the party—they said that the hall was rented until noon the next day. But if the carriage had arrived, I had to go. In the end, a feather bed at home was softer than flooring. What if I caught a cold on the floor?

Sighing, I moved my extra few pounds into the carriage that was waiting at the entrance, was painfully stung by something in the darkness, cussed out the cab driver (who smelled like a fishing tacklebox), and sharply fell asleep.

I didn't remember the moment I nodded off: there were neither twilight glimpses of consciousness, nor visions—nothing. I closed my eyes and then opened them under a high ceiling with a dome. The blue sky could be seen through broken fishnet windows without glass, and I felt cold. It was no longer summer.

Shivering, I realized first that I lay not at home, second that it was in an unknown place, and third that I was completely naked.

And then all the liquid I took imperiously demanded to be let out.

"Lie down quietly!" a voice commanded from the off-stage. "A horrible curse will not let you move."

I gently patted myself, found nothing (no pants, either!), and sat down. I wondered whether they really expected me to fall for such a stupid joke.

Two (white mages, by all indications) stared at me in shock. They were kind of chewed up, and because the body's physical health directly depends on the condition of the soul, I concluded that they were experiencing mental stress. Especially bad looking was the guy nearest to me with a spear in his hands. His eyes shone feverishly, his cheeks were sunken, and his hair tousled. The spear looked genuine and antique, though he held it as casually as a whisk.

"We do not fear thee, sorcerer! The teacher has killed your magic; now you cannot hurt anyone."

What a clown.

They looked painfully familiar, and the zombies of White Halak suddenly surfaced in my memory. Of course! That meant he would easily jab a spear into my chest without thinking twice, if I let the situation slip into fisticuffs. On the other hand, maybe they wouldn't dare. How could the captain say that they were "gullible, suggestible, and industrious"?

I had not known that the need to go to the bathroom could stimulate my thoughts that much.

"You betrayed your souls, miserable freaks!" I announced in a tragic voice. "You are the same as zombies, and the dead are at the mercy of dark magicians. Obey! I curse you on the first star, the sepulchral fog, and guts of a black cat! Ow-ow! Let you lose the true vision and skill to separate illusion from reality! Let it be!"

I said that and snapped my fingers, intending to cause a sheaf of colored sparks. Instead, I puffed up a huge ball of fire above my palm. I quickly shook it off under the table—it started smelling of smoke.

In short, it was time to get away.

As expected, the enchanted mages couldn't critically think of the situation. While the white fools clapped their eyelids at me, wasting time, I gathered an armful of clothes and was gone. I didn't care what was going to happen with them; it was their fault anyway.

I got out of the building into the junkyard, pulled on the crumpled clothes, and looked around. The place that I had left was a public use building, about to be demolished, but still quite sturdy (foliage on its marble steps, peeling colonnades, dome devoid of glass). A greenish-turbid river rolled its waters around: we were on the island in the middle of it. Now I understood why no one had noticed the hideout of those fools—water barriers greatly weaken magic background.

I felt surprisingly well: no trace of hangover, my head was fresh and body was energetic and pleasantly itching. I experienced an urge to start a fight or do some trick. If it was an effect of the white "killing magic", then give me more of it. I strongly disbelieved that the white hobbyists were able to invent something fundamentally different from the centuries-old practices of the Inquisition. It remained to discover what their ritual was called in plain English to make sure it was nothing outstanding.

I had made a fireball instead of sparks. Before, I had revived a zombie, without any special effort. Something was wrong with me. We were lectured on what magicians' "errors" could look like. It was scary even without pictures. Obviously, my troubles were related to the spontaneous Empowerment, and now, on top of it, the white had performed some rituals on me! My inflamed sense of responsibility required to find the culprits and explain their wrongdoings, to teach them a little with my feet.

But where to look for them?

Something crackled cozily inside the building, and a white streak of smoke stretched over the roof. Firemen and NZAMIPS would be here soon. Did I want to deal with NZAMIPS? A stupid question.

I hobbled along the chipped pavement, logically assuming that a bridge to the mainland should be somewhere close. There was a road, and it should lead somewhere, right? Soon I noticed the arch of a beautiful stone bridge with a double-crossed banner at the entrance: "The College of St. Johan Femm." I had heard something about that place, but didn't have time to think—I was almost running into the fire crews.

I thought I needed to check whether they had robbed my apartment and, if not, take some money from the cache. Redstone is a big town and I could not reach my home on foot, but cab drivers wouldn't give me a ride on trust. Though the thought of a cab gave me a brilliant idea. What was the cab company that served the banquet yesterday? I recalled that on standby there were mainly the dark blue carriages of "Rimmis and Sons"; they would hardly allow an outsider to pick up a customer. I needed to inquire with them about the yesterday's carriage! I decided to pay them a visit right away.

The first cab driver that caught my eye told where their stables were, and I got to the place on the steps of a tram, like I used to ride when being a freshman. The rest was "simple"—to find a man, whose face I had not seen, and learn from him what the name of the forbidden ritual was.

I could have begged and offered money for the information, but it was not my style. I undid a couple buttons on the shirt, pushed the belt to one side, uncombed my hair, and in that disheveled appearance walked into the office.

"Hello!" I began with aggressive pressure right from the door. "Where is your master?"

All of the people inside saw a dark mage in a militant mood, wearing expensive—albeit dusty—clothes and, obviously, suffering from a hangover. A walking nightmare.

"May I help you?" an office girl chirped.

I stared at the receptionist, trying to catch her gaze, but she stubbornly looked aside. Okay, apparently she had dealt with the dark mages as clients before.

"Help?" I asked mockingly. "Your guy left with my wallet! What else can you do for me?"

"What an unfortunate misunderstanding!" the girl sang in a high-pitched voice. "He did not do it on purpose. Are you sure you have not forgotten your things in a different place?"

"I'm not drunk!" my expressive objection raised knowing smiles on the faces of those present. "I do not like booze at all, and I had none of it yesterday. He picked me up at the restaurant 'The Black Dole', and I need my wallet back!"

"You will get it, sir, don't doubt," the noise and cries attracted the owner of the stables. "Who was on duty at the 'Dole' yesterday?"

The girl quickly checked her records: "Laurent, Mitchell, and Barto, sir."

"Sir," the owner turned to me, "can you describe the man who was driving your cab?"

I frowned and pretended to be carefully straining my memory: "Young. And looked... like a fish."

"Laurent!" the girl could not refrain from commenting.

"When is his shift?" the owner frowned.

"In the morning, but he did not show up, sir. Pinot has replaced him."

"The pilferer!" I said pathetically. "The damned thief. I demand that the police come to his house before he gets rid of my stuff."

"There is no need for the police!" the owner hurried up. "I will go to him immediately and personally deliver your wallet to you. Perhaps directly to your home?"

He wasn't making a fuss over anything—the main income of such stables was from the contracts with restaurants and pubs. Restaurateurs called certain cab companies in advance, depending on the number of customers, and kept the hired carriages on hold in the assigned parking spots. That was slightly more expensive than hiring independent cab drivers, but the restaurants relied on "their own" carriages' safe and sound delivery of a drunken customer. And suddenly—a theft. The owner needed time to look into the situation - fine with me! The fact that I had learned the name of my enemy was already a big success. I barely remembered him, and they could have recognized no one based on such meager description..

"Okay, you may deliver it to my home," I dictated the address to the girl (by the way, I live in a respectable area). I described the missing item—a wallet with keys. "If by this evening I don't get my wallet back, the police will hear my complaint against you!"

After all, I liked that wallet, and my landlady would kill me for losing the keys.

I waited near the gate of the stables, as if looking for something in the pockets. My patience was rewarded: I caught the moment when the boss departed in one of his carriages to Laurent's home.

"Quay Barco," he growled the address to the cab driver.

Excellent! That's how a real dark magician works! Just a couple of hours ago I had not known anything about my enemy, and now it remained only to clarify its house number.

I pondered if I should go and meet the guy in person. Had I gone home now, the concierge would've wrangled with me for the lost keys; then the landlord would've joined us and we would've argued the whole day. No, I wanted to know now what my enemy looked like!

I was ordered to get off the tram and threatened to be taken to the police (I hadn't bought a ticket). Misers! Well, it wouldn't seriously affect my plans—Laurent's work was close to his home. I walked to the waterfront of Quay Barco, gazing with interest at the column of black smoke billowing over the river— the College of St. Johan Femm was still on fire.

The buildings with Quay Barco's address formed the second line, hiding behind the hangars and warehouses of the North Creek, a relatively shallow harbor favored by owners of yachts and small boats and by amateur fishermen (imagine—people were fishing in that dirty river!). The blue carriage stood in front of a dull five-story building; I noted its number in my mind. To wait for Laurent outside could be waste of time. What if he doesn't come back? What if he feigned sickness and went out for some business? The marina, the island, the boats gave me some ideas. The shortest way from Laurent's place to the college was by boat. And he smelled of fish...

I turned to the docks. North Creek is not a commercial port: people in such places are kind of slow, know each other (even if they are not formally acquainted), and don't interfere in each other's business, but they always know who went with whom and where to.

Cozily nestling among the boxes and empty barrels, a group of fishermen was having breakfast on the dock. My stomach reminded loudly of itself at the sight of fresh bread and roach (yesterday's feast had already left my body). I needed to end this manhunt!

"Where is Laurent?" I confidently asked them, not bothering with a salute.

"There!" they waved in the direction of the long sheds.

Luck was with me that day. Maybe I could get my money back—I desperately did not want to trudge home on foot. A small side door was open, and loud voices could be heard inside—Laurent was not alone.

"Hey, morons!" I started talking right from the door. "Haven't expected me?"

Two athletic guys gazed at me in surprise. The third, a blond hunk in a white captain's jacket, lightly pursed his lips. Apparently, he swore to himself.

"The same to you, Laurent!" I nodded to him. "What else can you say?"

He looked at me with a mixture of disgust and perplexity, and my dark character immediately took a fighting stance. I hated snobs and copycatting captains! If you want to walk on my roof, show me your claws.

"You have a lot of nerve to come here..." he started wearily.

"What choice do I have?" I shrugged. "Your half-baked morons can't talk, and I need specifics. I had to drag myself here, teacher. On foot. By the way, I rubbed my feet sore!"

Who can tell me why I was in such a hurry? There were three artisans before me, the very same that had alarmed all of Redstone and stirred up the university. Moreover, one of them was certainly a magician, and not the last one in his gang. Wasn't I in the position of a lapdog barking at an elephant?"

But it was too late to retreat. Where power doesn't save, audacity will help!

"Confess what you have done, assholes!"

Laurent closed his eyes, as if demonstrating an abyss of patience, and tried to keep silence. He seemed to know little about the nature of the dark.

"Do not tell me that you are a magician-inventor. I won't believe you—you don't have the right physiognomy."

"Of course, I used nothing out of ordinary," the artisan refrained, "Only the shackles of deliverance! Is this term familiar to you?"

"Didn't you mess something up?" I asked strictly and shocked him completely.

I felt no discomfort (neither cold, nor emptiness, nor loneliness) from the loss of my Source. It was strange. I hadn't seriously considered magic as one of my limbs, but I thought that the infamous shackles should be sensed somewhat differently. Was that really the very same thing that dark magicians feared the most, to the point of hiccups? Enough to make a cat laugh!

"Do not doubt," he assured me. "You must feel sad about ending your magician's career so early?"

I wondered if he mistook me for someone else.

I shrugged. "Not really. Actually, I am going to be an alchemist. But I'll report on you to NZAMIPS anyway, as a warning."

They abruptly saddened.

"It looks," Laurent sighed, "like you do not understand what favor we have done to you by releasing from the pernicious influence of the Evil..."

I replied to him with an obscene gesture.

"...Or has the vice too deeply rooted in your soul? You're forcing us to resort to extreme measures!"

Did he threaten a dark mage? What a brazen white! Even if I did not have access to magic, I could still give him a fistfight, and I immediately told Laurent as much. Instead of a reply, the two muscles scowled and moved in my direction. Look at them, half-baked goblins of the dwarf species!

In a good fight three adversaries at a time would be a guaranteed defeat. If these were wicked city teens before me, I would turn around and run—the dark are not afraid to retreat timely. But these were just musclemen—cultured boys who decided to become cool through weight training; their combat skills hadn't been polished in dozens of minor skirmishes with broken noses and dark blue bruises. Against the ragamuffin from Krauhard's backwoods, they were like well-groomed pets against a stray alley cat.

While Laurent's friends clucked their beaks, I knocked off a barrel at their feet—they had to attack me one at a time now. The floor was swept very poorly, much to my advantage. Pretending to take a lower stand, I scraped a pinch of sand from the floor and threw it in the face of the approaching enemy. He was taken aback for a moment and recoiled, protecting his eyes, and immediately got a shoe kick on the knee from me—an inexpressible feeling, I knew for myself.

"Son of a bitch!"

They really had a bee in their bonnet about my relatives! I didn't have time to respond to the insult—the second opponent rushed to attack. I did not know where they took their combat lessons from, but the money was spent in vain: a one-on-one fight, without weapons, is not a fight but a pub brawl. And the techniques should be appropriate for the brawl. I grabbed him by the clothes, pulled toward myself, and in a couple of seconds he glided down on one of the boxes. I could have applied more skill to make his head meet the corner, but then there would be a warm corpse on my hands, and I wasn't accustomed to killing people.

I had underestimated Laurent; he had realistically assessed his chances against the dark—even if the latter wasn't a magician anymore. While his comrades were getting their asses kicked, he ran into the back room and was now ready to show his skill: "It's all over for you, accursed sorcerer!"

Laurent was holding an object, for the possession of which he could be jailed right on the spot for three years: a huge crossbow with an arrow, thick as a finger. Quite an exotic arsenal for a white magician. That thing hardly differed from the armory of a combat mage, except that the crossbow took more time to charge, and it did not leave aural imprints or require special abilities. The smooth arrowhead was stained with something greasy; I had no desire to test whether it was oil or poison.

Forgetting everything, I made the simplest ward-off weaving and threw it at my opponents.

A bright light ignited. I sensed a puff of heat and a rancid stench. When I was able to see again, it was very quiet around, and black flakes of soot were falling on the floor. My opponents could not be seen anywhere. I heard neither frightened screams, nor footsteps, nor creaking floorboards, nor slamming doors. Only black dust was powdered all around... When I understood what had happened, my blood drained from the brain, and the heart retreated to my heels. I rushed headlong from the hangar without looking to where I was running.

Yellowish smoke that scattered at the ceiling and flakes of soot were all that remained of a combat crossbow and three people who dared to argue with a dark magician.

The problem was not that I deprived someone of life (I wasn't cognizant of that fact yet)—things just happened very quickly and without any conscious effort on my part. Uncle's words about the armory curse surfaced in my memory. Was that a manifestation of my non-standard channel of power? But I had repeated that same curse many times in the classroom, and it only made balls bounce!

I rushed home like crazy: my apartment was at least six miles away, on the other side of the river. The concierge looked at me and silently gave a spare set of keys (she wasn't suicidal, apparently). I was hungry but couldn't eat. I was too emotional. Totally shocked.

I took a spoon of valerian and went to bed but didn't sleep for long. The doorbell rang; it was the owner of the stables. Smiling, he handed me my wallet: "As I said, it was an unfortunate misunderstanding. My guy did not notice in the darkness the thing you had forgotten. He had gotten sick."

By the time of their alleged conversation, Laurent was dead and could only be collected by shoveling. So the owner surely lied. I don't know how the enterprising boss managed to get into the apartment of the dead artisan, but he took out the only thing that could point to my relationship with the victim.

"Thanks!" I was sincerely gratified.

"Any more questions for us?"

"No! I'm really thankful to you."

I took more valerian and went to bed again. The doorbell rang; this time it was Captain Baer in black overalls, smelling horribly of smoke and breathing heavily. I said, "You stink," and closed the door. I went to bed again, the bell rang again, and Uncle was at the door, smiling, wanting to enter. I screamed and woke up. What an eerie dream!

CHAPTER 23

The infamous College of St. Johan Femm burned vigorously and for a long time.

Locomotive went there for the second time: two years ago, when Larkes was in charge, a few young scumbags castrated a kid—an uninitiated white—and were killed by the elemental curse, first and last in the short life of the white boy. Sixty-four students and attendants were slaughtered along with them, all of whom the dying wizard managed to douse with his rage. Who says that the white magic is harmless?

Firefighters poured nearly half of the river on the island, but if it had not been for the sake of the investigation, Conrad Baer would have let the fire frolic freely. It was a place nobody wanted to buy. Being a privileged school not long ago, the college was completely abandoned now. Sooner or later, the abandoned buildings always become infested with some yuck. Though Locomotive did not expect that it would be the warm-blooded yuck.

In the yard flooded with water and trampled by firefighters, healers calmed down a heavily burned white. He did not want to leave and assured everyone that he had lost his soul "here, exactly right here", and begged to help him with the search.

"Another fool got hit by a beam," the healer said to Locomotive with cynicism, typical for the police practitioners. "Perhaps, it will be better for him that way."

"Dragon tears?" the captain pointed to the injured white.

"No, more like a lobotomy. I will give more details after the examination—if he stays alive until then."

Locomotive nodded and went inside the building blackened by soot. It smelled disgustingly of smoke, water squelched under his feet and dripped on his head.

"Yours are there," a firefighter stowing a tarpaulin sleeve waved in the direction of the hall.

He found the senior coordinator in the hall that had clearly been an epicenter of the fire. The floor boards were burned through to the rocky foundation there, and Locomotive moved via flimsy footbridges, thrown by the firefighters over the structures that survived the fire. Everybody's attention was focused on the crumpled skeleton of a surgical table: around it, buried in black trash almost to the elbows, magician-experts and Mr. Satal personally crawled on their knees in search of evidence. All were unhealthily agitated.

Locomotive came up closer, expecting to see the charred remains.

"The same style as last week," Satal sighed, straightening up. "But there is a difference."

The captain looked at the ashes with understanding, but the dark magician smiled: "No, it's not about them. The artisans performed the shackles ritual last night, likely successfully, because this time their victim was an initiated dark."

Locomotive got a nasty sucking feeling in the pit of his stomach.

"The pump-sign stayed for eight hours, but then something happened," Satal gestured around the walls, gnawed by fire. "This couldn't be done by a human being. The channel is very different from the standard one; a magician with such a Source would not live through the Empowerment.

"A dark mage," Locomotive stated.

"Rather, an otherworldly creature. A mature one, rich in energy, confidently orienting itself in the material world, affecting the environment with rare strokes, not wasting its power. Perhaps it has a material carrier."

Captain Baer tried to picture such a horror walking along the streets of his city and failed.

"I don't understand another thing: how did those two men survive? They were injured later and only because they didn't get out of the fire in time," Satal mentioned and nodded to an expert that had dug some crumpled round piece out of coal. "Send it to the lab and let me know the result!"

"Couldn't that be the armory curse work?" the captain asked with an inner shudder.

Satal frowned. "I doubt it. The pump-sign broke up from an external impulse, but not due to the release of energy of the Source. The perturbation was extremely local, at least this time."

Baer realized that he had not seen typical human remains in the mud: "Where is the victim?"

"Obviously, he or she woke up and ran off," the dark shrugged indifferently. We haven't seen any belts; the victim was held onsite only by the pump-sign. Rather thoughtlessly on their part."

"Crazy psychos!" the captain could not resist shouting. "The third case. What do they want to accomplish?"

"Probably the same thing as Melons, had she not been arrested."

"One more artisan?"

"Not likely," the coordinator nearly spat on a pile of evidence, but managed to restrain himself. "That bitch seemed to coach a follower; he didn't make the grade by just a bit. He knew what

263

to do and how, but wasn't sufficiently accurate, so the first two victims died during the ritual. And he was not explained how risky it was to put the pump-sign on an initiated mage. Here's the result!"

The coordinator looked again at the blackened walls.

"And the white bastard is still at large," Baer added gloomily.

"Then go back to work!" Satal soared. "Look for witnesses; he didn't get here by air, did he? And I'm not done with evidence yet!"

Locomotive did not quarrel in response, although his patience was stretched to the limit. He was the head of Redstone's NZAMIPS, there were four hundred men under his command, and he wasn't going to lisp with a milksop—even if the latter was a dark magician. He wouldn't be a scapegoat! None of the emotions raging in his soul reflected on Captain Baer's face. He turned around and walked to the door in silence, habitually pondering whether he should immediately quit. Yes, five more years remained until his full pension, but he had already surpassed the length of service for an officer, and an old bachelor like him wouldn't need a lot. Numerous relatives would welcome an uncle from the city; he wouldn't be bored. Locomotive saw only one obstacle: if he left, he would completely lose the chance to influence events.

A young policeman in motorcycle goggles and gloves trampled on the steps of the college. He got agitated, seeing the captain, and started waving his hands. Not a moment of rest! Baer pushed his way through scurrying firefighters and approached the policeman. The guy's face expressed embarrassment.

"Eh, sir..."

Locomotive looked down and cursed in a fit of anger.

"Damn, it's all dirty here, too! What else do you have for me?"

The motorcyclist handed him a piece of mail, and Baer realized that shit was about to hit the fan. What could happen in the town that the chief of NZAMIPS had to be notified by courier? Locomotive pulled out of the dense envelope a letter, read it, and wished he carried a poison: in full compliance with the statute, the team of instrumental control informed the authorities about a powerful surge of magical activity around Quay Barco. Had they missed the alpha and omega?

"Pass it to Senior Coordinator Satal, okay?"

The policeman saluted and briskly splashed through the water on the sodden floor. He didn't know what a mine he was carrying.

While a striped NZAMIPS car was making its way through the crowd of firefighters, Locomotive intensely pondered the situation; none of his subordinates would guess that behind his usual mask of calm was carefully suppressed panic. Not without reason the artisans hid on the river: the magic activity in Redstone was traditionally tracked well, mainly because of the presence of the university. Amulets scattered around the city were officially regarded as protection against the supernatural, but they could also fix any spike of magic background, regardless of its nature. On a daily basis the monitoring team recorded dozens of small flashes, but there were plenty of magic artifacts on the streets that could cause them; records of the place and time of the outbursts assisted in NZAMIPS investigations from time to time, and that was it. The magic surge was very serious, if the magicians on duty recalled the statute and decided to play it by the book.

The driver brought the captain to the Quay Barco in less than ten minutes. Locomotive expected to see signs of panic and destruction, but the street was quiet and sparsely populated.

Still, that didn't mean anything in the case of a magic attack. A policeman, meeting NZAMIPS cars, waved his hand, inviting them to turn toward the docks.

The situation at the docks was peaceful and sort of ordinary. A police officer questioned a company of drunken fishermen, and a criminal police van was parked to the side, meaning there were victims. The cops pulled a striped ribbon around a large boat hangar and chased the curious away. Locomotive went inside, not stopping for talk.

Well, the hangar consisted of nothing ordinary. There was neither blood on the walls, nor a cadaveric stench, nor traces of fire, nor damage, except for an overturned barrel. And piles of dust were all around. Magician-criminologists were rummaging there, too, but of a lower rank, local from Redstone. One of them habitually saluted: subordinates respected Locomotive.

"Amulets of instrumental control recorded an outburst of magic of level eight, no less, at 2:32 pm. There appear to be human remains—ashes. I cannot say yet how many people died. I'd like to show you something interesting."

Carefully avoiding forensic specialists, rustling with their brushes, and stacks of boxes, the magician-criminologist took the captain into the back room. A seasoned professional, Locomotive whistled in surprise: against the wall there was a rank of crossbows, cocked and ready for firing; three or four more in the process of assembly were laid out on a long table; two uncovered boxes labeled "Hardware" predatorily gleamed with familiar parts. Boards on the far wall were pierced with bolts: the assembled weapon was tested in action.

"Search from floor to ceiling," the captain ordered. "Do you have enough people?"

"The office has sent all people who haven't been taken by Mr.

Satal," the expert shrugged.

"Okay, I will get you some of the coordinator's people!"

"One more thing, sir," the expert stopped him. "The imprint of the aura at the crime scene is very unusual. I have not been able to identify it, but it's nothing like I've ever met."

Locomotive nodded and went out into the fresh air, the smell of smoke and ashes followed him closely. It seemed inconceivable that the otherworldly, even with a carrier, managed to get from the College of St. Johan to North Creek unnoticed, but two cases with fire and strange aura in one day... The timing of both events was appropriate. The frightening word "quarantine" slowly appeared in the captain's mind. Redstone was much bigger than Nintark; in order to put a cordon around it, one would need a lot more than four thousand people. Rumors would start panic and result in victims. Soldiers would have to shoot into a mob mad from fear.

On the waterfront a young officer reported to the senior coordinator; troopers jumped out of a truck with NZAMIPS logo. Locomotive quickly approached them; he wasn't going to let the dark magician terrorize his subordinates.

"I know what you think," Satal quickly said, "let's step aside."

The word "quarantine" was left unsaid.

"Please, wait!" the coordinator muttered quietly. "I know I cannot order you in this case. But the situation is not so obvious."

"The creature walks around the city."

"Listen, witnesses say the suspect had talked to them. Do you understand what that means? The supernatural cannot talk! The otherworldly are capable of thinking in their own way, but they cannot articulate words: it's a known fact."

"What do you suggest?" the captain interrupted him coldly.

"Give me a day! The quarantine will sow panic in the city; the artisans want exactly that. We would play right into their hands!"

"What will change in a day?"

"The carrier is likely the very same victim; there were no more people on the spot. We'll find him before he reaches the point of breakage, I promise. The pump-sign retained the imprint of the original Source; we'll find the name through the crystals and catch the carrier before the monster will completely suppress his will. Trust me!"

Trust the dark mage? Again?

"Probably, the last victims are somehow related to the sect," Locomotive noticed, trying to gather his thoughts. "There is a large batch of illegal arms in the hangar."

"We need to search the hangar!" the coordinator came to life.

Captain Baer frowned: did Satal doubt his professionalism?

"Twenty-four hours. You have exactly twenty-four hours. After that, I will inform the center that we have lost control of the situation."

CHAPTER 24

The artisans could burn half of Redstone and conduct long-lasting battles with NZAMIPS, but my lecture on alchemy began at 9 a.m., and I was on time for it—albeit battered and not fully awake.

The dim fall sun filled the world with moderate contrasts of heat and cold; golden leaves in the University Park established a lyrical mood. What should be done to the dark to draw him to the lyrics? A silly question! A couple of insignificant things would do the job: fleeing through the city on an empty stomach for a whole day, being enchanted (so that all of my magic turned inside out) and almost killed twice—nothing special, in short.

Quarters met me at the door (was he waiting?) and immediately began to dump on me the accumulated news. Where had he managed to learn so much?! By the time I took a seat in the auditorium, I already knew how intense the last weekend happened to be in Redstone. The police banned the rally in support of Melons, and nothing terrible occurred. Someone set fire to the abandoned huts on the island at the northern end, and the mayor had lost around a million crowns worth of burned real estate. Though nobody would pay him so much money anyway—the place was thought to be cursed. There were persistent rumors that NZAMIPS had ruined the artisan's nest (NZAMIPS, indeed!) and found such nasty things that battered cops refused even to whisper about them. Two mutilated bodies, found in the river, were certainly the work of the same gang, and now the townspeople wondered if there would be a third corpse. I nodded melancholically and pondered how many attempts the sect needed to make things right. And they were called "artisans", those idiots?! If they always acted like that, no wonder that so many people were killed in Nintark.

"...and the mayor's horse gave birth to a three-legged calf."

"What?!"

"I thought you weren't listening to me."

Entering the classroom lecture stopped me from beating the tar out of Quarters. Yes, that day I was in no mood for humor!

The lecture went awfully. I couldn't catch the meaning of the subject and had to scribble stupidly word for word. Even in the hospital I hadn't felt like that—I was weak, but not stupid. My mind was like jelly: the professor's speech was heard as if through cotton wool in the ears, and my eyelids needed matches to keep them open. If I found that those bunglers messed up my brain, I would devote my life to the extermination of their kind! You couldn't do things like that with dark mages! In the end, I managed to pull myself together to focus on principles of building electric machinery, and the lethargy receded.

To get rid of Quarters was more difficult. With unusual tediousness, Ron followed me right up to the university canteen; after yesterday's fasting I was tormented by a brutal hunger.

"Why do you stick around with me?"

My patience was running out. I wanted hundreds of unnatural things, but learning wasn't one of them. I was dying from the obligation to spend two more hours studying the theory of tension, but I couldn't leave. If I missed something important, I would be angered with myself. Though desire to visit a pub never left me for a second. I was cursed, probably!

"Tom, you're not sick, are you?"

"No, it's just a hangover."

"But the party took place two days ago!" Quarters was taken aback.

"I ate something bad. I had food poisoning—got it? Vomited all day yesterday."

"Sorry... you... left so unexpectedly then... Usually you stay until morning."

I suddenly realized that Quarters must have been plagued by anxiety. Sweet of him, but I didn't have the time.

"You are strange! You yourself told me to stop drinking. What else was I supposed to do there until morning?"

Quarters smiled (as if getting food poisoning was funny) and soon left me for some business of his own. Okay, I shook off one, but there were still two more left: the artisans and NZAMIPS. Whom did I fear most?

No one!

I began violently cutting a steak, imagining Laurent in its place. I couldn't care less about all the discontented (even more so if they were corpses), but the number of problems they awarded me defied comprehension.

First, how soon would NZAMIPS find out about those three? Unlikely that the owner of the stables would mourn the runaway carriage driver; that is, he would simply cross him out of the payroll, and that would be it. The two beefs were in no way connected with me at all. How much would NZAMIPS find out if they got to the hangar? True, the fishermen had gotten a glimpse of me, and the boss of the carriage drivers had my address... Who had pulled my tongue yesterday? I wondered whether the police would be able to connect the island, the hangar, and the dead artisans, but this was out of my hands, and

I decided not to worry about repercussions.

Second, I needed to figure out whether I was under the influence of the shackles of deliverance. It was simple: if the shackles were imposed, I wouldn't be able to use the Source, and all that happened yesterday would be the consequence of the homebrew ritual. NZAMIPS could not hold me responsible, even if it discovered my involvement. But if I had something on me, and it wasn't the shackles, well, that would be the "third" problem.

During the break between classes, I went to Rakshat and asked him to let me in the basement where they conducted the ritual of Empowerment, saying that I wanted to test myself again before resuming the studies. He didn't mind and gave me a frame and a whirligig to check my concentration. After five minutes of testing, I discovered a funny thing: the Source manifested itself, but only at times. It was not quite the Source, and it wasn't mine. Out of five attempts, it resonated twice, at best. The power sluggishly fluctuated somewhere around zero, but as soon as I focused on a simple spell, it burst with such strength that I barely managed to plug the channel. To continue casting spells would be folly.

That test supported the only conclusion: those half-baked macaques did mess me up. Seriously. They had not "killed" the magic, just broken it, the meager charlatans. What could I do with the Source now? Maimed magic is much worse than none at all. Disappointed, I habitually kicked the Source and, surprisingly, received a kick back, wrapped in a sort of anger—someone really expected me to be grateful and gave a hint that it had become bored. What the hell...?

The familiar feeling of the presence of another being set my hair on end. Holy priests, was Rustle sitting inside of me instead of the Source? Was that possible at all?

Hello, skeleton with brown foam...

I wanted to hang myself, fearing that forty days of quarantine would start anew.

Quietly, quietly, no panic! I read a book about Rustle, did I? To get rid of it was quite simple—I only needed to get to the garage... I rushed out of the basement bunker as if pursued by a hundred ghouls, ignoring Rakshat's surprised exclamations and the bewilderment of the oncoming students.

I wanted to run non-stop and not think why and where I was going! Otherwise, this time more than just vision would fail me. I needed to get to the junkyard where my motorcycle was.

It was like a bet not to "think about the white monkey"; an ordinary man would have lost it, but not a dark magician. Two thoughts dominated my conscience: the need to get to the garage, and absolute, all-consuming rage.

How had the monster dared to play its trick on me, me?! Okay, no one had managed to exterminate Rustle in the last one thousand years, but I was ready to fix that. Even without the Source. Indeed, I didn't need magic to kill the ghouls before! The complexity of the mission wouldn't scare the dark off. I would bring down on it the entire power of technomagic! I would find what the technomagic was about and use its might on the monster. Rustle seemed to become impressed.

I must have looked awful on the outside; nobody requested that I buy a tram ticket, and that says a lot. Judge for yourself: I hissed, spat, and cursed myself, and looked like a mage at that. No wonder I scared people. I broke into the garage and grabbed the saddle bag taken off the motorcycle after the "death" of the Dark Knight. In the bag I kept my combat mage's kit, including a powerful enchanted lamp—quite harmless to Rustle when it was inside me. But the lamp had a source of energy... I began violently plucking out the accumulator from the case, trying not to focus my thoughts on what I was doing. The zombie-dog skeptically watched my efforts.

There it was!

A painful touch stabbed my tongue, and my mouth became sour. Yes! Now I could think. In addition to the blue light, Rustle disliked electricity, so its victims were treated by... hmm... there was no point going into detail.

Cold and resounding emptiness reigned in my head. Perhaps, that's how life looks like after the imposition of the shackles: the apotheosis of solitude. Given the alternative, I felt incredible relief. As they say, everything is relative.

The first round was on me. Nodding to a puzzled Max ("alright, ciao!"), I took the battery and got back to the apartment. It didn't make sense to return to classes; tomorrow I would claim illness.

* * *

To get to the central NZAMIPS lab, wisely located in a separate outhouse, the captain had to cross diagonally the entire police building. When Locomotive reached the place, he understood how fortunate he was: waiting in his office for the expiration of the twenty-four hour timeline, he had a good night's sleep, unlike all the others.

Gray from fatigue and looking ten years older, Satal sat in his chair, relaxing, and sipped something that resembled poorly made tea.

"How are you?" Locomotive called to him cautiously.

The coordinator did not waste energy on the greeting.

"We pulled out of the pump-sign the imprint of the aura, selected fifty candidates from the database, and are examining them now."

"What if he is a visitor?" Baer asked practically. The dark are usually quite mobile people; they do not like sitting in their gardens as the white do.

"That would mean no luck," Satal dropped indifferently.

"I've sent officers to the university and local services to inquire whether they saw a new mage. It is unlikely that the initiated magician is a tramp."

"Watch," the coordinator put the cup up to his head, "if there are any eccentrics on the streets. The time has come for that."

"What do you mean?"

"Did you get at all what had happened?"

Locomotive shrugged uncertainly—he had never dealt with such exotic cases of supernatural encounter, and the experts' report had not been provided yet. Actually, that was the purpose of his visit to the coordinator.

Satal majestically waved his cup (fortunately, it was nearly empty): "In conjunction with the pump-sign, the shackles do not inhibit the Source, just tear it from the controlling willpower. The energy channels are left open-loop, and the initiated magician in such condition may try to get energy from the outside."

Baer nodded: that he knew, but the burned-to-ashes corpses didn't look like they had been sucked by a vampire.

"If at this moment some otherworldly creature offers itself as the Source, the monster will have access to the etheric body of the mage, bypassing all his natural defense mechanisms. Like manure directly into the vein! In that case, the infection cannot be stopped; the body resists for some time, but then the otherworldly wight totally subdues the subordinate's shell and destroys its host. If we don't find the carrier before his willpower has failed, we would have to deal directly with the thing that played in the hangar, so to speak. Got it?"

Locomotive did get it—his protective suit was not designed for that level of defense. With the risks so high, the dark was delaying the quarantine?! He had to start notifying the services immediately: plain soldiers from the barracks wouldn't be enough to collect a really strong combat group; the "cleaners" would need time.

"Sir, there is a match!" a junior magician put his nose into the room.

The coordinator rushed from the place so quickly that he got into the lab before the captain. A pile of recorded crystals and cartons lay on the table; hopefully, they wouldn't confuse the records afterwards. The dark mage was already comparing two muddy balls.

"I have two pieces of news for you: good and bad," Satal began.

"F*ck you!" Locomotive could not refrain. "What's there?"

"It looks like it's our friend. That would be logical. What a strange crystal..."

"It cannot be! I checked on him last night!"

Satal snapped: "What was he doing?"

"He seemed to be asleep."

The coordinator froze for a second: "Okay. Take a group, go to him. I am exhausted now, but he knows you. Try to make him drink an inhibitor: that is his only hope. I'll call Fatun—let him bring his guys to town."

Locomotive trotted to the garage, where the operative group was waiting for his orders. Let's hope Satal would manage to get a call through to the "cleaners". Baer had not had a chance yet to work with the magician that replaced Colonel Grokk, but they said he was an intelligent man.

* * *

I accurately paid for a tram ticket, politely shook hands with the concierge, and tried to compensate everyone for my crazy look with good behavior. No need to test human patience beyond what was necessary! My fingers trembled unpleasantly. Passing the mirrored windows and seeing my reflection, I even started: a real psycho looked back at me. The body's physical health directly affects the condition of a magician's soul, and I was getting into scrapes, one after another, one after another! Even a dark with a very strong spirit has a limit to what he can stand. I ordered myself to look more cheerful and decided not to drink coffee: chemical stimulants in my condition would only hurt.

What a bobble came out with Laurent! Even if I had roasted him slowly, enjoying his cries and stretching his agony, he couldn't play a meaner trick on me in reply. Why did all this happen to me? Because one fool, rather than going to professionals, got engaged in self-treatment, as if the problem would go away by itself. Yeah, indeed! Out and back.

But my decision was firm: I would exterminate Rustle.

At first I was full of optimism. Why not? There were plenty of people kissed by the monster! If I did not touch the Source, it wouldn't climb out of there, would it? True, the day after tomorrow I was supposed to resume my classes in magic. How my spellcasting would look in that situation, I didn't dare to picture. Hence, I would need to withdraw from the class; it would be shameful, but necessary. Next I would need to find a specialist in Rustle, perhaps even pay some combat mage. I was not crazy and understood that I wouldn't get out of such trouble alone. What if the lesion started progressing?

Nothing happened for a few hours, and I finally relaxed; after all, the entire morning had passed on without any problems.

There was no entertainment in my rented suite; all class assignments had already been done. I could go take a nap, but sleeping at noon was a clear sign of sickness. Bored, I took from the bedside table a book wrapped in yellowish newspaper—it was that very same rarity of Uncle's (I hid it in the most visible place, according to the ancient spy methods), and began reading. Its pages breathed antiquity and magic; they must have been hiding something very important. It was a pity that I could not decipher what secrets they kept.

And then the strange faded scrawls formed in my mind a clear sentence: "The perimeter leaks in three spots."

A wave of panic swept over me. Throwing the book off, I retreated to the far end of the bed, but the mysterious squiggles still danced in my mind. The perimeter leaks in three spots. The perimeter of what?

Maybe I dreamt that because I was nervous? It happened to me sometimes, like a short circuit in the brain. I opened the book randomly and looked at another page.

"Salem assures us that there is no threat," the anonymous author had written in haste. "His ability to anticipate the attack is scary, but it's our only hope."

It seemed that if I wanted, I could see the unknown author, look over his shoulder, admire his mysterious perimeter, and maybe even move there, becoming a hero of the past and living his life, again and again. I wrapped the book in three layers—with my shirt, a blanket, and a bed sheet—and shoved it in the darkest corner of the cabinet.

I felt reluctance to learn anything from the book.

Childish curiosity touched my consciousness, as if the monster wanted to understand why.

Because!

And I realized that stupid tricks weren't all that Rustle was capable of.

I heard a kettle whistling in the kitchen. I had no habit of drinking tea and didn't use the main gas (Quarters' uncle's business) at all. Hot drinks weren't a tradition in Krauhard— our ancestors had no stoves to make them. Their meal was simple and artless. Surprised, I dragged my slippers to the kitchen and turned off the burner under the tinkling kettle. Pinch me, but I knew I was seeing that roundside copper kettle for the first time in my life.

And then, abruptly, without any transition, I found myself standing on the balcony. High railings saved me! Slowly, touching the walls, I got back into the room and began violently poking myself with the accumulator's electrodes. My arm ached displeasingly—I needed to find a less self-destructive remedy. I imagined a huge, droning electric arc and suddenly realized that I was poking my arm with a fork, and the accumulator lay on the table. At lightning speed I corrected the error. Also, I understood why I ended up on the balcony—the kitchen and balcony doors had been reversed.

My God...

I could not even imagine that such things were possible. Let's face it: the magic skills of the creature were impressive. And what would it do at night then? This thought made me freeze in my tracks. I couldn't sleep under the electric current every night for God knows how long. I would die from the nervous tension alone!

My deceased Uncle advised to go to an empath with any problem, but they belonged to the white and didn't know much about the otherworldly creatures. Now, when he passed away, nobody in my family would help me—even if I managed to reach Krauhard, refraining from sleep for two days. Chief Harlik was Uncle's friend, not mine, and it didn't make any sense to go that far to ask NZAMIPS for help. In any case, I would not dare to approach any people dear to me in that condition. God knows what the angry monster was capable of.

And the accumulator would be drained soon.

What did that beast want from me? The answer came instantly: its cold sticky tentacles greedily reached out to my mind, to the spot where memory is stored, where the source of my desires was, where the threads of my feelings converged. I plunged the electrode plates into the skin until it bled and kept it so until a chilling emptiness started reigning in my head. I'd rather die then yield to it!

I needed to hurry up.

I took Captain Baer's card out of my desk. My hands shook—I couldn't turn the door key on the first try. There was no sense regretting and repenting now. I wouldn't have time to find any other help; I would be lucky if I reached NZAMIPS sane.

I did not dare to catch a tram—I was afraid that I would go in circles, but any cab driver in Redstone knew the building on Park Road. I had never thought that I would call that address of my own free will.

The entrance to the police headquarters looked impressive: its glass windows weren't broken and the copper was not faded.

There were surprisingly few people in the lobby. Last time I ran out of there so fast that the interior was not imprinted in my memory, and Captain Baer was taking me in through the service entrance. They were obviously well-funded! A beautiful blue-gray carpet lay on the floor. Why not? Redstone's police headquarters is not a municipal police station; they don't deal with drunken revelers there. But my imagination stubbornly put under the carpet a few protective pentagrams. I was practically sure that if I lifted up the rug's corner, I would see them.

I approached the wall with the hanging office plan and realized that most of them belonged to the staff of the fiscal service. Oh, yes, besides NZAMIPS, there were also the criminal police, customs, the vice squad, and the alchemical control; all of them live their own very intense life, and bribe-takers and prostitutes are of no less concern to the society than the mages. That thought, for some reason, cheered me up. But I needed to find my captain.

"Are you looking for someone, sir?" the officer of the day asked.

I mutely put the captain's card on the reception desk.

"Do you need particularly Captain Baer? He just left for an assignment."

My resentment broke the bonds of depression for a second. It was outrageous! I came to report on myself, and he was absent. What were they doing here?

The officer on duty did not wait for my answer and dialed some internal number: "Sir, I have a visitor to the captain," he said into the phone. "I don't know; he doesn't say. Will do, sir!" And to me: "Please take a seat! Mr. Satal will be with you in a moment."

I hesitated, deciding whether the soft leather chair could be dangerous. In that condition I was afraid of everything...

A group of tough men in gray business suits walked by, politely moving me aside. Their leader should have carried colors of the Guard of Arak, if only his hands hadn't been occupied by a plump leather bag. The strange detachment marched silently up the marble stairs to the second floor. Watching them, I did not notice right away that the same dark magician I saw in the junkyard, in a similar suit but of a darker tone, appeared in the foyer. Mr. Satal, yeah. He carefully gazed round me, stared without irony at the accumulator, and calmly nodded to the officer on duty: "Thank you, Officer Kennikor. Please find Captain Baer and ask him to contact me. I'll be in the office. Come on, young man, we'll wait for the captain in my office. Do not be afraid; I will not bite!"

I wasn't afraid of him at all! Reluctantly dragging behind, I was figuring out once again how to start the conversation. Confessing right away about Laurent seemed undiplomatic. Some blurry silhouettes flickered on the border line of my vision, and on the suspicion that Rustle was ready to take its revenge, my hair began to stir with horror.

Perhaps one look at me was enough for the magician to draw conclusions. He searched in the drawers and pulled out an elaborate bottle with a blue label; not hiding it, he dipped the potion into a glass, splashed water from a carafe to top it off, and handed it to me. I emptied the glass. Why would I play the fool? The flickering in my eyes abruptly stopped.

"You are so upset because of Locomotive?" the magician asked gently. "He's gone to you; have you met him?"

I shook my head: "Missed him."

Hearing my reply, the magician visibly brightened: "That's excellent! He is not a compassionate man: plays by the book. You'd better tell me what's bothering you; maybe I can help."

What was going on? A dark mage expressed sympathy to another dark, offering help and support?! I even shed a tear.

And then I confessed everything to him. About Rustle, about the book, about the black flakes in the boat hangar... everything. I only hoped my death would be painless.

Instead, he sighed and said, "Forget it!"

"What?"

"It would not be a bad idea to interrogate those morons, but it's okay as it is now: for the attempted theft of the Source they would be sentenced to death anyway. Also, they tortured to death two more people before you. Let's consider that the execution had been done onsite. Or you thought that the law worked only against the dark?"

"What are you talking about?! I have a monster sitting inside me. When I try to cast a spell, it throws them at people. And it seems to be trying to eat me, too."

"That's normal. It's a standard response when contact between Rustle and a dark magician is reinforced with the shackles. Don't panic! You're not the first infected mage, nor the last one. With regard to the shackles: if the curse is not re-imposed at least three more times during the first month, its blocking effect will dissipate in three weeks. Then the behavior of your Source will be predictable again. As I remember, your doctor has forbidden you to conjure? Let's say the ban is extended for another month, I will guarantee to you the absence of magic. As to Rustle, you will have to get used to it; it is impossible to completely shut down its access to your mind. You had coped with the Source; you will manage Rustle as well. Most importantly, do not play up to the monster."

I expected a totally different reaction from the dark mage. My white upbringing skewed my perception of the world.

"That means you won't penalize me?"

"Why not? We will," he was surprised. "We'll leave records in your file; when Locomotive returns, you'll testify. Right after that we'll prepare a contract—you will work for me."

"No!" I was horrified. "I have one more year until graduating from the university and a contract with Roland the Bright's Fund thereafter. I want to be an alchemist."

"Who's stopping you? You'll serve as a magician-reservist— you'll be set in motion when necessary; that way it'll be easier for you, and NZAMIPS will save some money. I will settle the issue with the Roland's Fund; I'm on close terms with the guys from there. Do you," he frowned sternly, "seriously want me to institute criminal proceedings against you?"

I did not want to know what that meant!

In less than an hour I had become a NZAMIPS freelancer with the nickname "Dark Knight", and Captain Baer, with a deep sense of satisfaction, glued my photo to the folder of the illegal combat magician. Had I been sentenced, I would have served three lifetimes or had two death penalties. I didn't feel or observe the magic giving me shivers anymore. A very familiar looking lady earnestly congratulated me on a decent start of my career and tried to get details of the triple murder. She wondered whether I felt a little lonely. I dully replied, pondering what had been the turning point at which my fate took such a steep curve. Did it all start with Bella from BioKin? Or with Uncle's book? Or with the record of the first crystal? Or maybe from the moment I was born?

How the hell could I become one of NZAMIPS people?!

Part 5. DEVIL'S DISCIPLE

CHAPTER 25

Snowflakes danced slowly outside: flew to the window, sparkled shortly, and hid in the darkness. I tried to project for a second, to save their flight in my mind, but failed time after time.

"Tangor!"

Yes, yes, I was there. Where could I go now? What madness made me believe the speech of the dark magician and sign the damn contract? It must have been the trauma inflicted by Rustle, and the monster will answer for that! For about a month, I was in blissful ignorance of the trouble that I had gotten myself into—exactly until the moment I finished taking the course of the inhibitors. And then Mr. Satal called me, ordered to take Max out of the "quarantine" vivarium, and explained the content of the contract again.

For example, one of its points was about "training, free of charge", meaning that in order to withdraw from the course, I would have to pay a lot.

"Tangor, why are you slacking?!"

I had made a mistake: I would rather have gone to jail; they would have treated me with the course of inhibitors anyway. They didn't have a choice. In the end, to help victims of the supernatural was their duty! And now I was under the contract for five years and, quite likely, I would have to sign it again. Dark magicians always have to work pro bono for the public good. In the sense that society always thinks the dark owe it something.

I could have tried sabotage, but something was telling me that would make things worse.

"I've already finished, sir."

"You will be done when you report on the execution of the job!"

"Sir, I'm done."

"Good."

When Satal swears, it's normal; the foul language in his performance doesn't need to be taken seriously. When Satal becomes really dangerous, he begins to express himself in exquisitely literary language, with the hard-to-pronounce accent of a noble gentleman that treads his enemy into the dirt with his white gloves on. I had a vague suspicion that because of his high position, the coordinator pinched his dark nature too tightly before strangers, and his thirst for informal communication poured out on me. A sort of manifestation of his trust. What was I supposed to do? I just started taking responsibility for my white family and then turned again to the position of a disciple. Satal perceived my apprenticeship in the most archaic sense of that word (when apprentices endured beatings and washed their master's socks).

I wondered whether killing the senior coordinator would aggravate my punishment. Even if it would, I didn't care. The only problem was that I didn't have confidence in the success of my attempt—that bastard was too good in combat. I decided to act like a genuine assassin—hide my intentions until I could accumulate sufficient power and skills.

"Not bad," Satal noticed casually, examining my scheme (I spent over two hours on it!). We had not started practical training yet, because, in his opinion, I had to "polish my knowledge of theory".

"That's all for today. Dismissed!"

"Excuse me, sir," I had to be polite, "Christmas holidays are coming. I would like to leave Redstone for two weeks—is this possible?"

He frowned: "Why?"

"I promised my brother that we'd spend winter holidays together. My brother is white."

That was an important comment: all children would be upset when they are promised something and the promises don't come true, but a little white would take it hard.

"I got it. Apply in writing!"

In writing?! Wasn't I a "freelancer"?! What would happen next, then? Likely, he would start sending me on assignments! I needed to learn how to make undetectable poisons.

"Goodbye, sir," I was able to leave the room, keeping myself icy calm. I learned how to hide my feelings well!

The empath met me in the hallway, smiling. They must work in tandem.

"Hi, Thomas! How are you doing?"

"All is wonderful, Ms. Kevinahari. I have made great progress!" For example, I managed to lie while looking straight into the eyes of an empath.

"Yes, dear," she confirmed. "But if your smile is sincere, the outer corners of your eyes should go slightly down!"

I needed to learn the art of poisons and try it out on her.

The second, "authoritative" floor was quiet and dark. By the end of my classes, most of the staff in the police headquarters was gone; only officers of the night remained along with workaholics that were ready to sit until midnight. That bastard senior coordinator ordered the freelancer to work at least two days a month—that is, whole sixteen hours. Satal was not going to spend his weekends on me. I wouldn't get credit for my work for him, so I went to NZAMIPS on my more or less free weekday, Wednesday, and worked for four hours until my brains refused to accept any more information.

He should not treat another dark like that!

In return, Satal covered up the killings I had committed and the zombie I created, as well as my vast illegal practice of magic. From the point of view of justice, I was a persistent repeat offender, unworthy of mercy. The coordinator did not know about the rewritten memory crystal yet; collusion between a magician and a representative of the supervisory bodies was regarded as a very serious offense. And there was yet a whole six months until graduation...

The only thing that I stopped worrying about was my acquaintance with Rustle. Long ago, the clever otherworldly wight had found a way to interest itself in the most dangerous of its opponents, the dark magicians. The one who overcame the monster and didn't lose his mind would get a benefit: knowledge. Given that Rustle's age was at least ten thousand years, and its infernal body was present everywhere in the world, the prospects this situation opened up for me were exciting. Unfortunately, the statistics of the survivors was approximately one to forty-three: the majority became insane in the first one and a half or two years. No wonder, taking into account how the monster mocked me. The only way to avoid the increase in the number of senseless victims was to hide that interesting benefit of Rustle from the curious mages, and NZAMIPS was doing exactly that via rigid censorship.

In my opinion, the benefit of the long-lived monster was

questionable. First, Rustle was illiterate, which meant it wasn't able to recognize words, letters, and symbols, unless it had dealt with the subject in some way. I could read Uncle's book, because the monster ate a few people who had read it before and was now capable of precisely reproducing the sensations associated with each word. Second, that freak of nature had no idea what the calendar meant and what the date and time were today or in the past. There was no way to get any details from the monster. Responding to a question, Rustle used to dump a pile of random associations on the inquirer, the validity of which was almost impossible to check, and the monster wanted some interest for its work. I wasn't going to risk my sanity for such nonsense as some doubtful information from Rustle, and I immediately announced that to all interested persons.

Still at the mercy of gloomy misanthropy, I put a student jacket on top of a standard student suit and pulled down a typical student cap over my ears; it snowed, after all. Even my shoes were standard for a student now. I could, of course, come to NZAMIPS wearing an expensive black suit, but then Satal would certainly mock me. Did I need it? No, not until the poison would be ready.

"What's up? Is the boss pressing you?" Captain Baer, another workaholic, was coming down from the top floors.

I shrugged uncertainly.

"If you can't stand him, complain to the empath—she will reprove him."

The best piece of advice ever.

Having shouldered a typical student bag, I walked to the door, feeling with the soles of my feet the heat of protective spells under the carpet. I ought to think of something neutral—spells like that responded to hostile intent; it would be shameful to get arrested for the intended murder of the senior coordinator before even attempting it. There is a bright side to everything. In the end, I could forget about this nest of vipers until next semester—freedom!

I perked up and went to the tram stop, alone as always. The police headquarters were located in the commercial area and stretched for nearly a block, with one side facing Park Road and the other - Carriage Alley. A few more separate buildings (including the mortuary and a parking garage) were situated in the yard, but the majority of government officials worked till exactly 5:30 p.m. and then instantly disappeared. As the saying goes, only fools and horses work. There were neither pubs nor restaurants nearby, for obvious reasons, and I did not expect any company. Naturally, two men hiding in a gateway caught my eye, at least on a magic level. In one of the strangers I surprisingly recognized Quarters. Interesting: why did the lover of comfort suffer through heavy snow at night? Maybe he was driving a car?

I paused, waiting for the strange couple. Ron's friend was very short; the back of his head was hardly up to my chin and below Quarters' shoulder. I held a vulgar joke about bad weather at the tip of my tongue, because the small fry turned blue from the cold (with his body weight he should have given serious consideration to the choice of his clothes), but Ron was not in the mood to listen to new stories and didn't even say "hello."

"What are you doing at the police headquarters?" he demanded aggressively.

I raised my eyebrow—it was weird interest on his part, but replied, "I take lessons in combat magic."

"Give me a break! From whom?"

"From a visiting specialist. Edan Satal, have you heard of him?"

"He's the senior coordinator of the region!" Shorty sighed.

I wondered how come he knew so much. As for me, I hadn't been aware of Satal's rank until Kevinahari enlightened me.

"Well, he is not bad as a combat mage."

Though he was the worst teacher I ever had.

"You're lying!" the short guy said flatly. "Did you really come for some stupid magic at this time?! I would have believed it easier had you said that came to have tea there!"

I lost my breath from his statement. I suffered, and he saw that as a cause for jokes!

My mind still struggled to come up with a killing derogatory response, but the dark nature already started acting; my fist met the offender's jaw. Of course, I was in no position for a good swing, and my hit spared his nose, but made him fly backward to the ground. That is, onto the pavement; that is, onto the rocks. Only his hat and high collar saved Shorty from instant death.

Again, my reaction overtook my thinking. At least, I was in complete agreement with myself. That's how a dark magician ought to respond! Ironically, Quarters hurried to help his fellow.

"What's wrong with you? What are you doing?" he was outraged.

I shrugged, "What did you expect from me? If he wants to be rude to a dark magician, he should wear a helmet. Anyway, I don't recommend that you communicate with this goon. He is one of the artisan, obviously."

"Why did you say that?"

"Because!"

Never before had I witnessed paralysis of the brain in Ron. On the other hand, what should I expect from an ordinary person? Let him kiss his new boyfriend. If he started protesting, I would fight him. Before Ron was able to defeat me, but now Quarters wouldn't stand a chance; I was taking classes in martial arts and had already achieved some progress. Don't get me wrong, the inborn skills of the dark were usually enough to live a good life. But Satal had a picture on the wall where he held some shiny thing, wore a wrestling suit, and looked very pleased. That is, had I started a fistfight with him, he would have made mincemeat out of me.

I hate to fear people!

Suddenly Quarters came to senses; he decided not to run up on the cuffs and fully concentrated on the short guy who clapped his eyes in confusion. I turned around and walked to the tram stop, feeling sudden bitterness: when I was beaten up, Ron did not fuss so much.

My nerves became completely shattered. Imagine, I had a desire to go back and explain what was going on. But Rustle reprovingly protested, and a shameful moment of weakness safely passed. I decided to instill respect in the monster.

I've got a box. What an amazing box I have! What a mysterious box! And what's inside the box? I sensed that the naive creature was sticking its long nose into my thoughts. "And inside the box is... lightning!" Rustle disappeared as if it were blown away by the wind. If the otherworldly doesn't get brains from birth, then age won't fix the problem.

I came up to the tram, already feeling heated, angry, and perky.

* * *

Ms. Kevinahari was having mint tea in the office of the senior coordinator. From windows she did not see what was happening in the square, but something made her sadly shake head.

"Have you read your student's file carefully?"

Mr. Satal threw the last papers in the drawers.

"What do you mean?"

"He grew up in a house with a white mage and saw his dark relatives only occasionally. That affected his character."

"So what?"

"Don't you push him too hard?"

Satal rolled his eyes up: "What are you talking about? He is dark; if he is not shaken like a pear, he won't be doing anything!"

"There are other approaches..."

"For other approaches he's too old! Only in my way can I make something of him."

"Oh Dan, it seems you will get more than you expect."

"No problem; I'll survive," Satal grinned. "He asked permission to visit relatives on holidays. I will let him go to restore emotional balance."

The idea of mental equilibrium in a dark magician seemed to amuse the coordinator.

"Let's hope that their contact doesn't cause conflicts," the empath pursed her lips.

Satal, as is always the case with the dark, took into account interests of only one side; how the disturbed combat mage would be perceived by the juvenile white did not bother him.

CHAPTER 26

Students sat in the last lectures with martyrs' faces, but the spirit of Christmas holidays was hovering over the university: the white hung in the hallways traditional paper ornaments (very much like real flowers, just not fading), the walls were full of many-colored advertisements for parties, and magicians with artistic inclinations competed in the creation of ice sculptures. I took a hand in the holiday preparations, too - designed a device igniting the lights on the Christmas tree before the Faculty of Combat Magic. One might think that a dark magician and volunteering are incompatible things, but my desire to see how people would gasp with surprise proved irresistible. The Christmas tree was a live spruce; when they started to hang light bulbs on it— God knows; it took me a lot of time to find all of the control circuits. But now the garlands flashed in seven different algorithms, and the dean of the white mages bit his lip with envy.

With great satisfaction I looked at the fiery spirals, waves, and hieroglyphs dancing on the bushy branches. If Quarters had not stopped talking to me, he would have learned that the City Hall paid for the second such device, and it fully compensated me for all expenses related to the project. The trick was that the bulbs were contacting each other by chance for creation of the ornament; the sole task of the decorators was to hang them as tightly as possible. I noticed that some students tried to guess where the ornament would appear the next moment, and what its form and color would be. Useless! The process was controlled by genuine dark magic—spontaneous and unpredictable.

A surprise awaited me directly beneath the Christmas tree. I recognized the recent friend of Quarters by the back—his figure had a very characteristic shape. Once again the dolt wasn't dressed for the weather and had a freshman as company. The fact that he dealt with freshmen seemed strange; for a beginner, Shorty was a bit old. He looked like a frozen chicken: a white bird with blue legs.

I abruptly changed my course, came closer, and kicked him in the ass with my knee - I had an urge to see what his face turned into after my hit. Shorty turned around, intimidated. Oddly enough, he had no bruises on his face.

"Hi!" I greeted him, smiling very nastily. "How's your health? Don't you feel sick? Doesn't your head spin?"

"No, thanks."

"That means you aren't pregnant."

Gladdening him with the conclusion, I went on my way, whistling.

I wasn't aware where that fool came from (likely, from the very same Southern Coast where Quarters enjoyed going), but if he didn't get a scarf at least, he would not last until his return home. However, did I care about his pneumonia? A minute later I forgot about the frozen gnome, but he clearly remembered me. And took measures...

During a break between classes, I sat in the lobby of the lecture building and studied the rarity I recently bought in the bookshop: the work Toxicology by Master Tiranidos. I must say that the last distinguished inquisitor of Ingernika was a pharmacist, and his book could be read as a reference guide for a poisoner. I did not know how he managed to gather such factual material, but I heard that his grateful contemporaries tore him with their bare hands for it. Of course, the master did not describe the methods of poisons' manufacture, but it wouldn't take much skill to produce an extract of foxglove. I was reading in excitement about the symptoms of poisoning by toadstool (it seemed to be an almost perfect means, though I did not know where to pick the mushrooms), when Quarters showed up. He approached me indirectly, walking in circles with atypical nervousness for five minutes, looking at me and muttering something. Did he think that the dark magician would not notice him?

"Wow, Ron! Long time no see."

In fact, for four days. In some way that was a record.

"Hi. You don't... eh..."

I watched for Quarters, who had lost his tongue. I never thought it could happen to him!

"Do not harass Sam anymore!" Ron blurted out finally.

"Who?"

"The guy who was with me..."

"Oh, that one! You'd better tell me why he brought you to the police headquarters. It was his idea, yeah? As for me, I am not concerned with what you do in the evenings."

"Why do you ask?" Quarters started getting angry. "It does not matter where we walked."

"You are saying that you always walk around the police headquarters? Ha!"

Why did Ron bug me about some shabby boy, not even a relative? An incredible guess lit up my mind.

"Are you in love with him?" I shouted.

Quarters clapped his eyes blankly.

"Do not worry, there's nothing shameful in it. We live in a civilized country..."

Ron's face became so fearsome that any dark magician would envy him.

"Idiot!" he yelled, turned around, and almost ran toward the door of the auditorium.

Quarters was nervous; his painful reaction to my criticism was typical for this type of relationship. Did I guess right? I observed no such inclinations in him before; however, I didn't produce the first impression of a felon either. Let them do with each other what they want—they are adults! Already leaving the university, I noticed Sam in the company of some sophomores. What a sociable freak... Shorty glanced at me with some challenge, and I winked conspiratorially in response. It scared him half to death, I thought.

In contrast to Ron, preoccupied with my leisure time, I couldn't care less about his problems. I had already made arrangements for my vacation with Polak (it was easy); it remained to get permission from NZAMIPS (the most unpleasant part).

The police headquarters before Christmas looked strange. Its hall breathed austerity and almost a void of space; on the desk of the on-duty officer there was a spangled Bonsai Christmas tree in a scale of one to a hundred. Enhanced with white magic, the plant exuded a strong odor of pine needles. On the floor of the superior officers I saw no one, but distinctly heard the clink of glasses. Perhaps, in the wing that housed the offices of inspectors and investigators, the work was still in progress, but I did not go there—why would I want to spoil mood? Seeing people at work awakens unhealthy reflexes in me.

I decided to drop by the captain first to show my report—

wanted to make sure that the text was composed correctly. He would advise me instead of mocking. For some unclear reason, the chief of Redstone's NZAMIPS had his office on the fourth floor - level designated for miscellaneous non-essential staff. There, holiday eve was felt strongly: windows shone with tinsel, and the air was full of the treacherous smells of cucumber salad, freshly baked pastries, and vanilla. To the captain's office I marched under the interested gazes of lady accountants not overburdened by work (whenever I walked by their office, they were having a tea break). The main thing was to pretend that you were terribly busy; the last time I agreed to try a piece of cake I barely managed to run away. The brutal women, suffering without men, didn't care whether I was dark or white, or striped; more importantly, I was of age.

The captain took my appearance graciously, removed a cake from his desk, reviewed the text, and tapped his finger on the title of my report.

"Don't go to Satal; he's in a terrible mood now."

"I thought it was the norm for him."

"You do not know what you are talking about. We have received a petition demanding to find missing Laurent Pierrot."

"Oh!"

"O-ho-ho! The boss now writes a response that doesn't contradict the facts and looks true."

"Damn it!" I said "good bye" to my vacation.

"By the way, I am your boss officially. You work in Redstone's division."

"Can I go on holidays?"

"Go home for holidays?" the captain asked good-naturedly,

putting his seal?? in the upper left corner.

I nodded, "To my brother."

The captain paused, holding the document in his palm.

"Where does he reside?"

"He is at school in Mihandrov."

"It's not our district, is it?"

I nodded, though not quite confidently.

"And not even our region... Don't go anywhere; wait for me," Captain Baer grabbed my report from the desk and walked out.

I sat and wrestled with desire to disappear. Curiosity eventually won—I eagerly wanted to know what he was up to. The captain came back in about half an hour; he carried a bunch of sheets and a large paper bag. Judging by the distinct smell of brandy, he had managed to nip somewhere and spent his time well.

"Your vacation is canceled. You're going on a business trip instead."

"What?!"

"Here are your travel assignment and the order to Mihandrov's NZAMIPS. Sign it!"

I looked through the documents suspiciously. "'To investigate the work of primary and secondary educational institutions'?"

"That's it. Bear in mind, you owe me a report."

I groaned.

"Don't dare say no! Have you thought what would happen to Satal if you mess up there, and your past pops up?"

"I'm not going to mess—"

"Yeah, yeah. With your zombie you also weren't going to do anything special, as I understand. Either my way or no way; just stay in town."

For how long will I have to suffer from the moral terror? A normal dark would have rebelled long ago. On the other hand, had I gone to complain to Satal now, he could have beaten me up. What did I want more: to go on vacation or go to the hospital? Sighing, I signed the papers. Meanwhile, the captain emptied the bag.

"This is your temporary identity card—it does not give you any power but discourages others from asking questions. If you show it to any civilian, I will lock you in the basement for a week!"

How strict, my god!

"A traveling kit of a sorcerer: a marker with chalk emulsion, a salt shaker, a compass, mirror taps, a set of candles. You'll have to replenish everything you've used, got it? I give it to you, because it's in the rules, but I need it back."

I nodded vigorously; I understood about candles and mirrors, but how could he determine how much of the emulsion remained in the marker?

"A special emergency kit: elixirs. Well, you know that! Blue— inhibitors, green—supporting potions, red—stimulants. If you want to stay alive, do not touch them."

Hmm. Well put.

"The last one: an emergency call amulet; simply put, a "whistle". Click here and there, or bite off the nibble here (whatever you are capable of at the moment), and the nearest NZAMIPS division will send a quick response team. Do not even think about testing it—a false alarm will rack up a serious penalty."

What a pity. It would be fun to check it in action.

"Follow my instructions. If you go looking for trouble, I will turn you in to Satal, and you do what you want with each other!"

It was so cruel of him. Was he always so cold-hearted? He looked like a sweet man.

"That's all. Happy holidays!"

I briskly picked up my stuff and went out into the hallway. Enough of my bosses. A great deal of work was ahead of me: submit the three theses I finished yesterday, buy gifts for Lyuchik, make arrangements at the junkyard to have the motorcycle guarded, and bathe Max; the zombie would go with me again, and drying out that fur rug takes a long time.

That was another unexpected benefit of good relations with NZAMIPS: devoid of piety toward the undead, the "cleaners" darned Max's skin, trimmed his nails, and laid on its collar a special spell that compelled fur to grow on the dead body. The advantage was that the gray-red wavy hair hid under itself all of the characteristic features of a zombie, and we got a nice hairy poodle-like shepherd. The disadvantage of that camouflage was the need to regularly comb the long hair, bathe Max in a special preservative mix, and pour the egg protein into his throat (the zombie was not very good at licking and swallowing). I never thought that a zombie-dog would require so much fuss!

Slipping past the lady accountants, I walked down the stairs to the floor of the superiors and crept on tiptoes to the marble staircase that led to the entrance hall. Satal's office was just a few steps away; I saw his door but passed it unnoticed. It was time to run away, while my favorite teacher was busy with his report!

* * *

The senior coordinator came to Baer in the late afternoon, gloomy and fearsome; with somnambulistic precision he found an unfinished bottle of whiskey behind the cabinet and began to pour its contents into a teacup. Angry Satal either forgot that he could just call his subordinate on the phone or decided to walk before he would talk and let his irritation subside.

"Where is this underage fag? He was supposed to come today," Satal tipped the contents of his cup in his mouth, as into a sink.

Locomotive winced: a drunken dark magician wasn't exactly what he wanted for Christmas.

"He came to me."

"Did you let him go?!"

"No, I did not. I sent him on assignment," Locomotive decided that logical arguments wouldn't work at this moment.

"Where to?"

"To Mihandrov."

Satal suspiciously squinted his almost sober eyes. "How do you know about Mihandrov?"

"From the files. He's got a brother there."

"Ah!" Satal leaned back in his chair with a pleased countenance, immediately losing his battle fervor.

It was now Baer's turn to narrow his eyes suspiciously: "Is anything wrong?"

"Nothing," the magician waved vigorously, almost knocking the empty bottle onto the floor. "I will... no, better you call them tomorrow and alert that our employee is coming. Let them meet him."

"Is it worth it?" Locomotive hesitated, suspecting some kind of terrible villainy in that.

"Yes, it is!" Satal announced with drunken peremptoriness. "I'll go to the capital after Christmas. I hope that at least Axel will be on my side. Did he need a magician? We've sent the best one!" The coordinator hiccupped loudly and uttered with some effort: "Confidentially."

Locomotive figured out how much alcohol Satal had taken on per pound of weight and decided that his boss would last for five minutes, but then he would have to drag him to the guardhouse for the night.

"Do you think our guy will cope?"

Satal thoughtfully breathed through his nose. "I cannot deal with the white; they drive me crazy. Is his brother white? Yes! Exactly what we need. If Tangor did not kill his brother growing up, he will handle this."

CHAPTER 27

Protected by magic from any weather, the transcontinental express looked as if it had just rolled out of the train depot, as though it hadn't experienced the snowstorms of continental Ingernika, desert winds blowing over the capital's neighborhoods, and alternating sun, rain, and frost in between. Against the backdrop of Polisant's grassy hills, the train looked like a beautiful toy; only tiny human figures, bustling around the sleepers, betrayed its true scale. Hired carriages had already harvested newcomers and driven them through the hills to where the expanse of a great lake sharply glittered. Mihandrov was ready to welcome strangers who tired of snow and cold weather, and the express flew further into the arms of the humid tropics of the Southern Coast.

"Disgrace, what a disgrace!" a well-dressed gentleman lamented; he wore a pin, "Thirty Years in the Police Service," that he had obviously inherited.

"Do not worry, sir," a whiskered driver habitually comforted his boss. "It's not your fault! The station attendant on duty misled you."

"Ah, Alfred, I could have seen him with my own eyes if I had looked around a little!"

The driver did not argue with that. The only car in all of Mihandrov rolled along the winding streets, cheerfully sneezing. Not too fast though, as Mr. Clarence had to exchange greetings with all the passers, and there were a lot of them on the eve of Christmas.

"Hello, Mr. Luhmann!... Uncle Barry... Aunt Melons... Happy holidays, Mr. Festor!"

Clarence knew half of Mihandrov's inhabitants from his childhood, and the other half was related to him. If the only town's policeman had not worn his famous badge, the trip would have ended almost immediately—he would be required to talk with each passer-by.

"It's already after 2 p.m.," the driver tried to reason with his superior (as a civilian employee, he wasn't paid for overtime). "It's Christmas Eve. Wouldn't it be better if we search for our guest tomorrow?"

"You do not understand, Alfred! Dark mages are very quick to take offense. We have not met him at the station, and what if he doesn't get the room because of his dog?"

"I think, sir, a dark magician can stand for himself."

"That's what I'm afraid of!"

The driver tried to hide his heavy sigh in the background noise of the engine; the car reached the intersection, and he had to deaden the engine: he could not afford to drive the wrong way—turning around on the narrow streets was simply not an option.

"Hello, Aunt Tusho!" Mr. Clarence called to a thin elderly woman in a bonnet with ribbons, mincing along the street with a plump parcel in her hands. "Have you seen a stranger with a dog?"

"Yes, yes!" Mrs. Tusho smiled, delighted by the attention of an important person. "They went to the Mrs. Parker's B&B."

"Thank you," Mr. Clarence kindly smiled, and Alfred pressed the gas pedal right away; he didn't want to waste half an hour, picking neighbors to pieces with the talkative old woman. Vain efforts! By the time they got out of town and reached the comfortable two-story mansion of Mrs. Parker, the guest was not there.

"The young man checked in and left," said the landlady, a stout middle-aged woman with sparkles in her hair. "He did not say where to. If I knew it was important..."

"Do not worry, madam, our business can wait till tomorrow!" Alfred resolutely took matters into his own hands. Noticing that his boss was ready to object, he quickly added, "Sir, I think the magician is off on a personal matter, and he'll not like it if we pursue him."

"Yes, you are right, my friend," Mr. Clarence gave up. "Nothing can be done today; we will have to come back tomorrow. Madam Parker, I rely on you! Our guest should not feel uncomfortable."

"Don't doubt even for a moment. Happy Christmas!" the hostess smiled coquettishly to Alfred and flew off to her own guests—the eldest son had brought her first grandchild for the holidays.

* * *

The boarding school of the town of Mihandrov looked impressive: delicately executed decoration on cast-iron gates (beyond comparison to the modern styles), heavily enchanted oil lamps (rare electric bulbs could shine so brightly), large light buildings, its own marina and park that even Quarters' uncle could not afford in Redstone. From the gate I saw cobbled walks fleeing into the distance, trees of great girth, a strange grove where flowers and fruits quietly grew side by side, a garden of flower beds where everything (absolutely everything) was in bloom. No comparison with Krauhard... I wondered how Joe was able to send Lyuchik to such a place without recommendation. Or had he managed to get some?

I suddenly discovered that I knew little about my stepfather, even less than I knew about my deceased father. For a dark mage such lack of curiosity was normal; but it started annoying me—when I was ready to ask the right questions, something prevented me from finding the answers. I missed my chance to talk to Chief Harlik, for example...

Deep in thought, I entered the gate and stood still with the silliest look; a leopard ending up in antelope paradise by mistake must feel that way. In the square outside the gate people were bustling (probably getting ready for Christmas), and they were all white, every one: students, their teachers, and those parents who decided to spend holidays with their children at school. In fact, educational institutions were recommended to keep the ratio of mages to ordinary people at fifty-fifty, but either the rest of the pupils left for the holidays, or the administration could not scrape enough ordinary children to follow the correct proportion. One way or another, even the porter meeting the guests in a spangled jacket and a cap with a large pink bow was one of the white. That was crazy...

I must say that I had not thought through the moment of my meeting with Lyuchik. At the university, all white mages were adults, and at home the white were my own family. But a crowd of unfamiliar white kids with an unknown degree of sanity was a different story. How should I conduct myself with them? I felt like falling into hysterics! Having made two deep breaths and filled voice with as much honey as my tin student throat could withstand, I approached the porter: "Hello. How can I find Luciano Tamironi?"

Well, at least I had managed to recall his last name, and only because Joe wrote me letters.

The porter looked at me with a mixture of confusion and

suspicion, which usually took place when a guess had not reached one's consciousness yet but was already scary. Sweet. And I hadn't done anything yet.

"Thomas!" it was a joyful cry from behind, and at the same moment Lyuchik jumped on my back (he seemed to put on weight).

"Hi, bro!" I said when I managed to regain my balance. "Here I am. Not too late?"

"Right on time! Come on, I'll introduce you to everyone." He already turned to the woozy porter, "This is my brother! He came to stay with me for the holidays."

And Lyuchik pulled me around to scare people.

"This is Ms. Aster, a teacher of botany. My brother came to me for the holidays! Mr. Tanat, a teacher of math. My brother, for the holidays! My classmates. My brother!"

And wherever we went, a tail of shocked silence waved behind us.

"Listen, what did you tell them about me?"

"That you are the best dark mage in Krauhard!"

Hmm. I hoped nobody would choke at the banquet table. The garden and the guests quickly left behind, but Lyuchik pulled me further: "Now we let the directrix know that you've come, and then I'll show you my room!"

Okay, the guests would have time to recover and decide where to run. Well, did I really care about their heart attacks?

Nevertheless, some incidents did happen. We had been searching for the elusive headmistress for a quarter of an hour already (I suspected that she ran after us, but was one turn behind), when a gray-haired, middle-aged white appeared from the depths of the park. The magician wore a slightly old-fashioned frock coat with a handkerchief in the upper pocket. He plodded, deep in thought, without looking around and, obviously, not in the direction of the Christmas party.

Lyuchik's behavior changed dramatically: he stopped jumping, ceremoniously took my hand, and muttered in a low voice, "This is our assistant principal, Mr. Fox."

Well, I could understand his timidity before superiors; even I, a fearless dark magician, committed the same sin, for example, in relation to Satal...

We, as cultured people, approached the gray-haired gentleman and politely greeted him.

"Sir," Lyuchik showed his best manners, "this is my brother, Thomas. I told you about him. He came to celebrate Christmas with us."

Mr. Fox allowed himself to notice us. His reaction was strange: when he looked at me, his eyes widened, and his face became contorted by a grimace of almost mystical horror—as if he met a speaking ghoul. Though it lasted only for a moment and was hidden by his curly white beard, I did notice his impression of me. The elderly man looked worse than deceased in coffin.

I even started feeling ashamed.

"Nice to meet you!" I held out my hand, but the teacher looked at it as if it were a live cobra.

Well, that was the first strikeout. I thought that the main problem would be the kids!

But as soon as I started to speak, Mr. Fox came to senses and, with some effort, pulled himself together. In short, he finally shook my outstretched hand.

"Thomas... uh?" he smiled questioningly.

"Tangor! Thomas Tangor," I tried not to shake his hand too vigorously.

"Luciano...?"

"We have the same mother but different fathers."

"I see..."

Mr. Fox's face slowly regained color.

"I've heard a lot about you."

"I'm flattered!"

"Have you ever been to Mihandrov before?"

"Alas, no."

"How do you like our town?"

"It's pleasantly sweet."

He stared at me as though he suspected a dirty joke. What did I have to say? "Not a bad village, but not enough brothels?" Wisely deciding to ignore my responses, Mr. Fox finally drew himself up a bit and even assumed a dignified air.

"I suppose you won't stay for the banquet," he said in a secular tone.

"What is your problem, a shortage of food?" I asked to clarify.

"Food has nothing to do..."

Ah! He must have seen a lot of drunken dark magicians.

"Do not worry; I'm not inclined to abuse alcohol!"

At least not in his company.

"We will not serve alcohol," he said with some glee.

"Even better." I always wanted to know how the white were having fun. "I can tell a few anecdotes."

"Please don't," Mr. Fox was very serious.

"Okay, I won't," I said agreeably.

At that moment Lyuchik found a chance to intervene. "Thomas will stay for the party," he said with some pressure. "I talked about him with Mrs. Hemul, and she didn't mind."

"She simply did not believe your brother would come," Fox smiled indulgently.

He was an atypically nasty white. What else would he say in front of the child?

"Do you possess telepathic abilities?" I asked with awe in my voice, trying to catch his eye (that used to be very unnerving to the white). "Are you so intimate with Mrs. Hemul?"

"Who spreads dirty rumors about me?" a melodious female voice cheerfully sang behind us. The local headmistress was young, pretty, and a white mage at that, as her daisy brooch of rock crystal clearly indicated; the brooch seemed to be a symbol of one of the schools of healers. Judging by her tense look, she was already informed about my visit and came to rescue the situation.

"You see, Mrs. Hemul, Luciano's half-brother came here for the holidays," Fox said pointedly.

Why was he talking about me as if I was absent? I firmly took the initiative, moved him aside with my shoulder, and smiled most charmingly: "Thomas Tangor, at your service! Unfortunately, I haven't been introduced to you. Lyuchik was telling me so much about the school that I could not resist the temptation to view it. I hope I did not cause any problems?"

"Not at all," she weakly protested, and I grabbed her hand and kissed it.

Mr. Fox almost winced. An old lecher!

"I will go and make arrangements for another seat," Mrs. Hemul flew off, flushing from embarrassment.

"Are you staying for just one day?" Lyuchik asked cautiously.

"Why?" I was surprised. "I will stay with you for the entire two weeks. You live in a gorgeous climate. I just got off the train; tomorrow I will bring gifts. If you do not like some, you'll give them to your friends."

Fox snorted indignantly. What did I say wrong?

We toured the school property, accompanied by the watchful assistant principal: we walked through the garden and greenhouse, looked at the pond and the brook (why did they need that parody of the swamp, when a real lake was a stone's throw away?), visited ponies in the school's stables, and sat in Lyuchik's room. I wished I lived like that... To be honest, that place was worth the money I paid.

The alcohol-free banquet promised by the assistant principal began exactly at a quarter past seven.

Naturally, they didn't put kids next to me (except Lyuchik), but that was even better: adults had longer hands when you wanted something to be passed over the table. I methodically tried every unfamiliar dish, placing on my brother's plate the most delicious (in my opinion) pieces. Among the treats, meat was clearly underrepresented but, thinking what could happen if the white kids saw a whole roasted piglet, it was certainly better to stay away from the meat.

Lyuchik didn't care about the food; he hastened to narrate the events of the past four months in great detail. I nodded as usual and wondered how he managed to remember not only what and where he saw things, but also what he thought about them at that moment. I wish I could dump on someone my own experiences, curse my teacher obscenely, grumble about the blatant monster (Rustle was inaudible today for some reason), and complain about my ruined youth. However, it would be induced psychosis, the dark do not behave like that, and excessive talkativeness for a combat mage is generally considered pathology. Preoccupied with those thoughts, I ate twice as much as usual and almost fell asleep.

There were no interesting neighbors at the table. A couple across from me discussed with their child the style of her summer dress ("white lace?" followed by "lace, lace!"), and it was all about the lace for ten minutes in a row. Edan Satal did not seem so vile at all, in comparison. Before I wondered who wrote strange books about talking rabbits, in which all the characters expressed themselves as if they had no brains, but hydraulic brakes instead. Good that alcohol was not served— from the first glass I would have lost control over my tongue, and the sweet children would have learned a lot about human physiology and student life.

Should I flee maybe? I mean finish the trip earlier. I would not stand two weeks in such an environment. But as soon as I recalled that Redstone was now cold, nasty, and snowy, and Quarters had become gay?... the company of the white didn't seem so bad.

After an unbearably long two hours at the banquet table, the guests were offered a break to warm up and dance. I was as good at dancing as a wild boar in ballet; besides, I ate too much. While pupils and their parents volunteered for an amateur orchestra, I managed to drag my chair to the opposite corner of the dancing hall and settle there in comfort.

I quickly gathered an audience around myself. Such attention did not bother me: the white were like sparrows; the worst they could do would be taking a dump on my head.

"Is it true?" the bravest kid had the courage to ask.

"What exactly?" I asked good-naturedly.

"That you are a dark magician," he blurted out, looking as if he demanded that I confess to cannibalism.

I experienced a rare attack of good manners: "You needed to say a 'combat mage'," I gently reproached the kid. "Yes, I am a combat mage."

Then came tense silence—I was closely examined to see if I had any unusual parts of the body. I wondered whether those guys had seen even one dark in their life?

"They believe," Lyuchik remarked caustically, "that a dark mage should be in a sorcerer's hat with a pikestaff in his hand."

I rolled my eyes. People, stop it!

"The staff is good only as a bludgeon, and the hat went out of fashion two hundred years ago."

"Have you seen a monster?" a little girl looking like an angel (big blue eyes, pink cheeks, and two large white bows on thin braids) got courage to ask.

"You mean a supernatural creature? Of course, I have seen them. A lot!"

"No way!" a skinny bespectacled kid objected fiercely, squeezing a teddy bear in his hands.

"It is true!" I recalled Captain Baer's warning not to show my

NZAMIPS card to civilians and showed it to the children. "NZAMIPS. Making the world better is our job! Nothing to worry, kids, Uncle Thomas will not let them hurt you."

The kids took over the card and began to twirl it, looking admiringly at the iridescent rainbow logo and delicate ornamentation around the enchanted seal. Carefully concealing malevolence, I watched as Mr. Fox on the opposite side of the room tried to convince Mrs. Hemul of something, angrily glancing at me. I was never good at lip-reading, but no skill was required in this case—the young headmistress believed that communication with the benevolent-minded dark mage would benefit their children.

"Like the little ones," Lyuchik muttered in my ear, and I heartily agreed with him.

All local pupils looked a lot younger than their age. Even my sister Emmy, who had not yet grown out of the childish defects of diction, seemed, by comparison, a model of prudence and common sense. That's what happens when the white lack breadth of communication! I was determined to help remedy the situation, as much as possible, for the entire two weeks of my stay.

* * *

"You are putting the lives of children at risk!"

"You are spouting nonsense," it wasn't easy to make a white mage angry, but Mrs. Hemul's patience was seriously depleted, "Luciano grew up with his dark brother by his side, and the kid has got no health problems."

"Our children are not ready to meet this sort of people!"

"And that is really bad, Mr. Fox. We must seize this great opportunity! The young man is very well-mannered and well-educated. Acquaintance with him will provide our children with a positive experience.

"Your predecessor had different views on this, Mrs. Hemul."

"My predecessor quit over a year ago, Mr. Fox, and you know why. We agreed that teaching methods should be changed. You've supported the actions of the Board of Trustees. Have you changed your position since then?"

"Take note of my words: this situation will end very badly!"

"It depends on us. I do not understand your position! If you cannot keep your pupils in sight, please say so outright. Ms. Ryman had enough courage to admit her shortcomings. We can apply to the Council for an increase in staff..."

As the door had closed behind the assistant principal, Mrs. Hemul shook her head. For a white, using power isn't a simple task, but ordinary people as candidates for the position of director were not even discussed by the trustees. Honestly, she did it solely for the sake of children. It was difficult to admit, but they should not live a life sheltered from the rest of the world, and the empaths were completely on her side in that regard.

CHAPTER 28

Next morning I got up with the first rays of the sun, which was unusual for me on holidays. Kids were sent to bed at exactly 11 p.m. yesterday (it was cruel, in my opinion), and I did not have time to find a place in Mihandrov where a lonely dark magician could have fun. Mrs. Parker, still sleepy, served coffee on the open veranda; Max lay at my feet and successfully imitated a bored dog. It was surprisingly quiet around, as if we were not in town. I could sit forever here in a squeaky rocking chair with a blanket on my shoulders and a cup of coffee in hand. Of course, such happiness could not last for long.

A car of characteristic striped colors with a squealing transmission drove up to my B&B. Why is it like that—an alchemist in a public employ is always a hack. I watched sadly as the driver and the hostess exchanged bows; for some reason I was sure that he didn't come for her. Indeed, receiving instructions, the newly arrived went to the veranda.

Max stretched and yawned widely; I hoped that the man did not manage to see its mouth in close-up.

"Good morning!" the driver lifted his hat.

"Same to you," I tried to portray a polite smile. Had they received a complaint from the boarding school on me, or were the local services displaying vigilance?

"We express our deepest apology for yesterday. We intended to meet you, but an unfortunate misunderstanding happened! We are very sorry."

To meet me? Oh yes, yesterday at the station some clowns

jumped around the baggage car, but since I had taken Max inside the sleeper, I didn't check in my suitcase.

That meant someone from Redstone had called here. Wow, what alertness! NZAMIPS in action.

"No problem," I shrugged.

He visibly relaxed.

"Mr. Clarence is asking when you can meet him."

I pondered it for a while. Two hours remained until Mihandrov's boarding school would open for visitors, and I had absolutely nothing to do.

"Now, let's go now; give me a second to take the documents!"

He started smiling, and I went to my room to lock up the zombie and pick up the travel papers. Maybe I could persuade the authorities to stamp the documents with both arrival and departure dates at once - it could save me time. I was pleased that Mihandrov's NZAMIPS was open on holidays at 9 a.m. They really worked hard! By the way, what were they busy with?

For the next half-hour, the driver intently steered the wheel along the narrow streets, cobbled at the time of the Inquisition, while I frowned and tried not to listen to the toil of the badly adjusted engine. I ought to check the car, purely out of compassion—they were just killing it.

The police office in Mihandrov nested in a nice one-story building, sandwiched between a hotel and a bakery. To the left of the entrance door, three doorplates hung, one above the other: the Criminal Police of the Town of Mihandrov, Mihandrov's Division of NZAMIPS and, for some strange reason, Mihandrov's Animal Cruelty Prevention. I had wondered how they all could fit there, but when I opened the door, everything fell into place: Lieutenant Rudolph Clarence (according to the plate) sat in a tiny office with one desk, being the sole head of everything, and he was an initiated white mage. Oh my God! What genius decided to put a white mage in charge of NZAMIPS?! It would be curious to learn who worked as "cleaners" here...

I closed eyes and started counting to ten, no, better to twenty. I had a feeling that my bosses had managed to find me a job for all of the holidays.

"So," I said calmly after a minute, "what kind of problems do we have?"

There were issues in this place—it was quite obvious.

"Eh," a disoriented lieutenant tried to recall what he was going to start with, and then brightened, "Rudolph Clarence!"

"Thomas Tangor."

We shook hands. I struggled with a feeling similar to delirium (the white have captured the world; they are everywhere!).

"You cannot imagine how eagerly we have been looking forward to your arrival! We've been waiting for you, waiting for quite a while; I went three times to the head office and personally filed requests, but Senior Coordinator Axel does not tolerate..."

I bravely stifled a groan: "Let us first discuss business!"

He readily nodded and stared at me. There was a pause.

"So what exactly has happened?" I could not refrain.

"Wasn't it explained to you?"

"Let's pretend that I want to learn everything from the source."

"It is wise," he agreed, fidgeted in his chair, and began, "it all started a year ago, after the scandal. NZAMIPS investigated the suicide of a graduate of Mihandrov's boarding school, and in the course of the examination it became clear that twelve former students committed suicide over the past eight years. Every one of them was a white mage."

The lieutenant's voice broke with emotion; my eyebrows went up. The suicide of a white is an extremely rare event. Well, to ruin themselves by drinking, to lose mind was typical of them, but laying hands on yourself had almost never happened before.

"What a nightmare!" Lieutenant Clarence seemed to wince in pain even thinking about those cases. "The former director resigned, a special commission worked on it, but that's not the end of the story. I participated in the investigation and pointed out that another four children went missing. Of course, those students were rather unsociable, without close relatives and friends, but the white are not inclined to go nowhere! Then I compared these facts with my own experience. You see, Mihandrov is not that small: all the residents know each other, but they are not so close as to watch everyone all the time. So, according to my observation, at least five white mages who lived alone had moved out somewhere for no apparent reason. To their relatives that do not exist, to a town which name no one knows, just on business, and no one ever heard back from them. Two of them left personal items in the apartments, and homeowners still keep their stuff in the event of the owners' return. Of course, it is my speculation, but all of this seems weird! I applied to the head office with a request to open an investigation, possibly for the presence of supernatural phenomena. Out of my three reports, they responded to one only; I was ordered to wait."

Naturally! No bodies, no file. It was normal practice, but Lieutenant Clarence looked genuinely distressed.

"They probably have a shortage of staff," I comforted him (I didn't tell the man that it was foolish of him to expect help if

320

there was no crime), "especially of the go-getters. In the last four years supernatural activity has increased, but the staff hasn't; growth has been cut off. At Redstone, things got better only after the ghouls had eaten the former chief of the "cleaners". I am not kidding."

"But you've come!" Lieutenant Clarence snapped.

Because I didn't know.

"My brother is a student at your boarding school."

My Lyuchik lived in the snake's lair! I had to take him out of here. But where to? Could there be a guarantee that another school would be better? And the chance remained that all the missing people lived happily somewhere on the South Coast... Hmm, alongside the suicides. No worries: I had two weeks to solve the problem and draw conclusions—but time was running out.

"Well, your suspicions are understandable, lieutenant. Though it does not look like the work of the supernatural. It rather reminds me a killer-maniac—we'll work on that. Do you have any information about the missing people?"

"Of course!" he smiled again. "I have compiled detailed files."

He took a cardboard box from somewhere under the table and started pulling plump folders out of it.

"Can I take them with me?"

"Yes."

"Another request: let my involvement in the case remain a secret. Why scare the townsfolk in vain? The presence of a dark magician is a serious challenge to their nerves."

I didn't mention that I could be denied access to Lyuchik, too.

"Of course, I understand," the lieutenant nodded with the look of a habitual conspirator.

"If people ask what I was doing at your office, please tell them that you are keeping an eye on me."

He nodded, twice as energetically as before. And we parted. Already at the door, I asked the question that was tormenting me: "Tell me please, who works in the 'cleaning' department here?"

His eyes became a bit guilty. Oh!

"I understand. Thank you. Goodbye."

To get out of this madhouse as soon as possible! I took just one folder—no time for more reading. I was curious to see what the police could dig out in principle about a person who did not commit any wrongdoing. The driver, who introduced himself as Alfred, took me back to Mrs. Parker. He could not refrain from standing up for his boss: "Do not think badly about Mr. Clarence, sir; he performs his duties with all diligence. He does a lot for the town."

"Uh-huh. For example, in the area of animal protection."

Alfred did not protest loudly but, apparently, he got angry. "Do you really think that if a man is kind, he will not be able to stand firm at the right moment?

I sighed and said frankly: "Lieutenant Clarence, as one of the white, is physically incapable of performing the work he has taken upon his shoulders. Successfully, I mean. You were lucky that nothing happened here! If I were in your shoes, I would buy some brochures on how to avoid the supernatural (Krauhardian NZAMIPS prints a lot of them currently), and rely on myself only. Everyone will be safer that way."

Alfred stayed silent. I hoped that he would ponder my words, at least.

Half an hour later I was back on the veranda of Mrs. Parker's mansion, but not in the same state of blissful indifference as before. I got further proof that there was no paradise on earth! I should not show my change of mood to Lyuchik—no need to scare little tykes. I sighed and began to recall some formulas for meditation—I was about to demonstrate wonders of self-control to the world.

* * *

Mrs. Hemul watched from the window the second visit of the dark magician, about whom pupils were whispering the entire morning. The awful monster, smiling good-naturedly, helped his brother unwrap the gifts. Given the amount of gifts, it was truly titanic work. Mr. Fox breathed heavily over the directrix' shoulder, constantly rubbing his palms and making her feel madly nervous. Had Luciano come to the thrilling meeting alone, it would not have attracted so much attention, but the white from Krauhard (a compilation of words that hardly made sense) brought a friend along.

"Petros is not poised to talk to the stranger!" Mr. Fox whispered indignantly in his boss' ear. "You know how susceptible he is!"

The skinny, sickly boy was thought to be a distant relative of the assistant principal and an object of his constant care.

Mrs. Hemul was inclined to disagree with her colleague: with uncanny insight, for some meager fifteen minutes, the dark managed to ingratiate himself with the child, gave him a bag of candy and a big glass ball with a Christmas unicorn. The beautiful, shimmering iridescent toy totally fascinated the kid. Taking a seat right on the walkway, Petros admired the run of the illusory horse, scooping handfuls of candy from the bag and, without looking, shoving them into his mouth. Before, the painfully shy boy took nothing from strangers! Had it not happened on the territory of the school, right before her eyes, Mrs. Hemul would have been the first to rush and rescue the child from a potential pedophile.

Luciano suddenly discovered that, when unpacked, the gifts occupied twice as much of the space, and the process went in the opposite direction.

Perhaps, if the situation with students had not been so alarming, Mrs. Hemul would have satisfied the request of the assistant principal. But there was something wrong with the school in Mihandrov, and even the best empaths weren't able to prescribe a medication to it. The director herself left her sons (two wonderful twins) in Artrom when she accepted the job in Mihandrov. For now, the parents of her students still believed the Board of Trustees, but if the alarming events, acknowledged by the commission, didn't come to a halt within a year, the authorities would close the school. No one wanted to be responsible for the possible death of students—and the oldest educational institution in the district would cease to exist. Less than six months remained until the end of the one-year probation.

But what were they doing wrong? The intuition of a practicing magician, a rather strong one, prompted Mrs. Hemul to think that the answer was closer than they imagined, and the dark stranger was a part of it. He had fumbled with the children for half an hour already, and from a distance it looked like he even enjoyed the kids' continuous chatter. It was not normal! Neither a harsh word nor an aggressive gesture from him. Indifferent like a cat.

Petros, wanting attention, clutched with his dirty hand the sleeve of the dark's light jacket. Now the dark would show his true nature... No, he leaned over, listening, and seriously replied. Appealing to both boys, he united them in conversation, and then left kids to talk to each other. A skilful trick! Gesticulating vigorously, Petros dropped the ball. Oh my God! The glass ball bounced harmlessly along the walk—protective magic in action. What foresight... She became uneasy by such mastery of the situation by the dark.

Mrs. Hemul decided: "You are wrong, Mr. Fox!" Noticing the change in her mood, the assistant principal slightly stiffened.

"I think Mr. Tangor's visit is our best luck this year. Perhaps he is our last chance to improve the situation in the school. We've tried everything—except asking the dark for help. If you have a different opinion, please keep it to yourself or appeal directly to the Board of Trustees. While I am the director here, Mr. Tangor will be free to visit the school and communicate with any of our pupils."

"Petros does not need the intervention of a rude, selfish..."

"Petros seriously lags behind in his development, even if we account for the initiation of his Source. Don't you agree that it is disturbing when the period of primary fragmentation of consciousness is delayed to ten years! Luciano is the only one with whom Petros communicates regularly, and his brother is the first adult in the presence of whom he doesn't hide in a shell, like a frightened snail. I advise you to appreciate it."

Her relations with the assistant principal were spoiled; Mrs. Hemul realized that by how resentfully the man had twitched his chin. People think that hierarchical concerns are the prerogative of the Dark, but the white mages are cut from the same cloth, and sometimes the whites' blood boils too. Mr. Fox thought of her as an irresponsible greenhorn. Whatever; perhaps, later he would understand her motives, although at his age... doubtful.

CHAPTER 29

My trip had a chance to become a real resort vacation. I got up at dawn, did some exercises, had lunch, came back to take a nap in the room, and by 10 a.m. went to school to entertain my little white. What could attract an adult dark mage to the white youngsters' company? One thing: with no effort on my part, they literally hung on my every word, and it was like a balm for my wounded pride. Deceased Uncle Gordon was right when he said that my lust for power was enormous.

Well, of course I thought about our conversation with Lieutenant Rudolph; however, I hoped he did not expect that one dark mage would solve all his problems. In my opinion, it would be much more productive to gather people to scour the neighborhood and the town; perhaps the missing just fell in some pit. Yeah, all nine people... My attempts to sort out the situation looked more like catching a black cat in a dark room. A totally counter-productive activity.

However, I was not afraid of the maniac—my Lyuchik was clearly not to his taste. But all these suicides...

For nearly a week, every day at 10 a.m. sharp, I came to the gates of the school and stayed put there until 5:30 p.m., even had lunch in the local cafeteria. We did nothing serious: played, walked, jump-roped (why am I even mentioning it?!), and talked. The flip side of the thin spiritual organization of the white was incredible tediousness—they could linger on every emotional experience for weeks, and not in a corner, quietly, but with everyone whom they could draw into conversation. Joe once explained to me that they needed to chatter over and rationalize any strong emotion, either positive or negative; otherwise it would put pressure on the nerves and drive them into the coffin. Lyuchik chattered without stopping, and I habitually nodded and thought about totally unrelated things.

For example, I thought about universal splendor. I ought to have gotten accustomed to the local beauty and returned to the dark mage's normal cynical and pragmatic mood long ago, but blessed idleness persistently entangled my soul. It was unnatural, like the pleasure from smoking marijuana, a forbidden joy that sooner or later you would have to pay for. When a dark magician experiences discomfort, the rest of the world should stock its amulets.

In a flash of brilliance, I realized I should ask Lyuchik's opinion about this place.

"You, yourself, do you like it here?"

My younger brother did not babble enthusiastically; instead, he seriously pondered my question (which already said a lot to me), then suddenly replied: "No."

"No?"

"It's boring here. And I don't feel like doing anything."

That was an answer worthy of a Krauhard's resident! He was bored and wanted to leave, despite all sorts of eye candy. I appreciated it.

"Then perhaps you'll go with me to Redstone? We'll live together; there are also schools for the white in there."

"What about the others? How about Petros?"

Hmm, Petros. My brother had managed to make a friend, whom, in the beginning, I took for an idiot: the boy a year older than Lyuchik continuously smiled, all the while shifting his beady little eyes and every now and then jumping up and down on the spot. Did he have some sort of tick? The dark mages, if they needed company, choose somebody on equal footing, but the white pick up all sorts of rubbish; it would be simpler to keep a pet for the company. The first time I met him, I could not resist the temptation to laugh at the boy—I reached out and began clapping him on the top of his head, like bouncing a ball. He stopped and somehow shrank. I ought to cheer him up.

"Exercising? Good for you! It's very good for your health. I was also ordered by the coach to jump-rope, but I don't know how."

"Really?" Lyuchik asked suspiciously.

"True!" I replied with some pride.

Not everything I say should be understood literally, but the coach did give me that advice. But who was pulling my tongue? On the same day they found somewhere a long piece of twine and began mocking me, talking in two voices, each on his own subject. I could not say now that I did not care about the coach's advice—that would have ruined my image. In between we played their favorite game. Guess which one? Me being their horse! And the school had six real ponies at that! By the end of the week I realized that the white kids were not so harmless after all.

Frankly speaking, only the presence of these splinters didn't allow me to dive into the blissful moronity, because you cannot sleep on a hedgehog. For some reason, probably due to the complete change in my life rhythm, meditation formulas quickly lost their strength, and I was poised for action.

I needed to distract the kids with something else, or they would totally exhaust me.

The problem was that there were no other sources of strong impressions nearby; the white do not create problems for each other. The boarding school reminded me of a dollhouse in which handsome doll-teachers talked about loftiness with younger dolls, but the kids wanted to run and fool around; it's in human nature to play at that age. And here I was, a typical genius: we should go camping, on foot, preferably with an overnight stay. Thus, children would be busy walking, and I could pretend I was thinking about the work, at least occasionally. What remained was to get permission from the local bosses.

* * *

Mrs. Hemul watched with interest as a group of younger pupils (those who spent the Christmas holidays at school) crawled under the green fence (they thought they were invisible), and the dark magician walked directly across the lawn from them, defying paved paths, shameless, as befitted a man of his nature. Passing by the children excitedly rustling branches, he clapped his hands and startled the kids, who poured out of the bushes with shrieks and laughter. Though, they did not run away too far.

It was a new entertainment for the youngsters, to watch the magician. Toys and books and previous play activities had been forgotten. As soon as the familiar figure—hands in the pockets—appeared at the gate, the children were blown away as if by the wind. All poured into the park, hiding in the bushes and peeping at the innocent amusements of Krauhard's brothers. Not every white mage would tolerate calmly so much attention, but the dark couldn't care less. He treated them as if he was a farmer and they were the annoying chickens, but children seemed to like his attitude.

And these were their white kids! Charming, cultured kids!

In other circumstances, this situation would be funny, but now it only intensified the anxiety. Children (especially the ones with the Source) can feel when something goes wrong. Deep down, they sensed their hope in that man, like Mrs. Hemul herself; the children suffocated in the school, and they were drawn to him as to an open window. The older ones got used to the school's spirit and became deaf to the inner voice, and that made them helpless before the obscure threat. Mrs. Hemul saw it quite clearly now. She was thinking of closing the school right away, in the middle of the school year, all the more so because half of the students had already gone home.

The dark ran up the stairs of the administrative building. 'Mr. Fox is alone in the teaching room at this moment; will they be able to come to an agreement?' But to intervene immediately meant to damage the dignity of the elderly assistant principal, so Mrs. Hemul patiently waited for ten minutes and then went after the dark.

She caught the guy when he came out of the office, looking quite pleased with himself, with a warm smile and brazen eyes. How could a man with eyes like that deserve children's trust? Mrs. Hemul felt like a little bird that was about to be caught by a sassy yard cat.

"How are you?" the impudent animal purred.

"Fine, thank you," she chirped, frightened.

He was gone. Wow, just with a glance he made the respectable teacher lose her balance!

Mr. Fox could stand meetings with the dark much better than her; he just looked a little more pensive than usual.

"I met Mr. Tangor in the corridor," the directrix began uncertainly, trying to calm her heart.

"Uh-huh. He wants to take children for an overnight trip outside the school."

"And...?"

"I advised him to take a tent and children's backpacks; we have some that nobody uses."

"A wise suggestion."

Did the assistant principal decide to halt the developing feud?

"Petros visibly perked up," Mr. Fox said suddenly. The acknowledgment of the obvious seemed to present a problem for him, especially taking into account who was the cause. "You know, yesterday he put a frog in my drawer."

"Did he?"

"Yes," the assistant principal smiled helplessly. "Of course, I explained that it was cruel to treat animals like that, and together we carried it back to the park. He said he loved me," Mrs. Hemul noticed that the teacher's eyes filled with tears, "and he looked so happy."

The director approached the coworker and gently touched his shoulder. Every teacher reached the moment when his or her student grew stronger, more independent, estranged, with interests of his own. Sometimes it was difficult to accept.

"Petros is very talented. He will be a great magician, if he decides to go through the initiation, but now he is a little boy. He needs a role model, a guiding star. It seems we are not a good fit to this role."

Mr. Fox took a deep breath.

"A strong core, balancing the astral plane. I should have guessed myself."

Mrs. Hemul smiled with relief: "Everything will be fine, you'll see."

CHAPTER 30

The kids approached the idea of a trip with naive enthusiasm. Lyuchik was too little when Uncle Gordon once dragged me out into nature and promised a walk along the Trail of the Brave, a historical landmark in Krauhard. I distinctly remembered how I cursed my long-legged ancestors. That was the last time Uncle managed to trick me into something like this, and in the absence of a grown-up dark magician a night-time walk around Krauhard was a steep extreme. I reasonably believed that after the trip to the hills the kids would forget about me for a long time. The main thing was not to knock myself out.

I entrusted Lyuchik with packing, as the most reasonable of us, and we left early—to buy some stuff for the trip, especially shoes (the ones that I had were not suitable for a long stroll). I needed to go shopping and at the same time to stop by the animal cruelty prevention office—to return the folder to the lieutenant and to check some of my theories.

The head of everything was available, as expected. On my appearance, he slammed a notebook (either he was reading or writing one) and stood up to greet me.

Instead of shaking hands, I handed him the folder and flopped into the chair for visitors.

"Lieutenant, what is the local situation with criminals?"

He shrugged: "There is no such situation—no crimes."

"And in the past?"

His gaze became clouded: "My father died in a bank robbery."

"Hmm. How were the robbers planning to flee?"

"I have no idea."

But that was an interesting question, given that one could get here only by train. Or did they intend to run away on horseback through the steppe?... With some effort I focused on the case. "Are the crime stats available?"

"Of course!"

He took from the drawer and showed me a folder with annual reports. I rustled through the papers for ten minutes.

"Are the dates of disappearance of the missing white available?"

Clarence took out of his desk a sheet filled with the names.

"Hmm. So ten years ago, after the first disappearance, the crime rate diminished. And then these suicides started."

The lieutenant nodded in silence.

I rummaged in my memory through mountains of information on general magic, learned at the university. Damn, I was going to be an alchemist! My knowledge of magic theory was limited.

"I give up. I cannot imagine a magical influence that could cause such an effect."

"I can," Clarence said quietly.

I suspiciously squinted at the lieutenant: "That is, you did notice a strange magic background in the vicinity of the town? With a palpably depressive effect on the psyche?"

"Anyone who has ever left the town and come back was able to perceive it, but the white can hardly recognize the external source of their bad mood."

Because we are suggestible, he meant. I banged my fist on the table: "Why didn't you say so? I have lost so much time!"

"To say what?" the lieutenant snapped. "I have no evidence to prove it but my senses! You got to feel it yourself."

I closed eyes and began counting. Up to thirty-five.

"So, what is it? Let's talk straight; we are short on time."

I felt an urge to beat him when the case would be over.

"In theory, a protective spell exists, a side effect of which is the emotional 'rollback' that inhibits aggression," Clarence explained. He took my rudeness in stride with surprising calm. "Putatively, the spell is deadly, but I cannot imagine a white mage using it on someone other than himself. Furthermore, nine times in a row, to explain all the deaths."

"I personally met one like this."

Deceased Laurent had exercised his deadly spell only three times; his colleague was more successful and, obviously, had set a record.

I pondered the lieutenant's version—the rollback inhibiting aggression, trying to assess the extent of its impact on reality. Never guessed that I would need knowledge of white magic! But the fact that Rustle stayed silent since I came to Mihandrov brought on some bad thoughts: the effect of the spell took away some very important component of the environment.

"Do you know how it could end?"

The lieutenant blinked—he did.

"Then why are you still here?"

"How about responsibility for the town, its residents?"

The white, what one could expect from him! He surely wanted to be a hero, if he was with NZAMIPS.

"Will you confirm my words?" Clarence perked up.

"It's useless," I waved, "we have only circumstantial evidence: statistics, our senses; there, real people die every day. Our superiors are morons," I visualized Satal, "they won't do anything until it is too late."

"What about their social responsibility?"

I rolled my eyes. He was just like a naive kid!

"Wake up, man! In Redstone, the "cleaners" didn't notice three ghouls, each over a century old. Doesn't it say anything to you?"

"But... what should we do then?"

He started panicking, and not without a reason. For me, the most appropriate solution was to grab Lyuchik with both hands and run. But when it blew up here, Satal would drown me in shit, and Lyuchik wouldn't be proud of his brother (the town will blow—no need to ask a fortune-teller).

"We will work on that," I tried to concentrate. I dropped by to check some suspicions and finished by taking obligations on my shoulders! "Perhaps you know the name of the murderer?"

Clarence shook his head. "No. It ought to be someone from the boarding school's staff, but plenty of people resigned after the scandal, so the guy might not be here any longer."

Lovely! The culprit ran away, and we had to clean up shit after him.

"It doesn't matter," I slapped my knee. "The shield has been accumulating potential for ten years; this we can't change. We will provoke detente!"

"What?"

"Detente. We need to get some of the "cleaners" in here and make them stay—under any pretext. Then we will educate residents and place ward-off signs around the town. There have been no victims for a whole year; therefore, the shield is about to fall apart, and it will be hot in Mihandrov. The supernatural that the spell drove out of here for ten years will run back at once."

"Do you think it is time to engage volunteers?"

"It needed to be done yesterday, and tomorrow will be too late. Are you familiar with the theory?"

He silently put a stack of brochures on the table. I leafed through one: the Publishing House of the Trunk Bay. Home, sweet home!

"That will do. Think of a reason; lie, mystify if necessary. You're a magician after all! I'll notify my superiors, but it will take time while they come to an agreement... As they say, if you are drowning, you are on your own. It's sink or swim."

And we parted at that. I came back to the B&B in a state of quiet madness. These are my holidays, guys, come on! Of all the options, I chose the shittiest town. If not for the two restless white kids with me, I would have been stuck here, like a fly in honey. Interesting who had advised Joe to send his son to Mihandrov.

* * *

Edan Satal was suffering from a hangover after the lengthy holidays, and he preferred to hang out at work, raising suspicion in Baer that the senior coordinator was afraid to scare his family. Locomotive looked into the swollen eyes of his chief and thought that the common salutation in this case would be a straightforward mockery.

"A telegram from Mihandrov."

Satal read through a piece of paper with one eye and pushed it away in disgust. "Nothing new!"

The captain was a bit surprised. "A magic phenomenon of such magnitude is a rather alarming sign. It could trigger a serious breakthrough of the supernatural energy..."

The coordinator groped for a mug on the desk with some murky dishwater inside (Baer was not good at potions) and took several big gulps—it helped a bit.

"Axel has got a full desk of such messages; Artrom County is famous for that. Half of them are the repercussions of weather spells; another half is unidentified ancient garbage. The wandering white magic is horrible stuff. Artrom is the place where White Halak stood! Tell him to dig deeper. Axel needs specifics. He asked to solve the problem, not to report it."

Locomotive neither slammed the door—that would be too petty, nor sent the valuable directions to Mihandrov (Tangor wasn't a fool; he would figure that out himself). But he forwarded a copy of the telegram to Artrom, just in case. Let them know that the reports were sent not only to them. Last year the amount of observed supernatural phenomena in Redstone increased by three hundred percent (in spite of all magic perimeters and ward-off signs), and Baer did not want to become famous as someone who knew about the impending disaster and did nothing.

CHAPTER 31

Some twists of fate make even dark mages uncomfortable; at the thought of a curse hanging over Mihandrov my skin began to itch. I almost forgot to buy a backpack but, by some miracle, managed to acquire walking shoes of a disgusting bright orange color. I had to pretend that it was intended like that and bought a shirt of the same horrible color. Now I looked like traffic lights.

Once again I thought over the chance to flee, but I would have to drag Lyuchik overcoming his resistance, and people around could misinterpret that. On the other hand, the safest place is always near a dark magician. And we will let the zombie-dog run ahead of the group; it would be a pleasant surprise for the maniac.

In the evening at the B&B, swearing softly but terribly, I tried to stuff enough grub for three people, socks, blankets, the traveling kit of an exorcist (nowhere without it!), and a canister of drinking water in the backpack. Plus a tent on top of everything... Well, I could leave it out and say that otherwise we wouldn't gain the experience of real hikers. Sleeping under the sky and stars—a hiker's dream! The idea of the trip did not seem as smart as before, but it was too late to retreat; moreover, it was vital to me to free up some time, and I did not know how to get it in any other way. I took Uncle Gordon's beads with a pair of student curses, in case the worst came to worst.

The next morning we left for the trip. I, wise and prudent, with the bamboo handle from a mop (yes – my staff), and the two white kids, hopping with excitement. Well, surely, they would not be skipping for long...

Honestly, I did not plan the route. Judging by Lieutenant Clarence's map, the area around the lake was quite the same in all directions (except for Mihandrov on the east): hills near the water surrounded by the steppe stretching for seven days of walking. We passed the territory of the school, got out through a fallen section of the fence (supposedly it was the security perimeter), and went on, maintaining a general direction towards the west, to the lake. Vegetation changed quickly and substantially: instead of lush park greenery, we now walked through gullies, dry standing grass, and weeds. It started smelling strangely; even touches of air to the skin felt differently than before. The wildness of the landscape awakened some ancient instinct that caused us to tread carefully and stay quiet; the white were silent, but their excitement sparkled around. New experiences and sensations are good stimuli for a child's mind!

I tried to keep track of time until we reached the boundary of the notorious defensive circle of the deadly spell (Clarence said it would be impossible to miss it). I wanted to get an idea of how the spell was distributed in the area. It was clear to me that its perimeters followed the signs' line, but the shields were set differently - along the axes in two directions, as far as the power would allow. In dark magic, the curses that generate shields exist for as long as the energy of the Source is pumped in; that is, only in the presence of a dark magician. In white magic, as I understand, the spells act differently: they create some distortion of the structure of reality, the longevity of which depends not so much on the input energy, but on the resistance of environment (there is not even one formula for that in the dark section of magic foundations). An experienced white magician could make his creation so natural that its influence would last for centuries. However, precisely that feature—the change in the environment—made the results of divination so ambiguous.

I was slowly losing my mind from attempts to sort out the

situation. Logically thinking, if there was a shield, then the pentagram that created it should be somewhere in the centre, too. If we found at least some trails of the pentagram, the arrival of the "cleaners" to Mihandrov would be guaranteed. It remained to understand where the middle of that white spell was...

After three hours and two stops for rest, the kids turned visibly sour.

"Hold on, boys, we have just a little bit left until the lake!"

The terrain started to slope, green grass replaced dry weeds, and rabbit burrows began to tuck under the feet—all that was an indication of our proximity to the lake. Therefore, we didn't need to save water for the tea and could even wash our feet after the walk—very conducive for relaxation. By the time the surface of the lake started shining ahead (they called it a lake? To me it was more like a rain puddle!), the kids were exhausted, and I had to set up our camp alone and in silence. The white fell asleep barely touching the ground.

Well, wasn't I a genius? No bustling, fussing, or excessive energy. We were going to have dinner, overnight sleep, and slowly go back tomorrow. And I will have a day off with no threat of the jump ropes for me (knock on wood).

The next moment I learned that my attitude towards the children was outrageous. I was sent to help people, but instead I scratched my ass for a week and played the fool. Clearly, the area of distorted reality had been left behind, because Rustle was back. But my personal monster forgot that I couldn't care less for its opinion. Imagine how comic the situation was: the supernatural creature criticized the dark magician for his sloppiness. Rustle's anger would have been righteous had I intended to work on holidays. The local NZAMIPS had ten years to sort out the situation, and now what—one poor student ought to work the whole Mihandrov's division? Ha-ha!

By evening, the kids perked up just enough to eat cereal, watch the sunset, say "Ah!" and get into their sleeping bags. Nice. As a final touch, I put an amulet on Petros' neck, warding off mosquitoes (otherwise, my white kids would look like leopards by the end of the trip), and crawled under the blanket. Coals smoldered in the neat fire hole, insects avoided flying around me (wise choice on their part), and the zombie-dog guarded us at a distance. I had rarely felt this good.

For the first time I realized that I did not regret becoming a magician. Magic abilities give me certain freedom, confidence in the future. It would be stupid to have Power and deny it, right? Now I could wander the expanses of Ingernika, not fearing loneliness and darkness, and lack of means...

The dissatisfied Rustle cut in again—I was bored without it— and said that all my thoughts were complete crap. In its view, it was time for me to make kids, not to entertain them, and, if I wanted to sleep outside, I should have a cool chick by my side, together in one sleeping bag.

With a surprise, I realized that the otherworldly wight was interested in sex. It missed that feeling, imagine that! Shit! Get out of my mind, you filthy animal!

Rustle maliciously hinted that at such a time and place (at night, at the campfire) I had no reason to show off.

I promised myself that when I came back, I would confess in necromancy and finish my life in the electric chair!

Rustle retreated, hiding in the inaccessible depths of my consciousness and indignantly broadcasting obscene pornographic pictures. Oh my God, where did it pick them up? Quarters was a fan of that stuff, but even he didn't see such perversion... So many people deathly fear that beast, but all it has on its mind is obscenities! And what shall I do when I really get a girlfriend, have a threesome?

That night in my dream I saw Rustle in the jar. What was interesting: the jar I remembered clearly, but how I put the monster in there I could not recall.

Needless to say that my white kids came back as heroes, tired and happy. They stuffed pockets with all sorts of rubbish (stones, dead beetles, last year's snake skins), managed to see a real fox and find an eagle feather (I declared it was an eagle). Walking at a slower pace but not stopping for rest, we reached the school before lunch. On the way back I lied with great inspiration about the King's Island, my work in NZAMIPS, my evil boss—a genuine dark magician (finally I had somebody to complain to!), about my student life in Redstone, and the kids compassionately sighed and asked hundreds of meaningless questions. We made a detour to enter through the main gates; I delivered the children to Mr. Fox and sighed with relief. Now they had a week worth topics for discussion!

"You turned our entire school upside down," Mrs. Hemul noticed, but she did not look unhappy at that.

More to come!

"You'd better repair the fence at the rear; a few sections were overturned," I suggested heartily. "You won't close the perimeter without them."

She thanked me very seriously. Lyuchik arranged for sort of a meeting at the square (even senior students came for it); Fox dragged Petros off to take a bath; I flirted with the idea of going to bed, but reluctantly went to town—it was time to get down to business that the kids didn't need to know about. I was going to please Rustle!

Clarence was in the office: the enterprising white magician drew propaganda posters, focusing on illustrations from the Krauhardian brochures. His pictures looked even more fearsome than the originals. I guessed that a man like him wasn't susceptible to any "rollback".

"Office, to arms!" I announced from the doorway. "Let's go gather evidence."

He began rushing around the office like a frightened rabbit.

"Freeze! Do you have a cart in your possession? We cannot take your vehicle—it would unmask us."

"My nephew has a two-wheeled gig."

"It will work! Take it and let's go."

The horse is not a car; it takes half an hour to harness it. By the time unhappy Alfred returned with the cart, Clarence had stuffed a whole field lab into his suitcase—from a magnifier to a spirit lamp. The purpose of half the objects in the suitcase remained a mystery to me. We climbed into the seats and pretended that it was casual: I, dirty like a pig after two days of camping, and the distinguished representative of the town's authorities were going somewhere on business together.

"We need to approach the school from behind, from the direction of the park. Can we?"

"There is no road in that area, but I'll try."

A curved dirt walkway barely conquered the hills surrounding the lake, made a steep turn, and disappeared in the middle of the clear steppe; from that point onward our hope was on the strength of the cart axis. The gig jumped on hummocks and wriggled between thickets of thorns, blindly hitting some holes and rocks hidden in the grass. I kept the suitcase on my knees, trying to quench the jolts and shocks—it wasn't altruism on my side; if not for that job, I would have to handle the horse.

"How far?" Clarence asked, his teeth clattering.

"My mate will meet us."

"What?"

"Come on, drive!"

The horse sensed the zombie first; it began to snort and jump anxiously from side to side.

"That's it, we have arrived! Tie up the horse—we'll walk from here."

"What's the matter; can you explain?" the white mage muttered discontentedly after I had returned his suitcase.

I sighed and tried to convey all the brilliant simplicity of my plan to the provincial policeman.

"I will explain it one time only: from the side of the lake, the transition to the 'rollback' zone is very sharp; we reached the place of 'normal appearance' in three hours. Under the 'normal appearance' I mean presence of animals, predatory birds, and blood-sucking insects. From the side of the railroad lane, the transition is almost imperceptible. Believe me. I conclude that a pentagram that generates the shield is somewhere around here."

"I should have taken more people for the search." When a white mage starts to snap that means he is extremely irritated.

"Don't fret, chief! My mate had already looked around."

Clarence wasn't convinced.

Max silently came out of the bushes; from the lingering grace of its movements one wanted to turn around and run away. You cannot hide the otherworldly nature! The monster that hid under the disheveled brown hair could not be seen but was felt quite clearly. Dear God, where could it pick so many thorns and spines in its fur? The white squinted warily and started unconsciously rubbing his hands against the jacket's pocket (perhaps he kept some amulet there). There was no sense in hiding my dog any further. We were in the same boat.

I called Max and presented it to the lieutenant: "Meet my mate." Clarence leaned over to stroke the dog. "It's a zombie," I finished, grabbing the shattered lieutenant by the elbow. "Quiet, quiet! Max is tame."

Max brushed its bangs to the side and squinted whitish, lifeless eye at Clarence with interest; the head of Mihandrov's NZAMIPS unsuccessfully tried to calm his heavy breathing. And this man was a salaried "cleaner"?!

"I was aware that all darks were crazy, but not to such a degree!"

"Well," I was sincerely offended, "my superiors are okay with it."

"But that creature is a zombie!"

"A silly superstition. A zombie is just a reanimated body, not a genuine supernatural phenomenon. Max is stable, that's the main thing, and extremely helpful! You will see."

"You should have warned me," the gallant officer muttered angrily and pretended that he could walk by himself now.

I shrugged and followed Max; now both of them—the suitcase and the white—were hanging on me.

By the way, Clarence was fundamentally wrong about "taking more people"—the problem was not in the scale of the search. Our enemy was a magician; hence, he was able to hide traces of his activity much more reliably than ordinary people. But not from the zombie—the reanimated corpse always finds another corpse, no matter if it's enchanted, or sprinkled with an odor-killing potion, or buried masterfully. Where hundreds of chartered detectives would have worked for a month, Max just ran around for half an hour. Now the dog trampled merrily on an unremarkable piece of grass, in the middle of a clear field, where there was absolutely nothing eye-catching.

"We will be digging here," I concluded with a straight face.

We marked up the plot according to archaeological science and began removing sod gently. The grave was shallow; just twenty inches under the surface my shovel groped a skeleton's hand.

"There it is..."

I heard only rustling of grass in response —Clarence rushed into the nearest bush, to vomit. The chief of NZAMIPS! What a joke! A quarter of an hour I spent bringing the white to senses, and then he lasted long enough only to make a formal report of the findings and test a couple of standard police spells on it.

"A young man, died three years ago, hard to say any more with certainty. There are traces of some magic; I'll take its imprint. I need to bring experts to find out more."

"Too early. For one corpse they will send ordinary criminal experts, but we need "cleaners". I do not think that the maniac dragged the corpse on his back, and the gig won't get here. We will search for the pentagram."

"It's getting dark," the lieutenant objected weakly.

"I don't care! Darkness sharpens the senses."

We split up and went along an expanding spiral; Max was helping us as well, but I did not rely on it, and this proved to be right. Clarence found the oddity, not by the magic trails, but for a completely idiotic reason; he did not like the bush.

"Mr. Tangor!"

I tried to remember the place where I stopped, gave up, and

went to the call.

"Well?"

"Don't you think they are sort of... wrong?"

"Wrong" was an evergreen shrub with spikes of such size that I got sick from just looking at them.

"What's wrong with it?"

"Too straight. Too dense."

And that was true—the wild bush looked more like a cropped hedge. It was a typical look for a garden, but completely unnatural in the wilderness. I carefully pulled apart the branches.

"Are we going inside?"

The white looked doubtfully at the prickly hedge.

"You'd better take the suitcase, or we will have to come back for it."

The bamboo stick I left in the police office would have come in very handy! The combat magicians of the past were experts at this. To say that we got scratched by the spikes was to say nothing: one spike cut through my arm almost to the bone, and I was struck with pure and sincere hatred for the villain who set that all up. Let me get to him: he will be mutilated!

Behind the dense ring of branches the bush sharply cut off, opening up nearly empty space thirteen feet in diameter, without a hint of vegetation. The magic background intensified, and I squatted, studying the dirt.

You would guess that such an impermanent thing as chalk lines would disappear without a trace after the first rain. Perhaps, this is true for the regular chalk, but if magic energy went through the contours of the signs, the traces of whitening would be stronger than after kindling a fire. Nothing would grow in their for a long time. Even if someone put sod on top of a pentagram, it would not change anything; the grass would wither and crumble into fine dust or would be strongly inhibited. In that place the grass dried out, but slowly and in patches, circles and triangles; using a pen knife, I was able to find traces of chalk on the ground. I stood up, looking at the drawing vaguely showing through the turf.

Excellent! It did not matter whether the pentagram was related to the disappearance of people or to a weather spell; we discovered the traces of a ritual, the corpse, and now we could call the combat mages.

"Make a record of it!" I ordered Clarence, smiling predatorily.

The poor lieutenant, looking very much like a ghoul, took the necessary tools out of the suitcase.

On the way back to town I rode the gig myself. The white could not pull himself together. Of course, I was no good as a cart driver, but the horse was eager to reach its home stall, and even if I wanted to I wouldn't be able to slow it down.

"Call Alfred now; do not wait until morning. Put evidence in the sealed envelope and send it by courier with the highest degree of urgency. I will write a cover letter to scare them. They will be forced to rush here!"

"And then what?"

"Let's make them search for the remaining eight bodies; it will take no less than a month without Max. During this time we will make noise, find journalists among the tourists or students' parents, and publish an article in the regional press with 'artisans' in every line. The scribblers are so sensitive to that word! We must turn things in such a way that for your 'cleaners' catching the perpetrator will be a personal challenge. And let the experts estimate for how long the shield will maintain the created effect. If we are fortunate, you will lose one of your jobs."

"I do not mind."

"And if we aren't, you will have to hire a private combat mage. It's not cheap, but you cannot leave town without the protection of a dark magician; this is not the case when you can count on luck."

CHAPTER 32

The next day I intended to rest and slept until 11 a.m. without any remorse. I deserved it! My vacation turned out to be a real business trip; I worked seven days a week, knocking myself out. Good that at least my hostess was compassionate: if yesterday night, after three hours of combing my zombie's hair, I couldn't take a bath (it was after one a.m.), I would have burned all of Mihandrov today. A nervous breakdown wasn't the exclusive privilege of the white mages!

Dropping by the school just to check, I discovered that my diversion with the trip brought unexpected results: instead of playing pathfinders and building huts, children enthusiastically argued. It looked hilarious in the performance of the white: they stood and talked very quickly all at the same time, perhaps not even catching the meaning of each other's words. I got so curious that came up closer to listen to them.

"Thomas!" Lyuchik finally noticed me.

I got surrounded by kids with such speed that I even started.

"Tell me, tell me," Lyuchik was tugging at my sleeve, "why the snake takes off its skin?"

"Because it has always done that," I shrugged. "Why not?"

"But I do not shed my skin!"

Dear god, was that the reason for their hysterical quarrel? No, I will never get the job of an empath; I cannot grasp such things.

"Bro, in fact, you are shedding constantly, and the snake only

350

once a year. It's questionable who is better off—you or the snake."

"Really?" Lyuchik frowned in puzzlement.

"Of course! The snake doesn't have to wash, and they don't stink." If I remembered correctly, the snakes did not have sweat glands.

"But the snake will get cold," sobbed a girl in bows. "They need clothes."

I pictured a snake in the coat and gave a raucous neigh. Perhaps it was wildly anti-pedagogical, but I couldn't stop.

"How about buttons?" I squeezed the question through tears. "How will they zip up buttons?"

The children became puzzled. What bedlam! Of course, I knew the white had a peculiar vision of the world, but not to that extent... I should be lenient and make allowance for age, after all. I tried to formulate my thoughts in a simpler way: "Clothes were invented by people because humans were bald, but the snake and mice do not need coats. In the areas where they live, their skin is exactly what they need. They're animals! Don't your teachers tell you anything about animals?"

"The snake is a reptile," a bespectacled kid with a toy bear corrected politely.

"Good for you! Then you know that the snake is cold-blooded. Why would it need a coat if it is heated from outside?" I ruffled Lyuchik's hair. "Do not worry! The snake has lived on earth for millions of years, so all that is necessary for their survival they have already acquired."

"Our teacher told us that some species of snake have become extinct," the four-eyed kid said.

That was where the problem originated! Quite a bizarre run of associations.

"Animals become extinct because people plough virgin lands and build houses. Animals need wilderness; if we do not interfere with them, they will be all right. Got it?"

Everybody calmed down. Good. I was lucky that the kids didn't ask the sacred question about a fried piglet; I cannot talk on this topic, but I know a bunch of jokes. Like, once a vegetarian married a butcher's daughter... 'Maybe the kids' moronity was the result of the rollback,' suddenly came to my mind. On the other hand, teachers also ought to think before they say something. Anything. I fished out my brother from the crowd of pacified whites and took him for a walk to the park, vaguely sensing the lack of something of great importance.

"Where is Petros?"

My brother sighed. "Mr. Fox does not let him out for a walk."

"How is it possible that he doesn't let him out?" I was taken aback.

"Mr. Fox said that Petros got sick, but Petros wrote me a note that he wasn't sick, only his feet hurt a little."

My God, they were exchanging notes already, teen-conspirators?! Should I have a serious talk with the assistant principal? If I wanted to get that crazy kid under my wing, then yes, I had to immediately rush into a quarrel. But a sudden idea came to my mind: if Petros disappeared from the horizon, it would be much easier to take Lyuchik away from Mihandrov. So I decided to act in a civilized manner.

"Let's go talk to the headmistress of the school."

Mrs. Hemul was glad to see me, but she looked tired and agitated. You know, the emotional and physical conditions of a magician are strongly related. As if by magic, a cup of jasmine tea and a basket of fancy cookies appeared on the table (Lyuchik began to dig into them, searching for the sun-shaped ones). She understood the meaning of my question at once, saying, "This is an unfortunate incident, a totally unacceptable situation. Mr. Fox unpleasantly surprised me. To put it bluntly, he reacted very painfully to your visit; however, I was sure that he was coping with his emotions. But it happened so suddenly—and absolutely without a motif! The problem is that Mr. Fox is the legal guardian of Petros; it's in his power to simply take the boy out of the school and leave. I need time to find Mrs. Kormalis and resolve this issue. Unfortunately, she is not in Mihandrov."

"Suddenly left the town, am I correct?" an unpleasant ache developed in my stomach.

"Just before the holidays," Mrs. Hemul nodded. "I'm sure she is about to come back."

Maybe she will return. I thought that Clarence's attention to the missing people and the commission's work calmed down the maniac, but what if they didn't? Though such complex coincidences just could not happen.

"I am glad that you are not letting the matter slide."

She became a little confused. "Regarding this, I have a favor to ask from both of you..."

I already knew what she was driving at.

"Mr. Tangor, could I ask you to refrain from visits to the school for some time?"

"What do you think, brother?"

A heavy fight between a few mutually exclusive desires reflected on Lyuchik's face. "If that is necessary for Petros... But for how long?"

"For a couple of days," Mrs. Hemul soothed him.

"Please keep in mind that I can stay here only until the end of the holidays," I warned her.

"Do not worry; the misunderstanding will be resolved very quickly."

"Good. I'll call tomorrow then."

Lyuchik and I finished the tea and said goodbye to Mrs. Hemul.

Lyuchik followed me to the gate; we sat in the park for a bit. I finally came to the conclusion that I would not leave my brother alone with the curse and the nutty teachers at Mihandrov. I didn't have custody rights, but I was paying for his tuition, and Joe would follow my advice.

"I'm being serious with you; think hard about changing schools. Redstone is a big city with plenty of entertainment and a zoo."

"What if everywhere is like here?" Lyuchik asked sadly.

"No, there is obviously something wrong with this place."

"And what do you think is wrong with our school?" Fox turned out to be near.

The assistant principal looked cheerful—no doubts tortured him. He seemed to be in a hurry to push me out of the gate. He hung over Lyuchik in such a manner that I could hardly restrain myself from hitting him with a curse. Watch out, Mr. Fox!

I shrugged indifferently. "For example—you. A normal teacher would not lie right in the students' faces."

He was taken aback. "I've never..."

"To Milos the day before yesterday? Why did you lie to him that his cat would be with him forever? As if you do not know that animals and humans have different life span!"

He was surprised; maybe he thought that I was blind and deaf to everything around me.

"Would you have had me say that his pet would die in his hands?" Fox softly smiled having recovered from the surprise.

"You should have said that the kitten was not invented for his entertainment. The kitten wants to walk on roofs, make love with she-cats, and piss to mark its territory. Wanting from the kitten something that does not conform to its nature is selfishness, and to demand its immortality is pure necromancy. Do you expect to raise a necromancer from Milos?"

Fox went pale. "The zombie is more up your alley," he almost hissed.

I did not argue: "Yes, I make them, but I can destroy them. But Milos will manage only the first part, at best. What will the guy do when he realizes that the animated corpse is not his pet?"

I sensed growing attention on me with all my skin; I was looked at from all sides, and I felt like making a speech. "The world must be loved for what it is; we must not pick out the most delicious parts of it, like raisins from a bread loaf. Not all of what we like is good, and not everything that hurts us is evil. Among your pupils there are girls—how will you explain to them what childbirth is?"

He even turned green at that.

"Don't you like babies?" I purred softly. "Don't you know where they come from?"

Fox turned and fled. I showed him us—the dark! All the white minnows in the park ran to the side with a soft shur-shur-shur. I beat Fox with means specific to the white—I gave a different

355

explanation—and now kids would not calm down until they determined which of us was right. Poor teachers! To be honest, the phrase about the bread loaf was prepared ahead of time; I came up with it when tried to get rid of the nightmares caused by visions of White Halak.

The dark, having nightmares! If I said that to anybody, I would be laughed at.

"If you decide to stay here," I told Lyuchik, "never trust to what that guy says. He is crazy!"

"I thought so too," the kid nodded very seriously, "but I do not know why."

God knows how sick I was of their gooing!

"Don't be puzzled about 'why', " I chuckled. "Teachers must understand more than students, not just talk convincingly. He is a theoretician on life, damn it."

So, I finally got two days off. Now I had plenty of time to wander around and visit Mihandrov's barely any sightseeing spots. Still, the town itself was quite interesting. It was in the condition of "antiquity without decrepitude". I didn't mean miserable huts hanging onto each other in clusters. This condition is laid with the first stone of the foundation, ripens for centuries, and is lost if the ancient brew is diluted with even a drop of contemporary design. So, Mihandrov was soaked in the antiquity so strongly that its age was nearly impossible to determine. I was sure that the town was like that before the deadly spell, and it would maintain the same appearance many, many years later: white walls, slate roofs, low stone fences—like the pictures of ancient towns in school textbooks.

Vines did not grow in the neighborhood of Mihandrov (Alfred had said something to that effect, but I did not save it in my memory); however, there was a man living on the lakefront who regularly supplied the town with fresh beer. I knew the road to his pub, a stylish basement with huge barrels, wooden tables, and indispensable bundles of garlic. Compared to the best Redstone restaurants, it differed only by the absence of a fireplace (the latter was not needed here) and by a shorter menu list (mostly fish was present). I seriously considered buying a house in Mihandrov, although it will be scorching heat here in the middle of summer...

I know it sounds selfish, but I vitally needed a break in communication with the white. In the end, a mage's physical state depends on the condition of his soul, and my contacts with the white drove me crazy lately. Besides, the "cleaners" from Artrom were expected to come to town any minute now, and a sharp transition to communication with the combat mages could be harmful to my health. Who would need me then as a cripple?

I did not manage to get drunk on light beer, and stronger drinks were unavailable in Mihandrov at all. I was too lazy to drag to the train station for liquor and went back to the mansion to swing in a wicker chair, take a nap, and think how nasty Satal felt in Redstone now (it was freezing cold there). Clarence didn't bother me. Twilight began to darken, dinner was getting closer, and the smell of fried fish wafted from the windows of the kitchen. Fish was everywhere in Mihandrov.

And then it struck.

No, there was no sound; it just felt as if a big toothy saw touched the nerves of Max and me. The dog that had been soaking in a tub with some preservative since morning howled hoarsely. I told it to shut up and stay in the bath, clicked the "whistle" in my pocket, and ran to pick up my traveling kit. The unforgettable feeling that mauled my nerves could mean only one thing: the supernatural was hovering nearby.

With the staff and the suitcase in hands (just like in a fairy tale), I rushed to where my intuition strictly forbade me to go. In a hurry, I burst straight in, cutting corners on the slopes where one wrong move would make you fly headfirst to the lake below. Yet I was glad that I wasn't running in the direction of the school. Somewhere halfway up hill, I caught up with Fox, who wheezed on the rise. I wondered where the man was going to. Pulling up my socks, I overtook him, and while the white climbed the slope, I made a loop and broke into the overgrown park from the other side (first!). There it was! A large open space covered before with grass and bushes was now filled with ash-gray dust.

"Witch's baldness!" Fox breathed out, having made his way up through the thickets of the wild rose.

I wondered how come he knew what that was. Witch's baldness was a rare type of supernatural phenomenon, surprisingly difficult to get rid of: the source of the supernatural was deep underground. That is, a normal pentagram won't decimate the bald unless you draw it after removing the top five feet of dirt, standing right in the centre of contamination. I had to move backwards - the border of the baldness shifted significantly closer to me.

"I have never seen them growing so quickly!" I gasped in shock.

"What should we do?" Fox screamed in panic.

That was a good demonstration of his self-control.

"I will take care of it, and you run and tell people to get out of their homes. They are too close!"

"Close" was not the right word: roofs were already visible at the bottom of the hill slope. They were within a stone's throw! The NZAMIPS' "whistle" was of no use—they were too far to help. Alfred, sent as a courier to Artrom, wouldn't be able to come back earlier than in twenty-four hours, and I didn't need another white here. The lieutenant would be a burden.

The bad news was that I could not kill such a huge otherworldly creature alone, and at the speed it grew (thirty feet in diameter for half an hour that we took to reach the place) very soon the power of the combat mages of the whole Ingernika wouldn't be enough to cope with it. When the "cleaners" arrived at the place (if they hurried up), only one remedy would be left: the armory curse. It required five to seven victims - people who did not manage to get away from Mihandrov in time. Theoretically, one experienced dark mage would be enough to kill the supernatural with the armory curse. But I wasn't taught at the university on how to perform it.

I wasn't taught...

And then I thanked all the gods for putting in my way that loathsome creature, Edan Satal. No, he did not teach me the deadly curses—he was not suicidal—but he set my teeth on edge with all sorts of high-level shields and barriers. I recalled what I needed; however, my knowledge was purely theoretical. But when had it stopped me before? After assessing the growth rate of the witch's baldness, I breathed out a fire weaving that burned down bushes in a sixty-foot radius, took a marker out of the bag, and began to draw. That would be a perimeter, a simple ward-off perimeter, only turned inside out: it would keep the creature inside.

There was no time to measure out the sectors; I had to act by eyeballing it. As a result, instead of the minimal twelve signs per perimeter, I drew eleven. I hoped it would work anyway! The marker ran out before the last couple of lines were drawn—it was not meant for spells of that size—and I didn't have time to look for a replacement. No more than half a meter remained between the baldness and the line. Simple chalk was no good for such a surface, and to redraw the pentagram on a larger scale was meaningless. A perimeter of such size could not be activated. This was the end, not for me, but for most of the townsfolk for sure. Such a crowd of people would not be able to leave the town quickly.

I threw off the empty marker tube and screamed hoarsely, like an animal.

"This? This?" someone poked me in the back.

That was Lieutenant Clarence, white as chalk, with the exact same bag as mine and with the same token from the sorcerer's traveling kit. My God, what did he need it for?

I snatched from his hand the white tube and finished drawing in feverish haste.

"I-isabertana dar-ram!"

A wave of power from the Source, zonked from such treatment, swept through the line of signs, activating the spell—akin to what Uncle Gordon used to scare mice. Smaller in size, but with a higher price tag. The toothed crown of the three-dimensional perimeter soared above the ground and struck inward.

I had done what I could. If this failed, I would have to grab Lyuchik and run away. I heard a thump behind my back— Clarence fainted. Of course, he was drenched in my power! I looked—the witch's baldness stopped growing and even slightly leaned back from the burning line of signs—then I heaved the brave warrior on my shoulder and carried him to the road, bypassing the baldness.

Fox was waiting next to a striped police car; hence, he had not warned the residents of nearby houses. What a jerk! Well, at least he didn't run away.

"What's the situation?"

"I have locked the witch's baldness by a reverse perimeter; meanwhile, it's holding up, but I can't do any more alone. We have already called the 'cleaners'; they should be here soon. Can you drive? Go to the train station and wait! Bring Clarence to life and let him call the 'cleaners' and prepare for evacuation in the event of the armory curse. I will stay here and maintain the perimeter."

For a white mage, Fox recovered very quickly, but he couldn't steel himself to follow my orders.

"Why?" he demanded explanation.

I thought his question referred to the strange supernatural entity.

"Your town's suburbs are absolutely sterile—I mean, relative to dark magic. No disturbances, no complex flows. If an otherworldly creature comes into such environment, it begins to develop explosively. Have you ever heard of Nintark? Here you go! Something similar happened there. When you meet our team of mages, tell them about this; the 'cleaners' are not that bright and may not guess themselves."

It seemed he did not accept my answer. He wanted to say something but refrained, nodded, and finally left, and I went back to the baldness—to terrorize my Source and pour power into the perimeter. The waiting promised to be long.

The chalk marks were ill-suited for the long-term divination, and my asymmetrical, unbalanced perimeter powered out like a leaky tub. I had to update the curse virtually every fifteen minutes, to sit to the side and keep watching. How inopportune was that beer! It was getting dark and cold. A perked-up Clarence returned to me with blankets and sweet juice: a magician's first aid. I sent him for an alarm clock; I feared to death that I would miss the baldness' growth. The moon slowly drifted over the lake and down the hills, the east brightened, and it started smelling of trouble.

No, I wasn't tired; it just became awfully difficult to concentrate on the perimeter and even to remember to watch it. My thoughts ran like mercury balls; clearly, if the 'cleaners' did not arrive by the early morning express, I would have to flee. It would be even wiser to take the very same express myself, but that sound idea came into my head too late.

When I heard the familiar screech of Mihandrov's police car's transmission, I mistook it for the sound of the silly alarm clock. I would need to ask Clarence... But instead of the lieutenant some absolutely unfamiliar people came out of the bushes, and, judging by the fact that their very appearance aroused my irritation, at least one of them was a dark magician.

"Shit...!" a burly fellow with a crew-cut in a dark red field uniform expressed what they were thinking as they approached. With such a face he could only be the commander. "Sergeant Claymore," he introduced himself, shook hands, and jerked me, forcing to stand up. "Your work?"

To tell him it was not mine? Maybe he saw some other dark magicians here?

"Squalor," a thin sharp-nosed nerd with a goat-like squint muttered through his clenched teeth. Either he needed glasses, or he hadn't been beaten by the dark for very long.

"Stop talking!" the sergeant barked, the sharp-nosed shut up, and even I no longer wanted to object. "Remove the unauthorized persons. Where is Rispin?"

Another dark, younger, burst through the bushes with two huge trunks. Well, it looked like they were itching to climb the hill, but to go through the wicket—no way! Was there some hidden sense in that? I wasn't going to wait until they pushed me out and began a slow descent to the road. The trio left an elephant trail behind. At the bottom of the hill, Clarence gently helped me get into the back seat of his limousine; alas, he did not have a second blanket for me.

"What's going on there?" the lieutenant asked tensely.

I tried to shrug. My brains thawed slowly from the stress; I wanted neither to speak nor to think.

"Will they cope?" Clarence worried.

How should I know?

"You'd better U-turn your car right here," I advised him, "driving in reverse isn't speedy."

There were no streetlights in Mihandrov, so nights were very much like in Krauhard here: dark and misty. The lake breathed out fog, and a rather chilly breeze came out of the steppe; the sun rose fast, and day started instantly. I slept peacefully under Clarence's jacket for an hour and a half and was awakened by a strike of lightning, typical for the expelling curse. It blew off so strongly that the car bounced. The lieutenant ruthlessly pulled the improvised blanket off me. The sky was already bright.

The sergeant climbed down the slope, swearing, along with the sharp-nosed assistant with my staff in his hands! Their younger colleague, named Rispin, showed prudence and went through the gate—an extra one hundred meters, but much more convenient.

"In my twenty years of experience I haven't seen such a hefty creature before," the sharp-nosed guy said, trying to push me out of the car, but I tenaciously clung to the seat. Clarence's cabriolet was not designed for five, but it was not my problem. Let them sit on each other's knees!

"Gorchik, as you were!" the weary sergeant ordered and decisively took a seat beside the driver.

Rispin pushed on Gorchik with his hip, the compacted people compressed to the limit. And we were off. Personally, I was happy at how everything turned out; I even began to doze off again, and only Gorchik, sandwiched in from both sides, angrily sniffed and almost pinched us in annoyance.

"Drop me off at the school," I asked Clarence.

"No need to," the lieutenant advised. "Yesterday I warned Mrs. Hemul; it's all under control. And the perimeter is working; the gates will stay locked until 11 a.m."

I asked about the time—there was more than an hour before the school's opening—and I had to agree: showing up looking like I had a sleepover in the bushes would discredit the image I had created. And to stay awake for another two hours was beyond my strength.

"I'll be waiting for you in the office at seventeen hundred!" the sergeant shouted at our parting.

"It won't work," I warned him honestly. I would be sleeping, no matter what.

"Well," he displayed some compassion, "then tomorrow at ten hundred—no excuses!"

And they drove off. With a short delay, I began to feel resentful. Geez, he wasn't even my commander! And he wasn't at home! What right did the guy have to order me? But, on second thought, I decided that to learn about the plans of the long-awaited "cleaners" was absolutely necessary; hence, I had to go. But I would stop their every attempt to benefit at my expense! If the dark mages cut their way to higher status, they become absolutely unbearable.

In the mansion, the tender-hearted Mrs. Parker released Max from the bathroom. Either she was a secret necromancer or believed that the dark magician's dog had the right to be strange, one way or another. Mrs. Parker recognized in the preservative solution a remedy against fleas, and she washed and brushed Max's coat with a special homemade lotion that kept its hair not just shiny, but also tangle-free. With the thought that I ought to get the magic recipe from her, I fell into bed and slept for almost twenty-four hours.

* * *

Mrs. Hemul watched the assistant principal walking around his office, and tried not to display her concern. Mr. Fox no longer cast even a shadow of sympathy—rather, he frightened her. Where did he hide such a chasm of complexes and prejudices, and why hadn't she noticed them before? All his quirks and reservations from the last six months now acquired a much more sinister meaning.

"It's the dark mage's fault!" Mr. Fox insisted feverishly. "Our troubles started after his arrival."

Long ago, at the time of the Inquisition, it was proved that the occurrence of supernatural phenomena did not depend on the will of the dark, but on the properties of the environment. The arsenal of dark magicians has plenty of abominations, but guests from the other world are not part of it. But Fox rejected the truisms straightaway, and to reach out to his common sense was getting more and more difficult.

"Even if it is so, would you prefer that the breakthrough occur in his absence? We had lived for ten years without any supernatural manifestation; it was too long even for the capital."

"Who told you that?" Mr. Fox frowned in annoyance.

"Lieutenant Clarence came to see us yesterday. We talked."

It was the young policeman, pale from shock, who told her

about the need to lock the ward-off perimeter—not the experienced assistant principal, too busy buying train tickets to carve out a minute and call to warn her. In the morning the whole school had seen an ugly scandal: Fox yelled at her for not unlocking the gate for him to leave. The assistant principal did not accept the directrix' explanation that, if she unlocked the perimeter, they wouldn't be able to repeat the reactivation sooner than in four hours - he needed to go. Mrs. Hemul cowardly regretted that she hadn't let Petros out of the gate with suitcase earlier. They would have already been freed from the presence of Fox, who created problems for everyone, but the assistant principal hadn't informed her about his intention to take Petros out of the school, either.

"You have to forbid unauthorized persons from accessing the school territory!"

"No, I don't. I have invited experts from NZAMIPS to check the ward-off perimeter. After repairing the fence, some signs need to be replaced. In addition, I will arrange for a safety lecture. Do you think Mr. Tangor will agree to help?"

"It's irresponsible!"

"Irresponsible to repair the perimeter?"

"That insolent dark..."

"Saved Mihandrov. Did you want to say that?"

The mention of the young dark magician produced a strange reaction in Mr. Fox: he winced, grimaced, and began to shake his head. The white in general tolerate stress poorly, but that show looked more like a nervous breakdown. How else could one explain that, in rushing to save one child, he had forgotten about the fate of a hundred others?

"Nobody asked him about that!"

"Exactly. He showed concern for others, voluntarily and knowingly. His behavior must become a model for us."

"Do you blame me for something?"

"Yes, I do. Your duty as a teacher is to take care of the children. What have you done for that?"

"You are too young, girl; you still have much to learn. There are times in life when we must act decisively to save at least somebody. You'll lose plenty of people before it settles in your pretty little head!"

Mrs. Hemul smiled - a healer specializing in disaster medicine learns of inevitable casualties in the first place. Five years of experience, and no one better than she could walk the fine line between dead and barely alive, which would also die if left without help. She remembered the terrible fire at the Hotel "Palladium", a train crash near Turik, hundreds of smaller incidents; only the birth of her twins made her change the career path. But she never treated people like lifeless flesh, even if they had only fifteen minutes left to live. It seemed that Mr. Fox conceitedly considered as "inevitable victims" the entire boarding school.

"Have I missed something? Someone has died?"

It seemed he did not understand the meaning of her words.

"Mihandrov needs a dark magician. I was right, and you were mistaken."

Mr. Fox broke into an incomprehensible monologue about purity of thought and harmony of being. Interesting that yesterday he didn't even intend to call and warn her; on the contrary, if he could, he would have left without saying a word. Mrs. Hemul felt nauseous at the sound of his voice, but she patiently listened, occasionally pointing out errors in his reasoning. A white experiences unbearable difficulty trying to insist on something, unless he is obsessed. She wanted to calm down the tension, forgive his sins, and send him off, but it was better to let him make noise in her office than run around the school scaring students and staff.

She needed to get rid of that man, quickly and under any pretext. Unfortunately, having learned that NZAMIPS experts had eliminated the urgent threat, the assistant principal abruptly changed his mind and came into her office with strange fabrications about the inevitable evil. He seemed confident that it was Mrs. Hemul who ought to behave differently. Oh, yes! On the director's desk there was already a report, demanding rather than requesting the Board of Trustees to fire the inadequate assistant principal. In a few minutes a courier, called for that purpose, would take it to Artrom. It would be even better to talk to the trustees personally, but Mrs. Hemul could not leave the school while Fox was there. Her intuition literally screamed for caution in dealing with the mage-practitioner. She was doing that for the sake of the children, and the assistant principal wouldn't get young Petros either, even if Mrs. Kormalis wouldn't return home at all.

CHAPTER 33

I entered Mihandrov's office of NZAMIPS at half past nine as a civilized looking person. To be honest, I wanted to speak to the lieutenant, but the tiny room was already occupied by dark mages.

Gorchik sported a bruised face. If he had found such trouble in such a quiet town as Mihandrov in one day, he was a real combat mage! From Mrs. Parker (with whom we got along very well now), I knew that the incident occurred in the same local pub closing after the sunset. The visiting dark (with an exceptionally subtle body) quarreled with the owner, who had a surprisingly melancholic personality, and the former was thrown out to cool down outside. Gorchik was about to employ combat magic on the full-body brewer, but he was stopped by the other "cleaners" in time. I think the fear that they would have to stay sober until the end of the trip if the brewer was hurt stimulated them much more than the prospect of the shackles of deliverance on their mate. Now, a bitter wrinkle lay above the brow of the unfortunate magician; he was figuring out a way of getting into the pub again without losing his dignity.

There were not enough chairs, so Lieutenant Clarence was standing—not a very advantageous position psychologically. I carefully removed the flower pots from the windowsill and motioned him to sit beside me.

"Okay," the sergeant fidgeted, trying to settle comfortably on a hard office chair, "let's introduce each other."

I secretly poked the lieutenant with a finger and waited for a continuation. The "cleaner" did not notice the purposeful pause

369

and introduced himself first: "Master Sergeant Otto Claymore, my assistants—Philip Gorchik, Keane Rispin, of the Rapid Response Team, Polisant Regional Office."

"Aren't you from Artrom?" I clarified. It was important.

"Civilian mages are in Artrom, but we're from Polisant," Gorchik grinned contentedly. Obviously, it was some local twist, but their regional coordinator was still Axel.

"Thomas Tangor," I humbly introduced myself, "an out-of-staff employee."

"What's that?" the sergeant did not understand.

"It means I work two days a month."

The "cleaners" stayed silent for a while, trying to comprehend such blatant injustice. "Clever," the master sergeant commented, "I hope what we saw was not an example of your work?"

I shrugged and didn't stoop to meaningless excuses: he grasped the situation without my help, and I let him leave his gibes to himself. Sergeant Claymore finally started feeling tension and sat down a bit straighter. "I understand the case could be closed now."

It was very typical: they had just arrived and already intended to leave. And they would leave, if we gave them at least half a chance to throw their work on the other people's shoulders.

"Have you already found all the missing people?"

"Finding the corpses is just a matter of time. The combat group isn't needed for that."

"Excuse me, how has your assignment been formulated?"

"Never mind. We have expelled the otherworldly."

"What does the supernatural have to do with it? I don't care about the supernatural. You will be accountable for the artisans, not for the supernatural."

"Are you being rude?"

"Yes!"

Sergeant Claymore got behind Clarence's desk quite voluntarily; now, the same desk restricted him from coming and taking me by the shirt. Also, I was sitting in such a way that all three "cleaners" were before me, and the door was right beside me. It wasn't very conducive to the development of a conflict; however, the sergeant tried. He got up, and I did too. He defiantly stared at me; in return he got exactly the same challenging look from me. We were of the same height, and that greatly simplified the matter.

What happened further concerned only the dark; we disputed the question of whose will was primary—whose was poised to cause the enemy more problems and to make it through to the end. Strictly speaking, the majority of the dark are interested in just that, not in the nonsense about the law and the order. The sergeant saw the white lieutenant and, obviously, thought that the latter wouldn't be able to reprove him. He decided that they had done enough. But now Mihandrov was my town, and for my own territory I would tear anyone to pieces. Gorchik restlessly fidgeted in his chair, but I was confident that I could awaken my Source more quickly than he his. Do not tell me about arrogance! That kid did not see anything worse than the witch's baldness, but I had overcome three mature ghouls! I would even set my zombie-dog on them. There were eight corpses—and there would be eleven.

And Claymore faltered. He did not want to challenge his scope of duty, but to retreat in front of his subordinates meant to lose his indisputable authority. It would be bad for the discipline.

Evidently, the sergeant was looking for a way out of the conflict. His posture and body language—one shoulder slightly forward, as if taking a bow, head low, gaze on the enemy, but askance. Okay, sergeant! I closed my eyelids, breaking resistance, and Claymore immediately took advantage of me. "Hey, kid, relax! We will find that scum, clean up the neighborhood, and then will do what our superiors will order. We are soldiers."

I nodded, accepting the new terms. The sergeant was absolutely right; they didn't have a reason to go against the order. Hence, we would continue working together; I had a lot of interesting ideas in this regard.

The "cleaners" dragged themselves in single file to the door, looking at me warily. I poked Clarence with a finger again. I hoped he would not apologize! That would spoil the whole disposition—as long as they considered themselves on foreign soil, they would not be tempted to do a shitty job.

"Keep quiet, take your seat," I whispered to the lieutenant as soon as the door closed behind Rispin.

We sat in silence for a few minutes, while I pondered whether Gorchik had eavesdropped on us. Maybe I should check it out? My conflicts with the other darks had never reached that stage before, and the encounter with Mr. Satal was lost from the start.

The lieutenant broke the silence first: "That was outrageous!"

"What was outrageous?" I did not understand.

"All of that!"

"That they wanted you to sign the claims rejection?" I guessed.

"Exactly!"

The poor fellow felt abused.

"Hey Rudy, have you had any dark among your acquaintances?"

He shrugged uncertainly.

"I see. Remember (better write it down): the first thing a dark magician does when he receives an assignment is an attempt to get rid of it. To frighten him or appeal to his sense of duty would be useless, but to indicate the possible consequences of underperformance with an emphasis on personal responsibility is a must."

The lieutenant frowned. What a naive kid!

"Do not look at me. I grew up among the white; consider me a cripple. The real dark behaves exactly the way I described. Judge for yourself: why would they want to clear up mess that wasn't their fault?"

"But... what can we do now?"

"Let's follow the plan as before; now you know why the plan was like that. Your senior coordinator remains our goal, so look out for journalists. Ask the directrix of the school for help; she seems to be smart. And forget about these guys: as long as they know they are being watched, they will do their job in the best possible way. Do not flirt with them, or they will instantly make you do their job."

Poor old Clarence rubbed his eyes in confusion, trying to make his brain understand my logic. I think the white are unable to grasp the subtleties of the dark character, though empaths seem to cope with that somehow. "I'm stunned," he concluded finally. "I took a course on dark magicians—even attended a workshop. Nothing like reality."

"Theory without practice is dead! Go back to work."

* * *

Striped police ribbon carved out from the monotonous landscape a large rectangle, inside of which the grass was either mowed short or burnt out to the roots. A convenient wide passage was cut through dense thickets of thorns. The three combat mages were busy, each one doing the work that suited him best.

Rispin rustled through the brush in the location of the secret burial. The exhumed corpse had been thoroughly examined, described, and its parts wrapped in packing paper. He was an experienced criminalist, able to make the dead speak without the aid of necromancy. The credit for his hire by NZAMIPS, and not by the criminal police, should be given solely to Coordinator Axel; NZAMIPS doubled his pay.

Sergeant Claymore plotted on a sheet of paper a detailed plan of the crime scene, concurrently sketching a draft of his future report. His subordinates flocked to him with their findings.

"He was right, that kid," Gorchik came out of the bushes in overalls and goggles, the lenses of which made his face look like a fish tank. Needless to say, the dark did not like wearing glasses.

"What, someone called Rustle?"

Gorchik winced: naming the only monster that was more or less responsive to the call of the otherworldly liquidators was considered bad taste among combat mages.

"Shield, modified to specifically kill the white Source."

Claymore raised his eyebrow. An interesting picture! The dark Source could exist for some time outside the body, but the white one was not receptive to the fixation on the pump-sign. There was a time when inquisitors could induce spontaneous manifestations of white magic, but the consequences of that were so horrendous...

"It does not look like they tried to exorcise the possessed here."

"No, it doesn't," confirmed Gorchik. "The victim followed the killer to this place without any resistance, voluntarily called his or her Source during the ritual, and was murdered then. This requires either utmost dedication or an extreme amount of credibility to the murderer."

"Given the age of the victim," the sergeant nodded to the lovingly-wrapped remains, "one does not exclude the other."

"That means that our scum is a highly respected person. A man like this you won't approach without an order."

Claymore frowned. "Shit! It increasingly looks like the artisans. I hoped they weren't involved—so many years have passed, and Axel watches the white community thoroughly."

"The place already smelled bad a year ago, but the empaths decided that there was a collective magic resonance. I wouldn't want to be in the shoes of those nerds now!"

The dark mages exchanged malevolent grins.

"What, are you done?" Rispin broke away from the excavation.

"How about you?" the sergeant looked at his watch.

The forensics expert shrugged. "Nothing. The scoundrel works exceptionally accurately. The bones are not damaged; apparently, the victim died from a puncture to the soft tissue. I can't say anything more specific; the spell, accelerating decay, was applied. If the murders started ten years ago, it would be extremely difficult to find all the victims. The imprints of their auras will be hard to identify."

"I'm in a better situation!" Gorchik boasted. "There are some fragments suitable for identification, but they won't tell the overall picture."

"Shit," the sergeant spoke out. Hence, they couldn't find the murderer with magic. They would have to use good old police methods. "Can we identify the victim?"

"Yes."

"Compose his or her portrait, and we'll show it at school. He was young, so he must be one of theirs. We are done for today. Tomorrow we'll start to look for the rest. Can any of you ride a horse?"

For an urban dark, the idea of getting on a horse seemed unnatural.

"I see," the sergeant sighed, "that means we'll walk."

Rispin muttered under his breath something dirty that rhymed well with "Tangor." The sergeant himself could hardly refrain from swearing. No, in his mind he certainly understood the importance of catching the killer and the significance of their mission, but in his heart... Claymore wished with all his heart that the underage parasite would die in agony, infected with shingles. Well, he must have tried hard to find such a vile job for the three respected magicians! The sergeant did not doubt the success of the investigation—no villain escaped their team— but at the thought of how much time they would spend searching for the other corpses, he wanted to get drunk.

CHAPTER 34

A call from the school caught me lying under the car: I finally got into that squeaky vehicle! Of course, Alfred didn't let me work on the car right away; it was preceded by a thoughtful conversation about the benefits of front-wheel drive, the quality of local ethanol fuel, and the prospects of oil engines. Of course, he was not a professional alchemist and could not resist my obsessive charisma. I approached the adjustment of the carburetor with the piety that some people begin a prayer with, but then things got livelier. I started to feel great peace and happiness. The design of the machinery, clear and functional, was such a contrast to the intricacies of human existence that I sensed tears welling in my eyes. I officiated over the brake actuator (a critical part of cross-country driving) when I was interrupted.

Clarence came up, reporting, "Mrs. Hemul called and begged you to come to school. She seemed to sense that someone at the school cast spells this morning, and it highly disturbed her."

I almost threw a wrench at him. Could I have some personal time off? Which of us was the town's sheriff? Who was the head of Mihandrov's NZAMIPS? A unit of combat mages was grazing in the town, but he called for help a poor student on a business trip, a student who didn't even have a degree in magic!

But Lyuchik was at the school. I sighed and went to wash my hands off grease.

On the way to the school I was planning to tell the directrix all I thought of her. She hadn't known the words I was about to say! I had called her yesterday, but she discouraged me from coming,

377

hinting that she did not want to provoke Fox. And now everything seemed okay with her "boyfriend". Just when I was finally back to doing interesting things, he was readying his excuses! I hated that!

My self-control thinned completely. Now I understood why Coordinator Axel did not want to send his people here; Claymore with his mates would lynch him after such a trip. Satal would neigh at me when I came back "well-rested". However, I was ready to solve the problem with Satal in three hours. Very interesting grass grew on the flowerbeds at the school; the master of poisons, Tiranidos, would hang himself in envy. A full herbarium from "Toxicology", no doubt. I have to admit, Milky Widow blooms beautifully and looks great in the ridges, but, in my opinion, the gardener should think a bit more on his selection of species before planting them. There were children all around! I already dried out enough plants to fill half of my suitcase with interesting roots and flowers, and the thought of Satal's surprise when he learned what he was dying from brought my good mood back.

Do not believe the intuition of practicing magicians, no matter what people say about it. My gaze caught a narrow leaf with a distinctive silky sheen, because all the time I was searching for something like that. Not trusting my luck, I picked up the leaf and began looking around in search of the rest of the plant. Alas! Nothing like that grew on the nearby lawns, and a measly half a gram serving was obviously not enough for my goal. I was about to search the silage pit with the mowed grass. But the path where I found the treasure led to the back kitchen door instead of a park or a greenhouse. The cooks were busy with all their might and main: lunchtime was fast approaching. Not feeling any unrest in my soul, I mentally connected these three concepts: grass, food, poison. I shook the grass off my hands and wanted to go further on my business, but then a sense of duty prevailed. Perhaps that was nonsense, but the maniac that killed nine people was still at the school, and the artisans are like maniacs, in my opinion...

Clicking the "whistle" in my pocket (do not sleep, shitheads, do not sleep!), I burst into the kitchen door with a businesslike air, ignoring the blank stares and surprised faces; my eyes were fixed on the tables, and I did find on one of them the remains of the sliced green.

"Where is the rest?" I asked stupidly, thinking that I could still use some of the grass, perhaps.

The chef began to breathe air into his chest to make a perturbed retort, but my stupor was over; I pulled out my temporary certificate and jabbed it in his face. "The combat operation of NZAMIPS. This herb is poisonous. Where did you put it?"

Frightened eyes shifted toward a large soup pot.

I tossed a chromatic curse in the pot, which stained the contents with a threatening scarlet color (harmless, but impressive). "Who brought this stuff here? Name!"

They did not know, could not recall, and became horrified with it. It was a typical reaction to the masking spell.

"All kitchen supplies (all, got it?) are arrested until the experts' arrival. I hope no one tasted it? It is deadly poisonous."

A portly cook got very pale and gripped her chest.

"Wash out your stomach, quickly! And pray that the poison hasn't been inside long enough to absorb into the blood."

I waited until all the cooks left the kitchen and tied the door handles for safety with a cord I had found right there.

"What is happening here?"

It was the directrix. I gave her the damned leaf; she frowned, trying to identify it. Mrs. Hemul seemed not to know much about poisons.

"It is Opal Buttercup. Someone brought it in the kitchen and made sure that the plant got into the soup."

She still did not understand.

"Did you hear about the potion of Red King? Opal Buttercup, the main component, is harmless, but after the heat treatment it is transformed into a lethal poison—the antidote to which does not exist."

By the way, the growing of that plant without a license was punishable by three years in prison.

Mrs. Hemul became very pale. "Who could have done..."

"I do not know, but I've got one person in mind, who has some explaining to do. Come on!"

The rapid response team was still responding. I suspected that the "cleaners" went to Clarence to get his car (the one that Alfred and I had dismantled) and now they were giving him a "concert". Poor people of Mihandrov!

"But who could..." Mrs. Hemul was stuck.

The white cannot tolerate stress well, and they take a long time to respond to threats. They try to understand the reasons, but the dark do not need reasoning; they just get hit in the face and move on.

"There is only one employee at the school who has worked here for over ten years. I'm not saying he's guilty; I mean he should give us an account of his today's activities."

Some understanding glimmered in the eyes of the headmistress.

Five minutes later we stood before the assistant principal's office. I knocked, pulled the handle—it was locked.

"Perhaps he is gone," Mrs. Hemul suggested.

I looked through the keyhole—the key was inserted from the inside! Indeed he left!

"Step aside!" I was not going to ask permission.

My kick broke off the lock along with part of the doorpost (I was not that strong, it was just a good curse), and we entered. Quite a large room: two tables, bookcases, chairs and a sofa, comfortable and modest, unlike our dean's office or Satal's. A completely dead Mr. Fox (face up) and Petros (in an unknown condition—face planted) lay on the worn carpet in the center of the room. I didn't think that my talk with Fox would turn out like that.

"Oh my lord!" Mrs. Hemul rushed to the child first. "How do you feel, my dear?"

The kid was breathing—that was a good sign. While she lamented, professionally checking his pulse and pupils, I feverishly looked around the room for the cause of death. No bloody knife, no empty glasses, no smoking censers could be seen, but there was surely something that killed the big guy and nearly killed the boy! Some black fragments crunched under my foot—that was my ward-off amulet. The realization dawned on me like lightning.

"It's magic! Mr. Fox has a spell on him. Find out which ritual he had used!"

Mrs. Hemul indignantly shook her head. "Fox was a white mage!"

"Was" was the appropriate word choice.

"I do not care who he was! Look for it, or let me do it."

"You are mistaken," she murmured through her tears, but the brooch on her jacket began to glow, "you are deeply mistaken. You just cannot imagine how wrong your idea of white magic is..."

Sergeant Claymore (no, he didn't break in - it would be unprofessional) cautiously peered through the door. Ensuring that there was no need to fight anyone right now, he came in, forcing me to make room for him. He nodded to Fox: "Your work?"

"No, he did it himself. Have you searched the kitchen?"

He chuckled. "It's not just a kitchen, it's a necromancer's dream—one could murder a whole army. We'll have to throw out all the contents and re-floor the room. As I see, the suspect kicked the bucket?"

"To hell with him!" I did not care that we had spoiled Artrom's crime statistics.

"This face looks familiar," the "cleaner" said thoughtfully, "though not from that angle."

Surely Fox developed his skills somewhere. I shrugged and attempted to leave the room.

"I'll be waiting for you at the office at nineteen hundred," the sergeant said to my back.

I nodded silently and went off to look for Lyuchik. The square in front of the main entrance was crowded with frightened white kids. The teachers tried to calm the pupils, the staff and cooks were whispering—huddling at the fountain—and Gorchik grimly guarded them all. Lyuchik sat next to him on a bench with a very serious look, and I could see that he was there for a reason.

On seeing me, people became agitated.

"Stay still!" Gorchik barked.

"He says please to stay where you are, for the sake of your safety," my brother perked up.

Ah, he had latched onto the "cleaner" as an interpreter! Gorchik looked at me with grim doom; I smiled back without any sympathy.

I had some business to Lyuchik.

"Hey, they aren't serving lunch today. Let's go find something to eat in town?"

"Can we take Petros?"

At that moment, I realized that the kids should not know the details. "He will be fine; Mrs. Hemul is with him now."

The kids put their necks out to listen to our talk; someone could not resist saying, "What happened? What's going on?"

I cleared my throat diplomatically. "I cannot violate the confidentiality of the investigation. You'd better direct your questions to Sergeant Claymore; he is the boss. I am sure he wouldn't mind holding a press conference." I knew that one mention of the press conference would stall his brains. "I can only say that the danger is over, but the school is poised for change."

"We've been experiencing an entire year of 'changes', " one of the teachers muttered.

"You are mistaken; nothing has changed since the commission's work. But there will be changes now, and I'm sure, for the better."

That was it. If they had any brains, they would understand the hint, and if not, it would be better for them to keep the state of blissful ignorance.

Lyuchik didn't go with me; he decided to stay with the white to support them morally. I made sure the "cleaners" understood the simple idea that Lyuchik was my brother and then portrayed myself as a battle-worn warrior and went off. I could no longer look at the white and the "cleaners" together! I came back to the garage and worked on the famous Mihandrov car until evening. I enjoyed the work as a cat delights in valerian, and I was late for a meeting with Claymore by half an hour.

By the time I arrived, the atmosphere at NZAMIPS had reached a fever pitch. Lieutenant Clarence was nowhere to be seen: he had either fled or gone to work with the townsfolk. It was twilight already: they could kill me and secretly throw in the lake.

"So, the press conference, you said?" the sergeant roared in place of a greeting.

It was my turn to stand awkwardly and look askance—I wasn't going to fight with him over nothing!

"I did not want to bypass the senior officer."

He pondered it and decided to forgive me. "Judging by the imprint of the aura, that corpse was Fox's work," the sergeant magnanimously told me. "Why we don't record imprints of the white magicians, too?!" He was very cheerful; hence, they found a reason to flee from here.

"It's unfair," I agreed.

"Let's drink to this!"

Bottles of fresh beer and a bag of lovingly-packed snacks appeared from under the table, and my account of events gradually melded into the booze on the occasion of the successful completion of the case. It was the first time I shared a table with a company of combat mages, and their nasty reputation was not confirmed. Normal men, not any worse than Quarters! We knocked back, sang a few songs from the army's repertoire; Rispin told a few fresh anecdotes, Gorchik started to squint with both eyes, the beer was over, and we parted peacefully. They went to their hotel, and I - to Mrs. Parker's mansion. The naive sergeant could afford to sleep tight, but I had to get up at dawn tomorrow: a brain-twisting intrigue, spun by me with an eye on the coordinator, entered its final stage.

* * *

An encoded telegram bearing the name of Satal came at the last moment; the senior coordinator intended to leave Redstone for the capital and was nervous and swore all morning. Sparing the nerves of his subordinates, Captain Baer personally delivered the telegram to the boss—a half-sheet of text; obviously, the sender didn't try to save money on the letters. As soon as the coordinator read it through, his face brightened, and lips twisted in an arrogant smirk.

"That's another story! A priest that was making human sacrifices got caught and decimated in Mihandrov. The central database identified him as Sigismund Salaris, an artisan; he was wanted for fifteen years."

The captain gasped: "The same Salaris? Nintark's confessor?"

"Yeah," Satal good-naturedly allowed his subordinate to read the telegram. "By the way, your Larkes swore that he saw him dead."

"Why is he mine?" Locomotive was offended.

"He ruled here all this time, the talentless parasite let business slide!" the dark mage became a bit gloomy. "They will say that it's Axel who caught the artisan."

"Not a big deal," Locomotive comforted his boss, "you have caught two artisans."

"True, but no one believes that they were the artisans," Satal objected reasonably. "However, I am sure that the center of their interest is not Polisant. The death of the living legend of the cult will make them more active," the senior coordinator rubbed his palms in anticipation, "now they'll come to us in flocks!"

Locomotive pictured artisans thronging to Redstone and shivered. God save us, no!

CHAPTER 35

The rambling holidays were finally over; my ill-fated trip had come to an end. I could stay for a couple more days (nobody would kill me for that), but then I would have to attend the funeral of Mr. Fox. That was Mrs. Hemul's idea—the deceased assistant principal should not remain in the memory of the children as an evil person.

"Anyway, he was their teacher; they learned a lot from him. You cannot say to a child, 'Remember this and do not remember that.' The children must realize the ambiguity of his personality themselves, separate in their minds the right and the wrong. I know you see this as over-complacency, but his death closes all accounts, and we need forgiveness for ourselves in order to live on."

Well, maybe for the white it is so, but I could not picture myself grieving about artisans—even after a liter of beer.

And yet, Mrs. Hemul wanted to know the results of the investigation, because the achievement of clarity is a fundamental feature of the white; they physically cannot disregard or forget something important. The wise directrix chose the easiest way to reach her goal; she invited all interested parties to dinner at that same pub, at her own expense. Claymore's eagles came in full strength. I did not want to go, honestly; I was too proud for that. But I was asked by Clarence to be there. Max came with me: I had already introduced it to the "cleaners", and an extra set of teeth during the meeting would be helpful.

The sergeant expounded readily and in detail the results of the investigation, half of which was done by someone else. The main achievement of the "cleaner" was identification of Fox— the nice nelly—which provided an objective basis for my fanatical ravings about the artisans (I was very grateful to him for that). "By joining the artisans' cult, he took the alias Sigismund Salaris, under which he became famous, in some way. He was the mastermind behind the branch of the cult that decided to openly challenge the authorities and establish a community in Nintark. Of course, later he was considered dead and was searched for without passion, but all the time he was hiding here."

Mrs. Hemul took the news of the artisans with amazing composure, having practiced for years approaching horrific news with a stone face. I wondered what she was before she came to Mihandrov.

"I confess I always perceived the artisans as mentally ill, but now I see that my ideas were too primitive. Fox talked sensibly and consistently, but he was able to do absolutely unthinkable things at the same time. And most importantly: why? For what purpose?"

" 'Why' is clear," I could not refrain, "he wanted to protect bigger things by sacrificing the smaller ones, so to speak."

"To protect them from whom?"

I had my thoughts on this topic, though to voice them in their entirety meant to reveal my sources. Did I need it? In abbreviated form, my speculation looked like this: "Do you know that Petros' father - Fox's relative - was killed during an armed bank robbery?"

Clarence slightly frowned.

"Yeah, yeah, that same robbery! Three months before the birth of his first and last child, among other things. The first victim had gone missing a few days after the incident. You can rummage through the archives—a lot of strange things happened at that time. I do not know what Fox was trying to fight off with that shield, but he obviously liked the effect and, grieving and weeping, began to let his pupils die under the knife. Of course, he selected those whose death would affect as few people as possible. Orphans, in short."

The sergeant nodded: "A typical artisan's logic."

"But the children! Why did he try to poison them?"

"That is clear, too. What the otherworldly phenomenon was Fox knew well, I suppose, from his experience in Nintark. He lost control of the situation: his followers were killing themselves, but the shield did not hold for long, human sacrifices were required more and more frequently, but the school's leadership had changed, control had tightened. The white tolerate stress poorly! Eventually I showed up and started spoiling his flock, planting a bit of common sense into the children, and I helped Petros in a way he could not. Where you saw hope, he saw only depravity and degradation. Mourning and weeping again, he decided to save everyone from a collision with the real world—to put them to sleep like terminally ill pets, purely out of compassion."

"All of them come to this, sooner or later," Claymore growled. "This is the only logical conclusion of their philosophy."

"You'd better cheer up," I suggested, "that everything ended so well."

"Well?" the directrix did not understand.

"Uh-huh. The children are alive, and Fox's suffering has ended. Just think what would have happened if he had been jailed!"

"Execution by burning has not been abolished yet," Gorchik

commented to the point.

"A scandal will start again," Mrs. Hemul sighed.

"It's in your favor! The situation is critical: if NZAMIPS does not send a regular team to Mihandrov, all of Fox's fears will be realized. In addition, we must knock some sense into the heads of the townsfolk. You need help of empaths and additional funding, but under the current circumstances you will get these either after a massacre or in the wake of a public scandal. In your shoes, I would cooperate with the town authorities and pursue a preemptive tactic. The best treatment is prevention!"

Mrs. Hemul slowly nodded. "I see your point."

"I don't think that I'll sign it," the sergeant growled. "So far, all this talk about the shield is your personal opinion. As for the dark magic background around the town—maybe it's there, maybe it's not, I'm no expert, I won't lie. The town has a NZAMIPS representative," he nodded at Clarence, "we have liquidated the phenomenon, the killer is found, the report is sent out; now we are waiting for the order. What they say, we'll do. Address your complaints to the coordinator."

Clarence was silent, although he clenched his jaw so hard that his cheeks became white. I only shrugged melancholically: "Well, Mr. Axel is not suicidal and understands that if he loses the town after two warnings, the official investigation, and his subordinates' report, the shackles of deliverance will be a lucky escape. The moon will be the only place for him to emigrate to."

"Who is going to tell him about this?" Claymore chuckled.

I kindly smiled to the sergeant.

"You, and you have already told him."

He didn't get it, and I explained: "You sent off your report to
390

the authorities yesterday, didn't you? Right when I was there. Likely, you didn't count pages before putting them in an envelope."

"Right, but how..."

At that moment Max sent him a contented canine grin. It wasn't difficult for the zombie-dog to jump into the window of the second floor, was it?

Sergeant Claymore quickly put two and two together.

"You fag!" the sergeant exclaimed.

I pretended that it was about my zombie.

"What does it mean?" Rispin got frightened. "We're stuck here?"

"We'll see," the sergeant sullenly broke him off.

Mrs. Hemul hid a contented smile behind a cup—a white mage was not supposed to rejoice at other people's misfortune.

Luckily, I did not have to experience the anger of the combat mages on myself; that evening I left Mihandrov. Without Lyuchik. Mrs. Hemul tried to convince me fervently and at length that all would be well at the school from now on; Petros would be taken care of even if they didn't find Mrs. Kormalis. For my brother, it would be very important to see a happy ending of the story and the triumph of justice. I thought about it and backed off; after all, it wasn't such a joy to coddle a white youngster. I was doubtful, though, regarding the triumph of justice.

I didn't take Lyuchik to the station. My zombie-dog waited for me there under the supervision of Mrs. Parker. What if the kids would want to cuddle him? The lieutenant personally gave me a lift in the car that now moved without squeaks or squeals, but with a soft predatory murmur. Gorchik and Rispin were in the back seat (surely they were going to the train station for vodka). The sergeant apparently still hung on the phone, trying to catch his report before it would reach the desk of Senior Coordinator Axel. Good luck to him! I was interested in nobody and nothing anymore, except for the train and the departure horn.

My escort barely lifted my luggage onto the steps of the sleeper, Mrs. Parker waved, and the combat mages burst into indistinct cries and vigorous gestures. Assholes... After saluting everybody, I followed to my compartment, longingly poised for the conductor's usual show: "Please put your animal in a cage." All conductors are terribly predictable: no matter how much you pay for the ticket, they still try to lock your dog in the baggage car. Why would I buy the second ticket, if I intended to follow their advice?

The conductor rolled my suitcase into the compartment and broke into a saccharine, idiotic smile. "Let's put your dog in a doggy house!"

I looked at him as if he were a birdbrain. His face maintained a strange expression for a couple of seconds, and then he turned a bit pale. "Excuse me, sir! I beg your pardon! The white usually travel with pets, and I decided that you were...

Oops!

The question of placing Max in the cage was no longer debated.

In the state of quiet madness, I locked myself in the compartment and started biting my nails.

What was going on? People had started taking me for a white! What a shame... I was lucky that none of my friends witnessed that. I would hardly ever come back to Mihandrov.

I must urgently undertake something to improve my image: the first thing in Redstone I would have a good fight with Quarters. Also, I could catch Sam (if he wasn't in bed with the flu) and cram in feathers behind his collar. Oh! I could also piss on the steps of the police headquarters. Will they identify me by a puddle of urine?

The platform and my escort left behind; Rustle gently tossed in my head, trying to figure out what I had been busy with in its absence. My life was slowly getting back to normal. In the suitcase I carried five kilos of dried fish and two dozen bags of wax paper with quite harmful ingredients: souvenirs from Mihandrov.

One more thing hid inside the suitcase: a letter from the deceased artisan. The next day after the death of Fox, I received a mail with no return address, no note inside, but the sender's identity could not be doubted. At the top of the weighty package there were yellowed newspaper clippings a decade old with reports of strange events (the mass death of bees, the disappearance of gerbils, the rabies of horses) and an article about a bank robbery committed with extreme cruelty. Do you remember that story with the robbery in Mihandrov? I wondered how they were going to slip away. They weren't: two farmers shot their families and continued having fun in town, imitating the characters of a then recently acclaimed thriller. The locations of the incidents from the clippings fell on the map along a straight line, accurately pointing to Mihandrov. I do not know; maybe in his shoes, I would not stand it either.

Why did he not turn in his allegations to NZAMIPS? Perhaps his habit of conspiracy let him down, or Fox, like myself, was confronted with incapacity of the local authorities. And you know, I couldn't care less about his circumstances, especially because he did not want to discuss them with the investigators of the robbery. I have never encountered a situation that could not be turned around in the direction a trained magician wanted.

From the perspective of the dark, the artisan just lost his battle again (once in Nintark, the second time in Mihandrov), and if anybody wants understanding and sympathy, go to an empath.

* * *

Gorchik looked at the departing train with a characteristic goat squint. The dark magician was habitually outraged. "He could have finished the job, that hack! His zombie marked only six graves, and where can we find two more?"

"I wonder which group he belongs to?" Rispin was thoughtful. "I had never met him before. I would like to have a better look at his zombie..."

"No problem, we'll meet him in the office! Axel must be happy this time."

Lieutenant Clarence decided to demonstrate his knowledge of the situation (he was tired of the boorish guests, treating him as a speechless vegetable). "He's from Redstone."

Gorchik turned to him, surprised, as if a zucchini had started speaking. "What does Redstone have to do with us?"

"He came from Redstone," the lieutenant explained patiently, already regretting that he had gotten into the conversation.

"What the hell did he do there?" Rispin wondered.

"I do not know," the white tried to look independent, "but his traveling document was issued by Redstone's division."

For some time they stayed silent. "Why was he sent in?" Gorchik cautiously clarified.

"To study the work of educational institutions. I'm not kidding! It said so in his papers."

Lieutenant Clarence could not decipher the expression that

showed up on the faces of the combat mages.

"Hmm," Rispin summed up, "we won't get our bonuses again."

"Why? Witch's baldness has been cleaned out well!" Gorchik got angry, but his colleague looked askance at him with compassion, and the former was forced to face the truth. "Well, at least the boss will not beat us this time."

Lieutenant Clarence tried to keep a straight face and vowed to himself never to deal with that nutty company again. Let them do with each other what they wanted!

EPILOGUE

The monotonous rumble of wheels continued day and night—the transcontinental express barely made any stops. The conductor was perfectly polite and attentive after realizing his mistake. I flipped the pages of the deceased artisan's notebooks, which Fox did not want to leave to NZAMIPS for some reason, and I tried to sort out my feelings.

My soul was dull, as if something had been stolen from me, but I could not understand what exactly. Amidst the pages of the notebooks, the last record in which was made twenty years ago, I discovered a large yellowed photograph. The age-faded picture rescued images of people posing on the background of a strange pedestal. A photographer must have captured the graduation moment of some educational institution: three teachers and eight students. Fox, young and cheerful, in a light coat with a handkerchief in the upper pocket, sat first to the left of the teachers. Behind the backs of those in the front row, a girl and boy were hugging; the boy's face was carefully painted out. He wore a stylish black suit, and the girl looked vaguely familiar; the note on the reverse side read: Millicent MakKoran. It was my mother. Joe was not in the picture.

I couldn't ignore so many oddities.

I thought if the artisan had told me anything, I would have not believed a word from him. But now I needed to know who my father was and how he died. Why had mother run with me into the backwoods? What was Uncle Gordon silent about, and what was that moronic book about, over which he was killed?

Outside the window rain transformed into wet snow—I was returning to Redstone.

www.ingramcontent.com/pod-product-compliance
Lightning Source LLC
Chambersburg PA
CBHW070904260626
47162CB00007B/2559